## HOW WELL DO YOU EVER REALLY KNOW THE FAMILY NEXT DOOR?

**BUCOLIC NEWPORT COVE,** where spontaneous block parties occur on balmy nights and all the streets are named for flowers, is proud of being named one of the top-twenty safest neighborhoods in the United States.

It's also one of the most secret-filled.

Kellie, Susan, and Gigi are long-time residents and close friends. But behind closed doors, each woman is hiding something. Kellie has just returned to work after a decade at home, and she finds herself relishing the attention of her very handsome, very married male colleague. Susan is a single mom and a small-business owner, but late at night, she's stalking her ex-husband and his new girlfriend. Gigi is poised to become the perfect politician's wife—except she has skeletons in her closet, which are in danger of being brought into the light now that her husband is running for Congress.

Then a new family moves to the neighborhood. Tessa seems friendly enough to the other mothers, if a bit reserved. But when no one is ever invited to Tessa's house, it becomes clear that she is hiding the biggest secret of all.

# The Perfect Neighbors

Also by Sarah Pekkanen

*Things You Won't Say*

*Catching Air*

*The Best of Us*

*These Girls*

*Skipping a Beat*

*The Opposite of Me*

# The Perfect Neighbors

a novel

SARAH PEKKANEN

WASHINGTON SQUARE PRESS

New York   London   Toronto   Sydney   New Delhi

Washington Square Press
A Division of Simon & Schuster, Inc.
1230 Avenue of the Americas
New York, NY 10020

First Washington Square Press trade paperback edition July 2016

WASHINGTON SQUARE PRESS and colophon are registered trademarks of Simon & Schuster, Inc.

For information about special discounts for bulk purchases, please contact Simon & Schuster Special Sales at 1-866-506-1949 or business@simonandschuster.com.

The Simon & Schuster Speakers Bureau can bring authors to your live event. For more information or to book an event, contact the Simon & Schuster Speakers Bureau at 1-866-248-3049 or visit our website at www.simonspeakers.com.

Manufactured in the United States of America

10   9   8   7   6   5   4   3   2   1

Library of Congress Cataloging-in-Publication Data

Names: Pekkanen, Sarah, author.
Title: The perfect neighbors : a novel / Sarah Pekkanen.
Description: First Washington Square Press trade paperback edition. | New York : Washington Square Press, 2016.
Identifiers: LCCN 2015046232 | ISBN 9781501106491 (softcover)
Subjects: LCSH: Interpersonal relations—Fiction. | Neighborhoods—Fiction. | Housewives—Fiction. | Domestic fiction. | BISAC: FICTION / Contemporary Women. | FICTION / Family Life. | FICTION / Literary.
Classification: LCC PS3616.E358 P47 2016 | DDC 813/.6—dc23 LC record available at http://lccn.loc.gov/2015046232

ISBN 978-1-5011-0649-1
ISBN 978-1-5011-0650-7 (ebook)

*For the cousins (in order of appearance):*
*Jack, Sophia, Will, Ellie, Adam, Dylan, Sylvia, Danny, and Billy*

# Prologue

*Lovely 3-BR Cape Cod w/finished basement on a
cul-de-sac—no thru traffic! Located in one of the 20 safest
neighborhoods in the U.S.! Immaculate condition! Wood
floors! Southern-style porch overlooking fenced yard!
~~Tranquil neighborhood Gorgeous neighborhood~~*

Kellie Scott frowned, her fingers hesitating over her keyboard. "Peaceful neighborhood," she murmured. "Serene . . ."

"Bucolic," Miller Thompson suggested, leaning over her shoulder while he read the flyer copy on her computer. He exhaled and she felt a brush of warm breath against her bare arm.

"That's it," she said. "Thanks."

She watched Miller stroll away, then she finished the flyer before going into the kitchen for a cup of coffee. It was only her fourth day on the job, but she felt confident she could sell the kitchen in this office as a vacation property to harried mothers (as if there were any other kind) of young children. She imagined the copy she'd write: *Floors that don't crunch disturbingly under your feet! A spotless refrigerator with sodas and bubbly water lined up like little soldiers! A table that isn't covered in dried Play-Doh and sticky juice boxes!*

Her blood pressure seemed to drop twenty points every time she walked in here and realized she didn't have to clean rotting vegetables out of the crisper or make dinner for a ten-year-old girl who refused to eat much of anything except cheese or bacon and a seven-year-old boy who seemed to subsist on baby carrots and celery.

"My daughter is on the Atkins diet and my son's trying the supermodel diet," she'd joked to her in-laws during their weekly family dinner last Sunday. Her sister-in-law had responded quickly (some might say aggressively) by ladling a large helping of broccoli and rice onto her own son's plate.

Here, though, in this hushed office with tasteful beige walls and mahogany furniture, no one judged her. Here she was Kellie 2.0—a sleeker, improved version of herself. She curled her hair and wore mascara and skirts. She never had to hide in the bathroom and whisper when she needed to make an important phone call. No one wiped runny noses on her sleeve.

"Ready for lunch?" Miller asked, poking his head into the kitchen.

"Lunch?" Kellie repeated. She had a peanut butter and jelly sandwich and an apple in her shoulder bag. She'd planned to eat at her desk.

"Don't tell me you're planning to eat at your desk," Miller said. "It's tradition for the senior agents to take out the new hires during their first week."

She felt her cheeks heat up. The last time she'd gone to a restaurant alone with a man was when she and her husband, Jason, had dined at the Olive Garden three weeks ago. He'd ordered the carbonara Never Ending Pasta Bowl and had complained of a stomachache afterward.

"Sounds great," she said lightly.

This was all part of reentering the workforce after being a stay-at-home mom for a decade. You bought a pair of high heels. You made intelligent conversation about interest rates and whether kitchen renovations held their value in a resale. You ate lunch with colleagues—sometimes tall, distractingly handsome ones whose woodsy cologne lingered after they walked away from your desk.

Besides, Miller probably just wanted to learn more about the neighborhood. Kellie's home was right down the street from his new listing, which was why he'd asked her to write the flyer copy and assist him with the open house. She could tell prospective buyers that Mr. and Mrs. Brannon had lived there for nearly fifty years, and that the neighborhood was called Newport Cove. That it was the kind of place where children played hopscotch on the wide sidewalks, and residents greeted one another by name and collected newspapers for each other when they went on vacation. Where all of the streets were named for flowers, and neighbors held block parties on balmy summer evenings. "Bucolic." That *was* the perfect word.

"Sell it to good people," Kellie's best friend, Susan, who lived five houses down, had urged. "Make sure they have kids."

"I will," Kellie had promised.

A contractor was repainting every room in the vacant house and replacing the wall-to-wall carpets with modern, glossy wood flooring. A stager would bring in bouquets of bright flowers and accent pieces on Sunday morning. Kellie was going to bake chocolate chip cookies so the kitchen would smell irresistible.

The house reminded Kellie of a girl getting ready for a school dance, slipping into a new dress, fastening a sparkling bracelet around her wrist, dabbing on perfume. Wondering if someone across the room would smile at her, then make his way over and offer his hand.

The house deserved a good family. A special family. Kellie hoped whoever was meant to find it would come soon.

• • •

"A Southern-style porch overlooking a fenced yard!" Tessa Campbell read aloud to her husband, Harry. "A bucolic neighborhood!"

"What is a Southern-style porch, exactly?" Harry asked.

Tessa frowned. "Maybe one with pillars? But the point is, it's in one of the twenty safest neighborhoods in the country. Plus it's on a cul-de-sac."

Harry sighed and scrubbed his hands through his short salt-and-pepper hair. "Are you sure this is the right thing to do?" he asked. "Uproot the kids? Leave our friends?"

"Are you kidding me?" she asked. "What's the alternative? Stay here, with all the . . . the *reminders*?"

They spoke this way to each other now, in a kind of code. To anyone watching, they'd appear to be a normal couple enjoying a lazy summer evening on their wooden deck. A casual observer wouldn't notice that Harry was on his third gin and tonic, or that the circles under Tessa's eyes were the dark purple of an eggplant, or that Harry had a new, compulsive habit of tapping his foot against the floor.

Tessa gently closed her laptop.

"A fresh start is exactly what we need," she said. "School doesn't begin for a few weeks. It's only a half day's drive. We could head down Saturday night and stay in a motel. We'll book one with a swimming pool, turn it into an adventure. We'll spend the day checking out the town and the schools. If we like it, we could try to settle on the house fast."

"If we move all of a sudden, won't it look . . . ?" Harry began.

"No," Tessa said firmly.

Harry drained his glass and Tessa wondered if he'd refill it again. Rat-a-tat-tat thrummed his foot against the wood floor.

"We need this," she repeated.

Relocating wouldn't be an issue for Harry's job; his IT

company's headquarters was based across the country, in California, and he flew there for a few days every week or two but worked the rest of the time from home. Money wasn't a concern, not since his generous stock options from his last job, a technology start-up, had kicked in. They didn't have any family nearby, and the kids were young enough that they'd make new friends quickly. There were a dozen little reasons why a move wouldn't be a bad decision. And a single enormous one why it was vitally necessary.

She could hear the kids arguing inside and she gauged the intensity with an experienced ear, determining that it didn't require her intervention yet.

The sun eased lower in the pink-tinged sky, and the aroma of meat grilling on their next-door neighbor's barbeque drifted over. She liked their neighbors; they were a retired couple who brought by extra tomatoes and zucchini from their garden. She liked this house, too. Tessa had stenciled artwork onto her children's bedroom walls and had finally found the perfect shade of slate blue for the living room. They'd expanded eighteen months ago, bumping out into the backyard and creating a master suite and a cook's kitchen that spilled into the family room.

She desperately wanted to walk away and never see any of it again.

Harry stood up and went to refill his glass. He'd lost weight, and his khaki shorts sagged around the waist. Tessa watched her husband take another long sip of his gin and tonic. The cold glass was sweating in the warmth of the August air and a few droplets rolled down Harry's fingers before splashing onto the wooden deck.

Suddenly, she saw him again as he'd been on that night, reaching down to touch the dark red blood his shoe had tracked onto their kitchen floor, his eyes dazed. *What happened?* he'd asked her over and over. *What* happened?

Lost in the vision, Tessa didn't realize Harry had spoken

until his damp fingers clutched her arm. She flinched, then hoped he hadn't noticed. She didn't want him to think she was afraid of him. She had to be the steady one now; to convince him she could guide them through this.

"Okay," he said. "We'll go Saturday."

She stood up, picking up her own wineglass, which was still half full. She'd dump the remainder in the sink. One of them had to stay sharp and between her insomnia and Harry's drinking, it would be too easy to slip. "I'll tell the kids," she said. "We'll have fun."

Fun. An impossible concept. But the kids might enjoy the trip, at least. And once they were settled in a new place—in a safe place—she and Harry could try to find, if not joy, some measure of peace. A respite from the memories that were everywhere.

She left him there on the porch, sipping his drink too quickly, his eyes as blank as the darkening sky.

*I'll save you*, she thought. *I'll save all of us.*

# Chapter One

*Four Weeks Later*

## Newport Cove Listserv Digest

*Drivers Beware!

A friendly reminder that school starts today, so please be on the lookout for our students, especially the wee ones, and remember to come to a full and complete stop at every stop sign. Remember—A Normal Speed Meets Every Need! —Sincerely, Shannon Dockser, Newport Cove Manager

*Dog Poop

Would the owner of the VERY LARGE DOG (judging from the size of its leavings) please be considerate enough to clean up after your pet so that I don't step in a disgusting mess when I'm in my own yard? Canine fecal matter not only contains parasites, it attracts rodents. Please treat your neighbors' yards with the same respect you would accord your own. —Joy Reiserman, Daisy Way

*Honda Mechanic?

Can anyone recommend a good mechanic for a Honda minivan? —Lev Grainger, Crabtree Lane

• • •

"Hurry up, sweetie! You don't want to be late for the bus on the first day!" Susan Barrett called up the stairs.

She grabbed the leash hanging on a hook in the coat closet and her shaggy gray mutt, Sparky, who had supersonic hearing when it came to the rattle of a leash or the creak of the oven door opening, came running, his nails scrabbling against the wooden floors.

Susan ran through a quick mental checklist: Cole's new Spider-Man lunchbox was packed inside his matching Spider-Man backpack. A sheaf of three-ring paper filled his binder. His water bottle had been rinsed and filled.

She checked her watch. Sparky looked hopefully up the stairs. And Cole finally came racing down, his face clean but his shirt on backward.

Susan expertly flipped it around and they stepped outside into the golden September air. Later it would grow very warm, but right now the weather was mild and clear. This was the best part of Susan's morning, the few minutes she and Cole spent ambling to the bus stop, calling out hello to neighbors while Sparky greeted his canine pals. At the beginning of a fresh day, it was easy to make resolutions: She wouldn't eat carbs. She'd go to bed at a decent hour. She'd stop stalking her ex-husband, Randall, and his awful girlfriend.

A dozen yards ahead was her best friend, Kellie, shepherding along her daughter, Mia, and her son, Noah, who was conveniently Cole's best pal. As Susan drew closer, she heard Kellie saying, "Just try two bites of a granola bar. Two little bites! I'll pay you a dollar . . ."

"How come I don't get paid for eating?" Cole asked Susan.

"Oh God, pretend you didn't hear that," Kellie said to Susan.

"Mrs. Scott, you said 'God,'" Cole informed her.

"I beg your pardon," Kellie said, winking, as Susan shrugged.

Who knew where Cole had picked up that chiding tone? Maybe from Randall's girlfriend; when in doubt, Susan found it convenient to assign her blame.

As Cole ran ahead to catch up with Noah, Kellie moved over to let Susan walk alongside her. But Kellie nearly stumbled as a sidewalk crack snagged one of her shoes.

"How long does it take to get used to walking in high heels when you've been in flip-flops for a decade?" she asked.

"Two weeks," Susan said instantly. She and Kellie had an ongoing game in which they delivered bogus answers with complete authority. It had started when one of the kids—Susan couldn't remember which one—had asked where Santa went on summer vacation. "Australia," Susan had said, at the exact moment Kellie had responded, "Bermuda."

"You made that up. It's already been five weeks. Now tell me the truth, is this outfit okay?" Kellie asked. "Does it say I'm trustworthy yet savvy, the sort of woman you need to buy a house from? Mia, honey, don't pick that flower. It's part of Mrs. Henderson's garden."

"Mom, I would never pick someone else's flower. That would be *illegal*," Mia huffed. Ten-year-old Mia had a dozen Girl Scout badges and was certified by the Red Cross as a mother's helper, facts she didn't so much tell people as accost them with.

"You look great," Susan told Kellie honestly. She could see hints of the high school cheerleader Kellie had been in her heart-shaped face and thick blond hair. Kellie had been in the popular crowd, Susan knew, but she was one of the nice girls: the kind of teenager who'd ridden on a homecoming float, flashing a dimpled smile to the crowd, and whose yearbook pages were filled with notes from friends. Susan had had a very different experience in high school. She'd been one of only nine black students in her graduating class, and she'd spent most of her Friday nights with a book for company. ("You were class valedictorian, weren't you?" Kellie had asked after Susan had slaughtered everyone in Scrabble on game night. "No!" Susan had protested, honestly. She'd been salutatorian.)

"Oh my gosh! Look!" Kellie said.

She grabbed Susan's arm and pointed across the street, to the empty house with the SOLD! sign staked in the front lawn. Ever since Mrs. Brannon had died of cancer and her husband had moved into an assisted living facility, the Cape Cod had seemed lonely. Sure, the lawn was kept trimmed and the gutters were cleaned. But missing were all the little touches that had made it a home. Mr. Brannon's polished walking stick was absent from its usual spot by the front door, and the flowerpots that had once held Mrs. Brannon's begonias had been removed from the steps. The well-used wooden rocking chairs had disappeared from the porch. Now, though, the house was thrumming with activity, awakening again.

A silver minivan was parked in the driveway and a huge moving van laid claim to the curb, its back doors flung open. Three men were wrestling a couch down a ramp. The house's windows were open, and a soccer ball lay in the front yard.

"I saw that couch in Crate and Barrel a while ago, but it was three thousand bucks, which guarantees Cole would spill grape juice on it the first day," Susan said. "Didn't you say they have a couple of kids? What are they doing with a three-thousand-dollar couch? In cream, no less?"

"Maybe they like to live dangerously," Kellie said. "And look, they're at the bus stop already. Tessa!"

Kellie gave a little jump as she waved, nearly turning her ankle as she landed.

"Did I say two weeks? I meant two months," Susan said.

Tessa, who'd been standing at the bus stop flanked by her daughter and son, a little apart from the other families gathered there, was waving back. A tentative smile broke across her face. Tessa looked nervous, Susan thought. It was tough moving to a new town.

"You're here!" Kellie said when they reached Tessa.

"We are," agreed Tessa. She was a woman composed of edges, the sort a child might draw, Susan thought, taking in her blunt-cut hair, her sharp chin, and her straight, dark eyebrows. Tessa was enviably slender in her khakis and simple blue blouse. Susan made a mental note: No carbs *or* sugar today!

"We got into town this weekend," Tessa was saying. "We've been staying at the Marriott but we'll be in the house tonight since the furniture just arrived."

"I'm Susan Barrett. Welcome to the neighborhood," Susan said, offering her hand. "How old are your kids?"

"Bree is nine," Tessa said, touching her daughter's head. "And Addison just turned seven."

Both kids had that scrubbed, first-day-of-school look. New clothes with the creases still showing, combed hair, clean backpacks. Except Addison was trying to hide a fat, wiggling worm in his pocket. That detail alone made her sure that he and Cole would become fast friends.

"Great names," Kellie said. "And Addison's the same age as Noah and Cole! Who's his teacher?"

"Um . . . Miss Klopson, I think?" Tessa said.

"That's who Noah and Cole have!" Susan said.

"That's wonderful," Tessa said. But her smile seemed to require an effort. Her expression, like her voice, was flat—almost restrained. Was she sick? Or maybe she was just wiped out from the move, Susan thought.

There was a little awkward pause, then Mia tugged on Kellie's arm. "Can I interview them?" she asked.

"Oh," Kellie said to Tessa. "Sorry, Mia writes the 'Kids' Corner' column for our neighborhood newsletter. Would you mind if she asked you a few quick questions?"

"Um . . . sure?" Tessa said. She tucked her hair behind her ears and frowned. Mia was already digging into her backpack for her official reporter's steno notebook and pen.

Mia cleared her throat and uncapped her pen. "First question," she said. Some of the other parents and kids turned at the sound of her voice ringing out. "WHY did you move here?"

Tessa staggered back, as if she'd been pushed.

"What?" she whispered.

Kellie stepped forward, steadying Tessa by her arm. "Are you okay?" she asked. "You look like you're about to faint."

"I'm fine," Tessa said. "I didn't—I didn't eat any breakfast."

"Here," Kellie said. She dug in her purse and came up with the granola bar she'd been unsuccessfully pushing on her kids. "Try this."

"Is she going to get paid for eating it?" Cole wanted to know.

"Shh," Susan said. She grabbed Cole's water bottle from his backpack and offered it to Tessa. He could drink from the fountains for a day.

Tessa took a small sip. "That's better. I was just dizzy for a moment, but it passed."

"I need to ask my 'w' questions," Mia insisted. "Who, what, where, why, and when."

"Mia, quiet," Kellie said.

Tessa didn't look better, Susan thought. She was still ashen. It was a good thing Kellie hadn't let go of her arm.

Susan was about to suggest that Tessa sit down when a little boy shouted, "Bus! Bus!"

Parents exploded into activity, kissing children, retying loose shoelaces, shouting reminders about piano lessons and soccer practice, and waving as the kids climbed aboard. Susan touched her index finger to the corner of her eye, then her heart, then pointed it at Cole. *I. Love. You.* She saw his smile through the bus window, then the vehicle lumbered away, belching a cloud of exhaust. The group of parents echoed the noise with an equally loud sigh of relief. They peeled away, heading to the blissful quiet of their offices or homes.

"Are you up to walking?" Kellie asked Tessa. "We can wait here with you if you're still shaky."

"No, really, I'm much better now," Tessa said. "I should get back and check on the movers."

"Well, we're heading in the same direction, so we'll give you all the neighborhood gossip on the way," Kellie said. "You wouldn't believe the scandals. The intrigue!"

Susan punched Kellie in the arm. "She's kidding. We're actually quite boring."

"Sadly, it's true," Kellie said. "Well, we do have our ladies-only Wine and Whine night, and that tends to inspire some unexpected confessions, but other than that we're a pretty tame bunch."

"You'll have to join us at the next one," Susan said. "It's Gigi's turn to host, and she's your next-door neighbor."

"Have you met her yet?" Kellie asked. "She's the one with the Susan Sarandon vibe? Picture Thelma just before she and Louise drove off that cliff. Gigi's husband, Joe, is running for Congress in the special election—our congressman resigned because of a sex scandal with a prostitute, you might've heard—and Joe's always busy campaigning so you probably won't see him much, but Gigi's really great."

Tessa gave them a faint smile. "Well," she said, "here's my house." She handed the superhero water bottle back to Susan. "Thank you again."

Susan watched as Tessa walked up the front steps and disappeared inside.

"I repulsed her, didn't I?" Kellie asked. "I always babble too much."

"No, you're charming," Susan said. "I bet she's getting the flu."

"So what did you think of her?" Kellie asked as they resumed strolling.

"A spotless beige couch with two kids?" Susan said. "It screams 'control freak,' but I'm reserving judgment."

"She seems . . . pleasant, I guess," Kellie said. "But shy. She was like that when I met her at the open house, too."

Susan shrugged. "Busy day today?" she asked.

"Sadly, no," Kellie sighed. "I don't have a single listing yet. I earned a little something for helping with the Brannons' house, but I wasn't the main agent on it. I've been working for a solid month and I've barely recouped the costs I spent to get licensed and for my business cards."

"You're just starting out," Susan said. "It'll take time."

"I guess," Kellie said. "How long did it take you? I mean before your business really exploded?"

"Oh, a little while," Susan said vaguely. She didn't want to tell her friend that her company, Your Other Daughter, had been an instant success. Susan's idea for a part-time job coordinating services for the elderly, like taking them to doctors' appointments or visiting them in nursing homes, had somehow grown into a booming franchise in four states. Early on, there had been an article about her in *Black Enterprise* magazine, and then a write-up in the Duke alumni magazine, which had helped launch her company. Now she had a syndicated weekly radio show in which she dispensed advice about elder care to callers. She gave speeches at five hundred dollars a pop. Even Mr. Brannon had become one of her clients; she'd helped the widower sort through his accumulated decades of belongings and choose an assisted living center. She visited Mr. Brannon every week to make sure he was comfortable. That service was off the books; Mr. Brannon, with his courtly manners and sad smile, had a special place in her heart. He seemed so alone in the world.

"I'll spread rumors about asbestos at Wine and Whine night, to get the neighbors we don't like to move away, and then I can sell their houses," Kellie said.

"Great idea," Susan said. "I'll bring a few bottles of Chardonnay. Last time Gigi ran out."

"Maybe she didn't think it would be good for her husband's

congressional campaign to have a dozen drunk women lurching out of his house," Kellie mused.

"Oh, come on, it never hurt Bill Clinton," Susan said. "How's this for a plan: we'll get Tessa drunk and she'll spill all her deep, dark secrets."

"I'm in," Kellie said, laughing.

# Chapter Two

**Newport Cove Listserv Digest**

*Halloween party & parade!
  It isn't too early to begin planning for everyone's favorite holiday—Halloween!
  This year at our annual Newport Cove party we'll have a moon bounce,
  tasty treats for all (including gluten and nut free!), and a parade through our
  neighborhood for all of our little goblins and ghosts! "Opal" the fortune-teller
  may make a surprise visit to read fortunes (please remind your children to
  refrain from pulling on Opal's hair so we avoid painful incidents like last
  year's)! Please email Shannon Dockser if you'd like to volunteer for the snack
  committee or activities committee. —Sincerely, Shannon Dockser, Newport
  Cove Manager

*Re: Honda Mechanic?
  I don't have a Honda, but I bring my Chrysler LeBaron into Michael at Auto
  Repair Unlimited. He's a well-mannered young man, not like some these days,
  and his prices are reasonable. —Tally White, Iris Lane

*Re: Dog Poop
  I'd like to second the comment by Mrs. Reiserman. I can't imagine any Newport
  Cove residents would be so uncourteous as to leave canine filth in their
  neighbors' yards, but several times a year I step into something most unpleasant

when I'm out gardening and have to hose it off my shoe. Let's all try to be better neighbors. —Ralph Zapruder, Blossom Street

• • •

Gigi Kennedy rolled over in bed, lazily stretching out an arm and connecting with a cold sheet instead of a warm body.

She yawned and blinked and the world came into focus. Her nightstand with a hefty political memoir and a treatise about microbusiness loans stacked atop the juicy novel she'd been yearning to read—but hadn't found the time—for weeks. An expensive pot of eye cream that she'd begun to use religiously, though she suspected the cost was due to the French name rather than the quality of the ingredients. And her monthly planner filled with scribbled reminders of phone calls she needed to make, places she needed to be, people she needed to woo.

She despised that planner with its bright red cover.

Red signaled power, according to the image consultant her husband, Joe, had hired. Apparently crow's-feet did not, and the eye cream had been delivered to her along with the business card of a hairdresser who'd banished the strands of gray from Gigi's auburn locks before trimming off eight inches.

"Oh," she'd murmured, staring in the mirror when he'd spun her around with the flourish of a game show host. She'd always worn her hair down to her bra strap, and it had never bothered her that it got big and frizzy in the humidity. She'd liked the easy, bohemian style. But the hairdresser had applied a horrible-smelling chemical that made it look sleek and shiny and not at all like her.

Her mother had burst into laughter when she'd seen Gigi. "I'm sorry, honey," she'd said. "It's just that you look like a"—Gigi had waited patiently as her mother had succumbed to more giggles—"like a shorn sheep!"

Two years of therapy, and her mom could still light up her
buttons faster than a toddler at an elevator control panel.

Gigi yawned again and checked the bedside clock. Not
even six a.m.

"I wish they all could be California girls," Joe's off-key voice
warbled over the rush of the shower.

*Careful*, she thought. *Don't want to alienate the voters on the
East Coast.*

When she and Joe had first met, back in college, he was
famous for sleeping through his morning classes. Not missing
them, but actually sleeping in the last row, his head bobbing,
an occasional snore whistling through his nostrils. Now Joe
woke up at five a.m. to run three miles before drinking a green
smoothie, standing up, while he read the papers.

But she'd changed, too. Didn't everyone say the key to
a happy marriage was changing together? Or maybe it was
growing together. In any case, she'd begun to match Joe's runs
with her own Zumba and Pilates classes, and now that he es-
chewed dessert, so did she. So technically, they were shrinking
together. Except for the chips and brownies she snuck from
the snack drawer reserved for the kids' lunches, but she gobbled those standing up and buried the evidence in the trash
can, so they obviously didn't count.

The kids. She climbed out of bed and reached for her robe.
She needed to make sure this morning went smoothly, to
avoid stepping on any of the emotional bombs her teenaged
daughter Melanie loved to lob in her path. Late this afternoon
a photographer was coming over to capture a family photo
for Joe's congressional campaign brochure and website. Their
twelve-year-old, Julia, would cooperate. Of course she would;
Julia had been a happy, gurgling infant whose disposition had
never changed. She was an honor roll student and captain of
the soccer team. Julia would put on the sundress Gigi had laid
out and brush her hair without being asked. But fifteen-year-
old Melanie . . . well, the best case was that she'd demand

to wear all black and refuse to take out her nose ring. Gigi wouldn't think about the worst case until she'd fortified herself with coffee.

She'd make Melanie's favorite banana-pecan pancakes, the ones her daughter had adored when she was a little girl, Gigi decided.

She padded into the kitchen, her feet hitting cold tile, wishing she'd put on socks but feeling too tired to go back upstairs for a pair. She stroked the head of their sleepy golden retriever, Felix, before popping a pod of Starbucks Breakfast Blend into the Keurig. While her coffee spurted into a mug, she reached into the pantry for ingredients and began lining them up on the counter: flour, bananas, milk . . . She was dropping a pat of butter into the warm skillet when she sensed a presence behind her.

"Your hair looks ridiculous."

"Good morning, honey," Gigi said, trying to block annoyance from her tone. She smoothed down a few spiky bangs that seemed determined to defy gravity. "I'm making pancakes."

"I'm not hungry," Melanie said.

Gigi turned off the burner.

"How about just a banana, then?" she said. Melanie wouldn't get a break for lunch until almost noon. She had to eat something.

"I said I'm not hungry."

Gigi flinched. If her husband routinely spoke to her in that tone, she'd divorce him. If a friend did, she'd cut off contact. Only Melanie, with her sad eyes and defiant expression, could heap emotional abuse on her mother.

Still, she couldn't let Melanie get away with acting like a brat.

"Watch your tone," Gigi said, but when she caught a glimpse of Melanie's face, she regretted snapping back. Her daughter was clearly in pain.

When had Melanie's kohl-rimmed eyes changed? They looked to Gigi like black mussel shells. There was something in the center of those eyes reminiscent of the glistening fragility of a pearl, but try as she might, Gigi couldn't crack through the hard exterior and reach it.

Melanie grabbed her backpack off the kitchen table and shoved her binder inside.

"You don't have to be at school for almost an hour," Gigi pointed out.

"Raven is picking me up."

Raven. It couldn't possibly be a real name, could it? Gigi wasn't even sure if Raven was a girl or a boy, and an early glimpse of him/her hadn't helped clear things up. Raven hid behind a sweep of dark hair and seemed incapable of smiling. Gigi wanted to ask Melanie, but was afraid of her reaction.

Melanie was almost out the door. She hadn't eaten. She looked tired. She was wearing a long-sleeved shirt and black jeans and the mercury was expected to reach 80 today.

"Honey? Do you want to change your shirt? It's supposed to get pretty hot."

"God! Can you just stop nagging me?" The door slammed on Melanie's final word.

Gigi sank into a chair, blinking hard. Felix nudged her hand with his cold nose and she curled an arm around him, grateful for the comfort.

Gigi knew that whenever she reached out to touch her daughter, or asked Melanie to put away her phone and talk, Melanie viewed Gigi as a giant chicken relentlessly pecking at her. She could see it in the way Melanie shrank from her, or exited a room moments after Gigi entered.

Whenever she spoke to Melanie, all her daughter heard was this: *Peck, peck, peck.*

Why couldn't she hear what Gigi was really saying? *I love you, I love you, I love you.*

# Chapter Three

*Before Newport Cove*

WHEN HER DAUGHTER, BREE, was just seven months old, Tessa called 911 for the first time.

It was a rainy day, and the house had felt stuffy, so Tessa had walked upstairs to open a window. She'd left Bree on the living room rug, encircled by toys.

She'd been gone for sixty seconds, she'd insisted later. Ninety at most. She couldn't get the timeline exactly straight, though. Had she paused to pick up Harry's dirty socks off the bathroom floor and toss them in the hamper, or had she done that earlier in the day? She might've shaken out the comforter and smoothed it over the sheets instead of leaving it crumpled. An unmade bed had always nagged at Tessa.

The truth was, she had no idea how long she'd left Bree alone. Jagged patches of time had begun to disappear from her memory, like sinkholes forming in the fog of her exhaustion. Bree hadn't slept through the night, not even once, since coming home from the hospital. Bree was fussy. Sensitive. Spirited. Whatever the politically correct term was nowadays. Instead of nursing contentedly, like all the other babies in their Mommy and Me class, Bree always took a few sips, then yanked herself away from Tessa's breast as if she'd been scalded.

"It must be something in your diet," a lactation consultant had said, looking at Tessa with accusing eyes. "Are you eating a lot of broccoli? Chocolate? Caffeine?"

Tessa had mutely shaken her head at each fresh charge. She wasn't eating much of anything other than toast and water and bananas. She was far too tired to cook, and she'd gone off coffee during her first trimester and certainly knew enough to avoid drinking too much of it while breastfeeding. Still, Tessa was certain she was the source of her daughter's misery. Tessa would pace the house in the middle of the night with a squalling Bree in her arms, mindlessly chanting nursery rhymes, timing the beat to the throbbing in her head. Harry had been working for a software development firm back then and his job had required him to travel nearly every week, so she couldn't even hand off the baby for a break.

Tessa had wanted a child so desperately. She'd endured two miscarriages before having Bree, the second when she was nearly twenty weeks into her pregnancy. She'd tried to do everything right. She'd read a dozen books on child development. She'd washed Bree's tiny onesies in Dreft before folding them into the drawers of her pink-and-white dresser. She'd spent an entire weekend crafting the butterfly mobile that hung over Bree's crib. Yet every time she looked down at Bree's red, miserable face, she felt as if she was failing her daughter.

When Bree turned four months old, Tessa finally gave up breastfeeding. Whenever she hid a carton of formula in her grocery cart, she'd felt like she was stashing crack beneath her romaine lettuce and organic chicken. Breast was best—everyone knew that.

But miraculously, the formula had seemed to help. Bree had begun to cry less. She'd actually slept for a blissful five-hour stretch one night. She'd even begun to bestow a gummy little grin on Tessa that could've been gas but Tessa decided was a smile.

"Maybe it was just colic," Tessa had said to Harry two weeks before it happened. He'd returned home from yet another business trip and had picked up Thai food on the way in from the airport. Tessa's last shower was a distant memory—two, maybe three days earlier? She'd been wearing one of the drawstring pants and shapeless cotton T-shirts that had become her wardrobe staples. But as she'd crunched into a spring roll and taken a sip of cold, crisp wine, she'd felt the bright stirrings of hope.

"The worst is probably over," she'd said as she watched Harry feed Bree bites of a steamed yam. Bree had inherited her father's sweet tooth—she spit out green vegetables but at least she loved pears and yams.

As soon as Tessa had uttered those words, she'd felt an icy twinge work its way down her spine. She'd tempted bad fortune. And sure enough, it arrived the next day when Bree's cries took on a sharper, more pained tenor, so alarming Tessa that she'd rushed Bree to the pediatrician's office.

"She's teething already. An early achiever!" the doctor had joked as he'd examined Bree. He had white hair and a round belly, like Santa. His kids were all grown; he probably slept deeply for eight hours every night. Tessa hated him and his jolly laugh more than a little bit.

Baby Motrin didn't help, not nearly enough. The tooth took forever to come in and no sooner had it broken the surface than the one next to it began to embark on its jagged, torturous path through Bree's soft mouth.

Tessa rubbed Baby Orajel on Bree's red, raw gums, and gave her cold rings to gnaw on, but Bree seemed to feel pain so intensely! Every cry was a jab to Tessa's heart. Bree began waking up every three hours again, bleating the plaintive cry of a kitten. Tessa's vision grew blurry. Most of her meals were bowls of soggy cereal gobbled over the sink. Once, at a stop-light, the blare of a horn jerked her awake. She'd glanced back at Bree, safely asleep in her car seat, and she'd shuddered. What if her foot had slipped off the brake? She drank more coffee—three, four, sometimes five cups a day.

The mornings were the worst. Tessa would blearily look around at the cluttered kitchen, at the bottles she needed to wash, at the clothes she needed to launder and fold, at the counters she should declutter, and feel herself sliding into a gray gloom. She'd always been organized; she'd worked as an accountant. She'd untangled complicated taxes for clients, she'd unloaded the dishwasher with one hand while cooking a stir-fry with the other, she'd effortlessly kept a running men-tal to-do list with a dozen revolving items. She'd run three half-marathons! But she couldn't manage one tiny baby and her house, even with—and here was the truly embarrassing part—monthly maid service. Sometimes Tessa felt like her cleaning woman, who was middle-aged and had four kids, was judging her as she lugged the vacuum cleaner up the stairs and emptied Tessa's overflowing trash cans: *Get it to-gether, lady.*

So on that rainy, stuffy afternoon, things were blurry. Sixty to ninety seconds? It seemed like the limit on how long a con-scientious mother—a good mother—would leave her baby alone.

It was quiet when Tessa had come back downstairs. Bree was exactly where Tessa had left her, playing with wooden stacking blocks, chosen because they were made with natural materials and nontoxic paints and were too big to be choking hazards.

Bree had been making a funny face. Her mouth had been twisting like it sometimes did when Tessa tried to spoon in pureed green vegetables. Tessa had come closer and seen her purse lying next to Bree instead of on the chair where she'd left it, its contents spilled out. Her hairbrush. Her wallet. The bottle of Advil, with a few of its tiny mauve pills dotting the carpet.

Advil, with its sweet coating.

Bree had been reaching for a pill on the carpet. Tessa had pried it out of her tiny hand and Bree had opened her mouth to scream.

Bree's tiny tongue had been stained mauve.

"No," Tessa had whispered. She'd run to the phone to dial the emergency number.

"Send an ambulance!" she'd gasped.

The ensuing minutes blurred by: the frantic trip to the hospital, punctuated by the laconic wail of the ambulance's siren, the EMTs bending over Bree's tiny body, taking her vitals, the young doctor shining a light into Bree's eyes while quizzing Tessa.

"You don't know how many she took? Didn't you check the bottle to see how many were left?" he'd asked.

"No, but the EMTs said I should bring it so you could check the ingredients . . . ," Tessa had said.

The doctor had snatched the little plastic bottle out of her hand. "It says it holds sixty." He'd shaken the pills out onto the stark white hospital sheet, his index finger jabbing at each one like an accusation. "There are still fifty in there. Was it a new bottle?"

Tessa had shaken her head. "No. I—I remember I took two right before I went upstairs. I must not have closed the lid properly."

"Did you check the floor to see if any were there?"

"No," Tessa had whispered. "Wait—yes. There were some on the carpet."

"How many?" the doctor had demanded.

Tessa had closed her eyes. "Um . . . five?"

"So the most she ingested was three," the doctor had said. "Less if the bottle had already been open when you took two. Was the bottle already open?"

Tessa had nodded, her mind feeling thick as it struggled to grasp the simple subtraction problem. "Um . . . it might have been. I think so."

The doctor had exhaled loudly. He had patients who needed him. He didn't have time for this nonsense.

"She probably spit it out once she sucked off the coating; it's pretty bitter inside," he'd said. "I doubt she even ingested one."

Bree had been maybe two minutes away from having her soft little stomach pumped, all because of Tessa's inattention. The doctor's expression had changed as he'd stared at her, probably wondering if she was one of those women who faked her children's illnesses to get attention. Then he'd walked away without a single word.

As Tessa had left the hospital, Harry had called her cell phone, responding to the frantic message she'd left.

"I'll fly back tonight," he'd said, even after she'd reassured him that Bree was safe. Tessa had wondered if he still trusted her with their baby.

She'd hung up and looked around. To her left was a big parking lot; to her right, a busy street. But there were no cabs in sight, and even if she'd spotted one, it wouldn't have a car seat. She had no idea how she was going to get home.

She felt her throat constrict. *I'm sorry*, she'd thought, looking down at her baby.

A moment later, Bree had begun to screech in her arms.

Six months later, Tessa called 911 again.

# Chapter Four

**Newport Cove Listserv Digest**

*Re: Dog Poop

I'd just like to second Mrs. Reiserman's point about cleaning up after your dog. Oftentimes, dog walkers will drop a bag of poop in my trash can if it is by the curb on trash day. Whilst this might seem like an appropriate way to clean up after your dog, let me assure you it is not. If the can has already been emptied, these small bags end up on the bottom, where they can become stuck. The stench is most unpleasant. —Tally White, Iris Lane

*Re: Dog Poop

It's MS. Reiserman, not MRS. Reiserman. —Joy Reiserman, Daisy Way

*Lawn Bags!

Large brown lawn bags will be distributed to all Newport Cove residents on Saturday, Sept. 18 to assist with your leaf collection throughout the fall season. If you would prefer to not have bags delivered, please simply reply to Newport Cove Manager Shannon Dockser (no need to "reply all" to the entire listserv!). Thanks! —Sincerely, Shannon Dockser, Newport Cove Manager

*Re: Lawn Bags!

I don't want any lawn bags. I burn my leaves. —Mason Gamerman, Daisy Way

**\*Re: Lawn Bags!**

It's far more efficient to simply mow your leaves when you're cutting your grass. No need to risk injuring your back by raking and bagging. —Tally White, Iris Lane

. . .

"I'll be back around nine, nine thirty at the latest," Kellie told Jason as she looked in the mirror and fastened on a silver hoop earring.

"Sure you will," he said. He was lounging on their queen-sized bed, flicking through television channels. Kellie had shepherded the kids through homework and dinner before getting them changed into their pj's. Now they were eating bowls of vanilla ice cream in the kitchen.

"No, I'll be early," Kellie said. "I have to work in the morning, remember?"

Jason didn't respond; he'd settled on the Discovery Channel where a lion was selecting a dinner entrée from a revolving buffet of antelope and zebra. Jason had shed his clothes like a snakeskin on the floor, and Kellie suppressed a sigh as she bent down to pick up his Levi's and red polo shirt with the logo of the small hardware store he co-owned with his father. Kellie tossed the shirt and jeans into the laundry hamper in the closet. Jason had a half dozen identical shirts; he wouldn't need to wear this one to work tomorrow.

"If you could get the kids to put their stuff in the dishwasher," she said.

"Sure, just a sec," he said. She looked at him lying there in his blue boxers and white athletic socks, the only man she'd ever loved. Ever slept with. Sometimes, days—entire weeks, even!—would pass when she'd be so distracted by the busy rhythm of their lives that she'd hardly register her husband's presence. Then, bam! At the most unexpected times, she'd be drawn up short by unexpected details that conjured tenderness in her: Faint smile lines radiating out from Jason's eyes. Arms still as thick and strong as when they'd first wrapped around her in high school. A few dots of gray in the stubble around his jaw.

He seemed to feel her gaze and looked up. "C'mere," he said. She lay down next to him, snuggling into his chest, feeling his steady heartbeat against her cheek. He dropped a kiss onto her head, already reabsorbed into his television show.

That lunch with Miller Thompson had meant nothing. She'd been foolish to feel nervous. Miller had taken her to a seafood place, a nice one with tablecloths, but they'd mostly chatted about work. Miller was married and had three kids. He'd flipped open his wallet to show off their school photos. It had all been perfectly innocent.

"And honey, please have the kids in bed by eight thirty," she said.

"Yup," Jason said.

She climbed off the bed, went to kiss her children good night, and took a clean wineglass out of a kitchen cupboard. This was one of the inspired rules of Wine and Whine night—everyone brought her own glass, so cleanup was minimal for the hostess. Kellie's was a special one Jason and the kids had wrapped and tucked into her stocking last Christmas. It was comically oversized, and the words painted near the rim read: "Oh, look. It's wine-thirty!"

Kellie stepped outside, locking the door behind her, even though crime was practically nonexistent in Newport Cove. *Parenting* magazine had designated the neighborhood as one of the "20 Safest Communities" after crunching statistics for violent crimes per capita. Cash stolen from the glove compartments of unlocked cars, a mailbox-bashing by bored teens, an occasional UPS package missing from a doorstep—that was the extent of it.

She strolled down the sidewalk, noticing the Harmons, who had five boys, had left open the sliding side door of their minivan again. The floor mat was nearly hidden beneath snack wrappers, crumbs, and small plastic toys. Kellie reached out and pulled the door shut so the interior light didn't drain the battery, then continued on toward Gigi's brick rambler. The houses on their street were an eclectic mix. A few had been torn down and replaced by McMansions crowded onto the narrow lots, but for the most part, the original Tudors, Colonials, and Craftsmans still dominated the wide, sweeping roads.

"Beautiful evening!" Kellie called to Mason Gamerman, who lived across the street from Gigi and was watering his front lawn with his garden hose. She raised her giant, empty glass toward him, and he grunted in response, which was about as enthusiastic as Mason got. On Halloween, he grimly dispensed pennies to trick-or-treaters.

Kellie was walking up Gigi's steps just as her husband, Joe Kennedy ("No relation to the famous family," he always explained), came out the door. He wore a dark suit, crisp white shirt, and blue-and-gold-striped tie—campaigning clothes.

Joe smiled, his teeth flashing. Gigi had confided that the image consultant Joe's campaign director had hired had suggested Joe get his teeth professionally whitened. They'd laughed about it, but apparently Joe had followed through.

"Where are you off to?" Kellie asked.

"Door-to-door canvassing," he said.

"Sounds exhausting," Kellie said.

"It's rewarding, though," Joe said. "I get to sit down one on one with people and talk about the issues that are most important to them. Education, government spending, the economy . . ."

*Yawn*, Kellie thought. Last year, Gigi and Joe had come over for dinner and Jason had shown them the new Ping-Pong table they'd set up in the basement for the children. Someone had cracked a joke about how in a few years the kids would be using it for beer pong, and Joe had confessed to never having played. Ten minutes later, the four of them were clustered around the game table, Joe's face red and sweaty as he slammed down his paddle, bellowing, "Drink, sucker!" at Jason.

"Well," Kellie joked, "you've got my vote."

Joe reached for her hand and pressed it between his own. His brown eyes radiated sincerity. "Thank you," Joe said reverently. "Let me know if you'd like a yard sign. I can get you a discount."

He walked a few steps away, then turned around and winked. Kellie, who'd been standing there openmouthed, burst into laughter. He'd gotten her.

Joe continued on his way and Kellie pushed through the front door, still smiling. There were more than a dozen women clustered in small groups throughout the living room and kitchen, but the first one Kellie saw was Tessa. Kellie hadn't been sure if Tessa would come. Yesterday at the bus stop, Kellie had suggested that Addison pop by after school and join Noah and Cole, who were going to set up a soccer net in the backyard.

"I'm sure there'll be an extra spot on their team, if Addison wants to join," Kellie had said.

"Oh," Tessa had responded. "Um . . . I was going to take the kids shopping with me after school. But thanks."

It hadn't escaped Kellie's notice that Tessa had the same deer-in-the-headlights look as when Mia had asked her (admittedly in a loud voice, perhaps bordering on strident—she really needed to talk with Mia again about modulating her tone) why they'd moved to Newport Cove. Maybe her boisterous family was overwhelming Tessa's. Kellie had decided to back off, so she hadn't reminded Tessa about the neighborhood women's gathering tonight.

But here was Tessa, wearing a navy blue sundress and rosy lipstick. She was more dressed up than most of the other women, which struck Kellie as sweet, as if Tessa was trying to make a good impression. Tessa was clutching a glass of Chardonnay, ensconced in a conversational circle with Susan, Gigi, and—uh-oh—the community manager, Shannon Dockser. Kellie poured herself a generous splash of Sutter Home from an open bottle on the kitchen counter and eased into the group.

"So you see, Newport Cove is actually a municipality," Shannon was telling Tessa, who was nodding politely. Susan's eyes were a little glazed, which Kellie suspected wasn't from the wine alone. "It was designated one in 1982. That means our little neighborhood is kind of like a corporation. So we can hire private services just for us! You wouldn't believe how quickly we get plowed when it snows. At eight a.m. the next morning, the trucks come zipping through. And you know we've contracted with a trash service to do pickups twice weekly instead of once, right?"

"I didn't," Tessa murmured. "But that's great."

"Think about running for a spot on the neighborhood council," Shannon said. "We'll have a few openings when the current terms end. I can email you some more information about it."

"Don't get sucked in," Gigi warned. "That's how Joe started."

"By the way, his teeth look great," Kellie whispered. Gigi grinned and elbowed her in the ribs.

"Oooh! There's Marcy! Excuse me just a minute, ladies! I need to talk to her about the holiday decorating committee!" Shannon flitted away.

"Where does that woman get her energy?" Kellie asked.

"I hear she steals her children's Ritalin," Susan said.

"She made that up," Kellie told Tessa.

"Don't worry about the neighborhood council thing," Gigi said. "Just tell her you'll think about it for next year."

"That's what I've been saying for the past decade," Kellie said.

"It's not that I don't want to contribute . . . we just need to settle in first," Tessa said.

"Tell me about it," Susan said. "I moved here years ago,

and I still have a dozen boxes in the basement I haven't even opened."

"Everyone has been so welcoming, though!" Tessa said. "Bree was already invited to a birthday party next week, and someone left a casserole on our doorstep this morning. I'm so glad we found this neighborhood."

She turned to Kellie. "I'm sorry Addison couldn't play with the boys the other day, but maybe Noah and Cole would like to come over this weekend to watch a movie?"

"Sure," Kellie said. She was a little surprised by Tessa's sudden warmth, but her timing was excellent. Mia had been invited to a friend's house on Saturday. If both kids were busy, the house would be quiet for a few hours. She'd take a bubble bath, maybe give herself a manicure, and catch up on episodes of *Orange Is the New Black*. The thought sent a little shiver of delight through her body.

"And don't forget about the soccer team," Kellie said.

"Right . . . ," Tessa said. The smile slid away from her face. "Does one of the parents coach it, or . . . ?"

"Actually, we hired a professional coach," Kellie said. "I know, I know, it's completely ridiculous, but it actually costs next to nothing when you split it twelve ways and he's really good at teaching the kids skills. We had a dad doing it last year, but he got way overcompetitive."

"He had the kids doing wind sprints," Susan explained. "Have you ever seen little kids doing wind sprints? I haven't, either. They all got distracted by dandelions midway through, and then one kid decided to tackle the others. They ended up in a scrum while the dad stood there frantically blowing his whistle."

"Also, the guy we hired is about twenty-five and he looks like Liam Hemsworth," Kellie said. "Susan cheers whenever he wears shorts."

"Now she's making stuff up," Susan said. "I only cheer when he bends over to pick up his water bottle."

Tessa laughed. "In that case, I'm going to make Addison join the team," she said.

"I may join it, too," Gigi said.

"Gigi's younger daughter is a great soccer player," Kellie told Tessa. "Their team was the county champion last year."

"How many kids do you have?" Tessa asked Gigi.

"Two," Gigi said. "Melanie and Julia."

"Do they both play sports?"

"No," Gigi said. She drained her glass of wine. "Just Julia."

Kellie reached for the bottle again. "Another?" she offered.

"Please," Gigi said with a sigh.

"Long day?" Kellie asked.

"Just, you know . . . high school is tough," Gigi said.

And it was tougher when your daughter was going through a difficult stage, Kellie thought. Sweet Melanie, who'd always worn hair ribbons that matched her clothes when she was a little girl and had been a mother's helper for Kellie when Mia was a toddler, had transformed into a young woman Kellie would've sworn before a jury couldn't possibly be the same person. A few weeks earlier, Kellie had been walking down the sidewalk when Gigi's Ford Fusion Hybrid had pulled up. Melanie had gotten out of the passenger's seat, yelled something at Gigi, then slammed the car door and run inside the house. Kellie had waited for her friend to exit the vehicle, planning to make a joke about hormones, but Gigi had stayed in the driver's seat, her head in her hands. Gigi had sat there for so long that Kellie became worried her friend would be embarrassed if she knew she was being watched, so Kellie had turned around and walked the other way.

"Oh, Susan, I met your husband at school yesterday," Tessa was saying. "Randall's his name, right? He was helping out in Ms. Klopson's class. She said he volunteers every week. What a nice guy."

Susan smiled without showing her teeth. "Ex-husband," she corrected.

"Sorry," Tessa said. "Anyway, he was working with Cole and another boy on math, so . . ." Her voice trailed off.

"Who else should we introduce Tessa to?" Kellie interjected quickly. Tessa obviously didn't know yet that Susan was divorced—or the awful reason behind her divorce. But surely she'd seen the way Susan's face had tightened, causing her soft brown eyes to narrow.

Gigi glanced around. "There's Reece Harmon—she's wonderful but a little frazzled, since she's got five boys, so we should probably give her a chance to chug her wine before we make our way over there—and, oh! Jenny McMahon lives right around the corner. She's probably the one who left you the casserole."

"How'd you know?" Tessa asked. "I think that was the name on the card."

"Because she's the nicest woman on the block," Gigi said. "She adopted three orphans from Peru. They're in college now, so she's the foster mom to homeless kittens. She even chats up Mason Gamerman. The Dalai Lama wouldn't have the patience to talk to Mason."

"I've met him," Tessa said. "He yelled at Noah to get off his lawn when Noah was just trying to retrieve a Frisbee."

"That's our charmer," Susan said. "I call him my boyfriend, so hands off."

Tessa laughed again, and something shifted in her expression. She'd been holding herself so tightly before, her shoulders rigid and her fingers clenched around the stem of her glass, but something—perhaps the wine, or the warmth of the kitchen, or the sounds of murmured voices and women's laughter—seemed to have untwisted something in Tessa. Her face looked younger. She was actually a pretty woman, with her dark, straight eyebrows and sculpted cheekbones, Kellie realized with a jolt of surprise.

"You know, I've been meaning to ask," Tessa said. "Did the elderly couple who owned the house before us have just one child?"

Kellie frowned. "I don't think they had any."

"I've been here forever, and they definitely didn't have kids," Gigi said.

"Oh," Tessa said. "It's just that I found this little stepping stone in the garden, the kind with a kid's handprint on it. I didn't know if Mr. Brannon had forgotten it when he moved."

"Probably a gift from one of the neighborhood children," Kellie said. "Everyone loved Mrs. Brannon. She used to make these amazing caramel apples at Christmastime and invite everyone over to decorate them and sing carols. See, I told you your house had happy memories."

"I can ask Mr. Brannon if he wants it next time I check in on him at the assisted living center," Susan said. Then her voice dropped. "Incoming, incoming. Nine o'clock."

"Who?" Kellie asked.

"Tally White," Susan said. "The neighborhood busybody. She comments on every thread on the listserv. She knows exactly how many bottles of wine are in your recycling bin . . . Oh, thank God. Jenny McMahon just started talking to her. That woman really is a saint."

The women stayed in their group of four for another few minutes, then Susan took Tessa off to meet Jenny, and Kellie chatted with a few other neighbors before heading out. As she walked slowly down the street, feeling pleasantly buzzed, she detected fall's first faint nip in the air. It was a lovely night; the full moon hung low in the clear sky. She was happy, Kellie realized as she climbed the steps to her home. Thoroughly, ridiculously content. Going back to work had been the right move. She found herself looking forward to the morning, when she'd shower and put on a nice outfit and go into the office. And chat with her colleagues.

It wasn't until she'd unlocked her own door and walked in, stripping off her shoes so her footsteps wouldn't wake the kids, that a thought struck her.

When she'd first started dating Jason as a senior in high

school, she'd have given anything to be alone with him. They'd created elaborate ruses to slip away from their parents' homes, complete with code words spoken over the phone. An hour in the backseat of his beat-up Mustang, steaming up the windows, was her wildest fantasy.

But when Tessa had invited Noah over and Kellie had begun to imagine what she'd do—conjuring the things that would make her feel relaxed and happy—she'd imagined being alone.

When had her husband disappeared from her dreams?

# Chapter Five

**Newport Cove Listserv Digest**

*Re: Lawn Bags!
   Just a friendly reminder to all Newport Cove residents that the burning of leaves is
   prohibited by ordinance C-5238 due to fire hazard. Proper leaf disposal methods
   include bundling leaves into the large paper bags provided free of charge by the
   Newport Cove Manager and leaving bags at your curb for pickup. Alternately,
   you may choose to place your leaves on your compost pile. A little tip: Shredded
   leaves break down faster! Thank you! —Shannon Dockser, Newport Cove Manager

*Dry Cleaner Recommendation
   Can anyone recommend a good dry cleaner? The one on Forsythia Lane "lost"
   my best cashmere sweater although my synthetic-blend ones, which were
   dropped off at the same time, were miraculously not misplaced. —Melinda
   Morton, Tulip Way

*Re: Dry Cleaner Recommendation
   I've used the dry cleaner on Forsythia Lane for many years, and I'd like to state
   for the record that they've never misplaced any of my belongings. —Tally White,
   Iris Lane

• • •

Susan's favorite day of the week was Friday. Not because of the impending weekend—anyone with young kids had to reshape expectations of what days off meant—but because Friday was her long walk day. After taking Cole to the bus stop, she always led Sparky on a looping trek of about four miles, giving them both a good workout. When she'd first begun the ritual, she'd returned business calls during those walks, and had checked emails on her iPhone. But one day, Susan had realized she'd returned from her walk with no memory of it. Not a single recollection of a leaf that was changing color, a bird singing on a tree limb, or a cool gust of wind tightening the skin on her face.

Now she left her phone at home. She tried to breathe deeply, to soak in the delicate texture of the petals on a magnolia tree, to really see the vibrant green of the grass. To live in the moment. Once in a while, it actually worked.

Today, though, she was seething. That innocent comment from Tessa about Randall volunteering in Ms. Klopson's classroom had been enough to put a damper on the evening for her—and it had been a night she'd looked forward to all week, since she went out so infrequently.

She quickened her pace, charging up a hill, Sparky bouncing along by her side.

She imagined Randall standing up from a tiny chair in Cole's classroom, extending his hand to Tessa, smiling that smile. He was so handsome, with his milk chocolate skin, almond-shaped eyes, and broad shoulders. Men liked him. Kids adored him. Women loved him most of all. Susan had been charmed when they'd first met, too. The bottom of her paper bag had torn as she'd walked from a supermarket toward the parking lot, and her carton of orange juice had fallen out. Of course Randall had been there to scoop it up and carry it to her car, the big jerk.

She couldn't stop Randall from volunteering in Cole's class, from coming to all of his soccer games, from putting on a ridiculous white chef's hat and serving up pizza in the school cafeteria on special occasions and making the kids laugh with his silly fake French accent. Actually, she wouldn't want to stop him; it made Cole happy, and that was the most important thing. Far more important than her peace of mind.

She realized she was gritting her teeth, and added buying a night guard to the mental to-do list she wasn't supposed to be keeping because she should be focusing on the changing leaves. There! An orange one. Well, orange-ish. She could feel her neck muscles loosening up already.

She continued on, found herself ruminating about Randall again, and gave Sparky's leash a little tug to the left to take a shortcut home. She'd try the walk again this afternoon, when she was in a better mood.

If Susan had adhered to the Friday ritual, it never would have happened. In the past, when there had been close calls, Susan had crossed the street, or turned around and retreated. But she was so deep in thought, so *not* in the present moment, that she didn't look up until Sparky yanked on his leash, lunging ahead to greet a cute little French bulldog puppy with a comical overbite—the kind of dog Randall had always wanted.

Attached to the *other* end of the leash was her. She. Daphne.

Susan reared back, her heartbeat quickening. It wasn't supposed to happen like this, not while she was wearing old jeans and a long-sleeved T-shirt with Keds on her feet. Keds, for Christ's sake! There was even a hole in one of the toes.

Daphne was biting her lower lip, like a nervous schoolgirl.

"Hi, Sue," she said in that low, melodious voice.

Susan had always been envious of Daphne's voice. "She sounds like one of those radio hosts who come on late at night, doesn't she?" Susan had once said to Kellie.

"Oh, I know who you're talking about—the one who takes sappy dedications for love songs," Kellie had said. "Not that I listen to those shows."

"Me, either," Susan had said. "Just when I'm doing dishes or something."

"Me, too," Kellie had said. "Oh God, did you hear the one last week when the little boy dedicated a song to his father—?"

"The soldier?" Susan had interrupted. "He was deployed to Afghanistan, and he missed his son's fifth birthday . . ."

Both women had wiped their eyes, then looked at each other and burst into laughter. "Anyway," Susan had said briskly. "That's the kind of voice she has."

And now here was husky-voiced, lip-chewing Daphne, looking tragically beautiful in her slim-fitting (designer!) jeans and belted black sweater. Looking as if *she'd* been the wronged one. Sparky was showing a distressing lack of loyalty by enthusiastically sniffing the butt of Daphne's dog.

"Excuse me," Susan said as she tried to untangle her leash from Daphne's. It required the two women to perform a complicated, dancelike maneuver, but they finally got the dogs straightened out and Susan turned to go.

"Sue?" Daphne said again.

Daphne was the only one who had ever called her by that nickname. Susan froze.

"I'm . . . Could you . . . ?" Daphne began.

Susan whirled around and raised a single warning finger. "Don't."

She stood there for a moment, staring at her younger, thinner replacement. Randall had even upgraded Sparky to a cuter model.

When Daphne's eyes dropped, Susan turned and walked away, yanking on Sparky's leash to get him to follow.

# Chapter Six

**Newport Cove Listserv Digest**

*Re: Dog Poop

Just wanted to add to the discussion that for only $20, I picked up a little gizmo
called an "ornament grabber," I guess for those hard-to-reach ornaments on the
top branches of your Christmas tree! Anyhoo, I use it to reach down and grab
the little bags of poop if they get stuck to the bottom of my trash can. Once you
tuck the bag of doggie leavings into a larger trash bag, our collectors will carry it
away—no problem! —Jenny McMahon, Daisy Way

*Seeking Used Car

Does anyone have a used, sturdy car they're willing to sell? My teenaged son just
totaled mine. Will consider a trade: my son for your car. —Liza Edelstein, Iris Lane

*Re: Seeking Used Car

Will also throw in one or more of my five boys, free of charge! —Reece Harmon,
Daisy Way

• • •

Gigi's stomach muscles clenched up when the doorbell rang.
Strangers swarmed into the house—Joe's campaign man-

ager and press secretary and the image consultant, along with the photographer and his assistant and another guy whose role wasn't entirely clear to Gigi. Everyone immediately began to order everyone else around.

The photographer positioned them all on the front porch steps, an American flag billowing in the holder over Joe's head. Zach, the campaign manager, who looked about twenty-two years old, told the press secretary, who appeared to be even younger, to move a pot of red geraniums and put it next to Joe. "Too busy," sniffed the image consultant, who demanded that the geraniums be moved to the other side of the steps. The photographer's assistant sprang forward to pluck a brown blossom from the plant at her boss's directive. Someone adjusted Gigi's shoulders from behind, tilting her closer to her family. Someone else dusted imaginary lint off Joe's suit lapel.

"Smile!" the photographer finally commanded. He snapped a few shots, then began issuing commands.

"Joe, sit up a little straighter. Megan, can you put your hand on your father's shoulder?"

"It's Melanie," Gigi corrected, before wondering if Melanie would be irritated she hadn't let her daughter speak for herself. This *was* how women in abusive relationships felt, wasn't it—all the second-guessing, the fear of missteps?

But Melanie showed remarkable restraint, at least for a few minutes. Then the photographer said something in a low tone to his assistant, who ran off and came back with a makeup bag.

"Just a little touch-up," she said, pulling out a tube of pink lipstick and moving in toward Melanie.

"But I don't like makeup," Melanie said, leaning back. Gigi wasn't sure, but she thought she saw Melanie's eyes flick toward Zach, who was a very handsome young man, with sun-streaked hair and broad shoulders. He looked like he'd be more at home on a surfboard than volunteering on a congressional campaign.

"You'll look really washed out in the photos otherwise," the photographer said. "Even your dad has some on!"

Before Melanie could respond, the assistant said, "At least let me cover up this blemish."

"This is so stupid!" Melanie shouted, leaping up and running into the house and slamming the door.

"Did you have to say that?" Gigi snapped at the assistant.

She looked at Joe. She wondered if one of them should go after Melanie. She wondered if Joe really did have on makeup.

"I can probably Photoshop her in," the photographer said. "Maybe use a filter to give her a little color wash."

"Fine," Joe said. "Let's give her a minute to cool down and I'll go talk to her."

Was Joe's congressional campaign going to harm their already fragile family? Gigi wondered.

When their congressman had been indicted for the phone sex incident dubbed Tootsie Takedown (the congressman spent much of the secretly videotaped hotel room encounter discussing his fetish) and Joe had floated the idea of running in the special election, Gigi had nearly laughed out loud. Joe, a politician? Sure, he'd served on the Newport Cove council for a few terms. He'd even run for the school board, and lost by such a narrow margin it had almost felt like a victory. But this would be a sea change.

"Do you really want this?" Gigi had asked. They'd just finished making love on a lazy Saturday morning—their sex life had always been zesty—and they were lying in bed together, her sweaty leg draped over his. One of the things that Gigi adored about Joe was that he never rolled over and fell asleep afterward. Some of their most intimate talks had been postcoital.

"Yeah," he'd said. He'd nodded, as if to confirm his decision. "I do."

Gigi had known Joe was frustrated with his law firm job for an environmental organization. He believed in the cause, but his boss was a control freak and the organization felt stagnant. He wanted to do more. Maybe this campaign was his destiny. Joe's mother had been a huge fan of the Kennedy family even before she married a man who shared the common surname, and she'd named her son after Joe, the oldest of the four Kennedy boys—brother to John F., Robert, and Ted. Joe had been the one his parents had pinned their hopes on to be president, but he was killed in World War II.

Joe wasn't the only one who wanted his life to feel more meaningful. Since moving to the suburbs and having kids, Gigi had felt a little . . . watered down. She'd been working as a part-time art teacher at the community center, which helped fill her days, but Gigi had found it more and more difficult to suppress her yearning for her old self, the woman who had marched in support of Planned Parenthood and who had helped stage a sit-in to save an ancient redwood tree near her childhood home in California.

This would be Joe's campaign, but she would stake a claim in it. They'd always worked well as a team. This would be their next adventure together.

Gigi had rolled over and kissed him. "Okay," she'd said. "I'm in."

She was the first voter he'd had to sway, and he'd done it effortlessly.

The primary would be held in November, at the same time as the general congressional elections. If Joe won the Democratic nomination, he'd proceed to the special election against the Republican candidate in the spring. It felt like a long way away, but already Joe's calendar was filling up with events, as was hers: ribbon cutting ceremonies and Rotary Club meetings, school fairs and fund-raising dinners.

To Gigi's surprise, early reaction to Joe had been even more positive than he'd hoped. He was running on the promise of reform. He'd be one of the negotiators in Congress, a fresh face with real-world experience who would break down the gridlock and actually get things done. At least that's what his candidacy statement promised.

What Gigi hadn't expected, though, was the intrusion of so many other people in their lives, the constant honing and shaping of not just Joe's message, but of Joe himself. Of their family.

"Chin up, Gigi," the photographer called.

And so they left an empty space in their family portrait for Melanie, a little hollow corner on the edge of the steps where she'd once sat and played patty-cake with Gigi, near the garden where Melanie had long ago planted sweet peas with her adorable miniature trowel. The warm earth under their bare feet, the taste of sweet, tart lemonade, Gigi's belly, beautifully swollen with her second daughter . . . Gigi could still see Melanie tugging at the hem of her shorts, her brown eyes shining with delight over her pudgy cheeks as she tended to her plants. "Mama! They growed!"

Gigi felt a touch on her shoulder. Julia. She covered Julia's hand with her own, blinking back grateful tears. *At least I still have one*, she thought.

Maybe, she thought as the camera clicked again and again, the photographer could work a little magic on her, too. Erase the sorrow from her eyes and the tightness from her smile. Add a smiling Melanie to the shot and make them a picture-perfect family, at least for one frozen moment.

# Chapter Seven

**Newport Cove Listserv Digest**

*Re: Dog Poop

Here's an idea. Let's photograph the people who don't bother to clean up after their dogs and post their pictures on this listserv. A little public shaming might help our neighbors be better citizens. —Bob Welsh, Magnolia Street

*Re: Used Car

I don't have a used car for sale but I know someone whose daughter had success with CarMax. —Tally White, Iris Lane

• • •

Moving to Newport Cove had been the right thing to do, Tessa thought as she smoothed the blue down comforter over Addison and eased the Matchbox race car out from his fist. There were no reminders here, no kitchen floor that still seemed to bear faint bloodstains no matter how obsessively Tessa scrubbed them, no driving past the house that had been sealed off with yellow crime scene tape.

Tessa paused, watching Addison sleep, as she had on so many nights recently when her insomnia had struck. She wished she could slip into his dreams to see if they were happy. She waited for him to make a small sound, or smile, but his face remained soft and inscrutable.

It had thrown her when Kellie brought up having Addison join the soccer team. Tessa knew Addison would love it, but he'd be around other adults—strangers. Still, soccer practice was held outdoors. Tessa could sit on the sidelines. She could watch over her son.

She'd realized after she'd reacted so strangely to Mia's question at the bus stop that simply moving to another town wasn't enough. They needed to prepare so they didn't call unnecessary attention to themselves. So she and Harry had been practicing. At night, after she was certain the children were asleep, they'd go into the living room and fling questions and accusations at one another. Harry wasn't very good at the role play. He jiggled his leg when he recited his story, and his eyes always drifted up to the left. Police called those tics a "tell." If the female detective who'd questioned them before they'd moved ever interrogated Harry, she'd hone in on it.

Last night, Tessa had come into the kitchen, where Harry had been doing the dinner dishes. She'd decided to start without giving Harry any warning.

"Where were you on the night Danny Briggs died?" Tessa asked, just as he'd reached to flick on the garbage disposal.

"What?" he'd asked, flinching, his hand freezing.

"Dammit, Harry, you've got to get better at this," she said. "You look guilty!"

"I *am* guilty!" he'd shot back.

She'd decided to ease off. He was still so fragile.

But this neighborhood—well, had they moved here a year ago, things would have been very different. She'd have drunk three glasses of wine at the neighborhood gathering instead of the single one she'd slowly sipped. She would've done an impression of Mason Gamerman ordering Noah away from his rosebushes. Tessa was really good at impressions, a talent she always used to trot out at cocktail parties. Her Sarah Palin was almost on par with Tina Fey's. She would've offered to host the next Wine and Whine night, where she would've mixed up a giant pitcher of her special sangria. But blending in, not standing out, was her goal in Newport Cove. So she smiled politely and asked questions but never revealed much about herself. At Back to School night, instead of volunteering to become the room mother, as she had every other year, she signed up to launder the art smocks and clean paintbrushes. It was a task she could do at home, alone.

She thought about Gigi's husband, Joe, whom she'd met when she'd come in to the Wine and Whine night. He'd tried one of the brownies she'd brought, still warm in their pan, and had been overly enthusiastic about their taste. He'd inquired about her family, and had heartily welcomed her to the neighborhood.

As they'd talked, Tessa realized she and Joe had opposite agendas. His was to stand out in people's memories, to make an impression. Hers was the opposite: To blend in. To not be noticed.

They were both campaigning.

# Chapter Eight

## Newport Cove Listserv Digest

*Re: Dog Poop
Newport Cove Council Members voted last night to install dispensers that will contain free plastic bags for dog waste! Starting next week, you can find these on the corners of several of our streets, including Tulip Way, Iris Lane, and Camellia Court. The dispensers will be marked with the icon of a squatting dog. Feel free to take a bag—or two!—whenever your furry friend needs one!
—Sincerely, Shannon Dockser, Newport Cove manager

*Bunions
—Tally White, Iris Lane

*Re: Bunions
Ignore that last email. It was in error. —Tally White, Iris Lane.

*Re: Dog Poop
Does this mean we're at the "tail end" of this discussion? —Frank Fitzgibbons, Forsythia Lane

• • •

The thing about being a real estate agent was, you actually needed a house to put on the market before you could make money. There were some homes—like the charming, well-constructed Cape Cod Tessa's family had bought—that practically sold themselves. You could stick a sign in the yard and accept a contract a day later. Others, optimistically called "fixer-uppers," were salvageable if you could just get buyers to see the potential. You did that by emptying out the clutter so they looked bigger, scrubbing the walls and floors and windows, and perhaps hiring an architect to draw very simple plans designed to inspire daydreams.

Then there were houses that fell into the third category: the Titanics. Kellie's first listing was on a collision course with an iceberg.

Kellie absently chewed on the end of a pen, conjuring a picture of the house in her mind and searching for the best way to minimize the visual assault. The house itself was low and squat and gray. It reminded Kellie of a mushroom, a food she'd always despised. Its roof was squished down miserably on top, like a hat a mother had stuck on the head of a protesting boy. The yard was long and narrow and landscaped in a spectacularly ugly way. There were brown pebbles instead of grass, and a few manicured shrubs that looked like overgrown bonsai. Most bizarrely, a miniature lighthouse stood proudly in the center of the backyard, despite the absence of water in the vicinity. The lighthouse had a set of stairs that led to a tiny upper room containing a straight-backed chair and small table beside a window.

Kellie had gotten the listing because Jason's father, who was one of the nicest men on the planet, had sold the owner the materials he'd need to construct the lighthouse, and the two had become friends.

"So what did he do with it?" Kellie asked during one of their weekly family dinners while Mia nibbled on a slice of

American cheese and Noah heaped nothing but raw baby carrots onto his plate and Jason's sister's son devoured Caesar salad in what seemed like a deliberately ostentatious way.

"His kids used it when they were young, as a playhouse or something," Jason's father said. "After they were grown I think he mostly sat in it and looked out the window."

*That's so sad*, Kellie thought, picturing a lonely man, perhaps one who'd dreamed of living by the ocean, forced to scale down his hopes, dying inside a little bit more with each passing day, yearning to feel the spray of salt water against his face one last time. She looked at Jason to see if he was thinking the same thing, but he was focusing on buttering a roll.

She and Jason had never experienced the ESP some long-married couples seemed to share. It hadn't bothered her in the past. But lately, Kellie had been flipping through the *New York Times*' Real Estate section at work, and she'd found herself covertly turning to the Style section to read the stories of newly married couples. She'd scour the details like a private detective, trying to puzzle out why people were drawn to each other. Some of the men were ridiculously romantic. One actually said of his bride, "I need her like I need oxygen." Kellie wondered if, after a decade of morning breath and debates over whose way was the most efficient to load the dishwasher, the groom would still be making such declarations. Passion always yielded to contentment, didn't it? Fireworks fizzed into gentle sparks. It happened to everyone.

Still, it would be nice if Jason did something unexpectedly romantic once in a while. She hadn't felt this absence of a quality in him before. Jason was a good guy, through and through, cast in the same mold as his father. Unlike some of the other dads Kellie knew, who tried to be the fun parent and cherry-pick all the desirable activities, like taking their kids to the park, or out for ice cream, Jason actually scheduled dentist appointments and drove the kids there. He bought gifts for them to take to birthday parties. For years, Noah had been the hit of the toddler party circuit because of the real tool belts filled with tiny screwdrivers and nuts and bolts Jason had assembled for gifts.

"More roast?" Jason's father asked.

"Sure," Kellie said. "Thanks."

Her father-in-law reached out with the tongs, rejecting the first piece he scooped up in favor of one that looked a little more rare, which she preferred.

"Here you go, honey," he said, sliding it onto her plate.

Jason's mother was talking about taking all the grandkids out on a nature walk this weekend, where they'd surely gather flowers and grasses for some sort of craft project she'd create, and his father was turning to Jason to discuss a new distributor he was thinking of using while Jason nodded and chewed his roll. Kellie looked at the faces of her family while they finished eating, thinking of how much she loved them.

Oh, they were all so pleasant! Even Jason's sister was only smug about the eating thing, and it could be Kellie was imagining that. Maybe she was overthinking things. Or not thinking about them enough. Something was off. But sugar always helped when you felt out of sorts.

Kellie stood up. "I'll bring in dessert," she said. She'd gotten a box of brownies from A Piece of Cake, the best bakery in town, which was just down the street from her new office. Everyone groaned in mock protest, but she knew the brownies would disappear in two minutes. These weekly family dinners followed a routine. A roast. Jason and his father discussing work. Jason's mother fretting about whether the roast was too dry. Kellie reassuring her it wasn't, that it was even juicier than last week. Everyone insisting they were too full to eat dessert. Everyone devouring dessert. It was always the same.

"You're so domestic!" Kellie's irresponsible younger sister, Irene, had exclaimed when she came to visit from L.A., where she was pursuing a career as an actress. It hadn't sounded like a compliment.

Kellie slipped into the kitchen but instead of picking up the white cardboard box from the counter, she reached for her iPhone and began to tap out a text. Seeking the advice of a more experienced real estate agent was the logical next step. She had a lemon of a house to sell and she wanted to move it quickly. Should she tear out the lighthouse? Have someone take up the pebbles and replace them with sod? It was hard to know how much to invest in the house. She needed an expert opinion.

It was only natural she ask Miller.

# Chapter Nine

**Newport Cove Listserv Digest**

*Re: Dog Poop
Can we "bag" this discussion now? (Last one, I promise.) —Frank Fitzgibbons,
Forsythia Lane

• • •

Susan swept through the doors of Sunrise Community Assisted Living Center, carrying a copy of a new large-print novel and a small canvas bag.

She took the elevator, which was wide enough to accommodate three side-by-side wheelchairs, to the second floor. There were probably stairs somewhere around here, but she'd never been able to find them. She made her way down the long hall to Mr. Brannon's room. He shared a suite with another man, also a widower, named Garth.

Susan had tried to tease Mr. Brannon (he'd insisted she call him Charles, but she privately always thought of him as Mr. Brannon) when he'd moved in, saying that he and Garth would be the Casanovas of the second floor. "You'll be fending off the ladies," she'd said. "Look out!"

Mr. Brannon had smiled, but the warmth hadn't reached his eyes, and Susan had felt guilty for making the joke. She wondered if he'd wanted the suite, rather than the private room he could afford, because having another person close by was a comfort. On lonely days he could pretend the shuffle of slippers across the floor simply meant his beloved wife was in the next room.

Susan knocked on the open door to the shared living room. Garth was busy tinkering with something on a table—he'd been an engineer long ago—and it took another two sharp knocks for him to hear.

"Hello, Susan!" he bellowed (Garth was a bit deaf). "Charles, your granddaughter's here!"

Garth persisted in thinking she and Mr. Brannon were genetically related, despite copious visible evidence to the contrary (Mr. Brannon was as white as the inside of a biscuit, for starters). But Susan didn't mind. Her own parents lived in Germany now, where her father had been born, and her grandparents were deceased. It was nice to have a surrogate.

Mr. Brannon lifted his head from the book he was reading in the easy chair by the window. He was wearing slacks, a crisp white button-down shirt, and dress shoes. He always dressed well. Soft white tufts of hair floated above his ears like clouds.

A smile broke across his face, transforming it.

"Hi, Charles," she said.

"Miss Susan." He struggled to get up while she silently waited. She'd learned long ago that it was an affront to his dignity to suggest that he stay seated when a woman entered the room. When he had straightened up as much as his curved back would allow, she crossed over to him and kissed him on the cheek, breathing in a whiff of Old Spice.

"I brought you treats," she said. She reached into her sack

for a tin of cookies and set the novel atop a stack on the table next to his chair.

"You spoil me," he said.

"My granddaughter doesn't bring me treats," Garth said mournfully.

"It would be my pleasure to share," Mr. Brannon said.

Garth made a swift emotional recovery, taking a surprisingly large handful of cookies for a man who had arthritis. Susan made a mental note: *Next time, bring two tins.*

"Shall we?" Mr. Brannon said, offering Susan his arm. She walked with him to the elevator, then through the doors of Sunrise Assisted Living. She'd parked right in front of the entrance so he wouldn't have to go far to reach her car, and she helped him into the front seat of her Mercedes.

"It's so pretty out," she said as she settled into the driver's seat. "I thought I could get us some tea and we could go for a drive." Those lines were part of their charade. Earlier on during her weekly visits, she'd taken Mr. Brannon places— to restaurants, movies, and bookstores. Then one day she'd driven past Newport Cove high school and she'd seen something transform his face, a naked yearning. She'd slowed for a stop sign, and he'd stretched out his hand against the glass pane of his window.

"Did you go to school there?" she'd asked, but he hadn't answered.

"Would you mind . . . Could you . . . ," he'd begun, the words seeming to take a great effort. She'd pulled over and turned in to the entrance to the school.

"Thank you," he'd said as she'd driven slowly down the winding driveway, past the athletic fields and bleachers. They'd sat in the parking lot while she'd wondered about the school's pull on Mr. Brannon. Maybe he'd met his wife here. Maybe he'd been a star football player, or a shy band member, while she'd been in Home Ec class. Something had told her not to ask, though.

"We can go now, dear," he'd said after a few minutes, and as she'd driven away, he'd released a soft sigh.

Later, Susan discovered other places that exerted a similar gravitational effect on Mr. Brannon: a casual pizza restaurant, a nondescript redbrick house about a mile away from Sunrise Assisted Living, and the local hospital. She and Mr. Brannon talked before and after their drives, but not while he sat vigil outside his four spots. Those moments felt sacred.

Now Susan steered into the order lane for a drive-through Starbucks and bought two Chai Tea Lattes, then she set off, following the trail of Mr. Brannon's emotional landmarks.

Maybe, she reflected as she took a sip of hot, sweet tea, she never questioned him because she had secret pilgrimages of her own. What would the people who called in to her radio show, seeking her sage, calm advice, think if they could see Susan stripped of her pride and restraint? Would they still respect her if they glimpsed her at her lowest moments? At least once a week, Susan lurked outside the house where Randall now lived with Daphne and his French bulldog puppy. Her vigils usually occurred on the nights Cole was with Randall, when Susan was alone and memories pressed in on her until she clutched her head, feeling nauseous from the swirl of her thoughts, from the recognition of all she had lost.

Susan had assumed she'd been drawn to Mr. Brannon because he had no family left. Because he needed her. But maybe that wasn't it.

Maybe the reason was because he seemed broken inside, too.

# Chapter Ten

*Before Newport Cove*

BREE WAS A LITTLE more than a year old when the next incident occurred.

Harry had been away on another business trip. He'd been traveling more lately. Sometimes Tessa wondered if he wanted to escape their messy home, his unhappy wife, their strained life. She'd thought about asking him, but she was afraid of his answer.

That afternoon, she'd spent an hour trapped on the couch while Bree had dozed on her chest. Bree resisted sleep with the fervor of an escaped convict being dragged back to prison, so it had felt like a victory when she'd nodded off in Tessa's arms after her bottle. Tessa hadn't been able to transfer Bree to her crib, though, because it would have woken her. So even though Tessa had needed to flip the laundry from the washing machine into the dryer, and straighten the living room, and bundle up all the newspapers and magazines for the recycling truck that would come through tomorrow, she'd lain on the couch, her head at an uncomfortable angle, letting her daughter rest.

When Bree had finally awoken, Tessa had a kink in her neck and an uneasy mix of agitation and boredom churning through her body. She'd needed to get out of the house. She'd packed some cold drinks, since the day had been warm, bundled Bree into the stroller, and had taken her daughter to the park, thinking fresh air and the swings would do them both good. There was an elementary school nearby, and school had just let out, so the playground should have been empty.

As she'd approached the park, Tessa had noticed a group of kids at T-ball practice. The children were adorable; their team T-shirts must have been ordered in a size too large, making them resemble Charlie Brown and his gang. Tessa had settled Bree into a bucket swing. The gentle motion was one of the few things that soothed Bree, but it had to be a real swing. Naturally, the mechanical one Tessa had bought for their living room, the one that had cost a hundred dollars—and would free up her hands—only irritated Bree.

She'd been thinking about Harry, wondering what he was doing in California at that exact moment. It was late afternoon on this coast, which meant it was lunchtime there. Perhaps he was eating in a nice restaurant. Sushi, maybe. Tessa hadn't had sushi since before she'd gotten pregnant. It had always been her favorite splurge—the dash of searing wasabi, the tangy crunch of seaweed, the soft rice. After a good meal and then an afternoon of meetings, Harry would head back to his hotel room, where the newspaper would be crisp, the minibar filled with tempting treats, and the sheets on his bed snowy white. Perhaps he'd take off his shoes and flop on the bed and watch a little television, or sneak in a catnap. Maybe the maid had left him a minty piece of chocolate.

Sometimes she almost hated her husband.

Out of the corner of her eye, she'd seen a man coming from the direction of the parking lot. He was maybe in his sixties, with graying hair. He'd been moving slowly, weaving through the trees as he headed toward the T-ball field.

But then the man had stopped a few dozen yards away from the field. He'd positioned himself behind a tall, thick tree, leaning against it with his left hand while his right hand slipped into his pocket.

"Ma!" Bree had yelled at that moment.

Tessa would've liked to pretend that Bree was calling her, but she knew it was Bree's way of saying, "More!"

She'd reached out to give her daughter another gentle push, then she'd swiveled to fix her eyes on the man. He was a little disheveled-looking, now that she was getting a closer look. He wore a battered baseball cap, khaki pants, and a plain blue T-shirt.

There had been something in the hand that was coming out of his pocket. Something shiny that had glinted as the sun caught it.

A cell phone? No. A small video camera.

Tessa had glanced again at the children. A dozen or so little boys and girls, about five or six years old. The man had lifted the video camera to his eye as a little girl in a skirt walked to the batting tee.

The little girl's skirt hiked up, revealing her small, chubby thighs, as she swung for the ball and missed. Why was that creep hiding behind a tree, filming a little girl as she bent over?

A nanny had been pushing a child on the swing next to Bree's.

"Do you see that?" Tessa had asked. She'd pointed at the man. His hand was back in his pocket now.

The nanny had squinted and frowned. "What is he doing?"

"He's taking videos of those kids! He's a creep!"

"Is he a grandfather?"

"No!" Tessa had said. "Why would he be hiding? The parents can't see him because he's behind that tree."

The nanny had shaken her head. "That's no good."

"Can you watch her?" Tessa had said, gesturing to Bree. "I'm going to talk to him."

The nanny had nodded and taken over pushing Bree. Tessa had moved three long strides toward the man before she'd frozen. What would happen if she confronted him? He might attack her. More likely, he would simply walk away. She'd never know where he came from, or who he was. He'd go prey on other children.

She'd reached into her pocket for her cell phone and had dialed 911.

"I'm at a playground and there's a strange man lurking around here," Tessa had said, her voice sounding official. It was her job to protect her child—to protect all children. She was part of the village! "He's taking videos of a little girl. He doesn't seem to be with anyone."

"Address, please?" the emergency operator had said, and Tessa had given her the name of the park and the precise location. She'd described the man and said she'd wait by the swings until a police officer arrived.

She'd kept a close watch on the man. He'd put the video camera away, but he was still staring at the children, hiding behind that tree, one hand resting on it as his face peered around the side. His other hand was still in his pocket. Tessa hadn't been able to see his face clearly, but she'd committed his general height, weight, and hair color to memory.

The police came within five minutes, the squad car's tires grinding against gravel as it pulled in to the parking lot. The lights and siren were off, but a male and female officer had gotten out quickly and walked toward the swings. Tessa had pulled a protesting Bree out of the bucket seat, settling her daughter on her hip as she went to meet them.

"I'm the one who called," Tessa had said. She'd felt a little thrill of excitement—finally, something was interrupting her dull existence!—as she pointed to the man. "He's right there."

"Please stay back here, ma'am," the female officer had said. She was young but had a competent, no-nonsense air about her. The two officers began walking toward the man, spreading apart slightly, which Tessa had suspected was so that they'd be able to cover more angles in case he tried to bolt. He didn't even notice them until they came up beside him.

Tessa hadn't been able to hear what they said, but after a moment she'd seen the man spread out his arms, palms up. *I didn't do anything!* the gesture had seemed to say.

*Check his video camera,* Tessa had thought with satisfaction. *You'll see exactly what he did.*

She'd edged a little closer, despite the officer's warning. Most perverts were cowards; he wouldn't dare do anything to her now. Let him try! She'd sock him in the nose. The officers were still talking, and now the man was pulling his video camera out of his pocket and holding it up for them to see.

Tessa had stopped moving when she saw a woman running toward the pervert. The woman had put a hand on the old man's arm as she talked to the officers. Then the officers had stepped back, their posture relaxing. The woman had spoken to them for another minute, then looked over at Tessa. She'd shaken her head, her expression grim, and begun to walk over. Tessa's stomach had plummeted.

"Are you the one who called the police?" the woman had asked. Tessa had nodded mutely, her throat dry.

"My father fought in the first Persian Gulf war," the woman had said. Her eyes were bright and her voice sharp. "He has an old injury. There wasn't anywhere for him to sit down and his leg was stiffening up so he leaned against the tree for support."

Tessa had swallowed hard, feeling blood rush to her face. "I'm so sorry . . . ," she'd begun.

"Look, I appreciate you trying to protect our kids, but you really jumped to conclusions," the woman had said. Her voice had a little quaver in it and she was clutching her hands together tightly. By now the other parents at practice had all been looking toward the officers. "Why didn't you just ask my dad what he was doing? You embarrassed him."

"I'm sorry," Tessa had whispered again. She'd looked at the

nanny for support, but the nanny had quickly averted her eyes.

The little girl in the skirt had run over to the man, and he had bent over to give her a hug, and yes, Tessa had seen as he took a few steps, he was favoring his right leg with a limp. She hadn't noticed it when he'd been walking to the tree line.

The woman who'd confronted Tessa had walked away without a word. The grandfather had reached out to politely shake the hands of the police officers, a gesture that sealed Tessa's misery. He didn't look her way, not even for a moment.

Maybe one child was enough, Tessa had thought as she tried to get Bree into the stroller. She and Harry had discussed the possibility of another child, now that Bree was over her colic and most of her teething, but Tessa obviously had trouble managing just one. Bree had begun screaming because she wasn't ready to leave the swings, her arms and legs sticking out stiffly, and Tessa had to force her into the stroller. Now everyone who'd been staring at the old man was watching *her*. Judging her. She wasn't a natural as a mother; she was a crazy lady who couldn't comfort her baby and rushed her to the hospital when it wasn't necessary and called the police on an innocent grandfather. She wasn't any good at this!

They should just stick with one child, and hope they didn't mess her up too badly, Tessa had thought miserably.

The next month, Tessa discovered she was pregnant.

# Chapter Eleven

• • •

Early one Friday afternoon, Joe came home unexpectedly and announced that he wouldn't be campaigning at all that Sunday so they could have family time. "Maybe Chinese food and a movie?" he suggested. Then he handed Gigi a pint of salted caramel ice cream, which was her favorite.

"So," she said after hiding the carton in the freezer, behind the frozen spinach, where the kids would never find it. "Are you planning to tell me what's going on?"

Joe tried to give her an innocent face, but she just arched an eyebrow. She'd seen him talk his way out of speeding tickets. She knew his innocent face.

"I know you're not going to like it," he began, "but it would just be for a few months."

"Go on," Gigi said. This sounded like it was worth more than a measly pint of ice cream.

"Remember my new campaign manager?" Joe asked. He loosened the knot on his necktie and began to unravel the piece of silk.

Gigi thought back to the day of the photo shoot. "The young guy who looks like a surfer?"

"Yeah," Joe said. He slung his tie over the back of a chair and Gigi automatically reached to straighten it out. "His name is Zach."

"Right," Gigi said.

"So even though he's been working for me for the experience, he can't do it for free much longer. He's been crashing with a buddy but the friend's girlfriend is sick of it. I was thinking about our basement. It's empty." Joe began speaking more quickly now that he'd released the request. "You'd hardly even know he was here."

"Oh, Joe," Gigi said, folding her arms. "Really?"

She hated the idea of having a stranger in the house. And Joe's political campaign had already taken over so much of their lives. Already she'd tamed her hair and become the kind of woman who folded her arms when she was displeased with her husband. Did the campaign have to take over their home, too?

"It would just be for a little while," Joe said. "Look on the bright side, if I lose the primary he'll be gone even sooner."

"We'll have to ask the kids," Gigi said.

"C'mon, you know Melanie's going to freak out," Joe said. "She blows up when we tell her we're out of cereal. We can't present this as her choice. We either decide to do it and tell her, or we don't do it at all."

"Okay," Gigi said. "What if we don't do it at all?"

Joe exhaled. He looked exhausted. His eyes were red-rimmed, and the skin beneath them sagged, Gigi saw as her heart softened. He was juggling two jobs now, since he was still working full-time for the environmental company, and the strain was showing. It was only going to get worse in the coming months.

"He's good, Gigi. There are a lot of races around the country. He could leave tomorrow and join another one," Joe said. "I feel like I could actually win this thing. People are starting to recognize me."

"So how long are we talking, exactly?" Gigi said.

"Just through the general election, max," Joe said.

A few months, then. Definitely worth more than a pint of ice cream.

"Fine," she said. "But you have to be the one to tell Melanie."

Joe jumped up and came over to stand behind her, putting his hands on her shoulders. "Thank you," he whispered in her ear. He began to knead her shoulders, his thumbs seeking out knots of tension and digging into them. Joe could have another career as a masseuse; the man gave world-class back rubs. That reason alone could have cemented her decision to marry him.

"We're going to be on the road a lot," Joe said. "He just needs a place to crash at night. If I get elected I'll have a salary for staff and then he can afford an apartment, but for now . . ."

"I know, I know," Gigi said. She tilted back her head and let it rest against his chest as Joe's touch became lighter and his fingers came around to her front, grazing the tops of her breasts. Her breaths grew more shallow.

"Joe," she said.

"Mmm?"

"Is this what you expected?" she asked. "The campaign, I mean?"

His hands paused. "Some of the time," he said. "I don't know . . ."

"What?" she prompted.

"The other night I was door-to-door canvassing and this guy invited me in and I got stuck talking to him for half an hour," Joe said. "I couldn't figure out how to get the hell out of his house. And he was nuts. He kept telling me everything that was wrong with the government, and he made no sense, and whenever I tried to respond, he just talked over me. I finally started edging toward the door and escaped, but the whole time I'm thinking, *I'm missing a night with my family for this shit?* But I had to be polite. If I'd met that guy at a cocktail party a year ago, I would've blown him off after two seconds. But I can't do that anymore. I have to be more careful about offending people."

Gigi nodded. "You know what I think it's like?" she said. "Having a baby."

"My congressional campaign is our third child?" Joe asked.

"The expectations get too idealized," Gigi explained. "It's like when you're pregnant for the first time. You pick out the cute outfits and you make a birth plan and you imagine this snuggly infant sleeping on your chest. You don't think about the fourteen diaper changes a day and the sleep deprivation and all that other crap."

"Yeah," Joe said. "Exactly. I kept thinking about being in the Capitol and casting an important vote. I didn't expect to spend hours talking to people who think Obama is an illegal immigrant. The other day I had to explain the concept of global warming to someone, who told me she hasn't voted in fifteen years and doesn't plan to anytime soon."

"If you ever decide it's too much—if you ever want to quit—" Gigi began.

"I don't," Joe said. He hesitated. "Not yet."

"Okay," Gigi said. She sighed. "Julia will be fine with it. But do you really think Melanie's going to accept Zach moving in?"

"Sure," Joe said. "She'll squawk a little but she'll be fine."

But Joe didn't know how bad things could get with Melanie.

Melanie still adored her father. She reserved her worst rages for Gigi, for the moments when they were alone. Sometimes Joe would go into Melanie's room to say good night and Gigi would hear the murmur of Melanie's voice behind her closed door and she'd feel a spear of jealousy through her heart: *What are you telling him that you can't tell me?*

Joe's fingertips resumed making slow, electric circles beneath her collarbone. Gigi tilted back her head to look at him, this man she still loved so passionately. Sometimes you crashed into people, propelled by a surge of chemistry, and sometimes you drifted into them. Her relationship with Joe had been a long, slow slide that began in friendship and turned into like, and then lust, and finally love. She adored him, but more than that, she believed in him. He supported raising the minimum wage—one of Gigi's pet causes—and he believed in a woman's right to choose, another one of her priorities. Maybe the voters saw a man giving a winning smile with bright new teeth, and speaking in the sound bites that were catnip to reporters, but she knew the real Joe. Her Joe. He was the man she was voting for.

She wondered what the voters would say if they knew that Joe had smoked pot in college. That Gigi *still* smoked pot sometimes, leaning her head out the bathroom window while the water ran into the tub and her scented candles burned.

She glanced at the clock over the stove. It showed they still had almost an hour before the girls would get home from school.

"Follow me," she said, beckoning with her index finger.

She grabbed a spoon and the pint of ice cream, then beckoned for Joe to come upstairs, into the bathroom. She began running the water for the tub, then unbuckled his belt and tugged his slacks down over his slim hips. As Joe pulled his shirt over his head, Gigi lit her scented candle and reached for the Ziploc bag hidden behind an old electric toothbrush in the lowest drawer of her vanity.

She wiggled the bag in the air. Joe needed this; he was so stressed. After a joint and a soak in the tub and some sex, she'd convince him to take a long nap.

"For old times' sake?" she asked. "I can open a window to let the smell out. Pot and ice cream always was our favorite combination."

Joe smiled and slid into the tub.

Let the campaign photographer get a glimpse of *this*, Gigi thought as she put the joint between her lips.

•  •  •

### Newport Cove Listserv Digest

*Accountant

Can anyone recommend a good accountant? —Barry Newman, Forsythia Lane

*Re: Accountant

I highly recommend Randall Barrett as an accountant (he's the father of Cole, who's in my son David's 2nd grade class). Randall has been doing our taxes for years. You couldn't ask for a nicer guy! —Linda Hawthorne, Tulip Way

*Re: Accountant

TurboTax is also a helpful device, or so I've heard. —Tally White, Iris Lane

•  •  •

Susan's company, Your Other Daughter, was born when a sixty-seven-year-old woman tripped over a library cart.

An hour later, Susan was on the phone with her old college roommate, Bobbi, whose mother had broken her right hip and wrist in the fall. A librarian had called an ambulance, and Bobbi's mother had been taken to a hospital just twenty minutes away from Susan's home. Cole was two months old at the time, and Susan was still on maternity leave from her law firm.

"I hate to ask this," Bobbi had said, her voice tight and frantic. She was in the back of a taxi, racing toward the airport.

"But she's going into surgery before I can get there, and she's absolutely terrified of hospitals—"

"I'm on my way," Susan had said, already reaching for her car keys and Cole's diaper bag. Bobbi's mother had been warm and welcoming when she'd visited Bobbi at Duke; she'd invited Susan to join them for brunch, and had chatted with her whenever Susan answered the phone.

Bobbi had made it just in time to see her mother open her eyes in the recovery room after her doctors had placed three pins in her hip and encased her right arm in a cast. Susan had stepped away to give them some privacy, and when Bobbi had emerged into the hallway fifteen minutes later, she'd wrapped her arms around Susan. "Thank you," Bobbi had whispered.

They'd sat down together on a bench and Susan had handed her old roommate a fresh cup of coffee from a vending machine.

"Precisely what I needed," Bobbi said, taking off the lid and breathing in the steam. "You're a lifesaver."

While Bobbi drank her coffee and Cole dozed in his car seat at her feet, Susan had tried to help her friend formulate a plan. She knew how difficult it was to think clearly in a crisis, when anxiety and stress twisted through your mind.

"The doctor told me she's going to be in a cast for eight weeks," Bobbi had said, massaging her forehead with her free hand. "She'll need help bathing, and she'll need physical therapy. I can't stay that long . . . My job, the kids . . ."

Bobbi worked as a civil rights attorney in New York City, and she and her partner had twin sons who were toddlers. "And she can't come stay with us," Bobbi continued. "We've got too many stairs and our place is so crammed she wouldn't be comfortable. The guilt is killing me, Susan. How can I stick my mom in a rehab hospital?"

"Some of them are quite good," Susan had said. She'd reached out to touch Bobbi's arm, knowing her friend was close to tears. "And you can call her every day."

Bobbi had shaken her head. "She took care of me for eighteen years. After my dad left, she didn't even date until I'd moved away to go to college. This is the first time she's really needed me. She just looked so . . . so fragile in that hospital gown . . . She's getting old, Susan. How did she get old so quickly?"

Susan had rubbed Bobbi's back while tears had rolled down Bobbi's cheeks. The solution was simple: It was a relatively quick drive for her. She still had another two months of maternity leave, and Randall had a flexible schedule since he owned his business and set his own hours. She looked at her friend's anguished face and made a quick decision.

"So let me be there for you," Susan had said. "I'll visit her every other day. You can come for a weekend every two weeks or so. I'll bring her treats and talk to her doctors and make sure she's okay."

Bobbi had lifted her head. "You would do that?" she'd whispered.

And Susan had smiled and squeezed her friend's hand. "Of course I would."

It was a favor for a dear friend, not the inspiration for a business plan. But one afternoon after delivering a new book on tape and a slice of fresh apple pie to Bobbi's mother, Susan had stepped into the elevator to find a woman brushing away tears. Susan had given her a sympathetic smile, and suddenly, they were sharing a bench outside the rehab hospital, with Susan rubbing the woman's back just as she had Bobbi's. The woman's story had poured out—people had always seemed to want to confide in Susan; Kellie swore it was because Susan had the kindest eyes she'd ever seen—and her dilemma was remarkably similar to Bobbi's. She lived five hours away, had a family of her own, and could only come to visit her ailing father every other weekend.

"Would you—?" the woman had begun, then she'd stopped and gathered herself. "If you're willing, I'd like to hire you," she said.

Susan had blinked. "Hire me?"

"To be another daughter to my father, too," the woman had said. "Just for a few months. Please. I'll pay you whatever you think is fair."

*Well*, Susan had thought, *I'm coming here anyway* . . .

Soon the nurses began recommending Susan. It made their jobs easier when they had happier patients who weren't ringing their bells every ten minutes. Within a few months, Susan had so many clients that she needed to hire an assistant, and she'd given her notice at the law firm.

She delivered homemade mac and cheese and hot pot pies and milkshakes from Ben & Jerry's. She brought in e-readers and chenille bathrobes and decks of cards and needlepoint sets. She carried her laptop into the hospitals and rehab centers every time she made rounds, letting patients Skype with their far-flung families. Sometimes she brought Cole with her on visits. Seeing his little face seemed to cheer up some of her patients. During her second year of work, Susan added therapy pets. She had a volunteer who brought in a sweet golden retriever and cuddly guinea pig for patients who seemed in danger of falling into a depression.

Most of her work was short-term, focusing on patients with repairable injuries, but soon Susan expanded to include permanent clients. She had a steady roster of people who were determined to stay in their homes. Hiring Susan was often a compromise that appeased worried sons and daughters who lived too far away to look in on their parents regularly. So Susan made sure the food in refrigerators was fresh, and that front walks were promptly shoveled in the winter. She called families whenever she noticed something worrisome—a ninety-year-old man who'd begun to repeat himself; an eighty-five-year-old woman who'd started to shout, which could indicate hearing loss; an ammonia smell in the home of another couple, which could mean incontinence and required a doctor's checkup. She hired a third employee, then a fourth.

Within a year, she was out-earning Randall. Within two, she was making triple his salary.

Was that when their problems had begun?

He'd seemed proud of her, at least in the beginning. She'd commandeered the guest room in their old house for her office, installing a top-of-the-line computer, printer, and fax machine. She'd gotten a second cell phone devoted solely to her business.

Susan had always loved to cook, but the dinners she'd once enjoyed making—slow-cooked ribs and savory three-bean chili and turkey Bolognese—gave way to simpler meals. Sometimes Randall would come home after work, wander into the kitchen, and sigh when he discovered another foil-wrapped plate of a prepared meal Susan had picked up at Whole Foods.

*If you want ribs so badly, cook them yourself*, she'd think, pushing away a stab of guilt.

If his shoulders had slumped a little when she'd told him she needed to work some Saturdays, if he'd eaten more take-out, if there had been more nights than not when he'd stayed downstairs alone watching television while she'd caught up on paperwork in her office—well, that hardly justified what Randall had done. Plenty of men would love the fact that their wives were successful! She was pumping up their 401(k) plan, saving for Cole to go to college, paying off their cars.

Randall's fortieth birthday, though . . . she did feel guilty about what had happened that night.

# Chapter Twelve

A PIECE OF CAKE was the perfect spot for a casual meeting. It was warm and cozy, with little round tables forming a half circle around the bakery's floor. Vanilla and melting butter perfumed the air.

The two women wearing white aprons and working behind the counter were busy kneading dough and transferring loaves of French bread from heavy metal trays to the display racks; they took no notice of Kellie after she said she was waiting for someone and would order after he arrived.

Kellie was early, so she chose a seat by the window and watched people pass by. One guy staring at the screen of his iPhone walked directly into a parking meter, winced and rubbed his chest, then quickly looked around to see if anyone had noticed. No one had; most of them were on their phones, too. A pretty girl sauntered by, her sheaf of red hair swaying as she walked. For a moment Kellie thought the girl was staring back at her, then she realized the girl was admiring her own reflection in the glass.

Kellie had once looked that good, two children and fifteen years ago. Her hair was shorter now and not quite as bouncy (sadly, the same could be said for her boobs), but she'd lost

eight pounds since starting work and her waistline had recently emerged after a long hibernation. She'd felt charged
up lately; invigorated. In her knee-high boots and blue wrap-
around dress, she felt pretty for the first time in a long time.
No—an even more exhilarating sensation. She felt young
again.

Miller was coming down the street.

Kellie sat up straighter, gripped with indecision about
whether to smile at him or pretend she was engrossed in
something fascinating in the display case and hadn't noticed
his arrival. She opted for the smile; she was a terrible actress
(something put to the test in the weeks after every Halloween,
when her children accused her of dipping into their candy
stashes and she tried to deny it).

Miller's long strides brought him to the doorway of the bakery quickly, and just before he pulled the door open he caught
her eye and smiled back. She dropped her head, feeling her
cheeks grow warm, and reached for the yellow legal pad and
pen she'd slipped into her shoulder bag. If she took notes, this
meeting would reek of professionalism.

"Hi," he said as he sat down across from her. He must've
been meeting with clients today; he always wore a suit on
those occasions. On days when he just came in to the office to
make calls and catch up on paperwork, he wore jeans and a
button-down shirt.

"Thanks so much for meeting with me," she said. She
cleared her throat and sat up straighter. "This house . . . well, I
emailed you the photos. I need all the help I can get."

Miller winked. "You need more than that; you need a mir-
acle."

"Can I get you a coffee or something?" Kellie offered.

Miller shook his head. "I'm okay, but you go ahead if you
want something."

"No, no," Kellie said. So this would be a short, brisk meeting. She'd better get right to it. "So, I thought about having

the lighthouse torn down, but that'll be expensive, and then there'll be this gaping space in the yard. I could fill it in with more pebbles, but that seems ridiculous." She gave a little laugh. "Who wants a yard filled with rocks?"

Miller leaned back in his chair, resting his right ankle on his left knee so that his legs formed a triangle.

"The land is valuable," he said. "It's a tear-down."

"That's what I thought at first, too, but my clients are the kids of the couple who lived there," Kellie said. "Their father just died, and they inherited the house, and they don't want to see it destroyed."

"So they say now," Miller said. "But they're in mourning. They're attaching a lot of emotions to the house."

"So you think I should give it a little time to let them come around to the idea of it being a tear-down?" Kellie said.

"Here's what you do," Miller said. He put both feet on the ground and leaned forward, putting his arm on the table between them. His hands were large and well shaped, with a few dark hairs on the spaces between his knuckles, Kellie noticed, before yanking her gaze away. "Don't do a thing to fix up the place. Talk to the kids who own it, tell them you understand their feelings. Then hold an open house next weekend. See what happens. My bet is you won't get a single bidder."

"That's a safe bet," Kellie said.

"So then you put out a call to a few builders," Miller said. "Ask them to bid on the property. Bring the bids to the clients."

"You think they'll change their minds that quickly?" Kellie said.

"Maybe not immediately," Miller said. "But when they see an actual offer, the seed will have been planted. It's hard to walk away from money on the table. You can talk them through it, make them understand that a new house will be built and a family will live there again. That'll be better than the place staying empty. Real estate isn't just about selling; you have to be a little bit of a counselor, too. Buying a house is as big an emotional decision as a financial one."

Kellie nodded. She wished she hadn't taken out the legal pad. She hadn't written down a single thing and it seemed silly now.

"You're right," she said. "That's exactly what I'll do."

"And within a month or two, you'll have your first commission," he said.

"You make it all sound so easy," Kellie said. More than that, he made her believe in herself. "Thank you."

"My pleasure," Miller said. He glanced at the bakery case, then leaned toward her with a grin. "Have you ever tried their brownies? They're addictive," he said. "I've sworn off junk since I'm training for a half-marathon, but how about we share one? And maybe I'll grab a coffee after all."

"Absolutely," Kellie said. As he started to stand up, she motioned for him to stay seated. "It's my treat this time," she said. "I'm the one who asked for your help."

She walked up to the display case to order, thinking of how much Jason had loved the brownies she'd brought to the family dinner. He'd eaten two and had gotten a smudge of chocolate on his chin. Jason had always been a slightly messy eater; she'd grown used to wiping down the table around his plate after dinner.

Later that night, she'd gone into Noah's bedroom with a load of fresh laundry and she'd seen that Jason had fallen asleep while reading to Noah. His arm encircled their son, their heads with matching sandy-colored hair close together on a single pillow. The tiny smudge of chocolate was still on Jason's chin.

Thinking of it now, she felt strangely like she might burst into tears.

• • •

## Newport Cove Listserv Digest

*It's Halloween!

Please join your neighbors at our annual Halloween party 'n parade starting at 4:30 p.m. at bottom of the cul-de-sac on Daisy Way. We'll have a caldron of witches brew (simply red Kool-Aid, you can explain to your little ones in case they're prone to nightmares), tasty treats, a moon bounce, fortunes told by "Opal," and a parade down the street! Remember that tonight after dark our little ghosts and goblins will be out trick or treating, so drivers beware! Remember: Don't be the "driving force" behind traffic accidents! —Sincerely, Shannon Dockser, Newport Cove Manager

*Need Jump Start

Our minivan's battery is dead again. Would someone mind popping over and giving me a jump start? I swear I'll teach my kids to close their doors . . . someday. —Reece Harmon, Daisy Way

*Re: Need Jump Start

Be there in a jiff! —Jenny McMahon, Daisy Way

• • •

Halloween was Tessa's very favorite holiday. It was easy to feel like a failure on Valentine's Day, which was fraught with expectations (candlelight dinners and roses and sex!). Thanksgiving just felt like an elaborate meal with grace, since she wasn't a fan of either turkey or football. And Christmas was exhausting—Harry's parents always wanted to come visit that week, which stirred the competitive juices of Tessa's mother and older sister, Claire, who wanted Tessa's family to travel out to Colorado to be with them (though somehow Claire and Tessa's mother weren't quite so keen on packing up and traveling to visit Tessa). Tessa was always trying to juggle school break days and airline tickets to be fair to both sides. She usually ended up disappointing everyone and bursting into tears of exhaustion on Christmas Eve, right around midnight when she was stuffing stockings, though thankfully she always recovered enough to enjoy Christmas itself.

But Halloween was magical. What Tessa loved most was that it celebrated imagination. Kids got to choose their own costumes and decide exactly who they wanted to be—pop star or physician, princess or pirate—and everyone had to play along, at least for a single night. It was the one time of year when adults had to conform to the world of kids, rather than the other way around.

On the Sunday before the holiday, she and Harry had taken the kids to a farm to pick pumpkins and go on a hay ride. Addison had gotten his face painted, and Bree had convinced Tessa to buy a giant sack of Granny Smith apples to make a pie. They'd wandered around for hours, sipping hot cider, munching salty-sweet kettle corn, petting barn cats, and feeding cups of grain to greedy goats. When they'd returned home, Tessa had gone into the basement to retrieve the giant Tupperware bin of Halloween decorations: wispy ghosts to dangle from the pillars on their porch, cardboard tombstones for the yard, an orange lightbulb for the porch lamp, a black witches' caldron to hold the candy.

She and the kids had decorated the yard while Harry had made a giant pot of black bean chili, then they'd all watched *It's the Great Pumpkin, Charlie Brown*. At bedtime, as Tessa was brushing her teeth, she suddenly stopped and gripped both sides of the sink basin as a realization had struck her: it had been the first entire day that had felt normal since they'd moved. She'd experienced the same dizzying sensation a few years after her father had died of a heart attack, when she'd been sipping her morning coffee and had realized with a start that she hadn't woken up with a terrible ache in her heart, the sensation that something deep and vital was missing in her life, for the first time since his funeral.

Time didn't heal all wounds, but at least it layered buffers around them.

She'd believed—hoped, anyway—that their day at the farm had marked a turning point. Maybe this house, this neighborhood, *was* magical. She'd felt it the first time she'd driven down the street with the flowering dogwoods and pink and white crape myrtles arcing overhead like a canopy. Their Cape Cod was much smaller than their last home, which had boasted three expansive levels after their renovation, but Tessa was glad to downsize. Here, everyone in the family was within calling distance of one another at all times. They were snugly tucked away, safe and protected.

On the morning of Halloween, Tessa walked her Ninja Turtle and her veterinarian to the bus stop. Kellie was already there with Mia, who was dressed as a cheerleader with a megaphone (a prop that seemed more dangerous than the swords some of the boys were wielding), and Noah as an Angry Bird. A few minutes later Susan came along with Cole, who was a Transformer, and Sparky, who was wearing a hot dog costume he kept trying to wiggle around and bite. The Ninja, Angry Bird, and Transformer immediately began to argue about which one of them would prevail in a to-the-death battle while Mia and Bree turned cartwheels on the sidewalk.

"Are you coming to the parade this afternoon?" Kellie asked Tessa.

"Definitely," Tessa said. "We're really looking forward to it."

"It's a lot of fun," Kellie said. "Jenny McMahon makes this incredible iced pumpkin bread and brings a huge pot of cider. And Mason puts up string around his yard with stakes so that kids don't trample his grass. Last year he took down a few parents who stumbled off the sidewalk. He's got a BB gun, and he uses the tipsy parents for target practice, too."

"She made that up," Susan said. "At least the part about the BB gun. And the stumbling parents are totally Kellie's fault. She brings along a flask of rum for adults who want their cider with a little kick."

"It's my own special contribution," Kellie said. "It makes trick-or-treating a lot more enjoyable."

Tessa laughed. "So what's the plan for tonight? Do all the kids go trick-or-treating together after the parade with us parents following along behind, or . . . ?"

She saw Kellie glance at Susan before answering. "It usually starts off that way. You guys are welcome to join me and Jason and the kids."

Susan appeared to take a deep breath. "Cole's going trick-or-treating with his father," she said, enunciating each word crisply.

"Ah," Tessa said, feeling herself flush. First she'd called Randall Susan's husband, and now she'd put her foot in it again. Figures that she would embarrass herself in front of Susan, who was one of the most impressive women Tessa had ever met. Maybe it was something in Susan's posture; she always stood up straight, her neck in perfect alignment with her spine, and when she gestured, her long fingers moved with the graceful fluidity of a conductor's baton. She had the stance of a ballerina. Tessa hadn't realized how often she'd slouched until she'd met Susan; every time she bumped into her neighbor, she instinctively stood up taller.

"I keep telling Susan to join us," Kellie was saying. "We'll make it a party."

"Thanks, but I'm going to stay home and hand out candy," Susan said. "And probably eat one mini Snickers for every one I give out. I always hate myself every November first."

The bus approached, groaning and lurching toward them as it did every morning, and the parents began calling out good-byes and instructions, as usual—"Don't step in that puddle!" "Let Emma get on the bus first; she's smaller!"—which the kids ignored, as usual.

"Good-bye, Addison," Tessa called. "Have a great day, Bree."

She caught a last glimpse of her children's small, pale faces through the panes of glass as the bus pulled away and she stood there until the vehicle was out of sight, feeling a familiar crimp twist her stomach. It never loosened until the afternoon when the bus reversed its route and her children were safely back home.

"So, the parade!" Tessa said too brightly, to make up for her earlier misstep. "We'll see you there."

Later she'd wished they'd skipped the parade. Why had Tessa ever thought they could start over simply by moving to a new town? You couldn't outrun your past. It was like sprinting on a treadmill—as soon as your legs faltered, you'd discover you were in the precise place you'd been trying so hard to escape.

Moving to Newport Cove was nothing more than putting on a Halloween costume. Tessa had been swept up in the imagining, in the pretending to be someone else. But once the disguise was off, you no longer fooled anyone, least of all yourself.

# Chapter Thirteen

**Newport Cove Listserv Digest**

*Headless Barbie?

Did someone misplace a Malibu Barbie doll? I found one—along with its head a couple of feet away—in my front yard. There was also a mustache drawn on Barbie, and what appear to be tattoos on her knuckles. —Jenny McMahon, Daisy Way

*Re: Headless Barbie

My daughter lost her Malibu Barbie yesterday, but its head was still attached and she was mustache and tattoo-less. —Savannah Nichols, Daisy Way

*Re: Headless Barbie

My sons will be delivering a new Malibu Barbie to your daughter, along with an apology, tonight. —Reece Harmon, Daisy Way

• • •

Susan and Randall's custody agreement had been hashed out in a mediator's office during a half dozen sessions. They'd met in a space that was designed to look like a living room, with a cozy couch, leafy plants, and abstract artwork on the walls.

Perhaps the theory was that pleasant surroundings would inspire similar emotions in their clients.

Their mediator, Judy, had a low, soothing voice, and she repeated Susan's and Randall's names constantly, which was probably a psychological device to ensure that everyone felt heard.

"So, Susan, what you're saying is it's important to you to spend as much time with Cole as possible," the mediator would say, frowning earnestly, before turning to Randall. She was a pleasant woman in her sixties who looked like she did a lot of yoga. "And Randall, what you're saying is that you want to be an important presence in Cole's life, too."

Judy would take a sip of soothing chamomile tea and write something down on a pad of paper while Susan sat on the couch, as far away as possible from Randall, clutching a throw pillow in her lap, her fingers convulsively twisting the fringe.

Maybe it would have been better if they'd met in a courtroom, letting out the ugliness like steam from a kettle as they screeched accusations at each other. She could've hired a female lawyer with a jutting chin and flinty eyes, one who'd seen the worst and thought all men were scum, instead of Judy with her CD of Tibetan monks' chants. It could have been cathartic. And then maybe she would've been out on a date instead of sitting down the street from Randall's house, her Mercedes headlights switched off, her dog Sparky on the seat beside her, when Randall called to discuss Halloween plans at six p.m. on a Saturday night.

Cole was at a classmate's birthday party, which Randall probably knew, since he'd seen Cole that day. He'd probably planned this call accordingly. Susan took a perverse satisfaction in knowing that she could watch Randall's new home during the entire call. Maybe that figure passing in front of the window was him pacing as they talked. She heard the rattle of dishes in the background and imagined Daphne in the kitchen, sliding silverware into holders in the dishwasher, shooting Randall a sympathetic look: *Is she being difficult again? You're doing great, sweetheart!*

"I know Tuesdays are technically my nights with Cole," Randall said. "But you're welcome to come trick-or-treating with us. Cole would probably love to have both of his parents with him."

"Please don't use our son to manipulate me," she said, but she knew Cole *would* like it. Randall would probably like it just as much if she came along, though. He'd love for them to all be pals, for people to see him and Susan laughing together at school functions as they co-parented their amazing son. *What a good guy he is, that Randall Barrett!* they'd say, smiling. *He's even friends with his ex!* Other people's opinions of him had always been too important to Randall—probably the result of growing up with a father who was impossible to please.

Randall sighed, a long-suffering sound that annoyed her.

"Look," she said, tempering her voice. "Is she coming, too?"

"Daphne is coming trick-or-treating with us, yes," Randall said.

"I'll drop Cole off around six," she said.

That recommendation for Randall as an accountant on the listserv had really annoyed her. It had popped up on her iPhone when she'd been lying in bed in the morning, still drowsily scanning through her emails, awakening her with all the jarring force of a slap in the face.

"Fine," Randall said. He cleared his throat. "There's one more thing."

Did anyone ever reveal good news by starting off, "There's one more thing"? It seemed like the kind of phrase designed to make your abdominal muscles tighten. She looked at Randall's house, hoping for a clue.

"Daphne is pregnant," Randall said. "Cole's going to be a big brother this spring. We're going to try to get married before the baby comes, Susan."

It was like being at the beach, wading out into the icy water, and seeing a huge wave about to bear down on you. In a moment, it was going to hit you hard, and there was absolutely nothing you could do.

"Susan? Are you okay?"

She couldn't breathe. She was floundering, the wave pushing her deeper into the darkness, pressing all the air from her lungs, churning her around in circles.

"Do you want me to come over so we can talk?"

"No!" She held the phone away so he couldn't hear her gasping. When she put it back to her ear he was still talking. ". . . probably should have told you in person, but I wasn't sure how to—"

"It's fine," she said.

"I can hear in your voice that it's not," he said gently.

*Don't*, she thought. *Don't use that sweet voice with me.*

"I'm just glad you didn't knock her up while we were still together," she said. She was shaking. "Good thing our divorce came through two months ago. You got this in just under the wire." Let him try to play the good guy. They both knew better.

"Maybe we should talk more later," Randall said.

Daphne was probably coming over to stand beside him, putting a sympathetic hand on his shoulder while her other hand rubbed slow circles on her belly.

Susan needed to get off this call now, before she started to sob. The mediator had suggested that if one of them was becoming irrational or upset, the other should calmly find a way to end the conversation. What were the exact words she had modeled for them?

"I'm going to hang up now, but I'll talk to you soon," Randall said, and she nearly screamed. *Those* were the words!

She was still holding the phone, still shaking, when she heard the click that meant Randall was gone.

A French bulldog puppy. Another child. In less than a

year, Daphne had given Randall everything he'd ever wanted. Meanwhile, she was left living in a house where reminders of Randall were everywhere.

She rolled down her window and took a few deep, bracing breaths of the night air and then, because she couldn't think of anything else to do, she put her car in drive and headed home, where she could cry.

•  •  •

## Newport Cove Listserv Digest

### *Leftover Candy

If you have any leftover candy, I'll be happy to swing by and pick it up and add it to the box I'm preparing to ship overseas to children in an impoverished village in Africa. —Jenny McMahon, Daisy Way

### *Halloween Party

Thanks to all who came out to make our annual Newport Cove Halloween Party a big success! And a special thanks to Bob Kilpatrick for thinking so quickly and dumping a bottle of water over "Opal's" head after her wig caught on fire from a jack-o'-lantern! Whew—that was a close call, but "Opal" asked me to let you know that she's just fine and will be back next year! We're lucky to live in such a friendly neighborhood where we all look after each other! Happy November, everyone! —Sincerely, Shannon Dockser, Newport Cove Manager

### *GNOME!

Whoever STOLE my garden gnome bring it back TODAY or ELSE! —Mason Gamerman, Daisy Way

•  •  •

What in the world had happened to Harry at the Halloween parade?

Kellie had thought Tessa was the nervous one in their relationship. Kellie had invited Addison over a few times to play with Noah, assuming Tessa would drop him off, but Tessa had hung around the entire time. It wasn't that Kellie minded—Tessa was perfectly pleasant and Kellie was happy to make a pot of coffee and sit down for a talk. But she did feel a little judged. Was Tessa checking out her house—checking out Kellie herself—before deciding if she would leave Addison there unsupervised?

As for Harry, he had always been in the background, like Muzak in an elevator. No, no, that was unkind. It was just that Harry didn't stand out. He reminded Kellie of an absentminded professor. Sometimes in the morning, when he walked the kids to the bus stop, he'd look right through Kellie until she gave a little wave, at which point he'd snap to attention and smile.

Once you broke through his fog, Harry was pleasant enough. He'd even tried to convince Jason and his father to install computers at their hardware store rather than the old-fashioned cash registers they insisted on using (both Jason and his dad had recoiled, as if Harry had suggested hiring strippers to lure in customers).

At the Halloween party, she almost didn't recognize Harry. He was wearing a silly cap with long braids spilling down the sides. She complimented him on it when they bumped into each other by the line for the moon bounce.

"Thanks," he said. "I like your *Sharknado* hat."

She grinned and rolled her eyes. Jason had ordered them matching hats that made it look like a shark was about to take a bite out of their foreheads. They were ridiculous, but Jason was a fan of the campy movie—she'd come home just the other night to catch him watching it for the fourth or fifth time—so she'd given in.

"Have you gotten your fortune read yet?" Kellie asked, motioning to where Shannon Dockser had set up her little booth with a purple curtain.

Harry shook his head, his braids swinging.

"She'll probably tell you that you're going to come into a

lot of money," Kellie said. "Either that or to beware of a dark-haired stranger. I'm not sure if Opal is capable of telling any other fortunes."

Harry laughed, and after Noah and Addison finished bouncing, Kellie and Harry went their separate ways, and she hadn't given him another thought. Kellie had been trying to keep Mia from doing yet another cheer (really, was it normal for such a dainty little girl to have such a loud voice?) when she heard a man's panicked voice floating above the noise of the assembled neighbors.

"Addison! Addison!"

It was Harry. He was running after a little boy who was Addison's size and who was also wearing a Ninja Turtle costume. But Kellie knew that little boy wasn't Addison—Addison was dressed up as Donatello and the boy Harry was chasing was Leonardo (the two Ninja Turtles looked alike, but they had different-colored masks, a detail Kellie had absorbed from one of Noah's frequent lectures on the subject). Besides, that little Ninja Turtle was holding the hand of Fred Dutton of Crabtree Lane, which meant it was Fred's son Daniel.

As Kellie watched, Harry ran over to Daniel's side and grabbed his shoulders, trying to pull him away from his father. "Addison!" he yelled. "Let go!"

"Dad?" Daniel's high, quavering voice must have pulled Fred out of his shock, because he stepped toward Harry.

"That isn't Addison!" he said. "Please take your hands off my son!"

Harry released Daniel then, and Fred put his arms around his child and backed away. Harry looked around, scanning the crowd, his eyes wide. Kellie saw his face contort in terror beneath his hat with the long braids. His breath came in loud, ragged gasps.

"Addison!" he howled.

The scene was so bizarre it paralyzed Kellie; it was like watching a car accident unfold and knowing you were helpless to prevent it. Suddenly Tessa ran up to Harry's side, dragging little Donatello by the hand. "Harry!" she said, grabbing his arm and shaking him.

Harry seemed to regain his focus as he stared down at his wife. "Addison's right here," she said. Harry looked at his son as Addison pushed the mask off, revealing his face. "Dad?" Addison said. "What's the matter? I was just getting some popcorn."

"It's okay, Harry," Tessa said, her voice shrill. "Everything's fine!"

Kellie heard someone ask, "What happened?" And another answered, "I don't know. Is he a veteran? It seemed like a flashback." People moved back to make space around Tessa's family, leaving them alone in the center of a circle.

"We need to go now, Addison and Bree. Come on!" Tessa gathered up her kids and hurried off, ushering her family toward home. Kellie could hear her urging them on: "Hurry, hurry!"

"Well, that was certainly odd," Tally White said from behind Kellie. "Was he worried Fred was trying to kidnap that little boy? Doesn't he know we live in one of the twenty safest communities in the country?"

"I don't know," Kellie said. She excused herself and went over to Susan. "Whoa."

Susan shrugged. "Yeah."

They both stared at the retreating figures of Tessa's family. Tessa was almost running now, yanking Harry along by the hand.

"I thought something was a little off with her when they first moved in, but then she seemed to relax," Kellie said. "Maybe Harry's the one with the . . ."

She fumbled for the word. "Issues?" That didn't seem severe enough. Whatever Harry was dealing with was bigger. He'd been in a full-fledged panic at a neighborhood Halloween party on a sunny afternoon.

Kellie felt a tug on her shirt and looked down to see Noah. "Can Addison still go trick-or-treating with us or is he in trouble?" Noah's lower lip was trembling.

"Oh, honey, Addison didn't do anything wrong," she said, kneeling down to give Noah a hug. "His daddy just got scared when he couldn't find Addison."

"Like the time you lost me at the store?" Noah asked.

"Exactly," Kellie said (though technically "lost" was a subjective term, given that Noah had been hiding in the middle of a circular clothing rack, ignoring her as she shouted his name from two feet away).

Kellie frowned as she thought of something. Addison had come over a few times after school, always accompanied by Tessa, but she'd never seen any of the neighborhood kids go into Tessa's house. It wasn't that Kellie was keeping tabs, but she usually did the pickup in the afternoons after school and it was easy enough to tell when someone had a playdate, because a new kid got off at the bus stop.

And whenever she'd been out and about, driving down the street or biking with the kids or walking to the park, she'd never seen anyone go into or out of Tessa's house other than their family. Even Noah had only been invited there once, to see a movie. He'd stayed less than three hours. It stood out in this neighborhood, where kids freely floated from yard to yard.

"I'm not sure what's going on with them," Susan was saying, her voice low so no one else could hear, "but something definitely seems off."

• • •

## Newport Cove Listserv Digest

### *Re: Dog Poop

Are you kidding me? Not only is the owner of the apparently HUGE dog letting it poop on my lawn—which is bad enough—but now the dog owner isn't bothering to clean up when his dog poops on the sidewalk in front of my house. Do you have any idea of how disgusting it is to step in dog leavings when you're getting into your car to go to work? I'm with the person who suggested we start photographing the offenders and posting their pictures on the listserv. —Joy Reiserman, Daisy Way

**\*Re: Dog Poop**
Once we catch them, let's hang them in the village square! —Frank Fitzgibbons, Forsythia Lane

• • •

Some of Gigi's happiest mothering memories were of helping Melanie and Julia pick out Halloween costumes. The three of them would snuggle together on the couch, flipping through magazines for inspiration. "How about a shepherdess?" Gigi would suggest, her arms around her girls. "Or a wizard? Maybe Peter Pan?"

Early on, Melanie and Julia had been delighted by her suggestions. Gigi had painted their faces and pieced together outfits from odds and ends she'd found around the house: strips of an old sheet for the year Julia was a mummy, some gold glitter for Melanie's fairy dust. At age seven Melanie had dressed up as Dorothy from *The Wizard of Oz*, with Julia as her sidekick, Toto. Melanie had adored the movie, but the green-faced witch had terrified her. She'd bury her face in Gigi's lap whenever the Wicked Witch appeared on-screen. Back then, Gigi had had all the answers to Melanie's problems. She'd *loved* having the answers: "Of course there are no witches in real life." "No, a tornado could never take you away from me." "Don't you know I'd never let anyone hurt you?"

Even when Melanie was a preteen, and some of her friends were dressing in costumes too sexy for young girls—cats in black stockings and leotards, or pop stars in miniskirts and heels—she still seemed innocent for her age. Halloween remained a childish pleasure. At twelve, she went trick-or-treating as a pizza, wearing a giant cardboard box, then she came home and gleefully sorted through her candy, picking out Jolly Ranchers for Gigi because she knew they were her mother's favorite.

Somewhere between the ages of fourteen and fifteen, though . . . that's when Melanie had started to change.

Maybe someone had hurt Melanie. Some thoughtless boy— or girl. Gigi wasn't ruling anything out.

And Melanie was going through an awkward stage. Acne dotted her chin and cheeks. Her hair was frizzy. She'd put on some extra weight, too, and Gigi knew how awful high school students could be to their peers. It probably didn't help that Julia was turning out to be so lovely, and that Julia was always being invited to birthday parties and sleepovers. Melanie had never been in the popular crowd, but it hadn't seemed to bother her in the past. She'd always been content with a couple of friends.

Maybe kids were teasing her.

Maybe it was the hormones in milk.

Maybe it was just a phase. Ten years from now, she and Melanie could be sitting side by side on this very couch again, and maybe Melanie would lay her head on Gigi's shoulder and say she was sorry for all the worry she'd caused her mother. Maybe they'd laugh about it.

Or it could be drugs, in which case ten years from now Melanie could be . . . *No!* Her mind recoiled from the thought.

Bulimia. Depression. It could be anything.

The not knowing killed Gigi. How could she help when Melanie refused to talk to her?

The uncertainty drove Gigi into being the kind of mother she'd vowed to never become. While pregnant, she'd envisioned herself effortlessly dancing the tightwire between being overbearing and present. She'd certainly do a better job than her own parents, who'd managed to be distant yet perpetually critical. Gigi had grown up in a house with no rules, and little affection. Her father was a musician who endlessly ruminated about missing his big break; her mother brought cloth bags to the supermarket and taught yoga long before it was fashionable, and was a fervent believer in getting her "me time."

"Not now," was perhaps the most common phrase Gigi heard during her childhood whenever she approached one of her parents.

As a little girl, Gigi had marveled at the families in her storybooks, wondering how much of the tales between the pages were fiction. Did real families actually do things like make trips to a farm to cut down a Christmas tree, then come home and decorate it together? Did other kids sit around the dining room table every night with their parents, who asked about their days? Did real-life fathers tuck in their daughters and kiss them on the cheek and leave the door open a crack so their little girls wouldn't be scared of the dark?

As a teenager, Gigi didn't even have a curfew. It made no difference what time she came home—six o'clock, eight o'clock, two a.m. Her parents never checked on her. Sometimes they'd be around, and sometimes they wouldn't. There would be food in the refrigerator, or there wouldn't (though she could usually count on being able to scrounge up crackers and her mother's oily, awful-tasting healthy peanut butter in the pantry). Her mother and father never checked to see if she'd done her homework, or drove her to gymnastics practice, or gave her a safe-sex talk. When Gigi was fifteen and her boyfriend wanted to sleep with her, she'd asked her mother for advice.

"Do you want to?" her mother had asked.

"Um, I guess so," Gigi had replied, even though she wasn't sure.

"So go ahead, just use a condom," her mother had said. So Gigi did. It wasn't pleasurable; it had hurt. And two weeks later, her boyfriend had broken up with her.

"But they love you," Joe had said early on in their relationship. His brow had furrowed. "Don't they?"

"Yeah, sure." Gigi had shrugged. And she supposed they did, in their loose, unobservant fashion. She'd glided through her childhood and adolescence with remarkably few scars. And she'd married a man she'd adored, a man who cherished her in return. So even though she'd made mistakes, she'd gotten the most important part of her life right.

She'd heard people were unconsciously driven to repeat patterns, but she'd veered in another direction. She'd become the opposite of her own mother. She was too fluttery, too hovery, too worried. But how else could she be, when her broken-hearted/bulimic/hormonal/drug-using daughter was on the verge of . . . whatever it was?

Both of her daughters had curfews, even though Gigi suspected Melanie had begun to sneak out at night. Gigi hadn't caught her yet, but she'd noticed Melanie's bedroom window was open one weekend morning, with Melanie's shoes directly beneath it, as if she'd slipped them off when she'd climbed back in.

Maybe she should get a lock for Melanie's window. No, it would be better to catch her in the act.

Gigi's iPhone buzzed with an incoming message from a campaign volunteer, asking about the address labels Gigi was creating for Joe's new brochure. She typed a response, then went into the basement to flip a load from the washing machine into the dryer. After she turned on the machine, she walked past the small storage room that Joe had suggested turning into a bedroom for his campaign manager. Surprisingly, Melanie hadn't complained when Joe had discussed it with the kids—which fueled Gigi's suspicion that Melanie had a crush on Zach.

There were a few boxes of books in one corner, a dusty StairMaster that Gigi had bought in a surge of misguided optimism, and a rolled-up rug they hadn't gotten rid of even though it was the wrong size for the living room, because they'd paid full price for it.

But once everything was cleared away, the room would be sufficient for Zach. It lacked a closet, but there was a small attached bathroom with a shower, which was a more important feature, in Gigi's estimation.

She started to climb the stairs, thinking of the address labels she still had to print. They were hand-distributing five hundred copies tomorrow, in the hopes that the information would be fresh in voters' minds for the primary.

Gigi's foot paused on the first step, then she swiveled and walked back into the storage room. Joe would never ask her to clear out the basement. He'd come home tonight after a long day at the office with his insufferable boss and a night of campaigning in his suit. Some people would shut doors in his face and others would lecture him about the flaws in his beliefs and others would make jokes about foot fetishes. Joe would stagger home and he'd change and go into the basement and begin to fix up the room for his campaign manager.

Because Joe wanted to make the country better.

She bent down and began to pick up one of the heavy boxes.

*Lift with your knees, not your back!* She remembered the rule a split second after she felt the agonizing spasm in her spine, right at the spot of her decades-old horseback riding injury. She dropped the box and collapsed to the floor.

• • •

## Newport Cove Listserv Digest

### *Wreath Sale!

Newport Cove High School is having its annual wreath sale next week to raise funds for the basketball team. If you'd like to order a decorated wreath ($20) or undecorated wreath ($15), please contact me. I'll be taking orders through Nov. 15. —Connie Moran, Iris Lane

**\*Re: Dog Poop**

Isn't this discussion a "waste" of time by now? —Frank Fitzgibbons, Forsythia Lane

**\*Re: Dog Poop**

I'm glad you find this so amusing, Mr. Fitzgibbons. Perhaps you'll volunteer to canvass the neighborhood and clean up dog leavings in your spare time, since you seem to have so much of it? —Joy Reiserman, Daisy Way

**\*Re: Dog Poop**

My deepest apologies, Mrs. Reiserman. —Frank Fitzgibbons, Forsythia Lane

**\*Re: Dog Poop**

IT'S "MS." REISERMAN! —Joy Reiserman, Daisy Way

• • •

Maybe Harry *was* a veteran. Kellie didn't know. In fact, she didn't know much about the Campbell family at all.

She and Tessa always chatted at the bus stop, commenting on the weather and the Liam Hemsworth–ish soccer coach (Addison had joined the team after all) and their weekend plans, but those brief conversations barely skimmed the surface of their lives. That night at Wine and Whine had been one of the few times she'd felt as if she'd connected with Tessa. Afterward, Tessa had reverted to being polite and remote.

The day after Halloween, Tessa came down the sidewalk with her kids just as the bus pulled up—as if she'd deliberately timed it that way. She stayed about a dozen yards back while her kids ran ahead to climb aboard, then she waved to the other parents before hurrying to her house.

"Do you think she's going to do that all year?" Kellie wondered. "Hide from us?"

"Come here, Sparky. Don't go near Mason's yard or he'll shoot you. No, I don't think she will," Susan said. "Just act normal. She'll come around. She's probably just embarrassed."

"Okay," Kellie said.

"You look good today. Have you been working out?"

"Yeah, I'm training for a marathon," Kellie said.

"You made that up," Susan said. "That's a new dress, right?"

"I got it on sale," Kellie said. She could feel herself becoming flustered. "It's dumb to be spending more money when I'm not bringing much in, but I gave away a lot of my old work clothes to Goodwill after Mia was born, and I just figured I needed a few things so I look like a professional." She paused. "So the short answer is yes."

Susan laughed. "Don't worry. You've already got your first listing, right? The clients will come."

"Sure," Kellie said. "Who doesn't want a miniature lighthouse in their backyard?"

Kellie gave Susan a little wave as they split apart, then went inside her home to tidy up the kitchen before heading to the office. But as she was wiping down the counter, she noticed Jason had left his lunch sack by the refrigerator. She decided to run it by the hardware store on her way to work.

She got into her minivan and drove down the familiar streets, waving at Frank Fitzgibbons, who she always thought of as an overgrown frat boy, as she passed by. Every time she saw him, she remembered how he'd gotten rip-roaring drunk at a holiday open house at the Delfinos' home last year (both Gigi and Susan had sworn he'd tried to feel them up when he'd greeted them with hugs, leaving Kellie strangely insulted he hadn't tried to grope her).

Kellie pulled up against the curb in front of Scott&Son hardware store and cut the engine. The hardware store Jason's father had founded three decades ago was in a converted red-brick town house with a bright blue door. Inside were slightly dusty aisles lined with bins, and a little bell by the cash register for customers to ring if they needed help. In an era of big-box stores and overnight mail delivery, places like Scott&Son seemed on the verge of extinction. Jason's father had only one other employee, a white-haired man named Ed who cut copies of keys and specialized in lumber orders and who could, like Jason and his dad, lead you down a serpentine path of aisles to any screw, washer, fastener, mortar, or spring you requested.

She grabbed the lunch bag and got out of the car, stepping over a little pile of sawdust just inside the front door. She passed a man who was taking a loose screw out of his pocket and holding it up against a display to find a match. Kellie could hear Jason laughing and she looked down another aisle to find her husband chatting with a petite blonde with a red shopping basket looped over her arm.

Kellie started to step toward them and call out a greeting, but something made her stop. She moved back, camouflaging herself behind the aisle divider, and continued to watch.

"Definitely," Jason was saying, "or at least one of the Farrelly brothers movies."

The blonde burst into laughter again. Kellie could tell the woman liked Jason; her body language all but shouted it.

She watched as Jason reached up to the top shelf, his shirt gaping up to reveal a few inches of pale skin. He'd gotten thicker around the middle during the past few years, and he now wore his shirt out instead of tucked in. Jason grabbed a lantern advertised to light up a room in the case of a power outage—Kellie had two in her basement—then handed it to the woman.

"You'll need some D batteries, too," he said. "They're in the next aisle."

Before Jason could spot her, Kellie hurried to the front of the store and left Jason's lunch on the counter. Later, she'd tell him she hadn't wanted to disturb him when he was helping a customer.

If they ever divorced, Jason would be fine, Kellie thought as she got back into her minivan and started the engine. Another woman would snap him up, and be grateful for his kind, steady nature and his regular work hours and his willingness to tackle projects around the house.

Kellie wasn't the slightest bit worried about Jason's reaction to the cute blonde. She couldn't imagine Jason getting drunk like Frank Fitzgibbons and trying to cop a feel, or contemplating having an affair. Jason was so content. He loved working with his father, he loved the weekly dinners at his parents' house, he loved his family. He loved Kellie, too. He told her so all the time.

He'd loved her, and only her, since he'd been a senior in high school. Maybe that was the problem: in some ways, she felt frozen at eighteen around him. She wondered if Jason didn't adore that version of her, rather than the woman she'd become today. His parents still called her and Jason "the kids," and Jason enjoyed going back to their old high school to watch football games, sitting in the same bleachers they'd warmed two decades ago. He liked to go to the shore every summer for vacation and stay in the same motel. He liked football on Sundays and sex twice a week. Once, when they both felt like they should fool around but couldn't summon the energy, he'd suggested she squeeze into her old cheerleading outfit.

Kellie could see their lives stretching out, as straight and unremarkable as a swath of highway. Jason would take over the business when his father retired, but his father would still come in for a few hours every day to sit on a stool and chat with customers. His mother would be fretting over the juiciness of her roasts when Kellie was fifty-five. The thought of all those dinners, where everyone sat in the same seats, circling around the same conversational topics, made her chest tighten.

The other day, when Kellie had called her sister, Irene, in Los Angeles, she'd heard the clatter of the city in the background—the rush of cars swooping past and honking, the sound of a guy yelling, the yipping of a dog. All that energy swirling around, all of that *life*! An intense wave of envy had gripped Kellie.

It was strange, because Kellie was the prettier, older sister, the one who'd married one of the stars on the football team, the one with two beautiful children and a comfortable life. Irene shared a one-bedroom apartment with two other girls, and was selling cosmetics at Sephora. So far she'd been an extra in a dozen TV shows, had played Jane Doe #2 in an episode of *CSI*, and had gotten a small speaking role in one episode of a new sitcom that hadn't yet aired.

"I didn't get a callback for the part of the sister in that movie I told you about," Irene had said during their call. "Maybe I should give this up. I mean, I'm past thirty!"

"You're only thirty-two," Kellie had said, but what she'd thought was: *You're so lucky.* Irene's options were spreading out all around her like a sundial. Move to another city! Get engaged—or don't! Go to Greece and be a beach bum! Move to Thailand and teach English!

When they'd shared the brownie at A Piece of Cake, Miller Thompson had talked about the Italian lessons he was taking. He was planning a trip to Italy.

"I love good wine," he'd confided. "There's this class you can take at a third-generation family-owned winery in Tuscany. You stay in a little guesthouse on the back of the property, and spend a week learning about the grapes. You work in the fields, and eat fresh pasta every night. At the end, you make a dozen bottles that you take home and save for special occasions."

"That sounds incredible," Kellie said. The feel of rich, dark soil in your hands, the smell of grapes perfuming the air, the sun warming your shoulders as you worked. Then a sunset picnic in the vines, with cheese on chunks of bread torn from a crusty loaf, and sweet young wine.

Kellie had tried to imagine Jason sampling Chianti in Tuscany. He'd agree to do it if she suggested it, if he thought it was important to her, but he wouldn't truly enjoy it. He'd be frustrated by the lack of a television in their charming quarters, and secretly wish for a Marriott. He'd like the pizza, but he wouldn't want to spend hours wandering around unfamiliar streets, admiring churches and peering into shops. He'd fall asleep during the picnic. He'd snore.

Jason was a smart guy. He could build a playhouse for the kids without a blueprint, change the brakes in his pickup truck, and see a football play unfolding from fifty yards away. But he wasn't a particularly curious man.

It had never bothered her before, but suddenly, like a chip in a new vase, or a small ink stain on a silk sweater, her husband's tiny character flaw was all she could see.

# Chapter Fourteen

*Before Newport Cove*

WHEN ADDISON WAS SIX weeks old, Tessa hired a part-time nanny. It was ridiculous; she had only two kids, and she was a stay-at-home mom. Shouldn't she be able to handle this motherhood stuff better?

But Harry was still traveling, and Bree routinely awoke before six a.m., and Addison—though thankfully a cheerful baby who showed no signs of colic—wanted to eat every three hours. The nanny, Celine, had been recommended by a family down the street, who employed the nanny's older sister. She was young, maybe twenty-one or twenty-two, and had recently immigrated from France.

Later Tessa would berate herself. A recommendation for the nanny's sister was very different from the nanny herself. The family barely even knew the girl!

Although Celine understood English well, she didn't speak much of it. But Tessa was just grateful to have another adult in the house three mornings a week, even if her mother told her she was wasting money.

On one Wednesday morning, everything began to fall apart. Addison had awoken at five a.m., the dryer had stopped working with a load of soaking-wet clothes inside, and Tessa was out of milk and bread and everything else. When Celine showed up at ten a.m., Addison had just fallen back asleep in the bassinet in his bedroom.

"I'm going to dash out to the grocery store," Tessa had said. "Can you call my cell phone as soon as he wakes up?"

Celine had nodded but she didn't smile. Was she just shy, or sullen? It was hard to know with the language barrier. Even after nearly three weeks together, Tessa didn't have a sense of the young woman's personality. She always showed up on time, but she never sang or hummed, and she didn't seem to particularly enjoy being with the children. More and more, Tessa was asking her to do other things, like tidy the living room or prepare simple lunches for Bree, rather than help take care of the kids. She was beginning to think of giving the nanny notice, and looking for someone else, someone who would inject energy and good cheer into the house.

Still, on that sunny summer morning, as Tessa had breezed through the aisles of the supermarket, she'd felt grateful for Celine. It was remarkable how much easier it was to grocery shop with just a toddler, versus a toddler and an infant, and Tessa had whipped through her list. A helpful employee loaded the groceries into her trunk, and she returned to the house less than thirty minutes later. As she walked up the steps, Bree on her hip, and was about to insert her key into the lock, she heard Addison cry his usual low, drawn-out wail. He'd probably just woken up, Tessa thought, and since his bedroom was in the front of the house and the window was open, she could hear everything clearly.

Then she'd heard Celine say something in her gruff voice, and Addison made another sound—a high-pitched yelp. The only time Tessa had ever heard him make that sound before was when he'd gotten vaccination shots at the pediatrician's office.

It was a cry of pain.

Tessa had flung open the door and raced upstairs, her feet pounding against the steps. Addison was in his room and so was Celine. She was holding him. She looked startled to see Tessa. Startled—or guilty?

Addison's face was bright red and he was still wailing, arching his back, as if he were trying to get away from the nanny.

"What happened?" Tessa had asked, but the nanny just shrugged. She avoided Tessa's eyes, looking at the wall behind Tessa. Tessa had put down Bree and stretched out her arms for her baby. She'd stared down at Addison's tiny, sweet face, wrinkled in misery, and she'd felt rage swell within her. Had Celine pinched him? Or did she just hold him the wrong way, maybe bending his leg awkwardly? She was only a girl and even though the family that recommended her had said she had lots of experience with younger siblings and cousins, Tessa never should have left her alone with an infant.

Tessa had calmed Addison down, then kept Bree in the room with her while she undressed Addison and searched his tiny, helpless body for marks. She couldn't find any, but the echo of his shriek still reverberated in her mind. Tessa's purse was on her shoulder so she'd reached inside it, pulled out some twenties, and handed them to the girl.

"You don't need to come back," she'd said. "I don't need any more help. Good-bye."

She'd rocked her baby, whispering apologies.

Later that night, she'd called Harry and had told him what had happened.

"So he didn't have any marks on him?" Harry had asked.

"No," Tessa had said. "But something happened. I know it." The thought still made her nauseous.

"Maybe he had gas," Harry had said. "Maybe she was picking him up to comfort him."

Tessa had felt offended. Why was Harry taking the nanny's side when he hadn't even been here? "I don't think so," she'd said. "She looked guilty. And Addison never makes that sound when he has gas."

"Look," Harry had said. "You need someone to help you. Do you want to call a nanny agency? Get someone who speaks English and has a lot of recommendations?"

"Not now," Tessa had said. "I think I'd find it hard to trust someone. I'd rather just do it myself." But the thought of it made her want to weep. All those long, empty days stretching out in front of her, the mind-numbing chores, the broken sleep . . . If Harry had the regular hours of most fathers, he'd come home every night at six or seven. She could go out for a walk, or see a movie. She'd be free.

"Maybe you should talk to someone," Harry had said. "Look, I know I've been gone a lot, and with the colic Bree had . . . It hasn't been easy."

"I don't need a therapist, Harry," Tessa had said. Actually, she probably did—the idea of unloading her stresses to someone who was paid to be sympathetic was tantalizing. (Tessa's own mother had raised four kids and couldn't see what the fuss was all about. But back then, every mother on the block had stayed at home. They'd all gathered every day for coffee while their kids rolled around on a mat, and when the kids were big enough, they were sent outside to play while the mothers smoked and drank Tab. The isolation was what was killing Tessa.) "I'm doing fine, Harry!"

She'd hung up abruptly, and had gone to fix herself a cup of tea and a late dinner of cheese and crackers before remembering all the groceries, including the cheese she'd bought for the empty bin in the refrigerator, were still in the trunk of her car and had probably spoiled by now.

*I can't do this*, she'd thought, feeling the gray engulf her like thick, damp fog. *I can't do it much longer.*

# Chapter Fifteen

• • •

Gigi removed the heating pad from her back and eased off
the couch, hunching over like an old woman. The spasm that
had left her writhing on the basement floor was the legacy of
a horseback riding injury in her teens that had knocked a few
of her vertebrae out of alignment. Luckily, when she'd landed
face-first in the box of books, Gigi had had her cell phone in
her pocket. Joe had rushed home, helped her get into bed,

and gone to the pharmacy to pick up the muscle relaxants her doctor had ordered (sadly, her doctor was a bit stingy with the prescription and had only allotted her a dozen; Gigi would've liked to have tucked a few away for a rainy day). Then Joe had dashed back out again. More campaigning to do! More voters to sway!

More rest would probably do her still-aching muscles good. But Gigi didn't have any extra time. It was the first Tuesday in November. It was Election Day.

Gigi had already hobbled from her car to the polls this morning, noticing out of the corner of her eye that someone was snapping a picture of her. (The opposing candidate? A local newspaper photographer? It was infuriating not to be able to whip her head around and see.) She'd phoned in an order at the local market for veggie and meat and cheese platters and cases of bottled water and soda instead of the hors d'oeuvres she'd planned to make for their party tonight. So many of their neighbors had jumped in to campaign for Joe during the past few weeks. Today, Kellie and Susan had even taken the morning off from work to go to the polls to try to appeal to last-minute undecided voters. The least Gigi and Joe could do was show them some appreciation.

"We can't invite Tally White, though," Gigi had said yesterday. "She'll measure our dust bunnies and post the details on the listserv." She was in bed, woozily being entertained by *Wheel of Fortune.*

Joe had shot her an imploring look.

"Call an 'n,' you idiot," she'd said. "Fine, but I'm drawing the line at Mason."

"He probably won't come anyway," Joe had said, backing out of the room.

"You didn't invite him, did you? Joe? Joe! Get back here! I know you can hear me!"

Now Gigi made slow progress toward the dining room, where she'd heard voices. She recognized one as belonging to

Joe's press secretary, Devon, a slight young woman with a pixie haircut who'd just graduated from Dartmouth with a degree in political science. Gigi was continually amazed at the credentials of the people who'd volunteered to work for Joe. Zach had a double major in political science and world studies. Their faith in Joe, more than anything, made her realize what had seemed like an impulsive idea a few short months ago was rapidly becoming a very real possibility.

"Where should I put the extra brochures?" Devon was asking.

Gigi had almost reached the room when she heard Zach answer: "Right here on the dining room table. No, move those flowers. Just stick them on a chair."

"Hi," Gigi said from the doorway. She saw Devon's eyes flit up to the top of her head and Gigi reached up to tame her spiky bangs. Why had she ever allowed herself to be talked into this haircut?

"Actually," Gigi said, "those flowers were just delivered this morning from Joe's parents. Can you put them back and maybe just put the brochures over there?" She gestured to a little table under the window.

Zach frowned. "The thing is, it would be great if people could pick up a few pieces of literature. That way they'll have them on hand if anyone needs to know more about Joe. They can pass them out at the supermarket." Zach made a little gesture with his arm, as if he were giving someone a brochure. It reminded Gigi of Vanna and she bit back a giggle (oh, those muscle relaxants were gorgeous).

"I understand," Gigi said. "It's just that this is a thank-you party. I don't want to seem pushy when everyone has already done so much for us."

"Yeah," Zach said. "Except if we win tonight—"

"*When* we win!" Devon interrupted spiritedly, pumping her fist in the air. Zach didn't even look at her and Gigi realized from the red flush spreading across Devon's cheeks that the young woman had a crush on him.

"—we're going to need to go full speed into getting ready for the general election," Zach continued. "Max Connor is going to get the Republican nomination; he's sewn it up. So it's going to be him against Joe. Both parties are going to want this seat, bad. All the predictions are that Congress is going to be nearly evenly split after the election tonight. So we're going to get an infusion from the DCCC, and we can allocate those funds . . ."

Zach talked until Gigi was reduced to nodding. By then she could not have cared less about the flowers. Maybe that was his strategy.

"I've got to get back out," Zach said. "We've still got a few hours before polls close and I need to check on our volunteers at the library and elementary school—they're going to see a lot of traffic tonight and I have to make sure everyone's on message. Could I grab a sandwich or something? I'm starving."

"Sure," Gigi said. Wait—Zach wasn't going to expect her to put together meals for him when he lived here, was he? It would only be until the general election, she reminded herself. And if Joe lost the primary, Zach would be back on his friend's couch within days, but Gigi wouldn't let herself hope for that outcome.

"Help yourself," she said. "Food's in the kitchen."

She glanced at her cell phone and realized Melanie hadn't come directly home after school. She sent her daughter a text: Are you okay? Don't forget the party tonight for Dad's campaign!

Needy. She sounded far too needy. But it was too late to erase the text and the embarrassing smiley face she'd added at the end of it.

Devon was looking down at her own cell phone. "Someone from the Channel 6 news wants to be here to get live footage when the returns come in," she said. "This is awesome. I have to go tell Zach!"

She hurried off, slamming the door behind her.

"Um . . . okay," Gigi said. It would've been nice if Devon had at least checked to see if it was okay to bring in a camera crew. This was her home, after all.

But then another thought struck her. If a TV station was sending a cameraman, it might mean early reports from the polls were tilting in Joe's favor. They wouldn't waste all that time and personnel on someone who was destined to lose, would they?

It wasn't that Gigi had thought Joe would fail.

It just hadn't truly hit her until now that he was probably going to win.

•  •  •

Susan and Cole climbed the front steps to Gigi and Joe's home, both carrying heaping platters of her special buffalo wings. "You're our guest," Gigi had protested when Susan had offered to bring some food. "You're bedridden," Susan had countered.

Susan gave a little knock on the front door, but suspected no one would hear, since it sounded like the entire neighborhood was packed inside. She eased her way through the door, apologizing for bumping into Frank Fitzgibbons, who'd been animatedly chatting with one of the neighborhood au pairs, a comely twentysomething from Brazil (seriously, that man was trouble).

"Hey, Susan! Hiya, Cole!" Kellie said as she approached. "The other kids are in the living room scarfing down cookies," she told Cole, who handed Kellie his platter and took off like a rocket.

"This is amazing," Susan said, looking around as she followed Kellie into the kitchen, where they deposited the wings on the counter. "Everyone's here."

Joe swooped in, cutting through the crowd, and greeted Susan with a kiss on the cheek. The color was high in his face and his eyes were bright. He still wore a suit, but he'd loosened the knot of his red-and-blue-striped tie. "Thanks for everything," he said.

"My pleasure, Mr. Congressman," she joked.

"Oh, don't call me that," Joe said. "Sir Congressman is fine."

A young woman was tugging on Joe's sleeve. "The TV crew wants a shot of you watching the early returns come in," she said.

"Sorry," Joe said to Susan and Kellie. "Gigi's over there—I know she wants to see you."

Kellie waved him away. "Go, go, Your Excellency. I know you're busy tonight. Just give us a tax break to make up for it."

Susan poured wine into a small plastic cup, then watched as a cluster of neighbors formed a half circle behind the television camera as it filmed Joe. Joe was staring at the television set, watching numbers pop up on-screen.

"Shepherd is putting Joe Kennedy ahead of Rich Sappiro by five percentage points with forty-six percent of the precinct reporting," a newscaster was saying.

A cheer went up and someone began leading a chant: "Joe! Joe! Joe!"

"He's really going to do this, isn't he?" Susan said.

"Looks like it," Kellie said.

Susan felt a hand lightly touch her shoulder from behind and she looked back, a smile already forming on her face, expecting to see Gigi.

But Daphne was standing there.

"Hi," Daphne said. "I saw you come in. I just thought I should, um, say hello."

Susan took a step back. She felt the air rush out of her lungs.

"What are you doing here?" Susan asked.

"Joe invited us," Daphne said. That voice. How Randall must love hearing that low, sexy voice late at night when they were in bed. "Sue, I know Randall told you about the baby—"

Susan felt, rather than heard, Kellie's gasp, as her friend moved closer to her.

"—and I just thought maybe we could go out for a cup of tea. Or talk. It's been so long since we've talked. I wish . . ."

Susan shook her head. She felt tears pooling in her eyes.

"Will you think about it?" Daphne asked. "It would be good for Cole if we tried to reduce the tension between us."

Fury swelled in Susan. "Are you telling me what's good for my son? What gives you any right—any right at all—"

Daphne swallowed and lowered her eyes. Her face grew pinched and she blinked a few times.

"I'm sorry," Daphne said. "I shouldn't have said that."

Susan's body began to tremble. "You were my friend," she said, her voice cracking. "You were my friend first!"

She was aware of Tally White edging closer to watch, and a few other neighbors turning around, picking up on the uncomfortable new undercurrent churning through the party.

"I know," Daphne said softly. "Please. Will you just talk to me?"

Susan shook her head. She had to get out. The night was ruined. Her life was ruined.

Kellie was there, stepping between them. "Susan said she didn't want to talk right now," Kellie said, her voice low and firm. "I think you should leave her alone."

Daphne nodded, just once, and walked away, her head low. As she turned and Susan saw her profile, she realized Daphne was already beginning to show, just a tiny bit. Her stomach was swollen with Randall's baby. An ache pierced the middle of Susan's chest and she released a small, involuntary sound.

"Oh, honey," Kellie said. Her hand was warm on Susan's shoulder.

"I need to go," Susan whispered.

"Are you sure?" Kellie said. She must've read the answer in Susan's eyes. "Okay. Do you want me to come with you? Or should I bring Cole home for you later?"

"Can you bring him later?" Susan asked. Kellie nodded and

Susan pushed her way to the front door. She needed to be out-side, where she could fill her lungs with cold air.

Just before she reached the front door, she saw Randall. He was about to bite into one of the buffalo wings—*her* buffalo wings!—as he talked to a neighbor. He looked up and saw her expression and dropped the wing back onto his plate.

• • •

Tessa was walking toward Gigi's house when she saw someone burst out the door and run down the walk. She could tell it was a woman, but she didn't realize it was Susan until they'd nearly crossed paths.

Susan ducked her head, but not before Tessa realized her lovely face was streaked with tears.

"Are you okay?" Tessa asked instinctively. Dumb question—anyone could see Susan was in terrible pain.

"Here," Tessa said. She reached into her purse and pulled out a little pack of Kleenex. "What can I do? Do you want me to call someone?"

"I'm fine," Susan said, but she wrapped her arms around her stomach and bent over.

Tessa reached out and patted her back while Susan's shoulders shook.

"Want me to walk you home?" she asked.

Susan straightened up and blew her nose. She hesitated, then nodded.

• • •

They were settled in the kitchen at Susan's house, a bottle of Baileys and two steaming mugs of decaf coffee on the table before them. There was a reason the kitchen was called the heart of the house, Susan thought. How many confessions had been aired in snug little spots like this, while a teakettle whis-tled or a cork was coaxed out of a bottle? It felt so cozy to be sitting here on two stools, the rectangular knotted rug beneath their feet, the dishrag hanging on the sink, the little window by their table steamy from the contrast of cold outside and warmth within.

"Okay," Susan said. She sighed. "Here's what happened."

• • •

Newport Cove's manager, Shannon Dockser, was the one who'd brought Susan and Daphne together. She'd cornered Susan during a weak moment and had convinced her to sign up for the neighborhood welcoming committee.

Two weeks later, Susan had knocked on Daphne's door.

Daphne had opened it, wearing cutoff jean shorts that revealed her long legs and a red bandanna tying back her dark curls. She had the best cheekbones Susan had ever seen. She wasn't conventionally beautiful, but her face compelled your gaze.

Susan had handed Daphne a basket containing a warm coffee cake, paper plates, a bowl of hulled strawberries with mint, a bottle of fresh-squeezed orange juice, and two packets of instant Starbucks coffee.

"The morning after a move is always so awful, when you can never find anything you need," Susan had said. "So here's breakfast. Consider yourself officially welcomed to Newport Cove."

"This is so nice of you. Come in!" Daphne had urged.

"No way," Susan had said, laughing. "You've got enough to do without having an uninvited guest pop by. But my phone number's on the card. I live just a few blocks away. If you need anything, please call."

"Mmm," Daphne had said, inhaling the cinnamon coffee cake. "It smells divine. Did you make this? I'm a horrible cook . . . Would it be wrong if I ate this with some wine for dinner?"

"So wrong it's right," Susan had said, instantly liking her

new neighbor. So technically, Susan had fallen for Daphne's charms first.

• • •

"I don't think I've ever seen her," Tessa said.

"You'd remember," Susan said. That supple, reedlike body. That voice. Those cheekbones, which Susan later learned were an inheritance from her half-Cherokee grandmother. Daphne made quite an impression.

But Susan had never thought Daphne would be Randall's type. He liked busty, darker-skinned women. Randall was just five foot nine, and he didn't even like it when Susan, who was five foot six, wore heels. But Daphne stood as tall as Randall in her bare feet. It made no sense at all.

Susan wiped her eyes. "Can you pour me another drink?"

• • •

A week later, Susan had run into Daphne while she was out walking Sparky.

"Hi, Sue!" Daphne had called, and for some reason, the nickname Susan had never before liked sounded good in Daphne's throaty voice. They'd chatted for a few minutes, then Susan had impulsively invited Daphne to lunch.

"Do you like sushi?" Susan had asked. It was her favorite but Randall hated it.

"Love it," Daphne had said. "How about we go tomorrow?"

By the end of that meal, they'd talked about everything: Why Daphne had moved (a divorce). How she was adjusting to the new neighborhood (very well, the people were so friendly here). How much unpacking was left (quite a bit; did anyone ever get to the boxes they'd stuck in the basement? Did anyone even know what was in the boxes?).

There was one topic they didn't cover, though. Susan didn't say much about her husband at all.

She didn't tell Daphne that she hadn't made love with her husband in nearly four months.

Four months!

They'd hit an impasse in their relationship, and Susan didn't know what to do. Randall wanted more kids—maybe two. Susan had been an only child, and it felt right to her to have just one. Even if Susan could imagine going back to those early days of fractured sleep and exhausted arms from carrying around a ten-pound baby, she didn't want to risk it.

They'd learned when Cole was born that she and Randall both carried the gene for sickle-cell disease. Disproportionately common in African-Americans, the disease—named for misshapen red blood cells that prevent oxygen from traveling through the body—can cause health problems throughout a lifetime, including incidences of severe pain, organ damage, stroke, heart attacks . . . Had Cole inherited the gene from both of them, he would have required careful management. But he hadn't; like Susan and Randall, he had just one gene, which meant he was only a carrier.

Another child, though . . . Randall, the perpetual optimist, thought the risk was worth it, especially with the promise of medical advances. She didn't.

Besides, Cole was starting school and her business was taking off and her days already felt full to bursting. She'd heard that some people knew without a doubt that they didn't want to be mothers. There had to be other women like her, who definitively wanted a child but just one. Sweet, spectacular Cole, who'd inherited Randall's smile and her eyes, was all she needed.

She couldn't have sex with Randall because she'd had a bad reaction to birth control pills. She had a diaphragm, but the last time she'd slipped out of his arms to go to the bathroom and put it in before lovemaking, he'd asked what she was doing. When she told him, he'd grabbed a pillow and quilt and had stormed off to the couch.

So Susan had begun to work late into the night instead of cuddling with Randall while they watched HBO. It was easy to avoid him now that she had so much work to do. She'd crawl into bed after he'd begun to snore, and she'd slip out from under the covers the instant the alarm sounded, before his arm could snake around her and pull her close.

She knew Randall was upset, but he'd refused to go to counseling when she'd suggested it. "There's nothing wrong with *me*," he'd said.

"I'm not saying that, honey," she'd said, her tone reasonable, because she knew Randall hated to be yelled at. His father had done so much of it while Randall had been growing up that Randall carried permanent scars; he even turned down the volume on the television when the football announcers got excited about a play and began screaming.

She kept hoping that Randall would come around, that he'd realize their little family was exactly the size it should be.

Susan had given him a beautiful, perfect son. They had a wonderful life.

Of course he'd come around.

• • •

"So she swooped in?" Tessa said, sitting up straighter and frowning. "Like a vulture?"

Susan shook her head. "No," she said. "It was more complicated than that."

"My ex and I were married for ten years before we got divorced," Daphne had said with a sad smile over their lunch. "What about you? Have you been married long?"

Susan had looked down at her plate, toying with her chopsticks as her gold wedding band gleamed in the overhead light. "It's a little complicated now," she'd said. "We're going through a rough patch."

Daphne had nodded. "Well, if you ever want to talk about it . . ."

"Thanks," Susan had said, thinking maybe she would confide in Daphne when she knew her a little better. But she made a decision to keep her voice light and steer the conversation in a new direction, asking about the Bikram Yoga class Daphne was taking.

Daphne didn't meet Randall for another two months. Later, Susan would replay the details in her mind hundreds of times, torturing herself with how easily it all could have been prevented. She and Randall could have bumped into Daphne at the supermarket, or on the sidewalk. They could've pulled up side by side at the same stoplight. There were so many missed opportunities for Daphne to have seen Randall, to know that he was Susan's husband.

Randall had been at a bar downtown with a group of buddies. Daphne was there, too, one stool over, waiting for a new friend from the health club she'd joined. One of Randall's pals had jostled Daphne's elbow, spilling her glass of wine. A round of tequila shots had been ordered as an apology. Randall's buddies had been calling him R.B.—his high school nickname.

Randall's friends had left first. Daphne's acquaintance texted to cancel when her sitter failed to show up. Randall and Daphne had stayed on alone.

They didn't touch, not that night. But they'd confided in each other, in an hours-long, deeply intimate talk. They'd stayed until the bar had closed. Randall had confessed in one of the mediation sessions that he'd fallen in love with Daphne instantly.

"I wasn't looking," he'd said, seemingly bewildered. "I didn't mean for this to happen. It just . . . did."

Daphne didn't know Randall—R.B.—was Susan's husband. He'd told her he was getting separated.

But he didn't ask Susan for a separation, not until two days later. By then Susan knew Daphne had met a guy. She'd written about it in an email: I'll tell you everything over our next lunch, but he's incredible! All we did was talk but it was like I'd known him forever. I've never felt this way about anyone before!

I'm so happy for you! Susan had written back. She'd actually written those words.

The Monday after he'd met Daphne, Randall had stayed home from work. Susan had just gotten back from taking Cole to the bus stop. She'd shut the door, released the catch on Sparky's leash, slipped out of her shoes, and was walking down the hallway when she'd caught sight of him sitting on the living room couch. "Oh!" she'd said, putting a hand to her chest. "You startled me!"

Randall hadn't been watching television or reading the paper or checking his phone. He'd been motionless. Waiting for her.

But that wasn't the reason why her stomach had dropped. It was the look in his eyes.

• • •

"He moved out that day," Susan told Tessa. "I was kind of a zombie. I sat in the living room for hours. Kellie stayed with me that first night, but when she had to leave the next morning to take care of her kids, I called Daphne."

She gave a little laugh. "Can you believe we still didn't make the connection? Not then, anyway. But of course I didn't know Randall had met someone. I couldn't even talk. I just cried and Daphne made me tea with honey and brought a cold washcloth to put over my eyes. Then she went home before Randall came back so we could tell Cole. That was the worst moment. Even worse than when I realized who Randall had fallen in love with. It was seeing Cole's little face . . ."

Susan squeezed her eyes shut and swallowed hard. "I still think we might've had a chance, if it hadn't been for Daphne. If they hadn't been so in love." She tried to put a funny emphasis on the last two words, but it didn't work because her voice broke.

"When did she realize R.B. was Randall?" Tessa asked.

"A week or two later. She was over here and she picked up one of our family photos. She dropped it and the glass broke. Kind of a fitting metaphor, don't you think?"

"I'm so sorry," Tessa said.

Susan nodded. "Me, too."

Tessa didn't try to console Susan by telling her she'd meet another man, as so many others had done, and for that, Susan was grateful. She had instinctively known Tessa would understand—some things you couldn't fix, some wounds left forever scars.

# Chapter Sixteen

**Newport Cove Listserv Digest**

\*Joe Kennedy

Congratulations to Newport Cove's own Joe Kennedy on his victory in the primary nomination for Congress! We're all behind you, Joe! —Jeremy Kindish, Tulip Way

\*Re: Joe Kennedy

Is the listserv supposed to be used for political messages? I seem to recall a rule about using this medium for personal gain. —Bethany Roberts, Iris Lane

\*Re: Joe Kennedy

I looked up the listserv's bylaws and am reposting Clause 10: "In order to keep the Newport Cove listserv primarily a discussion list, posting of ads is extremely restricted. Free ads may only be posted by people who live within the listserv boundaries and the ads must be non-commercial in nature and not too frequent. Non-commercial means you cannot advertise something that benefits you via a sale. Exceptions include teenaged babysitters or recommendations for house-cleaners." —Tally White, Iris Lane

\*Re: Joe Kennedy

I don't see how the above clause relates to my message about Joe's primary vic-

tory. It wasn't a political ad; I was simply congratulating my neighbor. —Jeremy
Kindish, Tulip Way

**\*Re: Joe Kennedy**

I'd be curious to know if those objecting are Republicans, and if their objections
are in fact thinly veiled campaign strategies designed to promote their own
candidate. —Ruth Smith, Blossom Street

**\*Re: Joe Kennedy**

I resent your implication, Ruth. I assume you're a liberal Democrat? —Bethany
Roberts, Iris Lane

**\*Re: Joe Kennedy**

Can we start talking about dog poop again? —Frank Fitzgibbons, Forsythia
Lane

• • •

Gigi opened her eyes the morning after the primary election
and enjoyed two peaceful seconds before being engulfed by
a sense of doom. She'd experienced other wake-ups like this,
mostly back in college when she'd had too much to drink:
Once she'd kissed her roommate's ex-boyfriend, a man she'd
never even been vaguely attracted to. Another time she'd
streaked across the football field following a night game victory (she said a million prayers of gratitude that cell phones
with cameras and Facebook hadn't been invented during her
youth). But Gigi hadn't been drinking last night. She'd had,
what, one glass of champagne? She frowned, wincing when
the movement caused additional pain in her head.

Maybe two glasses, or two and a half, tops, but only because people had stuck the flutes in her hand and toasted Joe.
She certainly hadn't been drunk.

But the muscle relaxants! You were not supposed to mix
them with alcohol. She'd known that, but she'd hardly been
pounding shots. Should those slim flutes of champagne really
have affected her that much?

She had a vague recollection of trying to give a speech, and of seeing Joe's wide, worried eyes as he wrapped a firm arm around her shoulders and eased her out of the room.

Oh God. Gigi heaved her feet over the side of her bed and took in shallow breaths as she fought a wave of nausea.

Had Julia or Melanie seen? It would probably only make her older daughter hate her more.

The television camera had been there. That detail surfaced in Gigi's murky brain, making her stomach give another unfortunate lurch. She hadn't eaten much yesterday—or not at all? The muscle relaxants erased her appetite. No wonder the alcohol had hit her. She remembered a chipper young blonde clutching a microphone. Had the camera captured everything? What had she *said*?

She could hear Joe in the shower. He wasn't singing.

She saw a glass of water on her nightstand and she reached for it and greedily gulped its contents.

Another horrifying memory flash: the cold bathroom tile beneath her knees, her stomach clenching and bucking. She'd made it to the toilet, though. No one had seen.

But what, exactly, had she done before she'd thrown up?

• • •

"Where are you going?" Jason asked, glancing over as Kellie laced up her boots.

"Out to check out some open houses, remember?" she said. "It'll give me a better sense of the market and how to price my own listings. I'll be back in a couple hours."

He was sitting on their couch, his feet up on the coffee table, watching a football game. Mia and Noah were sprawled on the carpet, both engrossed in handheld electronic games.

"Can you get the kids off those games?" she asked. "Don't you think one screen is enough for them?"

"Yes!" Jason bellowed, pumping his fist into the air. His eyes were fixed on the television.

Kellie sighed and went into the kitchen. She'd made Jason and the kids pancakes that morning and the mixing bowl was still coated with batter and the plates, sticky with syrup, were piled up in the sink. A half-full carton of orange juice sat on the counter, along with part of a rapidly browning banana.

Kellie hated the smell of rotting bananas more than just about anything in the world. She felt irritation build within her as she picked up the slimy skin with two fingertips and dumped it into the trash can. "Yuck," she said, wiping her hands on a paper towel. She rinsed the glasses and plates and stacked them in the dishwasher, then she scrubbed down the counters.

She'd always done more around the house—a lot more—than Jason. It had made sense, when she was a stay-at-home mom. It wasn't difficult to throw in a few loads of wash and run the vacuum cleaner while the kids were in preschool. But now she was working, trying to squeeze in cold calls and network and lure in clients. It would be nice if Jason stepped up. She'd asked him, and he'd cheerfully agreed—Jason was nothing if not agreeable—but he never seemed to see the messes until she pointed them out. He had a much higher tolerance for clutter than she did. She had to give him specific directions: *Can you please switch the load in the washing machine into the dryer, then put away the clean stuff?* And of course, the next morning Noah would put on sweatpants that were two sizes too big, because Jason had mixed up his clothes with Mia's, and Kellie would notice it just as they were running late for the bus.

It was easier to do it all herself, she thought, banging the door of the dishwasher closed.

When the kitchen was clean, she went back into the living room. Jason's chin and cheeks were coated with stubble and he was wearing his grubbiest jeans. Sometimes on Sundays, if they weren't going anywhere other than his parents' house for dinner, he skipped showering completely.

"See you soon," she said.

"Huh?" he asked. "Did you see that field goal? Forty-six yards."

She was too annoyed to answer him. The kids were still engrossed in electronics, probably zapping their own brain cells along with zombies with every passing minute. She slipped out their front door, resisting the urge to slam it behind her, and got into her minivan. She typed the first listing's address into her GPS and drove to the house.

Miller was already waiting by his car, squinting into the sunlight as he looked in her direction. He gave a little wave.

"Hi there," she said as she got out of her van. Seeing him here, away from the office, felt very intimate.

"Hey, you," Miller said. "What do you think they priced it at?"

Kellie squinted at the house, a brick Colonial with a generous yard. "Five seventy-five," she guessed.

"I'm thinking five even," Miller said. "Loser buys coffee."

Kellie laughed. "Deal."

They began to walk down the sidewalk, side by side, toward the house.

An older man walking his golden retriever approached and Miller stepped aside, behind Kellie, to let him pass. She could feel Miller's presence as acutely as if electricity were arcing between their bodies.

"Gorgeous day," the man said.

"Sure is," Miller replied.

"Have a good one!" Kellie called as she and Miller turned up the front walk of the brick Colonial with the FOR SALE sign staked in the front yard.

Kellie wondered if the man thought she and Miller were married, if perhaps they were thinking of buying the house together. She turned her head to hide her smile.

# Chapter Seventeen

"THINGS ARE GOING TO start getting real now," Zach said as he stood in front of Joe and Gigi on the couch. He cracked his knuckles and Gigi winced. She'd always hated that particular sound.

"We don't have that long before the general election, and it's going to be tight," Zach said. He began pacing, and Gigi couldn't help but feel as though he were a professor and she and Joe his students.

Zach stopped pacing and squatted down, his hands on his thighs. Now he'd transformed into a football coach, intent on securing victory in the big game.

"I need to know anything in your background that could come up during the campaign," he said. He was looking directly at Gigi. "Ex-boyfriends who might make a stink? Drug use?"

She glanced at Joe, who frowned.

"Is this really relevant?" he asked.

"Yes and no," Zach said. "The other party is searching for ways to discredit you as we speak. You're squeaky clean, Joe"—except, Gigi thought, for that time when he was twenty-four and had nearly been arrested for public indecency for mooning a motorist who'd been stuck at a red light after the man had cut Joe off and nearly caused an accident; Joe had actually pressed his bare buttocks against the guy's driver's-side window—"so we have to be prepared for the possibility that they're going to come after your wife, especially since she's been pretty visible on the campaign trail. It's better I know everything now."

Joe stood up. "Tell you what, give us a few minutes alone," he said.

Zach pressed his hands together like he was praying and gave a little bow—an odd gesture for so hyperactive a young man—and left the room, checking his iPhone as he walked.

Gigi reached for her mug of tea and took a sip. "It's because of what happened on election night, isn't it?" she said.

Joe shrugged and sat down beside Gigi. "Maybe. Who cares. Look, you got a little tipsy and tried to give a speech. It was funny."

"Joe, come on," Gigi said. "Melanie told me I was practically falling down. She said I was slurring my words. It was awful."

"You were on muscle relaxants," Joe said.

"You realize that sounds like the excuse every celebrity gives right before they check themselves into a hospital for 'exhaustion,'" Gigi said. She put her mug back down on the table with a little thud and some tea sloshed over the side. She didn't bother to clean it up. Suddenly, she was furious. "Are we really going to do this? Tell this kid about the abortion I had when I was eighteen? Tell him that yes, I smoke pot and I've tried mushrooms more than once? Does he want to test my tea to see if I spiked it with vodka?"

It was humiliating. Zach would know intimate things about her, things that even her kids and some of her friends didn't know. And what would happen if he were stolen away by a competitor? People jumped ship all the time in political campaigns. Gigi wasn't ashamed of her past, but she didn't want it spread around.

The abortion: she'd been a freshman in college, and she'd made the choice that had seemed best for her, given the circumstances, which included the fact that her then-boyfriend had disappeared from her life as soon as he'd heard the news. The pot, the mushrooms: technically, she'd broken a few laws, but she hadn't hurt anyone. She'd never driven while under the influence. And a little marijuana buzz seemed far less dangerous than things she'd seen on campus, like kids doing beer bongs until they passed out in their own vomit.

If Zach drew out her secrets, he'd have a file on Gigi. Maybe not an actual one tucked away in a secret drawer, but there would be notes saved on an iPhone, or in the mind of a twenty-two-year-old guy Gigi didn't know very well, perhaps to be used in the future when he needed a favor. She wrapped her arms around herself, feeling cold and exposed.

Joe was watching her. "Zach?" he called out.

Zach came back into the room so quickly Gigi wondered if he'd been hovering just beyond the doorway, trying to eavesdrop. Suddenly she felt a flash of distrust for Zach with his golden surfer-boy looks and cold blue eyes. She didn't know him at all, yet he'd asked her to lay bare her history so he could pick through it like a salad bar.

"We're not going to do this," Joe said. "My wife's private life will remain private. If Max Connor tries to dredge up something on her, we're going to attack Max for having the low morals to go after a wonderful wife and mother."

Zach nodded, but he didn't look happy. "You're the boss," he said.

Gigi felt warmth creep back into her body as she felt Joe's hand cover hers. She looked at him and he smiled at her and she felt a little flutter in her stomach. *Put that in your file, Zach*, she wanted to say. *I'm still in love with my husband! In fact, I'd like to push him down on the couch and jump his bones right now!* The decisiveness and moral courage voters had seen in Joe was real.

"We've got the Optimist Club meeting to drop by in thirty minutes," Zach said. "Should I tell them we're going to be late, or . . . ?"

"Nope, we're done here," Joe said. He kissed Gigi and got up and left the room.

She sat on the couch, watching him go. As she did, a hazy memory returned to her. She'd tried so hard not to think about election night. But something had happened after she'd gotten sick and had collapsed into bed.

She'd felt something against her forehead. The briefest flutter of a touch, like the wings of a bird grazing her skin. At first she'd thought it was Joe. But she'd opened her eyes, and she'd seen someone bending over to set a glass of water down on her nightstand.

Her daughter. Melanie.

$$\bullet \quad \bullet \quad \bullet$$

## Newport Cove Listserv Digest

\*Snow shoveler
> I'm looking for someone to keep my sidewalk and driveway clear of snow, should we have any this winter. Will pay $3 per hour. Perfect way for a teenager to get a little extra exercise. —Tally White, Iris Lane

\*Farts!
> I love farts! —Reece Harmon, Daisy Way

\*Re: Farts!
> One of my sons got ahold of my laptop and sent that, obviously. Apologies to all. —Reece Harmon, Daisy Way

$$\bullet \quad \bullet \quad \bullet$$

"Mom, my teacher said she sent you an email," Cole announced as he stepped off the school bus.

"Great," Susan said. It was probably about a book fair or

fruit sale. "I'll read it as soon as we get home. Should we make our own pizzas for dinner tonight?"

"Yes!" Cole shouted.

It was one of their traditions. They bought dough and sauce and cheese from the Italian deli, then Susan put out toppings in little bowls: pepperoni and onion, red peppers and pineapple. Cole liked to make every slice a different flavor.

Cole bounced along beside her, chatting about what had happened at recess (apparently there was a flagrant violation of the rules at dodgeball that, shockingly, went unnoticed by the playground aide) and the silly book about a snorting pug dog that his teacher had read aloud. Cole loved his teacher. He loved Sparky. He loved this neighborhood. He loved Randall, and he loved his mama. Susan was proud of the fact that she'd never said a single negative thing about Randall or Daphne in his presence. Difficult moments kept piling up, like the one a few weeks earlier, when Cole had brought home a drawing. There was a little stick figure of Cole, and one of Susan holding his hand. On the other side of Cole was Randall and Daphne with a round stomach.

"MY FAMILY," he'd written in block letters.

As much as it pained Susan to see that sketch, there was some sweet running through the bitter. Her little boy was adjusting well. He was excited about having a new sibling—he was positive it would be a boy and he was coming up with a list of names. Susan had learned to clench her jaw so she wouldn't say, "Actually, he would be your half brother." The distinction would be important only to her, and Cole might pick up something in her tone that could distress him.

She'd run through fire for her son. Fling herself in front of a speeding truck to push him out of the way. So she could do this. She could speak well of his father, and smile when Cole talked about the adventures he had at Randall and Daphne's house. She'd turn away and pretend to cough so Cole wouldn't see the look on her face when he talked about building a gingerbread house with them (although she'd just bought gingerbread and icing and gumdrops for them to build a house together. That was *their* tradition, the thing she always did with Cole).

When they got home, she sliced a Granny Smith apple and spread peanut butter over four saltines, then poured a glass of lemonade and set Cole's snack out on the kitchen table.

"After you finish, we've got to run out to get stuff for the pizzas," she said. She took his backpack to the sink and pulled out his lunchbox, giving it a quick rinse to remove all the crumbs and tossing his crumpled milk box and uneaten cheese stick into the trash.

"Don't forget the email," Cole said.

"Right," Susan said, flipping open the laptop she'd left on the kitchen table. She frowned. It wasn't a flyer.

Mrs. Barrett,

Would you mind giving me a call at your earliest convenience?

Thank you!
Ms. Klopson

Susan glanced at Cole, who was swinging his feet on his stool as he plowed through his crackers, spewing crumbs all over the table. Despite the breezy exclamation point at the end of the note, an anxious knot formed in her stomach. She picked up the cordless phone.

"I'm going to check on the laundry," she said. "Give me a yell if you need anything."

She went into the basement and turned on the dryer, even though it contained no clothes. The noise would mask her side of the conversation.

She dialed the number at the bottom of the email. The area code was unfamiliar and she assumed it was Ms. Klopson's cell phone number, which seemed to add to the sense of urgency. She couldn't imagine teachers gave those out freely.

"Hi, this is Susan Barrett, Cole's mom," she said. "I just got your note."

"Oh, thank you for calling," Ms. Klopson said. She was a young woman of about twenty-five, exuberant and smiling—exactly the type of person you'd want teaching your second-grader. "It's nothing urgent, but a few little things have come up with Cole and I thought you should know. I'm a big believer in parent-teacher communication."

"Good," Susan said. "So am I."

"On the playground today, there was a little incident," Ms. Klopson said. "Cole mentioned your new relationship, and a few of the kids were teasing him, and I thought you'd want to know because he did get very upset, and it's my policy to call parents whenever a child cries."

"Cole cried?" Susan blinked. "About my new relationship?"

Ms. Klopson misunderstood her tone. "I mean, it's certainly none of my business who you're engaged to, and I—"

"No, no," Susan interrupted. "I'm not engaged to anyone. That's why I was confused. What exactly did Cole say?"

"Oh dear," Ms. Klopson said. "I should know by now not to believe everything little kids say. They have such rich imaginations! Well, Cole has been telling the other kids that you're going to marry Steve Kerr."

"Steve Kerr . . . his soccer coach?" Susan said, refraining from saying, *That kid?* Ms. Klopson was just a few years older than him.

"Cole has been very convincing," Ms. Klopson said. "He may have a future as a novelist. He says you all raked leaves together last night, and that Steve helped you change a lightbulb that you couldn't reach."

"Cole told you all that?" Susan couldn't believe it. It was one thing to fib. It was another to construct a multilayered, elaborate fantasy.

"I'm sure it's just a phase," Ms. Klopson said. "I just felt badly for Cole because one of the older boys told Cole that you were too"—Ms. Klopson cut herself off and readjusted her words—"that the age difference between you and Steve was too great, and he ran off the playground crying. I found him hiding in the closet in the classroom."

Cole had cried, and she hadn't been there to comfort him? Susan felt a pang in her chest.

"He didn't mention anything about that," Susan said. "He was in a great mood when he got home."

"Kids tend to live in the moment," Ms. Klopson said. "Most of them, anyway. I wouldn't worry about it too much."

"Thank you," Susan said, and she slowly put down the phone.

She stayed frozen in place for a while. If Cole hadn't had a father in his life, she'd understand why he seemed to be trying to procure one. But Randall was very present. Cole spent one full weekend day and night with Randall, usually Saturdays, and Cole also slept over at Randall's every Tuesday night. Plus Randall volunteered in Cole's classroom every Thursday. Randall phoned every night at bedtime to read Cole a story. Cole and Randall spent more time together than some other fathers and sons who lived in the same house.

It couldn't be simple hero worship of their soccer coach. Susan attended a lot of practices, and while the kids all liked Steve, Cole barely mentioned him.

What else could it be?

Susan turned the question over in her mind while beside her the dryer tumbled in fruitless circles, too.

Cole was grappling with something, but what?

# Chapter Eighteen

IN HIGH SCHOOL, TESSA had known a girl named Penelope who was so astonishingly beautiful she didn't seem human. She looked like she'd stepped out of a cosmetics ad. Every detail, from the curve of her eyebrows to the glossy sweep of strawberry-blond hair to the delicate shape of her collarbone was perfectly etched. Guys stared at her. Girls stared at her. Tessa had even caught a few teachers staring at her, their chalk halting in its movement against the board, before they caught themselves and continued their lessons.

During her senior year, Penelope had a boyfriend who was already in college, a detail that awarded her even more social currency. She drove a BMW. She wasn't catty, but she didn't go out of her way to be nice. She was a golden girl, living an impossibly charmed life. She seemed remote, which wasn't surprising, because how could mere mortals expect to coexist on the same plane as perfect Penelope?

Then, three weeks after beginning her freshman year of college, Penelope used a rope to hang herself in her dorm room.

The first thing that popped into Tessa's mind when she'd heard the news was: *But she was so beautiful!*

You told yourself stories about people, Tessa thought. You

took in superficial details and created a narrative: *Penelope must have been happy, because she looked so good.* But you were usually wrong.

She'd made the same mistake with Susan. She'd assumed Susan was a Superwoman. Pretty, successful, competent—a strong businesswoman who was also a great mom. Cole was polite and cheerful, and Susan had it all together. When Addison had tripped and skinned his knee on the sidewalk on the way to the bus, Susan had pulled a tiny tube of Neosporin and a Band-Aid from her purse. When Bree was struggling to remember state capitals in preparation for a geography exam, Susan not only recited them all, she gave her mnemonic tips to help her ace the test.

Now Tessa knew the truth: Susan had secret struggles, too. Sometimes Susan cried so hard that her pretty face twisted and she gasped for air.

*I know*, Tessa thought. *I've done that, too.*

The kids were in the living room, watching a video, while Tessa put together dinner. Harry had been away on business for two nights, and she wanted him to come home to a good meal. They'd been making so much progress lately. Before the incident at Halloween, neither of them had nightmares for a few weeks.

Tessa cut a butternut squash in half and drizzled each side with olive oil before putting it into the oven, facedown, to roast. She cleaned a chicken and slid slices of lemon and cloves of garlic under its skin before putting it into the oven next to the squash. There would also be rolls, and a big green salad, and hard apple cider for the adults. She'd light a fire, and put on music.

*Superficial details*, a voice whispered in her mind, but she ignored it.

When the phone rang, she was rinsing lettuce. Her hands were wet, so she dried them on the dish towel looped over the stove handle and scooped up the receiver without checking caller ID. That was her first mistake.

"Tessa!"

The voice on the other end burst out, bright and bubbly as champagne. Cindy. A friend from her past—from her other life, the one she'd taken for granted, even complained about.

"I've been trying to reach you forever, girl! Seems like you just dropped off the face of the earth."

"I'm sorry," Tessa said, her mind quickly searching for a reason to get off the phone. "Things have been so frantic, with the move, and Harry's been traveling . . ."

"Excuses, excuses," Cindy said, but there was no menace in her tone. Cindy had been the room mother, along with Tessa, for Bree's first-grade class. They'd gone walking together lots of mornings after taking the kids to school. She'd been a wonderful friend.

*Imitate the school principal doing morning announcements in your Sarah Palin voice!* she could still hear Cindy beg, and she could see her friend doubled over in helpless laughter, her shoulders shaking, tears streaming down her face.

Oh, how Tessa missed her! Suddenly other memories of her former life came rushing back: The little pencil marks on the kitchen doorframe she and Harry had etched to capture their children's growth—the painters would have covered those up when they'd gotten the house ready to put on the market. The lion she'd stenciled on Addison's wall to watch over him and protect him while he slept—Larry the Lion was probably gone by now, too. The small angel statue Tessa had bought for the garden, as a remembrance of the two babies she'd lost before they were born. The bushes in their backyard that, for two glorious weeks in late June, were filled to bursting with tart, sweet blackberries—their family had always vowed they'd pick enough for a pie, but they ended up stripping all the fruit off the branches to gobble down, their fingers and lips staining purple. Those sun-warmed berries were the best thing Tessa had ever tasted.

Tessa cleared her throat. "I'm glad you called," she said. She could do this. She could get through a simple conversation; it would be good practice. Cindy had left a few messages on Tessa's cell, but Tessa hadn't returned them. Instead she'd written careful emails to Cindy that were designed to appear chatty without revealing anything substantial. She'd read them through several times before hitting send, knowing that anything electronic could always be subpoenaed.

"How is everything back home?" Tessa asked, thinking she'd keep the focus on Cindy. That way she could talk less. But it was her second mistake.

Cindy sighed, and Tessa heard the whistle of her teakettle. Cindy constantly drank cinnamon tea because she was in an ongoing struggle to lose ten pounds and she'd heard cinnamon curbed your appetite. Except Cindy added a big spoonful of honey and a dash of cream to her tea, offsetting whatever gains she might make. It was one of the quirky, endearing details that sealed a friendship.

"It's been a strange few months," Cindy said. "The kids all miss Addison and Bree. I don't know, everyone around here is still pretty freaked out. Detective Robinson comes around and asks questions every now and then. She's always got that little black notebook out. She was here yesterday and I told her sometimes it just hits me that Danny is gone, and I'm so angry, because I want to—"

Cindy cut herself off. Tessa knew one of her children must've walked into the kitchen.

"Well, you know," Cindy continued lightly. "Those photos!"

Tessa could feel herself shaking. Why had she answered the phone?

"Yes," she murmured.

"But enough about that," Cindy said. "What's new with you?"

Tessa managed to talk for another five minutes before finding an excuse to get off the phone. "I'll call you next week!" Cindy had said. "Let's stay in better touch."

More memories were roaring back now, fast and hard. Tessa

sank onto a chair, her hands clutching her stomach, as images slammed into her: Harry staggering into the kitchen that night, the blood on his shoes, his face so pale . . .

"Your shoes," she'd said, pointing to them. Harry had looked down, seen the blood, and slipped them off.

"I have a plan," he'd said, his usually rich brown eyes appearing oddly blank. "Follow me."

Tessa had been in shock. She'd obediently trailed him up the stairs, feeling as if she'd floated outside of her own body. Harry had gone into their bedroom first, and he'd put his bathrobe over his T-shirt and shorts. He'd tossed Tessa her robe and motioned for her to do the same. Then he walked to the threshold of Bree's room. Harry had raised a finger to his lips. He'd slowly opened the door and had crept inside. He'd reached for the alarm clock on Bree's nightstand. She'd just gotten it the previous Christmas and was inordinately proud of her ability to wake herself up in time for school. As Tessa watched, Harry twisted a knob to flip the numbers back, changing the time from 2:54 a.m. to 12:29 a.m.

Harry put a hand on Tessa's shoulder. "Go to the top of the stairs," he'd whispered.

"What are you going to do?" she'd asked, but he just gestured for her to move. He stepped into the hallway with her. Then he slammed Bree's door—hard.

The noise crashed through the house.

"Daddy?" Bree had called. She'd always been a light sleeper. Harry waited a beat, then opened her door.

"Sweetie, it's so late," he said. "Have you been awake this whole time? Don't you know what time it is?"

Bree looked at the clock without waiting for an answer, then her head flopped back on her pillow.

"Here," Harry had said. He handed Bree a glass of water from her nightstand. "I bet you're thirsty. Drink some of this, then you'll be able to sleep."

But as Bree reached for the glass, Harry let it slip from his grasp. It landed on her chest and spilled its contents down her nightgown. She gave a little shriek and sat up. "Daddy, it's cold!"

"Oh, sweetie, I'm so sorry," Harry had said. "Tessa, can you get her a fresh nightgown? Bree, just run into the bathroom and change."

Even in her foggy state, Tessa realized what he was doing. If she'd immediately dozed off again, Bree might not even have remembered waking up. So Harry was making sure the details would be lodged in her brain that morning. Bree got up and went into the bathroom, and Harry turned on the hall light, which burned brightly.

When Bree returned, her voice sounded much more alert.

"You need to go to sleep," Harry said. "It's so late. See what time it is?"

He pointed at the clock.

"Look, the clock says one-two-three-four," Bree said. "It's twelve thirty-four."

"That means good luck is coming," Harry had said, and Tessa had clutched the door to steady herself against the dizziness engulfing her. Bree had always loved it when clocks showed sequential numbers, and had developed the superstition that they were a harbinger of a happy surprise. Bree would not only remember waking up, she'd remember the exact time the clock showed. Harry had planned this.

He was creating an alibi.

After they'd tucked Bree in, Harry had silently walked downstairs. He'd taken a paper towel and had wiped the blood off the kitchen floor, then he'd buried the paper towel in the trash can.

"I'll change her clock back when I'm sure she's asleep," he'd said.

Then he'd put his clothes into a plastic bag, even his shoes, changed into a new outfit, and had gone back outside. A moment later, Tessa heard the sound of his car engine starting up again.

# Chapter Nineteen

**Newport Cove Listserv Digest**

*Re: Farts!
   I love farts too! —Frank Fitzgibbons, Forsythia Lane

• • •

There were few things in life more disconcerting than being in your bathrobe, rubbing sleep from your eyes while you stumbled toward the coffeemaker, and nearly bumping into a man reading the paper at your kitchen table.

Gigi gave a little shriek, simultaneously releasing a small, unfortunate fart.

"Hi, Mrs. Kennedy," Zach said, turning a page.

Had he heard? He acted like he hadn't heard. Gigi wasn't sure if she should be more embarrassed by the way she looked or the sound she'd made. She needed to buy a nicer bathrobe.

"I'm just . . ." She waved her hand around, unsure of why she was gesturing. She buried her head in the refrigerator and started taking out eggs, bread, and butter.

Joe came bounding down the stairs a moment later. He'd

taken a leave of absence from his job at the environmental agency so he could campaign full-time. Just as Zach had predicted, the results of the congressional election had narrowed the numbers separating the Republicans and Democrats in Congress. This seat wouldn't tip the balance either way, but it was still highly coveted by both parties.

They were talking about having Bill Clinton come in to do a campaign event for Joe. Bill Clinton!

"I'll be gone for the night," Joe said. "We're hitting up the opening of a grocery store and a Rotary Club meeting. Then tomorrow morning we're going to diners to talk to retirees."

"Where are you staying tonight?" Gigi asked.

"Holiday Inn," Joe said.

"Don't get peed on by a baby," Gigi said, and Joe smiled. It had actually happened during one campaign event, when a woman had thrust an infant into Joe's arms. "Who started the whole politicians kissing babies thing?" he'd asked later as he'd changed out of his still-damp shirt. "Isn't that kind of weird?"

"Better than them kissing their interns," Gigi had said, just before Joe had tackled her onto the bed.

Now that Joe was the bona-fide Democratic nominee, more money had been made available to his campaign. He had to be careful how he spent it, and account for every penny, but almost a hundred thousand dollars had poured into his coffers immediately after the primary. Most of that would go for advertisements, but it would also cover his meals, gas money, and overnights at the Holiday Inn.

Joe picked up his stainless steel travel mug of coffee.

Zach picked up his stainless steel travel mug of coffee.

"Bye, honey," Gigi said, giving Joe a kiss. Zach gave her a salute and headed out the door, the newspaper rolled up under his arm.

"Oh," Gigi said.

"What is it?" Joe asked.

She decided to let it go. Maybe Zach was grabbing the paper

for Joe. "Nothing," she said. She could pick up another when she was out running errands.

"I told the kids I'd be home early tomorrow," Joe said. "Family movie night?"

"Sure," she said.

She watched him go, then fixed her coffee and sat down on the chair Zach had just vacated, relishing the few minutes of quiet before she needed to wake up the kids. Melanie had been surprisingly cooperative about Zach moving in. Her only rule, Joe had reported, was that Zach never be allowed to enter the second floor of the house. And in particular, he couldn't go into her room.

"That's all she said?" Gigi had asked.

Joe had shrugged. "I have the feeling she has a crush on him."

"I picked up on that, too," Gigi had said. "That day of the photo shoot—I couldn't be sure but I thought she got upset when the photographer pointed out her pimple because Zach was there."

"She could do worse," Joe had said.

"Joe, he's too old for her," Gigi had said sharply.

"That's not what I meant," he'd said. "It's just that he's smart and hardworking and idealistic. If that's the kind of guy Melanie is attracted to, more power to her."

"Idealistic?" That wasn't the word that came to mind. "Opportunistic," maybe. But she didn't know Zach well. Maybe she'd gotten the wrong impression.

Still, the way he'd squatted down to her eye level when he'd asked Gigi about her secrets . . . The expression on his face had been friendly yet serious. But for the briefest of moments, something had revealed itself in his eyes. A gleam that was almost predatory.

A charred smell alerted her that her toast was burning. She stood up and tossed it in the trash; she was no longer hungry.

A moment later she heard the sound of the shower turning on. Melanie must already be up. Gigi used to have to drag

Melanie out of bed, but she hadn't had to go into her daughter's room and shake her awake even once lately.

Gigi frowned, replaying Joe's words in her mind. He'd said Zach wasn't allowed to go into Melanie's room. Was that because she wanted privacy . . . or because she was hiding something?

Gigi crept up the stairs, hesitating at the landing. To the left was the running shower. To the right was Melanie's room. Her door was firmly shut, as always.

Gigi was convinced Melanie had installed security devices—pieces of tape stretched across the doorframe, maybe—because the few times recently when Gigi had gone in there to put away laundry, Melanie had known.

But maybe Melanie didn't take precautions when she was just taking a quick shower.

Gigi twisted the door handle and entered her daughter's room. She'd just take a quick look around, Gigi told herself. This wasn't snooping. She was searching for clues to help her solve the mystery that was her daughter.

She scanned the items on Melanie's desk. God, she was a slob. There were a few Sanpellegrino cans, an empty chips bag, lots of paper and books, and assorted junk like pencils and pennies. A few bras hung over the back of a chair.

Nothing here. What she needed was a diary, or a slip of paper with an email account and password. She peered under the bed and found only a few shoes, dirty clothes, and a book titled *Melt Away 20 Pounds Overnight!*

"Oh, Melanie," Gigi whispered. She looked down at the photograph of a skinny woman in a bikini on the cover and felt her throat constrict. She put it back exactly where she'd found it and straightened up and walked over to Melanie's dresser. She began rummaging through the drawers: clothes, bras, underpants . . . Gigi frowned as she felt something hard hidden beneath a pair of socks. She pulled it out. A pack of Marlboro lights, with a few missing.

Gigi hadn't noticed cigarette smoke on Melanie, but that

didn't mean much. Melanie rarely got close enough for Gigi to smell her.

Gigi put the pack back. She'd be grateful if a few cigarettes were all she had to worry about. But there had to be something else. Melanie couldn't have changed, seemingly overnight, from her sweet daughter to this . . . this *stranger* . . . without a reason. Gigi tore open the desk drawers. Nothing. Melanie's phone was on the floor, plugged into its charger, but it was password protected. She and Joe had never made rules about the kids' phones because they hadn't needed to. Melanie had talked to her until recently, sharing her problems with Gigi, wanting her mother's advice.

The shower turned off.

Gigi eased out of the room, shutting the door behind her. She went into Julia's room and switched on her closet light. The overhead one would be too bright and jarring for her sensitive girl. Julia had a Harry Styles poster on the wall and a Harry Potter wand in a prized position on her bookshelf. Gigi suddenly wondered if in another year or two, she'd find those accessories corny and embarrassing. If she'd find her mother corny and embarrassing, like Melanie did.

"Good morning, sweetie," she said.

Julia opened her eyes, yawned, and pulled the pillow over her head.

Gigi heard Melanie come out of the bathroom and pad into her bedroom, firmly closing the door behind her.

"Do I have to get up?" Julia mumbled through the pillow.

"You can doze for just a few more minutes," she said.

She sank down onto the bed, stroking Julia's long, soft hair, feeling inordinately grateful to be able to give her daughter a simple answer.

• • •

Experts insisted children needed to learn how to put themselves to sleep and should be taught to do so at a young age.

*Screw the experts*, Susan thought as she lay with Cole in his racecar-shaped bed, rubbing his back. She was going to enjoy cuddling him and breathing in the lavender scent that clung to him after his bubble baths for as long as she could. She probably only had a few years left before he would no longer seek out her touch. Already, Cole was losing his baby fat and his facial features were becoming more defined. His complexion was a few shades lighter than hers—closer to Randall's skin tone—but he still had Susan's big, long-lashed eyes.

"Ava is the meanest girl in my class," Cole announced.

"Why is that?" Susan asked.

"She hates everyone," Cole said. "She probably hates squirrels. But I bet she likes Cinnamon Toast Crunch cereal."

Cole's mind reminded her of a Twitter feed—random thoughts scrolled by, some connected and some completely off the wall. Actually, everyone's mind probably worked that way, Susan thought. Kids just hadn't learned to censor themselves yet, to streamline their thoughts into a defined channel for the sake of appropriateness. It was one of the things she loved best about their bedtime conversations, chasing the tail ends of his imaginings, trying to puzzle out all the pieces that formed her son.

"I bet she does," Susan agreed. "Everyone likes Cinnamon Toast Crunch."

"We should buy some," Cole said.

"Maybe tomorrow," Susan said.

"Plus I won at dodgeball," Cole said. "Ava wanted to win and she got really mad at me."

"Sounds like she was a sore loser," Susan said. She gave Cole's hair another stroke and he nestled against her like a baby koala, wrapping his arms and legs around her.

"Sweetie?" Susan said. "I have a question for you. Why did you tell Ms. Klopson that I was going to marry your soccer coach?"

Cole had been rubbing his feet together, but he suddenly went still.

"I'm not mad at you," Susan said quickly. "I'm just curious. Do you really like Steve?"

"Do you like him?" Cole asked, and Susan quashed a smile.

"He's very nice," Susan said. "And I think he's a good coach. I'm not going to marry him, though. I don't even know him that well."

"Oh," Cole said in a small voice.

"Are you worried I might get married to someone else?" Susan asked. "Someone you don't like?"

Cole shook his head.

"Do you know why you said that in the first place?" Susan asked. "About me marrying Steve?"

"I just thought maybe you would," Cole said.

Susan decided to let it go. They talked about a few other things—where fireflies came from ("I think Canada," Cole decided) and whether Cole should ask Santa for a fish or a frog for Christmas ("How about a stuffed frog?" Susan suggested, knowing the battle had already begun and that she was destined to lose it)—then Cole's chatter eased and his breaths turned soft and even. Susan held him for another moment, then she eased out of bed, leaving him bathed in the gentle glow of his night-light.

She crept downstairs to the dining room table where a pile of paperwork awaited. She paid taxes quarterly as a small business owner, so she needed to gather her receipts and calculate things like her estimated business mileage. But she found herself unable to focus. She picked up a receipt for a client's takeout lunch (chicken and mashed potatoes, Mrs. Anderson, in the hospital for three weeks following a heart procedure), then realized she was staring at the slip of paper.

Her mind kept circling back to the phone conversation with Ms. Klopson. Cole had been very specific about the things he'd said Steve was doing at their house. Raking leaves. Changing a lightbulb.

Actually, Susan had raked most of the leaves coating their

lawn while Cole was at Randall's. She'd stuffed them into the huge paper bags provided by Newport Cove. She'd saved some for Cole, though; her parents had been firm believers in chores, and Susan was, too. She'd pointed out the neat row of bags she'd done by herself, then she'd said, "We have to do the last two bags together. I did most of them, but I need your help now."

And that bit about Steve changing the lightbulb—that detail was rooted in something that had actually happened, too. The bulb in the hallway had burned out and Susan had climbed onto a chair to change it, but the fixture was just beyond her reach. Cole had watched her struggle to touch it. She recalled making a joke about wishing she were taller, but she didn't remember if he'd responded. She'd gone into the garage and brought out the stepladder and climbed onto it. Cole had watched, warning her to be careful. He seemed worried she'd fall, even though she'd assured him she wouldn't.

"See?" she'd said as she'd untwisted the bulb. And that had been the end of that completely unremarkable incident.

But apparently Cole had thought about these moments, adding and subtracting details before spinning them into something else entirely.

She pulled out more receipts, absently sorting them into piles. She'd almost worked her way through the stack when it hit her.

Cole wasn't looking for another father figure. He was worried about *her*. He wanted Susan to have a partner—someone to help her. Susan hadn't realized she was lonely, but her perceptive little boy had picked up on it.

She dropped the rest of the receipts and rubbed her eyes. She'd worked to model good behavior for Cole. She'd acted positive and strong, telling herself she was making the most of their little life together. She'd thought it had been enough— her son, her work, her friends. But Cole had seen deep inside of her and he'd known she was lonely. Maybe he even suspected she wanted Randall back.

Not that she did! She wouldn't take Randall back, not after everything that had happened. If he'd only agreed to counseling when she'd suggested it, if he'd only told her about meeting Daphne . . . if she'd only had the chance to go to Daphne after that first meeting and beg her to stop seeing Randall . . .

Randall and Daphne hadn't had sex until a week or so after Randall had moved out. Susan knew because Daphne told her. Daphne hadn't shared many of the details—perhaps she was trying to be considerate, given that Susan's own marriage had just been demolished—but there was no unseeing the look that had come into Daphne's eyes when she'd mentioned her new boyfriend. Or the way the look had transformed into horror a few minutes later, when she'd spotted the family photo.

She hated Daphne.

The words she'd spoken earlier, about the little girl who'd pouted when she'd lost at dodgeball, reverberated in her head. *Sore loser.*

That was different, Susan thought. That was something else entirely.

# Chapter Twenty

*Barking Dog

Someone let their dog out very late last night—close to midnight—and allowed it to bark for at least ten minutes, waking up my family. Please be mindful of the hours when you let your pet outside. —Barb Dixon, Forsythia Lane

*Re: Barking Dog

There's a noise ordinance pertaining to construction, which permits on-site work only until 8 p.m. Perhaps this rule should also relate to dogs? It seems like something for the Newport Cove Manager to investigate. —Tally White, Iris Lane

*Re: Barking Dog

Thank you for the suggestion, Tally! —Shannon Dockser, Newport Cove Manager

• • •

"We need a girls' night out," Susan announced at the bus stop.

"I'm in," Kellie said. "We should invite Gigi, too. I haven't seen her much lately."

"How about Thursday?" Susan asked. "Tessa, are you free?"

Excuses sprang to her lips: She and Harry already had plans. Thursday night was family night, and they always stayed in. She was feeling a tickle in her throat that might turn into the flu.

But her talk with Susan and the phone call with her old friend Cindy had ignited something in Tessa, a hunger for the easy, supportive camaraderie of other women. She'd be careful, she promised herself. She'd have one glass of wine, then she'd switch to seltzer water. She wouldn't slip up.

"I'd love to," she found herself saying, surprised by how much she meant it.

"Seven thirty at Sidecar?" Kellie said. "That way we can get the kids settled after dinner before we head out. Maybe we should take cabs, just to be safe. These days if I have even one drink I feel tipsy."

"Clearly you haven't been drinking enough, you lightweight," Susan joked.

"So let's remedy that!" Kellie said. "Thursday night at Sidecar!"

• • •

The plan was everyone would gather at Susan's house around seven p.m. and they'd all pile into a cab together. But Kellie's exit from her home was delayed because Noah had sloshed water over the side of the tub, and it was leaking through the cracks in the floors and dripping through the dining room ceiling.

"Jason!" Kellie called. She was in the kitchen, finishing the dinner dishes, when she heard a patter that sounded like raindrops against the floor. He didn't answer so she hurried upstairs to find her husband watching TV in the bedroom.

"I thought you were giving Noah a bath," she said. "He's making a mess."

"Sorry, babe," he said.

It seemed like Jason was glued to the television lately. Had he always watched this much?

She exhaled loudly and went into the bathroom, putting a few towels on the floor to sop up the water that had sloshed over the edge. Noah was still splashing around, a crown of bubbles on his head.

"Give me a kiss, sweetie," she said and leaned over— directly into the spray of water Noah aimed at her.

"Noah!" she cried. "Why did you do that?"

"Because you were a bad Transformer," he said. His eyes filled.

"Be more careful next time," she said, softening her tone. "Aim for the side of the tub, okay?"

"I'm sorry, Mommy," he said.

"It's okay," she said, feeling guilty. He was such a sensitive boy, tough on the outside, tender within.

She looked in the mirror. She'd taken the brunt of the splash on her left side—mascara streaked from that eye down toward her nose, and half of her bangs were flattened and damp. She glanced at her watch, saw it was ten minutes after seven, and reached for the phone.

"I'm running late," she said. "You guys can go ahead and I'll meet you there."

"No worries," Susan said. "We already opened a bottle of wine since we're not driving. Take your time."

Kellie fixed her hair and makeup, then went downstairs again to grab a coat, feeling her irritation at Jason mount. Why hadn't he stayed in the bathroom and supervised Noah? She'd cooked dinner and though he'd cleared the table, she'd also prepared the school lunches for tomorrow and had started a load of laundry. And it wasn't like Jason never went out; he played poker every week with a group of friends, and he regularly attended football and baseball games, sitting in the stands and drinking beer with his dad. She was about to call upstairs to remind Jason to take Noah out of the tub when she heard the floorboards creaking under Jason's footsteps.

"Hey, buddy," he was saying. "Let's get you dry and into some pj's."

Kellie breathed in, then out. Her shoulders relaxed. Mia was reading a book on the couch, so Kellie went over and dropped a kiss on her head. Mia didn't even look up, she was so engrossed in the story, which made Kellie happy. Mia had been a late reader, but she was making up for lost time.

"Bye!" Kellie called.

"Have fun!" Jason shouted.

• • •

It was too early for the bar to be crowded, and Kellie, Tessa, Susan, and Gigi commandeered a booth. U2 blared from the speakers, pool balls clacked together in the background, and a bartender shook a stainless steel mixer high in the air.

"Let's get fun drinks," Kellie said as she opened the menu. "This place has the best cocktail names. Ooh, I want a Happy Ending."

"Don't we all," Gigi said dryly. "I'm going to try an Angry German."

Tessa ran her eyes down the ingredients of different cocktails, trying to find one that didn't have too much liquor. "Set 'Em Up Joe looks good," Tessa said.

The waiter was at their table. "Ladies?" he said. They placed their orders and he committed them to memory.

"I used to be able to do that," Kellie said. "I could remember stuff before I had kids. Now? My brain is a sieve. The other day I couldn't think of the word for mitten. I was convinced it was early-onset Alzheimer's, so I Googled it. Turns out that the symptoms of motherhood mimic those of brain degeneration."

"You made that up," Susan said.

"Yes, but I think it's actually true," Kellie said. "We should come up with a name for the syndrome. Mommy Brain doesn't sound severe enough."

"Chips and guac to share?" Gigi wondered as she looked at her menu.

"Not for me," Kellie said. "And by that I mean you order them and I'll stare at them longingly until you tell me to help myself, and then I'll eat half."

Gigi smiled. "Tessa?" she asked.

"My answer's the same as Kellie's," she said.

"Two chips and guacs, please," Gigi told the waiter when he returned with their drinks.

"You look great, by the way," Gigi said to Kellie. "Did you do something different with your hair?"

"I got highlights last week," Kellie said. She touched her hair. "And layers. I've been wearing the same style since before the kids, so I felt like something different. Plus it was my reward. I just sold my first house!"

"Congrats!" Susan and Tessa said in unison. Gigi raised her glass. "Cheers!"

"Thanks," Kellie said. She took a swallow of her drink and Tessa saw a shadow pass over her face. "It was a little sad, actually. The house was so ugly, but the family loved it. The parents passed away, and the kids wanted it to be sold to a new family. But a builder bought it for the land. He's going to raze the lot."

"Seems like that's happening more and more these days," Gigi said.

"Yeah," Kellie said. She looked down at her drink. "The daughter cried when I told her it was the only offer we had. She said that house was her childhood. Her dad built this miniature lighthouse for her in the backyard because she really loved them. It was a gift for her tenth birthday. She said she was a really awkward kid and she didn't have any friends, and her happiest memories were of sitting up there and reading. I didn't know that. I just thought he was nuts for building it . . ."

Susan put an arm around Kellie's shoulders. "Are you crying?"

"No!" Kellie wiped her eyes and gave herself a little shake. "I'm celebrating. Miller—he's this guy I work with who has been really helpful—said it's better to have the house sold than to just have it sitting there. That way the kids can move on, Miller said."

"The daughter will still have all those memories, too," Susan said. "No one can ever take them away. That's what I tell a lot of my clients when they have to move to an assisted living center. Possessions are just stuff. They don't represent who we are."

Tessa nodded. "It's true. We left a lot of stuff behind when we moved. The kids had a great tree house and I finally had my dream kitchen . . ."

Kellie turned to her. "You know, I don't think we ever got an answer to Mia's question. Why did you decide to move, if you don't mind my asking?"

The guacamole arrived then, giving Tessa a few crucial seconds to compose herself. She took a chip and broke it in half but didn't put it in her mouth.

"A lot of reasons, really," Tessa finally said. She wanted to stick close to the truth; it felt important to be honest. "Something about this neighborhood seemed special. It just felt safe to me. It felt . . . right."

The other women were nodding.

"And even though we had lots of happy memories back at home, there were some unhappy ones, too," Tessa said.

Susan put a hand over Tessa's and gave it a little squeeze. It was the look on Susan's face—pure compassion—that told Tessa it was safe to open up. She wouldn't reveal everything. But maybe she could share a small part of herself.

"I had two miscarriages before we had Bree," she said. She swallowed hard before continuing. "And Harry and I created a flower garden in honor of those babies. It was in our backyard. We had butterfly bushes and a hummingbird feeder and a little angel statue . . . it was hard to leave that behind."

"Oh, sweetie," Gigi said. "I'm so sorry."

Tessa nodded. "I didn't know if we'd ever be able to have kids," she said. "The first one—I found out at the doctor's office. They couldn't find a heartbeat at twelve weeks."

A tear dripped down her cheek. Susan reached into her purse, came up with a tissue, and handed it to Tessa.

"Thank you," she said.

"Did you lose the second baby at around the same time? Twelve weeks?" Susan asked.

"We were almost at sixteen weeks, so I thought . . . Well, I guess I thought we were okay. Harry was away for work so I drove myself to the hospital," she said. "I hadn't bought much for the baby, because I was superstitious. But I'd seen these little yellow corduroy overalls that I couldn't resist. I still have them, tucked away in a box. Bree and Addison never wore them. I always thought of them as belonging to my other baby."

The waiter's cheery tone intruded, breaking apart the moment: "Ladies, another round?"

"I think we definitely need one," Gigi said. She gave Tessa a sympathetic smile.

"Anyway, it happened a long time ago, and I have Bree and Addison now, so . . ." Tessa said.

"But it still hurts," Susan said. "It's *allowed* to still hurt. You can be sad about what happened and grateful and happy for the family you have now."

Tessa nodded. "Yes." Somehow Susan had put into words exactly what Tessa had needed to hear. She'd felt like she was being greedy, mourning those babies when she had two perfectly healthy children now.

She took another sip of her drink. It was cold and sweet against her tongue. "I think it just . . . messed me up a little. I was so fearful with Bree and Addison. I kept worrying they'd get hurt, that I'd lose them, too. I was a little nuts when they were younger. I kept seeing danger everywhere. I felt like if I let down my guard, then something might happen again. And Harry was traveling so much, and Bree had colic and never slept . . ."

"Honey, being alone with two young kids is enough to drive anyone nuts," Gigi said. The other women were nodding in agreement.

"But I wasn't working!" Tessa said. "And I had a house-keeper once a month!"

"Yes, you *were* working," Susan corrected her.

"You had a colicky baby and a husband who traveled?" Kellie said. "That must've been so hard."

Tessa looked around at their faces in wonderment. She'd always thought she'd somehow messed up as a mother—failed because she'd struggled with the kids when they were little, and it seemed to come so easily to others. But the faces of her new friends contained only sympathy, no judgment.

"And now they're wonderful, healthy children," Susan said. "You did a good job, Mama. They're thriving."

"They are, aren't they?" Tessa said. She wiped her eyes. "Thank you. I knew we were right to move here."

"We've got a lot to celebrate tonight," Susan said. "Tessa moving here. Kellie's new career. And Joe's victory! How's he doing, Gigi?"

"You'd have to ask him," Gigi said. "He's off campaigning all the time. He sets aside a few evenings for family time, and he does make it home for dinner then, but that's about the only time I can count on seeing him these days."

"It's temporary, though, right?" Kellie said. "Just until the election?"

"Yes," Gigi said. "Then we'll get him back on weekends, at least. Meanwhile, I've got his campaign manager living in my basement."

"Is he the guy with the floppy blond hair who was ordering around the camera crew on election night?" Susan asked.

Gigi nodded. "Zach. I don't think he sleeps. The other night

I had insomnia and I went into the kitchen to get some chamomile tea. I heard this weird pecking noise coming from the basement so I looked down there and saw a blue light. Then I realized Zach was typing something on his computer."

"Is it odd to have a virtual stranger living with you, though?" Kellie asked. "Even a hot younger guy?"

Tessa thought she saw something flicker in Gigi's eyes, but Gigi just brushed off the question. "I hardly see him," Gigi said. "And it's just for a couple of months."

A year ago, if she'd been in this same situation, she might not have noticed it at all, Tessa thought. Susan was still in love with Randall. Gigi was upset about having the campaign manager live with them. Kellie was brimming with nervous energy and had given an odd little smile when she'd mentioned her coworker—odd especially because she'd been tearing up a moment earlier—and she'd checked her cell phone twice under the table. Suddenly it was abundantly clear to Tessa.

Every woman at the table had a secret.

•  •  •

Sidecar had gotten a lot more crowded in the past hour. They'd given up their booth after they'd finished eating, because a line of people were waiting to dine, and now the four women were clustered at the bar.

"I could only find one stool, and Gigi gets it," Susan said.

"Why, because I'm older than the rest of you?" Gigi joked.

"Because you have a bad back," Susan said.

"My senior bones and I will take it, then," Gigi said, sinking onto the stool.

The crowd was eclectic, mostly a mix of thirty- and forty-somethings along with a sprinkling of younger people. A few couples were dancing in one corner, and U2 had yielded to Beyoncé. The lights had dimmed.

Susan's second drink had given her a warm buzz, and she was working on her third. Her problems—how to handle

Cole's worry, Daphne's pregnancy, her grief over her imploded marriage—receded as she sipped the sweet concoction.

"Dance?" someone said near her ear.

Susan turned around and saw a not unattractive man. He was smiling.

Someone was nudging her from behind, pushing her closer to the guy, or maybe trying to steer her toward the dance floor. Probably Gigi, since Kellie had disappeared to go to the bathroom a minute earlier.

She wasn't going to dance with a stranger. She was out with her friends, having a wonderful time. She started to shake her head no.

The thing was, though, she really did love to dance.

"Sure," she said.

He led her to the floor and Susan began to move, twisting her hips to the beat.

"I'm Rick," the guy said, nearly shouting to be heard over the music.

"Susan," she said. She tossed back her hair and smiled. She was glad it was too loud for them to talk. How long had it been since she'd danced? Early on in their marriage, she and Randall had swayed to slow songs in their living room, by the fire. She used to pick up Cole and swoop him around, singing silly songs. But she hadn't even danced with her son in . . . months? Maybe even since Randall had left.

She pushed away the thought and tried to smile at Rick again.

But she couldn't clear her mind. She'd wanted so badly to set a good example for Cole, to be . . . honorable. But she'd forgotten to engage in fun. She hadn't laughed much during the past year. She'd carried around a dark weight, and though she'd tried to mask it, Cole had seen through her subterfuge.

The music changed to a song Susan didn't like as much.

The magic of the moment had passed. She didn't want to be here, with some guy who she could now see had adult acne and an overbite. She didn't want to go through the dating scene again, and participate in the whole exhausting charade of getting dressed up and meeting someone, then realizing you didn't have much in common, or he was still fixated on his old girlfriend (or worse, his mother), or that he was dull as paste.

The thought of starting over was so exhausting.

She'd finish this dance, then say she needed to get back to her friends.

To her left, she saw Kellie moving onto the dance floor with a handsome, dark-haired man. They were staring at each other in a way that made Susan do a double take. She watched as Kellie flipped back her hair and did a little shimmy.

So Kellie was flirting. Maybe she needed to let off a little steam, Susan thought.

But Kellie didn't seem to just be having casual fun. Her eyes were locked onto the guy's and she was a lot closer to him than Susan was to her dance partner. Kellie hadn't seemed drunk, but maybe she was tipsy.

The song ended, and Susan caught Kellie's eye.

"You okay?" Susan asked.

"Hey!" Kellie's cheeks were glowing and her eyes were bright. She walked over to Susan, trailed by the dark-haired man. "I'm great. I bumped into my friend Miller from the office."

Miller extended a hand and Susan shook it, then realized her dance partner was still there. "This is, um . . ."

"Rick," the guy supplied.

"Right, sorry. I'm going to head back to our friends," Susan said. "Rick, great meeting you. Thanks for the dance."

He inclined his head, but not before Susan saw disappointment and maybe a hint of embarrassment in his eyes. Oh, this was all so awkward. She hated that she'd hurt his feelings.

She walked over to Gigi and Tessa, who were deep in conversation, their heads bent close together. They broke apart when they saw her.

"Hey!" Tessa said. "Nice moves. I always thought you looked like a dancer."

"I took jazz for years," Susan said. "Thanks."

She finished her drink, thirsty from the exertion, and found her eyes pulled back to the dance floor. Kellie was still there. Miller bent down to say something to her, and she laughed, tossing back her head.

Kellie had mentioned his name earlier tonight, when she'd talked about selling her first house. It was a funny coincidence that Miller had shown up here. Susan craned her head to check if he had on a wedding ring, but she was too far away to tell.

"Another drink, Susan?" Gigi offered.

Susan shook her head. "Better not." She was hot now, and a little nauseous. She'd eaten too many chips and guac, and had downed her drinks too quickly.

"I'm going to switch to water myself," Gigi said. "All I need is to get tipsy and have someone put it up on YouTube. I'm still grateful that speech I tried to make on election night never surfaced online."

"You were on muscle relaxants," Susan said. "Everyone understands."

"Oh God, did you see it?" Gigi asked, putting her head in her hands.

"No," Susan said. Her eyes flickered and met Tessa's. "I'd left by then."

Susan wondered if Gigi knew Daphne and Randall had come to the party. Daphne had said Joe had invited them, which was fine.

Actually, it wasn't fine. But she couldn't—wouldn't—ever say that.

"Kellie's really having fun," Tessa said.

"Good for her," Gigi said. "He'll probably be disappointed to find out she's married."

"Actually, she knows him," Susan said. The other women looked at her questioningly. "She works with him. His name is Miller. Remember, she was talking about him earlier."

Gigi nodded, then craned her neck to check out Miller. "She didn't mention how handsome he was, though."

*Actually, she did*, Susan thought. Not in so many words, but something had conveyed that impression to Susan.

Susan grabbed a napkin and blotted her forehead. Someone bumped her from behind, jabbing a sharp elbow into her back. "Sorry!" a girl said when she turned around.

She gave her a nod and wished for a glass of water. The bartender was too busy to notice her wave.

She shouldn't have come out tonight. But what was the alternative? Sitting vigil in the cold outside Randall's again, imagining him and Daphne together, Randall stroking the outline of Daphne's face with a fingertip while he stared into her eyes, the way he'd done when he was with Susan?

On the dance floor, Miller reached for Kellie's hands and began to spin her around, doing a complicated series of moves that had her looping through his arms and ending with a little dip. His hands lingered on her rib cage.

Did anyone else see it? Susan wondered. The way Kellie stared up at Miller like a starstruck teenager? The way he seemed to be searching for excuses to touch her? Who the hell did they think they were fooling?

Susan didn't realize she'd begun to stalk toward the dance floor until Kellie looked up and caught her eye. The expression on Kellie's face—like she'd been caught doing something naughty—sealed Susan's suspicion.

"How's your husband, Kellie?" Susan asked pointedly. The music was so loud she practically had to scream it.

Kellie and Miller had stopped dancing by now and were standing a little bit apart. Miller had on a wedding ring, too, Susan saw.

"How's Jason?" Susan said. "He's at home with your children, right? What about you, Miller? Did you tell your wife you had to work late?"

Kellie's mouth had dropped open into a little O of surprise.

"I can't watch this," Susan said. "I'm leaving."

Susan turned and stormed out through the front door, ignoring Kellie, who was shouting her name.

A coy look. A dance. A conversation at a bar after your friends left and you found yourself sitting next to someone attractive. And suddenly, a marriage was splitting apart, and a family was wrecked, and a little boy was making up lies because he was worried about his mother. *It's not so innocent!* Susan wanted to shake Kellie by the shoulders, yank her away from Miller.

She wanted to scream at the top of her lungs: *This is how it starts!*

•  •  •

In some ways, Gigi felt like a big sister to Susan and Kellie. She was five years older, and had tipped the other women off about the best and worst teachers at the elementary school. She'd recommended a piano teacher for Noah and Mia (Melanie had been quite good, until she'd refused to continue playing and Gigi had decided to choose her battles). She'd given Susan the name of a wonderful karate instructor, and had recommended gynecologists and dentists to both women.

But she had no idea what to do after Susan stormed out and Kellie came back to the table, looking chagrined. Miller had disappeared by then.

"She just left," Kellie said. "I ran outside after her, but she was gone."

"She probably called an Uber," Gigi said. "I'll send her a text."

She tapped one out and asked Susan to let her know if she was safe. Do you want me to come over? she wrote.

A reply pinged back a moment later. No. Just in a bad mood. I'm in a cab now. Sorry.

"She's okay," Gigi told the others. "She caught a cab."

"I mean, that was ridiculous!" Kellie said. "All I was doing was dancing!"

Gigi nodded. She knew better than to get in the middle of it. She'd finished her second drink and was feeling tired. Melanie had to get up early every day for high school and Gigi always got up along with her.

Sleep deprivation couldn't be to blame for Melanie's personality change, could it?

Gigi sighed. Suddenly the music seemed too loud, the bar too crowded. The magic had evaporated from the night. "Should we go?" Gigi asked.

Tessa nodded. "Ready when you are."

"Oh, fine," Kellie said. "I'm not staying here alone."

They put on their coats and headed outside, into a brisk wind. Gigi wrapped her arms around herself and shivered, then checked her iPhone. "The cabdriver's just a minute away," she said.

The three women stood there in silence.

"I mean, it's not like I'm sleeping with Miller!" Kellie burst out. "We were just dancing."

"I think Susan's feeling a little sensitive because of . . . what happened to her," Tessa said.

"She told you about it?" Kellie asked.

Tessa nodded.

"I didn't know they were coming over on election night until I saw them walk through the door," Gigi said. "I would've warned Susan."

"Yeah," Kellie said. "Jason's still friendly with Randall, too. I told him I didn't want Randall coming to the house, because I don't want Susan to see, but they get together at bars to watch games sometimes."

She sighed and looked down. "I shouldn't have danced with Miller. This was supposed to be a girls' night and I blew it."

"It wasn't that," Tessa said. The other women looked at her in surprise.

"What was it, then?" Kellie asked.

"She misses Randall," Tessa said simply.

But it wasn't that, either, Gigi knew. Susan had regrets—a supple word that could bend and stretch to encompass a wide swath of emotions. You sent regrets when you couldn't attend a party, even if they were insincere. You regretted not telling someone—your mother, your father, a friend—you loved them before you lost them forever. And you could regret pieces of your past; brief, impulsive moments that nevertheless could have the power to shatter your husband's dream.

"She's a good friend, Kellie," Gigi said gently. "She was trying to help."

Kellie blinked hard a few times. "It's just—" she began, and then her cell phone pinged with an incoming message. She took it out of her purse and stared down at it.

Something told Gigi the text was from Miller. She watched as Kellie put the phone back into her purse without typing out a reply.

It was good Susan had interceded, Gigi thought. It wasn't too late for Kellie to avoid regrets of her own.

# Chapter Twenty-One

THE POLICE CRUISER PULLED up in front of Tessa's house on a Tuesday afternoon while the kids were in school.

Harry was out for a run, and Tessa was home alone. Tessa had been encouraging Harry to exercise because she hoped it might reduce his stress, but now she wished she hadn't. He came home sweaty and red-faced, often with reports of beating his previous mileage. Harry was up to something like thirty miles a week now, and his face was so thin his cheeks looked sunken. His transformation reminded Tessa of the one Matthew McConaughey had undergone for *Dallas Buyers Club*, where he'd morphed from muscular and healthy to sallow and fragile in a few short months. But McConaughey had won an Oscar for that transformation, then he had returned to a healthy weight. To himself.

Tessa wasn't sure what made her walk into the living room and look out the window—a sixth sense?—but when she did, the black-and-white car was parked by the curb. As if keeping surveillance.

She was grateful she wasn't holding anything, because her hands began to tremble and nausea rose in her throat. The doorbell hadn't rung, had it? She was certain she would have heard it. So the police officer must still be in the car.

What would an innocent person do, someone who had no knowledge of a crime? Would she run out to the car and ask the police officer why he was there, perhaps feigning fear at the thought of a criminal being on the loose?

No, Tessa thought. She'd wait, and look perplexed but eager to cooperate when the doorbell rang.

She went into the kitchen and ran cold water over a paper towel and dotted it against her wrists and the back of her neck. She took deep breaths and stared at her hands, willing them to stop trembling. The sudden silence of the house felt eerie. She could hear the almost imperceptible ticking of the kitchen clock.

When the doorbell rang, she nearly screamed.

She wiped her palms on her jeans, forced herself to slowly inhale and exhale once more, then went to open the door.

"Mrs. Campbell?" the young cop asked. He lowered his mirrored sunglasses and Tessa took in a shaky breath. He was a baby—maybe just twenty-two or twenty-three. They wouldn't have sent a baby cop if they knew.

"Officer, come in," Tessa said. She stepped back. Her voice was a little higher than usual but the cop wouldn't know that.

"Is everything okay?" she asked.

He stepped over the threshold and looked around. Their living room was neat and clean. The daily newspaper was spread across the coffee table, open to the crossword puzzle Harry had been working on that morning. There wasn't anything here amiss, nothing that would trigger suspicion.

"I'm Officer Chapman, just here as a courtesy," he said. "We got a call from Detective Robinson from your old town."

The female detective assigned to the case, the one with big, watchful eyes and an ever-present notebook.

"Yes," Tessa said. "I met her."

"She asked me to check in, see how you're doing," the officer said.

"How nice," Tessa said. "Can I get you some coffee? Or some cookies, or . . . ?"

Her voice trailed off.

"Actually, coffee and cookies sound really good," the officer said, and suddenly he was a boy again. He was of no threat to her.

Tessa hurried into the kitchen. She'd reheat this morning's coffee that was still in the pot so she wouldn't waste precious minutes brewing a fresh cup. Harry had been gone for almost an hour. He'd be back any minute now. She tore open a package of sugar cookies and put five on a plate, then snatched three back.

"Cream and sugar?" she called out.

"Please," Officer Chapman said.

She wondered what he was doing in the living room. If he was looking around.

She pulled the glass carafe off the warming burner before it was fully hot and sloshed some into a cup, then added sweetener and cream. She brought everything back into the living room and set it on the coffee table.

"Please sit down," she said. She could hear the kitchen clock ticking again. "Or actually, I can put that in a to-go cup if you need to get back to work?"

"Oh, I can take a five-minute break," the officer said.

Of course he could—Newport Cove was one of the twenty safest communities in the country. What did he have to do, other than give high-fives to little kids and respond to a report of a cat up in a tree?

Tessa sat across from him and crossed her legs and pushed the corners of her mouth upward, hoping her expression resembled a smile. She could see the street in front of the house. No sign of Harry coming down it.

"I guess you wanted to move away," the officer said.

"We did," Tessa said. "After everything that happened . . . well, it seemed like a fresh start was a good idea."

"You might want to give your contact information to Officer Robinson," the officer said. He dunked a cookie in his coffee and took a big bite. "She wasn't aware you'd moved."

"She wasn't?" Tessa said. "I'm sorry. It was sort of an impulsive decision. We just fell in love with this area."

Officer Chapman took another sip of coffee. *Hurry!* Tessa wanted to scream.

"What brought you down here again?" he asked.

Tessa suddenly went very still. The officer's eyes were fixed on hers. She'd let down her guard because he was so young. She'd been wrong to do that.

Out of the corner of her eye, she saw Harry jogging down their street. He stopped short when he saw the police car.

"Like I said before," Tessa said. "We just wanted a fresh start. And the weather here is a little milder, which is nice."

"You don't have any family here, though?" the officer said. He picked up a cookie and crunched into it, his eyes never leaving hers.

"No," Tessa said. "Of course, we didn't have any in our old neighborhood, either."

Somehow she felt certain Detective Robinson would be checking to verify that.

"Detective Robinson mentioned there wasn't a photo of your son in Danny's house," Officer Chapman said.

"No, there wasn't," Tessa said. *Meet his eyes*, she reminded herself. Don't volunteer unnecessary information. No tells.

"Is your husband home?" Officer Chapman asked. He finished the cookies and wiped his fingertips on his pants.

"Not at the moment," Tessa said. Her throat was so dry she couldn't swallow.

She heard the back door opening and coughed to mask the sound. Harry was in the house now. Would he come into the living room? "Well," she said loudly as she stood up. "I should probably start fixing dinner."

It was two o'clock in the afternoon. Another misstep.

Officer Chapman got to his feet. Any second now, Harry would walk into the room and he'd do something—run away or confess or start crying. He was so fragile.

Tessa strode to the front door. She held it open, knowing she was being rude—worse than rude, she was acting strangely.

She sent a mental message to Harry: *Don't move. Don't say a word.*

"Have a good day, ma'am," the officer said. "Thanks for the coffee and cookies."

Tessa closed the door behind him a split-second before Harry entered the living room.

"What's wrong?" Harry asked.

"Nothing!" she said. "Everything's fine!"

"Why were the police here?" he asked.

She looked him in the eye. "A fund-raiser. I wrote a check."

Harry nodded and she could see his body relax. "Okay," he said. "I'm going to take a shower."

Tessa managed to wait until she heard the water turn on upstairs before she allowed herself to fall onto the couch, her legs too weak to hold her up.

# Chapter Twenty-Two

**Newport Cove Listserv Digest**

*Happy Thanksgiving
  Happy Turkey Day, everyone! Gobble, gobble! —Shannon Dockser, Newport
  Cove Manager

*Re: Canned goods donations
  If anyone has canned goods to donate, I'll be happy to take them to the shelter.
  I'm making trips there every Friday throughout the winter, so just send me an
  email and I'll come by and pick up your boxed or canned food. I can also take
  extra coats, blankets and boots. —Jenny McMahon, Daisy Way

*Jump Start?
  Would someone mind popping by and giving me a jump start? Sigh. —Reece
  Harmon, Daisy Way

*Re: Jump Start?
  No problem! —Jenny McMahon, Daisy Way

• • •

Gigi pulled a tray of stuffed acorn squash out of the oven and
set the hot pan on top of a trivet.

"Are those done?" her mother asked, coming over and poking a finger into one of Gigi's squashes.

Her mother had arrived the previous afternoon, wearing a long tie-dyed dress with a purple knit cardigan over it. She'd brought along only a small cloth pouch, which made Gigi wonder if her mother was going to wear the same ensemble the whole three days she was visiting. Miraculously, she seemed to have stuffed several wardrobe changes into her little bag. But then again, her mother didn't need space for hair products or makeup or electronic devices.

"The insides don't feel very hot," her mother said. "Are you sure they don't need to go back into the oven?"

"Completely sure," Gigi said, even though she wasn't.

"It's too late for this year, but next year you should roast your turkey breast down," her mother said. "It'll be much juicier."

"I'll remember that," Gigi said. She eyed the unopened bottle of wine on the counter and wondered if it was too soon to pop the cork. Why had her mother been so disconnected for much of Gigi's life, only to now jump in and try to micromanage things? In the short time she'd been here, her mother had questioned the wisdom of everything from Joe's decision to run for Congress to Gigi's choice of a rug in the living room (the rug was from a store that produced goods in China, which resulted in a lecture from her mother on child labor and unfair trade practices).

"Where's Melanie? She's not still sleeping, is she?" her mother asked. "She's so like you at that age."

"No, I heard her take a shower a little while ago," Gigi said.

"I'll go check on her," her mother said.

*Good*, Gigi thought as she turned on water to boil the potatoes.

They were planning to eat dinner early, at one p.m., so Joe could go volunteer at a soup kitchen in the afternoon. That was Zach's idea; he'd said something about it being a nice photo-op, which cheapened the effort, in Gigi's opinion.

Gigi reached for the coffeepot and refilled her mug. Maybe she was just grumpy because she'd gotten up at dawn to put in the turkey. At least Joe had awoken with her to set the table and start the vegetable prep. They'd had to work quietly because Gigi's mother was asleep on the pull-out sofa in the living room, snoring. Zach was still ensconced in the basement.

"He's going home for Thanksgiving, right?" Gigi had asked hopefully the previous week.

Joe had shaken his head. "I offered to buy him a ticket but he said he'd just stay here and work through the holiday."

Of course they couldn't let Zach sit downstairs while they all ate and he inhaled the delicious smells. So she'd told Joe to invite him. But there was no way she'd let him stay for Christmas. Joe could get him a ticket home as a gift so he wouldn't be able to refuse it.

Gigi had been cubing bread for stuffing but she suddenly stopped moving and glanced at the ceiling. Was that laughter? *Melanie's* laughter?

"Hi, Gigi." Zach strolled into the kitchen wearing jeans and an electric-blue fleece pullover that matched his eyes. "Can I help with anything?"

"No, but thanks," Gigi said.

"Are you sure? I can wash these bowls," he said, gesturing to the mess in the sink.

"It's fine," Gigi said. "You're our guest. Why don't you just relax?"

She wished he'd go back downstairs, but instead he turned in the direction of the living room, where Felix was napping in front of a roaring fire. After a moment, Felix came padding into the kitchen.

*You don't trust him, either, do you?* Gigi thought, and slipped her dog a treat.

"Do you have stuff to make a pie?" Melanie asked as she came into the kitchen a moment later. Gigi turned to look at her in surprise. Melanie was wearing jeans and a black top, and her hair was brushed and out of her face. Her skin looked a little more clear, too.

"I do," Gigi said. She and Melanie used to cook together all the time, Melanie standing on a chair, a miniature apron tied around her waist while she mixed icing for cupcakes or kneaded dough for bread. Julia would help, too, although when she was really young they'd give her fake tasks, like whisking a few teaspoons of flour around in a bowl. Then the three of them would cuddle on the couch, reading books together. *Charlie and the Chocolate Factory* had been one of their favorites. Gigi had even set aside their dog-eared copy years ago with the thought that she'd give it to her first grandchild.

She and Julia had baked bread the previous month, but when Gigi had invited Melanie to join them, Melanie had just rolled her eyes.

"I've got apples and cinnamon and some pastry we can use for the crust," she told Melanie now, feeling a wash of sentimental emotion.

"Homemade crust is better," Gigi's mother said. "Have you ever tried it, Melanie? Melts in your mouth. You'll never eat the store-bought stuff again. Now, get me some butter and a little ice water."

Gigi turned down the heat on the potatoes and moved aside as Melanie opened the refrigerator and brought out the butter.

"What you want to do is mix up some flour with a little salt, then cut in the butter," Gigi's mother said. "You start cutting up the butter, Melanie. It's not organic? Fine, we'll make do. You want it to look like coarse crumbs. Go ahead, put some in with the flour."

"Like this, Grandma?" Melanie was asking.

"A little more butter," Gigi's mother said. "Then we'll start on the apples."

It was silly to feel left out when your mother and daughter were bonding, Gigi thought. If Gigi had asked to help, they probably would have let her. She could've cored apples, or measured the dry ingredients.

It was just that her children, along with Joe, were the loves of her life. Gigi had sung to them, nursed them, delighted in their first smiles, soothed their scrapes with magic kisses . . . Why hadn't anyone ever told her that one day the little girl who'd called out for her mommy whenever she had a bad dream would feel repulsed by her? Maybe this was what a divorce felt like. But you could always move on with a new man. You couldn't replace a daughter, nor would Gigi want to.

"Is this enough butter?" Melanie was asking as her grandmother peered in the bowl and nodded.

*Oh, come on*, Gigi thought, giving herself a mental shake. She wasn't in the second grade being left out of a game of hopscotch. She should be happy Melanie was baking with her grandmother.

"Mom?" Julia stuck her head into the kitchen. "Dad's setting up games in the living room. He asked if you wanted Scattergories or Catch Phrase."

It was one of their traditions. Every Thanksgiving they played board games. When the kids were smaller they'd done it in teams.

"You choose, sweetie," she told Julia. Julia nodded, then wandered over and grabbed a slice of apple and sprinkled a little cinnamon on it.

"Mmm," she said, taking a bite. "They're good this way."

"I've never tried that," Gigi said. "How'd you learn that?"

Julia shrugged. "I just figured it would taste good."

She offered Gigi a bite of the apple. She was right; it was delicious.

Julia gave her a quick hug, then wandered out of the room, singing a Katy Perry song.

Gigi moved her bread and the cutting board further down the counter, to give her mother and Melanie more room to work.

*She's so like you at that age*, her mother had said. True, Gigi had had triple-pierced ears and had been surly to her mother. But her mother was selfish and distant! She'd had good reason to be irritated with her!

And now, decades later, her mother still drove her nuts.

History didn't have to repeat itself, Gigi told herself as she cut the bread a little more forcefully. She'd find a way to break through to her daughter, to change this disturbing family dynamic before it gelled and set.

• • •

This year, Kellie and Jason were hosting the Thanksgiving feast. Twelve people were gathered in their house: Jason's parents; his sister Kim and her husband and son; Kellie's parents; her sister, Irene, who'd flown in from California; and of course their own family of four.

Everyone had contributed a dish. Jason's sister had brought a huge platter of roasted root vegetables, which her son would happily gobble up (not that Kellie was comparing), and her in-laws had brought wine and two pans of stuffing. Kellie's mom had made marshmallow-topped sweet potatoes and pumpkin pie, and Irene had unpacked a chocolate turkey to use as a centerpiece, which she'd pointed out could double as dessert. Despite the cloudy day, Irene had been wearing oversized dark sunglasses when they'd picked her up at the airport; she seemed to want to telegraph the message that she was from L.A. and in "the biz," as she called it.

"Happy Turkey Day!" Jason's father clinked his glass against Kellie's as they stood in the living room together. She smiled and took a sip of sparkling wine.

"You, too," she said.

"We've got so much to be thankful for," he said. He blinked rapidly a few times. Every holiday, Jason's father got a little teary. "This family is my greatest blessing."

Kellie's kids ran by, knocking against her hip as they argued about who'd get a drumstick (neither of them would eat the drumstick, they just wanted to win the battle), and then Jason came in, carrying an armload of firewood.

"It's getting nippy out there," he said. "It's cold enough for the first fire of the year."

They always had the first fire of the year on Thanksgiving, and like his dad, Jason was sentimental about tradition. Every time she saw Jason's father, she realized how much alike they looked. Jason had started to lose hair right in the exact spot on the crown where his father had a missing patch.

Kellie started at the knock on her door. She went to open it and there stood Susan, a foil-wrapped plate in her hands.

"Miss Manners says cookies are a suitable apology for an overreaction," Susan said. "But only if they contain chocolate chips."

Kellie smiled. "You made that up," she said, opening the door wider.

Susan stepped in and Kellie reached out and wrapped her arms around her best friend and held on tight.

"I know you'd never cheat on Jason," Susan whispered. "You were tipsy and being a little flirtatious, that was all."

"Yeah," Kellie said. "I'd had a couple of drinks and they really went to my head . . ."

"Just be careful around that guy Miller, okay?" Susan said. "He looked like he wanted to eat you up."

Kellie felt a little thrill. She wanted to ask, *He did?* but knew she couldn't.

"Look, why don't you come on in? We're about to sit down to dinner. I'd love it if you joined us," she said instead.

Susan shook her head. "Oh, I've got plans. I'm running late, actually. So we're good?"

"Always," Kellie said. "And thank you."

She gave Susan a final squeeze and watched her head down the walk before closing the door.

"Who was that?" Irene asked.

"Just a friend," Kellie said. "My best friend, actually. Susan. Hey, will you take these into the kitchen?"

She handed Irene the plate. The moment she walked back into the heart of the house she'd be enveloped by family. She needed a minute.

She'd been partially truthful with Susan. The drinks *had* gone to her head.

But it was more than that.

She had an enormous crush on Miller. And, thrillingly, he seemed to have a crush on her, too. He'd texted her when she'd been on her way out to Sidecar with the girls, and she'd responded, telling him of her plans. She hadn't invited him to join them, but she'd mentioned the name of the bar, leaving the next step up to him. He'd shown up an hour later, wearing jeans and a black V-neck sweater. She hadn't even been surprised when he'd walked through the door. Somehow it had felt predestined.

They hadn't kissed, though. They *wouldn't* kiss. She didn't want to kiss him, because this was better. The delicious anticipation of waiting for him to enter the office every morning. Passing him in the hallway and giving him a smile. Putting on a skirt and feeling his eyes skim over her legs.

Well, maybe she wanted to kiss him a little bit.

"Kellie? Is it time to take the turkey out?"

Not even her mother-in-law's voice could tear apart her fantasy. The images of Miller surrounded her like a warm glow. They smoothed out the rough edges of her life, making her feel warm and buoyant. She touched her cell phone, making sure it was in her pants pocket and set to vibrate.

They had dinner at four, like always. While Jason's father carved the turkey, Irene complained about her life as an actress ("I get callbacks all the time but they all say something different. I'm too young! I'm too old! I'm too all-American! I'm not blond enough!") and turned down the side dishes Kellie had made because she was carb-free. Mia knocked over her milk before she'd even had a sip, and Jason released a belch after gulping down a huge helping of potatoes. But none of it bothered Kellie.

Kellie sipped her wine and picked at a little turkey and some of the vegetables, but she didn't have much of an appetite. She hadn't for weeks. She'd lost another six pounds recently, without even trying. She was taking more pride in her appearance, after years of schlubbing around in stretched-out yoga pants and T-shirts. The crush might actually be good for her. And it wasn't like Jason never talked to women at his job!

She wondered what Miller was doing at this exact moment.

He was with his family, of course. She could see Miller sitting at the head of the table, next to his wife, his cherubic children beaming alongside them. His wife would be beautiful, of course—sleek and charming, probably. And young. What if she were much younger than Kellie? What if she were a pediatric surgeon who selflessly worked to save the lives of children? That would be the worst thing imaginable. No, no, it would be worse if she was a Pilates instructor.

"Excuse me," Kellie said, getting up from the table and hurrying into the kitchen.

She couldn't believe she'd never Googled Miller's wife before. She didn't know her name, but a quick investigation of Miller's Facebook page revealed it to be Jane.

Plain Jane. No, most of the Janes Kellie knew were pretty, as if in defiance of that old taunt.

She tried to access Jane's Facebook page, but the settings were private. *Do you know Jane?* Facebook asked her.

She couldn't friend her. That would be creepy.

But she could browse Miller's photos to see if he'd posted one of his wife. She began swiping through them. A house, another house . . . most of his pictures were of properties he was selling. There! A photo of a cute young woman with Miller and his two sons. Kellie squinted. That woman looked to be about eighteen. Oh, thank God. Miller had written a caption: "Fun with the boys' cousin Emily!"

"Kellie?" Irene was calling. "Could you bring in another bottle of wine?"

"Sure thing," Kellie said. A picture of a dog—Miller had mentioned his Lab before and she knew its name was Coop—and another of his kids on skis, perched atop a mountain. Miller was with them and so was a woman. But she was wearing bulky ski clothes, a hat, and goggles. She looked slender, and the hair spilling out from beneath her helmet was dark, but her features were indistinct. Kellie zoomed in, but the photo revealed nothing.

She'd die if Miller's wife was gorgeous, if he had a dozen photos of them together, his strong arms wrapped around her. She didn't want to see the pictures.

She had to see them.

"Kellie?"

"Hold *on*, Irene!" Kellie snapped. Maybe if she went back to last summer, there would be a beach shot. Damn it, why were so many of his pictures of houses . . .

"What are you doing?" Irene asked as she walked into the kitchen and snatched Kellie's phone out of her hand.

"Give it back!" Kellie shrieked. Irene danced backward and looked down at the screen. "Why are you staring at photos of houses for sale? No working at a family holiday dinner."

"I'm not," Kellie protested.

Irene ran into the dining room, still holding up the phone.

"I caught Kellie texting all her boyfriends," she crowed.

There was a moment of stunned silence.

"Irene!" Kellie snapped. "Give me that. I wasn't texting anyone."

Irene had always been immature and, truthfully, more than a little spoiled. Being the baby of the family could do that to you.

"Man," Irene said as Kellie wrenched the phone out of her hand. "Can't anyone take a joke? And where's my wine?"

Irene was tipsy, Kellie realized. She seized the chance to change the subject.

"Are you sure you need another glass?" she asked. She made sure her tone was light but she didn't conceal her annoyance. It worked; everyone stopped thinking about Irene's stupid comment and resumed eating. Kellie saw her mother give her father a resigned look: *The girls are bickering again!*

"I'm not driving anywhere," Irene said.

"Fine," Kellie said. "I'll get it for you."

"Don't take an hour like last time," Irene sang out.

Kellie turned off her phone and put it in her pocket, then brought out the bottle of Chardonnay. Jason was chatting with her mother and the kids were tearing into the chocolate turkey, having ignored everyone's suggestion that they wait a while.

"Here you go, wino," she said as she poured Irene another glass. She had to sound irritated at Irene, to keep anyone from asking why she'd spent so long on the phone in the kitchen. And it *had* been a while—everyone had cleared their plates.

Jason reached for her hand and she smiled.

"Good mashed potatoes, honey," he said, patting his stomach.

"I'm glad you liked them," she said.

She wasn't doing anything wrong, technically. But what if Irene had glanced down and seen Miller's Facebook page?

Tonight, she'd go into the settings on her phone and install a password, just in case.

• • •

What was one more lie, in the grand scheme of things?

Susan had told Kellie she had plans for today, and she sort of did. Earlier she'd gone to Sunrise Assisted Living to have a noontime meal with Mr. Brannon. Her evening plans involved HBO, a sandwich, and possibly a Xanax, which she normally took only when she flew on an airplane.

Cole was spending Thanksgiving with Randall and fertile Daphne. He was sleeping in the little bedroom Randall had prepared for him. It had a baseball lamp, and Fathead stickers of famous athletes on the walls, and a cozy rug where Randall's puppy curled up to sleep. Randall's parents were flying in from Florida, and possibly Daphne's family was in town, too. Daphne had two older brothers, and they both had kids. Maybe everyone would play football in the yard, and Cole would catch the winning touchdown, and Randall would toss him into the air while everyone beamed.

That would be good, of course, because Cole would be happy.

During their sessions with Judy the mediator, they'd planned out holidays. Susan wanted Cole for Christmas Eve and most of Christmas Day (though he would visit Randall for three hours in the middle of the day), so she'd conceded Thanksgiving. She hadn't thought it would matter. Thanksgiving was about food and gratitude, and she could just skip both of those concepts and make it like any other night. But as she walked home from Kellie's, her hands tucked deep in her pockets, her shoulders huddled, loneliness pierced her. Usually she could count on seeing other people out and about in the neighborhood in the late afternoons. Neighbors walked dogs, parents ran out to their cars to do the school pickup runs, nannies held the hands of toddlers as they made slow progress down the sidewalk.

But tonight the streets were silent.

She kept walking, past her house, knowing where she was going but helpless to stop herself, the way an addict keeps reaching for a cigarette. She hadn't dressed warmly enough for such a long walk, but she continued on, her feet growing cold in her thin boots, her cheeks feeling pinched. She turned down Randall's street and stopped. She wondered what the inside of the house looked like. She'd never seen it. She imagined he'd have Cole's artwork displayed on the refrigerator, like she did. There would be photos of Cole on the mantel, and some of Randall and Daphne, too. She wondered if Daphne would get pregnancy photos done, with Randall standing behind her, his hands wrapped around her belly.

She leaned back against a tree and closed her eyes.

She'd never been good at confrontation. She'd seen people erupt into rages at the slightest provocation—say, someone cutting in front of them in line—but that wasn't part of her emotional makeup. That's why what had happened with Kellie the other night had been so shocking. She'd never blown up like that at a friend before. She tended to think first, react much later.

Her parents had been a lawyer and a doctor, and they were calm, patient, almost overly formal people. Susan had never seen her father in his pajamas—when she was growing up, he'd always gone straight from bed into the shower and come downstairs dressed in a suit, or on casual days, an Oxford shirt with a vest over it. Her mother had liked classical music and she was an anesthesiologist. Her job centered around keeping things steady—breathing, blood pressure, vital signs. Over dinner they discussed current events and Susan's schoolwork and activities. She'd never had a sibling to squabble with; she'd never learned to fight.

Maybe if she and Randall had seen a counselor to talk about their differences before he'd met Daphne they would've stayed together. But the issue didn't seem to have any gray area. Randall wanted more kids. She didn't. She'd hoped that he'd come around, that he'd see her point of view. He'd hoped just as fervently for the opposite. And the truth was, she was so busy with work and with Cole that it became easier to push the issue aside, to ignore it and hope it would dissolve. To let their cold war stretch out, pretend it was just an ordinary marital dispute, like a squabble over their preferred settings on the thermostat.

She tilted her head back and felt two tears trickle down her cheeks. She knew she should get away from this place, she understood that what she was doing was intensifying her pain, but she was so tired. She wouldn't be able to sleep, though, and she didn't want to go into her empty house and watch television until it was time to go to bed.

She opened her eyes and noticed Randall had already strung up white Christmas lights in the trees, and the lamp mounted over his front door cast a golden glow across the porch. The house looked snug and cozy. Susan was glad she'd never been inside, because that would make the images in her head more vivid.

She hoped Randall had given Cole a drumstick, and let him pull the wishbone, and served him a big piece of apple pie that was still warm. Randall probably had done all of those things and more. He was a wonderful father, after all. And he'd been such a good husband, too.

When she was so cold she could think of nothing else but her discomfort, she turned, shivering, and made her slow way back home.

• • •

"Green beans?" Tessa asked, holding up a spoonful.

"Sure," said Addison. He was her good eater, the kid who never met a casserole or quesadilla he didn't like.

Tessa ladled some onto his plate. She knew better than to ask Bree if she wanted a portion. Bree was still a prickly child. She hated the little lines that ran across the tops of socks, so Tessa had to special order ones without seams. She didn't like mushy foods. She startled easily at loud noises, and she was afraid of the dark. But she'd mellowed out considerably since her early, colicky months.

Tessa had decided to fly her family to her hometown in Colorado for the holiday. The past few months had been so draining that when her sister had called and said, "So what's the plan for Thanksgiving?" Tessa had immediately responded, "We'd love to come to see you all."

Claire had sounded taken aback, but she'd recovered quickly. "That would be great," she'd said. "I'll set up the guest room for you and Harry. Do you guys still prefer firm pillows?"

Only Claire would ask for the pillow preference of her guests. She'd also make their mother's green bean casserole with fried onions on top, because that was tradition, and she'd light candles with the holders that had been in their family for three generations. She'd assign everyone seats, too, and make sure they all knew how much work she'd put into the meal, but suddenly, Tessa didn't mind. Her older sister was bossy but loving, and sometimes Tessa focused too much on the former instead of the latter.

"I can't wait," Tessa said, and was surprised to find herself meaning it, and not just because Colorado seemed like another escape.

They'd been crammed onto an overly full plane on the runway for ninety minutes before they took off, and a cold snap had overtaken Colorado, causing them to lament not bringing warmer clothes, but it was good to see her family again, Tessa realized. Bree and Addison had spent the day playing with their cousins, and Harry had watched football with Claire's husband, their feet up on the coffee table, cans of beer in hand.

"Tessa?" Claire was asking. "More stuffing?"

"I'm good, but thanks," Tessa said.

"Are you sure? You look so thin!" Claire said. "You and Harry both. Is your new town a secret dieting destination?"

Tessa laughed it off. "We do a lot of biking and walking, because the weather's better," she said. "It's easier to stay active."

"Well, that's one good reason for moving there," Tessa's mother said.

"Although it seemed so sudden," Claire added.

Tessa had prepared for this. It was the first time she'd seen her family since the move, and she knew they'd have questions.

"It was," Tessa agreed. She'd said all this before, in phone conversations, of course. "We drove down there on a whim—we just felt like getting out of town—and we saw this house for sale in the perfect neighborhood. Everything fell into place."

"You'll have to come visit," Harry said.

Tessa nodded, wanting to kick him under the table. The last thing she wanted was for her family to come to their new town. She could see Claire going for a walk and bumping into neighbors and chatting. Claire was careful to avoid mentioning Danny Briggs around the children, but she might let something slip about his death to another adult, and then Tessa would have to face the very sorts of questions she'd fled.

"I miss my friends, though," Addison said.

"Oh, sweetie," Tessa said. "But you've made lots of new friends, haven't you? Noah, and Cole . . ."

"What about you, Bree? Do you miss your friends, too?" Claire asked.

"Sometimes," Bree said. "But we still Skype and stuff."

"She has a computer?" Tessa's mother asked. She held the firm position that kids today were exposed to far too many electronics, and that they should be running around outside, playing kick the can.

"We have a family computer the kids can use," Harry said. This was his turf, since he was the electronics expert in the house. "Bree and Addison are allowed to use the computer with reasonable limits. I wouldn't let them get into a car at sixteen without any instruction and hand over the keys, and I'm certainly not going to let them go off to college without some training on responsible use of electronics . . ."

Tessa tuned out.

It wasn't until much later, when she and Claire were doing the dishes together, that Claire asked the question Tessa had been dreading.

"The children," Claire had whispered, glancing toward the

doorway to make sure they weren't coming. "Are they exhibiting any . . . ill effects from Danny's death?"

Tessa shook her head swiftly. "None at all," she said. It was important that they do this quickly, like pulling a tooth. She had to be firm and clear with Claire and tackle this head-on.

"The kids are doing wonderfully," she said, glad she could speak the words honestly. "It's like nothing ever happened."

"Good," Claire said. She squirted dish liquid into a roasting pan and added water. "Was that part of why you moved? A clean slate?"

"Yes," Tessa said, grateful that Claire understood. She couldn't understand all of it, of course—no one could except for her and Harry, because they were the only two who knew everything—but this made it easier.

Bree popped into the kitchen. "Mom, can we watch *How the Grinch Stole Christmas*?" she asked.

"Thanksgiving isn't even over, and they're showing Christmas specials," Claire sighed.

"Sure," Tessa said. "It's okay with me if it's okay with Aunt Claire."

"Fine, fine," Claire said.

When Bree left, Claire lowered her voice again. "Is Harry sick?" she asked. "You would tell me if he was sick, wouldn't you?"

"He's fine," Tessa said. "Just work has been stressful. And he's turned into a runner. I think he might be training for a marathon, but he's keeping it quiet."

"That's all it is?" Claire asked.

"I promise," Tessa said.

What harm would a few more lies do, given all the ones she'd already told?

• • •

Melanie had a crush on Zach.

Her neater hair, her friendlier attitude, her new clothing

style—Gigi's suspicions solidified when Zach asked Melanie to pass the gravy. Maybe no one else noticed, but Gigi was so attuned to searching for clues about Melanie's emotional state that she zeroed in on the shift in her daughter immediately. The slight pink in Melanie's cheeks. The way she giggled when Zach's fingers brushed hers as she handed over the gravy boat.

Gigi turned to consider Zach. He was a clean-cut, ambitious, hardworking guy. On the surface, he was everything a mother might want for her daughter, except for the fact that at twenty-two, he was too old for Melanie.

Yet he was too perfect, too polished. He said all the right things. He was exceptionally polite without being the slightest bit warm. Couldn't Joe see that?

Joe felt guilty that Zach was working for him for free to get experience, but Gigi suspected Zach was the one using Joe, that he'd get the better end of the bargain. She didn't trust the young man. How candid was Joe with him on their long road trips, when they were driving in the darkness, sharing a sense of weary compatibility? She needed to warn her husband to be circumspect.

"This was delicious, Mrs. Kennedy," Zach said after the last slice of pie had been eaten. "May I clear the table?"

"Thank you," Gigi said.

Joe jumped up. "I'll help," he said. "I need to work some of that off before we head to the shelter. Hey, Melanie, Julia—do you guys want to come with?"

"Sure," Julia said.

Melanie smiled. "I'll come, too," she said.

"That's my girl," Joe said. He gave Gigi a look: *Wow—she's in a good mood.*

"I'm going to change," Melanie said and headed upstairs. Gigi followed Joe into the kitchen.

"Honey," she began, but then she saw Zach at the sink.

"What is it?" he asked.

"I've got an old coat you can take to the shelter to donate," she said instead. She went upstairs to retrieve it, but she couldn't immediately find it in her closet. Finally she remembered it was in the attic. By the time she came back down, Melanie and Joe and Zach were preparing to head out. Gigi did a double take when she saw that Melanie was wearing lip gloss. The color was wrong for her; it was too red against Melanie's pale skin, but Gigi knew better than to offer a gentle suggestion that Melanie try a softer pink shade.

Gigi didn't have an opportunity to pull Joe aside. She wasn't even exactly sure what she'd say to him. *Watch our daughter*, maybe.

She stood on the doorstep, waving, as they headed down the walk. When they reached the car, Zach pulled open the front passenger's door and gestured for Melanie to step inside.

*Like a date*, Gigi thought, watching Melanie smile up at Zach as he gently closed her door.

No, she didn't trust Zach for a minute.

# Chapter Twenty-Three

## Newport Cove Listserv Digest

*Remove me from listserv?

Hi, I moved away from Newport Cove a year ago and still receive these emails. Can someone remove me from this listserv? Thanks! —Abigail Donohue, formerly of Blossom Street

*Maternity clothes—free!

Lots of casual clothes, well-worn but clean. Yours for the asking as I will definitely not be needing them again. —Reece Harmon, Daisy Way

*Re: Remove me from listserv?

Abigail, simply hit the "unsubscribe" button at the bottom of your listserv digest and you should be taken off the list. —Tally White, Iris Lane

*Re: Remove me from listserv?

There's an unsubscribe link somewhere near the bottom in every digest, just click and that should do it. —Bob Welsh, Magnolia Street

*A cheery reminder!

When replying to an individual's question on the listserv, there's no need to hit "reply all" if the question doesn't relate to the community at large. You can simply respond to the individual by clicking on their email address, which is embedded in their message, so that the entire listserv doesn't get multiple messages with duplicate information. —Sincerely, Shannon Dockser, Newport Cove Manager

*Re: Remove me from listserv?

Just hit "unsubscribe" at the bottom of the digest and you'll be taken off.
—Margaret Grainger, Crabtree Lane

• • •

You have 22 new matches! the headline of her email proclaimed.

Twenty-two sounded overwhelming, but it was better than none, Susan thought as she took a sip of her latte and clicked the button that would lead her to the dating website. She'd signed up for it the day after Thanksgiving, making her perhaps the only forty-year-old woman on the planet who wanted to begin dating to improve the emotional health of her son.

Maybe she'd meet a few guys for drinks. Maybe one of them would even be nice. Or just have all of his own teeth and speak passable English—she shouldn't set her expectations too high.

She navigated to the photo of her first match, whose ID was TheMan4U. His photo looked surprisingly normal. He was of Japanese descent, a triathlete, and an accountant. Nope, Susan thought. She was doing this to forget Randall, not to be reminded of him by a man with the same occupation.

She scrolled over to the next photo. This guy—BeachBum39—was extremely handsome. He was posing shirtless on a beach, a golden retriever by his feet. Susan began to read his bio: Note: My true age is 46, but I was getting contacted by too many women in their forties and fifties so I've changed my age to 39 in my profile. Be assured I look and act much younger than my real age!

*You act like a baby, that's for sure*, Susan thought as she instantly deleted the guy's face from her screen. So he wanted to date younger women—but he was dismissive of women who wanted to date younger men? On behalf of womankind, Susan felt like reaching through her computer, grabbing the Frisbee in his hand, and bashing it into his face.

By the time she'd gone through all twenty-two matches, she'd eliminated every contender except for two. And she wasn't all that excited by those guys. It was like reaching into a bin of reduced-for-quick-sale apples and choosing the two that were the least bruised. But maybe she should be more open-minded. Lots of people had trouble expressing themselves in writing, so she shouldn't jump to conclusions about Searching4Luv and his scant three-sentence bio. I love to be outdoors and all water sports. I have a big family, a steady job, and a ferret named Bo. You never know where chemistry will turn up so let's meet and see if there is a spark . . .

She'd send him a quick email, suggesting a drink. She'd make one of her friends come along with her and sit at a nearby table, just in case Searching4Luv was really Searching4AHostage.

Hi, she wrote. I love to be outdoors as well . . . Her fingers hovered above her keyboard as she tried to think of what else to say. Bo sounds nifty? Are ferrets in the weasel family?

She dropped her head into her hands. She hated this. She hated every humiliating moment.

Gigi had urged her to try online dating. "C'mon, everyone's doing it," she'd said. "Quality people are on dating sites because they're too busy to go out to bars and try to meet people like in the old days."

Susan scrolled down to the "Interests" section and discovered that Searching4Luv had been, in the last year alone, sailing in the Caribbean and mountain climbing. He'd done a Tough Mudder 10K and had the mud-splattered photo to prove it. He loved outdoor concerts and had been to see U2, Imagine Dragons, and Taylor Swift (that was my 10-year-old daughter's birthday present, he'd written).

Susan clicked over to her profile. She'd uploaded a candid photo from a family vacation a few years ago. She'd had to crop it to cut out Randall and Cole, but she didn't want to use her professional photo because it was on her website and on the radio station's website and there was too great a chance someone would recognize it. No matter how often she heard that online dating was no big deal, she couldn't shake a sense of embarrassment.

Under "Interests," she'd written: Reading, taking walks with my dog, and watching Downton Abbey.

I'm boring, she thought. Yawn-inducing boring. Searching 4Luv probably wouldn't even be interested in her!

Somehow, that made him marginally more attractive.

Terrific. Now *she* was acting like a baby. She closed the lid of her computer and got up and left the coffee shop.

Ten minutes of online dating, and she'd already frayed her self-esteem. Maybe it worked for others, but it had only made her feel worse. There were so many lonely people in the world.

There had to be a guy out there, a good man who would love her, she tried to tell herself.

*But you had that*, the traitorous voice in her head answered. *You already had that with Randall, and you threw it away.*

• • •

"We've got a problem, Mrs. Kennedy," Zach said, sitting down across from Gigi.

"What is it, Zach?" she asked. It bugged her that she called him by his first name while he refused to do the same. It didn't feel respectful that he referred to her as Mrs. Kennedy. It felt as if he were trying to be perceived as respectful, which was something quite different.

"A source has told me that Max Connor's campaign has some information on you," Zach said.

He'd asked to meet her alone, without Joe present, and

she'd agreed. She'd thought it might be easier to pinpoint exactly what made her feel uneasy around Zach if she could talk to him without distraction. And so, while Joe was attending the grand opening of a new civic center, Zach had stayed behind.

*Here it comes*, Gigi thought. She sat up straighter, trying to keep her face from revealing anything.

"What information, Zach?" Gigi asked.

"It seems they have a copy of an old arrest record," Zach began.

"For trespassing?" Gigi interrupted. "Yes. I was protesting the destruction of an old redwood tree. So were a dozen other college students. We were all arrested and let go that same day. No one even saw the inside of a jail."

"This is about another matter," Zach said delicately.

Gigi could feel herself blush, and it infuriated her. Who cared what some pipsqueak thought about her past?

The problem was, Zach was enjoying this, Gigi realized. What bothered her about Zach snapped into focus. He craved power. He didn't so much believe in Joe as he believed Joe could get Zach what he wanted.

Zach reached for a manila envelope on the couch next to him and handed it to Gigi.

"You have a file on me?" she asked, trying to smile to show that she wasn't the least bit intimidated by him.

"Well, Max's campaign does," Zach said. "A source in his campaign had this."

"Wait a minute—you have a source in Max's campaign who's feeding you information?" Gigi asked.

"She didn't exactly give me the information. She was indiscreet in where she kept it, and I, let's say, stumbled upon it," Zach said.

His eyes flickered briefly, revealing the unpleasantness Gigi had glimpsed before, and suddenly Gigi wondered if the source was a young woman who had a crush on Zach.

She'd seen the way girls acted around him—Joe's press secretary, even her own daughter! She tried to imagine how it had happened. Maybe they'd slept together, and Zach had gone through her belongings while she was in the bathroom.

Gigi didn't open the folder. "It was the shoplifting incident, right?" she asked.

Zach nodded.

"So Max's campaign is going to trot out this old misdemeanor and try to punish my husband for it?" Gigi said. "That's ridiculous."

"It is," Zach said. "But yes, they're probably going to leak it."

"Would a newspaper actually print that kind of junk?" Gigi asked.

"Your record is in the public domain," Zach said. "So technically, they can. But I doubt they would go for something so minor. I'm sure the conservative bloggers will be all over it, though. They live for this sort of stuff."

Gigi handed back the folder without looking at it.

"So if there's anything you want to tell me, anything we could use to offset this . . . ," Zach said. His fingertip stroked the folder.

Gigi held his gaze steadily.

"Nope," she said. "Seriously, Zach, you missed a campaign event for this nonsense?"

He smiled and stood up, conceding defeat graciously. "You're right," he said. "I can probably still catch the tail end if I leave now."

"I have some calls to make," Gigi said. "Excuse me."

Gigi went upstairs and waited until she heard the front door close before she came back down. She sat in the chair she'd just vacated, thinking about the contents of the manila folder.

It had been a scarf.

A silly scarf in a pattern she didn't even particularly like. She'd taken it from a snooty boutique. Like the sunglasses she'd grabbed the previous month, and the inexpensive earrings she'd pocketed the month before that.

The first time it had happened, she'd been in a department store to return a pair of wool gloves that made her hands itch. She'd been waiting for the salesgirl to finish with the customer ahead of her in line when she'd seen a display of earrings on the counter in front of her. A pair of chunky silver hoops had caught her eye, so Gigi had picked them up. They were almost the exact price of the gloves. She'd do an exchange, Gigi had decided.

The salesgirl had finished ringing up her customer, then walked over to the other side of the counter to wait on another woman who'd just stepped up with a shirt in her hand.

"Excuse me," Gigi had called, but the girl hadn't heard her.

Anger—more than the tiny affront warranted—roiled within her. Gigi had always railed against social injustices, but living in the manicured suburbs and caring for an infant hadn't given her much to protest lately.

She'd started to put the earrings back, then she'd let them roll into her palm and she'd closed her fist. She left the gloves with their receipt on the counter. She fully expected to set off the alarm at the security gate by the exit and be stopped by a security guard. She was looking forward to it, actually—she'd like to give the silly young salesgirl a piece of her middle-aged mind.

But she walked through the doors without triggering a sound.

She'd stood in the parking lot, wondering if she should go back. But then, unexpectedly, exhilaration had swept through her. The store would never miss the thirty-dollar pair of earrings. She'd done it! She'd lodged her own minor protest.

At home, the earrings seemed shinier, more enticing than her other pairs. Sometimes Gigi took them out just to look at them, remembering her tiny victory.

She wasn't tempted to do it again, though. The thought of

slipping an expensive chocolate bar into her pocket at the grocery store didn't tantalize her. She was never seized with the impulse to stuff an extra peach into the little square baskets that were sold for two dollars at the farmers' market.

The sunglasses, though.

Gigi usually just wore cheap Ray-Ban knockoffs purchased from the drugstore, and they were forever breaking. She'd had one pair for only a week when the tiny screw by her temple came out, separating the stem from the glasses. She'd popped into the drugstore to pick up a repair kit and she'd seen something that made her blood boil: There was a young mother ahead of her in line, juggling a toddler on her hip, trying to pay for a pack of diapers and a few other items. When the mother tried to pay with her credit card, the cashier asked for a photo ID.

Gigi was incensed. She'd shopped at this particular chain dozens of times, sometimes ringing up totals far higher than this young mother's, and she'd never once been asked to show an ID. It had happened because the woman was black, Gigi was certain. She'd heard about a similar incident happening to an African-American friend of hers. When it was Gigi's turn to approach the counter, she put down her glasses repair kit and deodorant and the few other items she'd collected. She paid with a credit card.

No one had asked for her ID.

On her way out of the store, Gigi had reached out and pulled a pair of sunglasses off the display unit. She was taking a stand, just like when she'd linked arms with other students to form a human barricade and save the old redwood tree!

Again, no one stopped her. Maybe store clerks weren't suspicious of her because she was white, because she looked comfortably middle-class. The notion incensed her.

She never even wore the sunglasses. They were oversized, with rhinestones, and looked completely ridiculous on her. But they served as a kind of trophy.

She'd shopped a dozen times before it happened again—quick trips to the mini-mart to pick up a quart of milk, and bigger excursions to Whole Foods. She'd gotten a new winter coat for Melanie. Temptation had never beckoned.

Until the day Gigi went into an upscale boutique with the gift certificate Joe's parents had given her for her birthday. Gigi had never set foot in the store before—it catered to a certain kind of woman, one who didn't wear Birkenstocks—and she felt uncomfortable the moment she breathed in the perfumed air and saw a tall, stick-thin woman approach her.

"Just looking," Gigi said. She reached out absently to touch a coat on a rack and snatched her hand back when she realized she was touching fur.

She'd once seen a documentary about the torture animals endured so wealthy people could strip them of their fur. Soft little creatures caught in traps, their limbs broken, plaintively crying . . . Gigi knew she couldn't buy anything here.

She approached the saleswoman. "I received this for a birthday," she said, handing over the certificate. "There isn't anything here I need, so I'd like to receive the cash instead."

The woman had raised an eyebrow. "I'm sorry, but that's against our policy."

Gigi had felt a slow burn. "That's ridiculous. May I speak to the manager?"

"I am the manager," the woman had said.

"You have got to be kidding me," Gigi said. "I don't like the clothes here. I won't wear them. I want a refund."

The woman had flipped over the certificate. "It says right here: 'Cannot be exchanged for cash value.'"

Gigi had snatched it back.

"Fine," she said. She wanted to tear it to shreds, but had a better idea. "I'll donate it to a women's shelter."

She'd started to stalk out then and, without even thinking about it, her hand had shot out and grabbed a scarf.

She'd made it four paces down the sidewalk when she heard the man's voice behind her:

"Ma'am? I'm going to need you to come with me."

Of course, with all that expensive fur, there had been a security guard in the store, Gigi thought as she froze in place, one foot outstretched, her heart thudding in her chest.

"Why did you do it?" Joe asked later, when he'd come to the police station.

He wasn't mad, but he was deeply confused. She was, too.

"I have no idea," she'd finally said. Reasons rolled through her mind, but none made sense. Because I was bored? Because sometimes I feel as if I don't matter, and the contours of my life are shrinking, and I want to mean more?

She was relieved Joe didn't know the worst part. She'd been alone when she'd been caught. But the other two times—at the department store and the drugstore—baby Melanie had been strapped in a carrier on her chest, sleeping, while her mother had blithely committed crimes.

# Chapter Twenty-Four

*Before Newport Cove*

AFTER THE INCIDENTS WITH the nanny and the Advil and at the park, things grew increasingly strained between Tessa and Harry. He called more frequently when he was out of town—three or four times a day—and took the red-eye home rather than stay away an extra night. Harry was six foot two, and he never could sleep on airplanes. He hated the red-eye. She suspected he no longer trusted her, even though the children had begun school full-time. Even though there hadn't been another incident in years.

But maybe he was right. Those early, panic-inducing scenes seemed to have changed something in Tessa. Or maybe years of sleep-deprivation and general anxiety had rewired her, leaving her jittery and easily startled. Celine was working with another family in the neighborhood and had been for years; Tessa saw her now and then in the park. The nanny still didn't smile much, but she seemed to be a diligent caregiver.

Tessa had seen danger everywhere when it hadn't existed. It made the ground feel unsteady beneath her feet. How could she protect her children when she couldn't distinguish an actual threat from an imaginary one? When her children were safely asleep, Tessa would wander out to look at the angel statue in the butterfly garden she and Harry had created.

*Help me,* she would pray beneath the moonlight. *Help me to . . .* But she never knew what to add after that. Get better? Relax? Learn to be the right kind of mother?

She insisted on walking her kids to school, even after Bree turned eight and her friends on the street were allowed to walk alone. Even though the school was just two blocks away, and didn't require crossing any major intersections.

She felt perpetually keyed up, as if she'd consistently had one cup too many of coffee. She tried to take up yoga, but her mind raced even more frantically in the quiet space. She threw herself into volunteering at the kids' school, which helped a little, but only because Tessa could surreptitiously sneak glances at her kids on the playground and in the lunchroom.

When one of Addison's friends invited him to join a local group called Young Rangers that was similar to Boy Scouts, Tessa was relieved to know parents were invited to attend all the meetings, as well as excursions like an overnight camping trip.

Tessa had driven Addison to the first meeting. She'd brought along a book in her purse, and had intended to sit in the back row, reading.

She and Addison had walked into the school rec room together that first night. A tall man with crew-cut graying hair had walked over to greet them. He appeared to be about sixty, a little heavyset, wearing a sweatshirt and jeans.

"Are you our newest Ranger?" he'd asked Addison.

Addison had broken into a grin. "Yup," he'd said. He could be shy sometimes, but something about this man had put him at ease.

"Excellent," the man had said. He'd reached out to shake Addison's hand, then he'd smiled up at Tessa.

"I'm Danny Briggs," he'd said.

# Chapter Twenty-Five

JASON HAD BEEN ACTING strangely.

Ever since Thanksgiving, when Irene had made her crack about Kellie's texts, Kellie had noticed the change. He'd gone from being a contented man who looked forward to dinner and the television after work to someone who seemed more . . . alert.

Last night, Kellie had come out of the bathroom to discover Jason staring down at her iPhone.

"What are you doing?" she'd asked.

"It, uh, rang," he'd said. "I was going to answer it for you but I think they hung up first."

"Oh," Kellie had said. "Probably just a telemarketer."

But when she'd walked over to her iPhone and typed in the code to unlock her screen, the register showed no incoming calls.

Had he been trying to check her messages? He wouldn't find anything incriminating. A bunch of work exchanges, some spam, and a few texts from Miller, including one that had arrived that afternoon that read: You look especially pretty today.

Well, maybe that was incriminating. If Jason worked in a normal office building, though, he'd probably go out to lunch with attractive women all the time. Just look at the way that blonde in the hardware store had acted! But because his father and old Ed were his only coworkers, it might be hard for him to understand that she and Miller checked in with each other during the weekdays and occasionally scouted houses together.

"Office spouses." There was even an innocuous term for her relationship with Miller, one that showed how common their relationship was in the workplace.

Still, something had compelled Kellie to get home early today, so she could hit the grocery store and get the fixings for dinner before the kids came home from school. Usually she dragged them along on errands so she could be in the office from nine to three, but today she decided to grill steaks, Jason's favorite, and make twice-baked potatoes.

Miraculously, Mia even put a tiny piece of steak on her plate, next to her pile of carrots and roll, and proclaimed it "Not awful."

"I'll take it," Kellie whispered to Jason. "She's tougher than Gordon Ramsay."

"Did everyone have a good day?" Jason asked.

"I did," Mia said. "Mrs. Dickenson had to step out of the room and she asked me to be in charge and report any bad behavior."

*Well played, Mrs. Dickenson*, Kellie thought. Mia must've been drunk with power.

"Did anyone misbehave?" Kellie asked.

"No, but I'm pretty sure Luke Dunhill was thinking about it," Mia said.

"Why did she have to leave?" Noah asked. "Did she have diarrhea?"

Kellie and Jason burst into laughter.

"That is so gross," Mia said. "Why are you laughing? You're encouraging him."

"Projectile vomit is worse," Noah said.

"Make him stop!" Mia said.

"Should we watch *Rudolph the Red-Nosed Reindeer* tonight?" Kellie asked.

It was one of their traditions. They taped tons of holiday specials, and watched them together before bedtime, one per night, between Thanksgiving and Christmas.

"Sure," Jason said. "Sounds great."

After the dishes were done and the kids bathed and in pj's, Kellie put oil in a pot to heat, then she dumped in popcorn kernels and set out the butter to soften before going into the living room.

"Move over, monkey," she said to Noah, bumping him with her hip. She plopped onto the couch and put an arm around him. Jason was at the other end, with Mia also in the middle, next to Noah.

"Finally!" Mia said loudly. "We've been waiting forever for you, Mom!"

Kellie was about to remind Mia to keep her voice down, but Jason spoke up first.

"It's okay, honey," Jason said softly. "She's here now."

Kellie's eyes drifted to his and he smiled. It took so little to make Jason happy. A piece of steak. A football game. Having his little family all on the same couch.

"Can we have hot chocolate, too?" Noah asked.

"Sure," Jason said. He leaped up. "I'll get it."

Jason never leaped up.

"Check on the popcorn?" Kellie asked.

"Sure," he said.

Jason was definitely more energetic lately. More tuned in. Was he trying a new kind of diet? Kellie wondered. He'd brought home a nice sweater in a navy knit yesterday; she'd seen him take it out of a shopping bag. Maybe he'd gone to the mall and had realized he'd inched up a few sizes over the past few years.

"You didn't tell us about your day. Was it good?" Kellie asked, kissing the top of Noah's head. He had the world's greatest hair—thick and full and sand-colored. Luckily, he was still at an age where he didn't mind her running her hand through it.

"Yeah," he said.

"What was the best part?" she asked.

"Recess," he said. "We played Power Rangers."

She loved the feeling of his warm body resting against hers. Noah was her puppy child, a floppy, happy-go-lucky bundle of deliciousness. A miniature version of his father, a third-generation photocopy. She stretched out her arm and grabbed on to Mia, pulling her in closer, too. She loved her children so deeply it felt like an ache sometimes. She could never do anything to cause them pain.

"Popcorn, madam," Jason said, handing Kellie the bowl.

"Yum," she said, scooping up a handful before passing it to the kids to devour.

"Four hot chocolates coming up," he said, disappearing again and returning a moment later with a tray of drinks.

"Fancy," she said, taking her cup. "Where'd you find the whipped cream?"

"In the back of the fridge," he said. "The expiration date said it expired last week but it still tastes good."

Kellie wrinkled her nose and took a sip, but he was right.

"Did you fart?" Mia asked Noah.

"Yup," he said.

"Eww! Mom!"

"Noah, I forbid you from ever farting again," Jason said, mock sternly. "Hold it in, son."

He reached for the clicker and started the video.

This was her real life, Kellie realized. Her messy, imperfect, wonderful life. Her crush on Miller, their mutual flirtation—that was just an illusion. It was like the airbrushed photos of models frolicking on a beach. Miller looked good to her because she didn't know any of his flaws. But if they ever were together—which was not going to happen—she'd discover all sorts of horrible things about him.

Maybe he picked his nose, for example.

No, she couldn't picture it.

Miller had worn a new suit to work today. The cut looked

vaguely Italian. She'd asked him if he'd gotten it in preparation for his dream trip to the vineyards.

"You noticed it's new?" he'd said, grinning.

Jason was looking at her with an odd expression.

"What?" she said. She reached up and touched her chin. "Do I have hot chocolate on my face?"

"No," he said. "Didn't you hear me? I was talking to you."

"Sorry," she said. "I just spaced out. What'd you say?"

A look she wasn't able to identify flitted across his face, and when he spoke again, his tone didn't match his words.

"I said, 'This is nice, isn't it?'" Jason said.

Kellie nodded quickly. "It is," she said.

Jason cleared his throat. "Are you working this weekend?"

"Just showing around a client for an hour or two on Sunday," she said.

"Shhh!" Mia said. "I'm trying to watch."

Kellie smiled at Jason and turned toward the screen again, determined to keep her focus on her family. Where it belonged.

• • •

Susan picked up the insulated shopping bag and her purse from the passenger's seat of her Mercedes and headed into Sunrise Community Assisted Living Center. As she walked toward the elevator, she noticed a group of about a dozen schoolchildren clustered in the lobby, singing carols.

Susan paused, drawn in by the ethereal sound.

"Silent night," the boys and girls sang in high, sweet voices. "Holy night. All is calm, all is bright . . ."

Residents were gathered around the singers, some in wheelchairs and others leaning on walkers. A frail-looking woman with white hair so thin her pink scalp shone through raised a shaky hand toward the children, as if she yearned to touch their faces. Susan saw a man sitting on the couch, an afghan across his knees, discreetly dabbing his eyes with a tissue.

"Beautiful, isn't it?" a familiar voice said beside her.

Susan turned to see Mr. Brannon in his usual white button-down shirt and pressed slacks.

"It is," she whispered, surprised by the catch in her throat.

They listened together as the song wound down, then joined in the applause. The children began to move through the audience, distributing little snowflake-shaped gift bags.

"Would you mind if we departed now?" Mr. Brannon said before the children reached him. "I don't mean to rush you."

"Of course," Susan said, hoping he wasn't exhausted from standing for so long. His treats would keep in the insulated bag; she could give them to him later. She went out and brought around the car and opened the passenger's-side door for him, then closed it when he was safely inside.

"Thank you," he said as she climbed in.

Susan patted his hand, then turned the heat a few notches higher and drove to their usual Starbucks. Once he had his chai tea in hand, she headed to the high school where he'd first asked her to stop.

"Shall we sit for a while?" he asked when they approached the entrance. He always worded his requests politely, but she knew by now how much these quiet minutes meant to him. Always at the high school, the house, the hospital, the pizza place. Always the vigils.

"For as long as you like," she said. She pulled into a visitor's parking spot and they stared at the large redbrick structure. A big outdoor sign proclaimed, HOME OF THE TIGERS—2015 ROLLINGWOOD COUNTY SOCCER CHAMPIONS!

They sipped their chai in companionable silence, and after ten minutes or so, Mr. Brannon turned to her.

"I'm ready now, my dear," he said.

Susan went to put her chai in the cup holder, then she remembered something. The garden stone Tessa had given her weeks earlier was tucked in her purse, wrapped in layers of tissue paper to protect it. She'd forgotten to give it to Mr. Brannon the last time she'd seen him.

She reached into her purse and pulled it out.

"The new owners of your house found this," she said. "They thought you might want it."

"Oh, what do we have here?" Mr. Brannon said. He unwrapped it and looked down.

"It was in the garden," Susan said. She hadn't looked at it carefully when Tessa had given it to her, but now she saw that along with the mold of a child's handprint was the name "Edward." What she'd thought was a design etched along the border was actually thin, spidery-looking letters.

"Edward," she said. "Was he a neighborhood child?"

Mr. Brannon released a sound from deep in his throat and her head dropped.

"Oh, no, Mr. Brannon," she said. She reached out and twisted in her seat so she could put her arms around him. "Please, Mr. Brannon, I didn't mean to make you cry."

She could feel his thin shoulder blades through the fabric of his coat. His body shook but he didn't make any more sounds.

She comforted him like she would Cole. "I'm so sorry," she said. "I'm so sorry you're hurting."

After a moment she drew back and reached for a napkin. He wiped his eyes and stared at the stone.

"How could I have forgotten this?" he said. He put his own hand up against the print. "Thank you for bringing it to me."

Gigi had said the Brannons didn't have any children. Edward must have died long ago, Susan thought.

"You must miss him so much," Susan said.

"I do," Mr. Brannon said.

Edward must have gone to school here, Susan thought as she looked up at the high school. The pizza parlor could have been where they'd celebrated his birthday. The old redbrick house—perhaps the Brannon family had lived there when Edward was a boy.

"It was my fault he is lost to us," Mr. Brannon said. Deep

grooves of sorrow were etched from the corners of his mouth down to his chin.

"It wasn't," Susan said, because she couldn't stand to see this kind man blame himself. "It wasn't your fault he died!"

Mr. Brannon looked up at her.

"Oh, no," he said. "Edward is still alive."

• • •

Mr. Brannon looked utterly exhausted, so Susan hadn't asked a single question. She'd just driven him back home. He'd held on to her arm as they'd walked to the elevator, one of the few signs of physical weakness he'd ever allowed himself to show in her presence.

It was dinnertime at Sunrise, but he'd said he was too tired to go into the dining room.

"They can bring me up a meal if I put in a request," he said once he was seated comfortably in the easy chair in his bedroom, his shoes off.

"We can do better than that," Susan said. "Just give me a minute."

Mr. Brannon's suite didn't contain a full kitchen, but there was a sink, a mini refrigerator, a hot plate, and a microwave in a little nook off the living area. Susan unpacked her grocery bag, stacking individual containers of casseroles and soups in the refrigerator. She put two tins of brownies on the counter, figuring Garth would snatch up the one labeled with his name when he returned from dinner. She prepared tomato soup and a grilled cheddar cheese sandwich for Mr. Brannon, then took one of the bottles of water from the fridge and arranged everything on a tray before bringing it to him.

"You're so good to me," he said as he dipped his spoon into the bowl. His hand was shaking, Susan saw.

Susan sat down across from him, on the foot of the bed. He'd put the garden stone on the bureau, but Susan wondered if he wanted to look at it every time he came into his room.

"Would you like me to put the garden stone away?" she asked. "I can wrap it back up and put it in a drawer."

"Thank you," Mr. Brannon said. "But it should stay there."

He ate a little more of the soup, then had a few bites of the sandwich and sipped his water.

"I'm sorry," he said. "This was very good . . . I just don't seem to have much of an appetite."

"Don't you worry about a thing," Susan said. She started to get up to remove the tray, but Mr. Brannon lifted a hand to stop her.

"I haven't seen Edward since he was eighteen years old," Mr. Brannon said.

Susan sank back down onto the bed.

"It was my fault," he repeated. "I . . . didn't understand things back then. I didn't understand him. Do you know what I'm saying?"

"I'm not sure," Susan said.

"Edward was our only child," Mr. Brannon said. "We wanted more, but it was not to be. It took us quite a while to have Edward. I was thirty-eight when he was born. My wife, she was younger, but still. We'd waited so long."

He paused and sipped some water. "Even as a little boy, he was different. I'd dreamed of playing catch with my son. I wanted him to know how to change the oil in his car. To be a gentleman as well as a man's man."

Susan nodded slowly.

"I was that way, you see," Mr. Brannon said. "I thought Edward would follow in my footsteps. That he'd be just like me."

"Yes," Susan said.

"He didn't like to get dirty," Mr. Brannon said. "He was shy. Didn't have many friends. But he liked to be around girls, more than he liked to be around boys, so I thought everything was okay. I was disappointed in him, but I figured maybe he'd change when he grew up. That he'd toughen up."

"But he didn't," Susan said, thinking, *He couldn't.*

"Now that I think about it, now that I've had so long to

think about it, I know he was scared to tell us," Mr. Brannon said. "He did this nervous thing when he was a little boy, this twisting of his right leg so that his toe dug into the ground. Whenever he got in trouble, you could see that leg going. He was doing that when he said . . . You see, my boy was . . ."

"Gay?" Susan finished.

Susan wasn't sure if he'd expected her to be shocked, but she just gave him a gentle smile. Her old college roommate, Bobbi, whose mother was Susan's first unofficial client, was gay. She and Susan had talked about it for hours in their dorm room, both of them sharing the stories of how they'd felt like outsiders in high school.

"What happened after he told you?" Susan asked.

Mr. Brannon was in his eighties. If he'd been thirty-eight when he'd had Edward, that would have meant Edward would've turned eighteen in the 1980s, at a time when attitudes were beginning to change, prejudices slowly beginning to crumble away. But Mr. Brannon was probably still stuck in the mind-set of an earlier generation.

Mr. Brannon shut his eyes tightly. "I told him it was unacceptable. I told him he had to change. I told him he"—Mr. Brannon took in a shuddering breath—"that he was an embarrassment, that he didn't deserve to share my name."

"Oh," Susan breathed. She imagined that sensitive eighteen-year-old boy, twisting his toes against the ground, working up the courage to come out to his parents.

"You see, in the army, we used to joke about guys like that. We had names for them . . . Well, I shouldn't say the names," Mr. Brannon said. "I didn't want that for him. My wife was upset, too, but not as much as me. She might've let him stay, but she still wanted him to change, too."

"I'm sorry," Susan said. *For all of you*, she thought.

Mr. Brannon shook his head. "I know he talked to my wife some through the years. On Mother's Day the phone would ring. But I never spoke to him again. He also came to see her at the hospital at the end. One of the nurses mentioned it to me."

"Did you ever try to reach him?" Susan asked. "To tell him you loved him, that you were wrong?"

Mr. Brannon sighed. "My wife told me I should try to see Edward. But I said not if he was still living that way."

Mr. Brannon leaned back against his chair. His face was ashen. This had been too much for him, Susan thought. The singing children, the handprint, these old memories. He looked on the verge of collapse. She didn't condone what Mr. Brannon had done, but people changed, and she knew he was deeply regretful now.

"I sent him a letter," Mr. Brannon said. "When I was moving out of the house. I wanted him to be able to find me, you see. I gave him my new address. I told him he could write back if he wanted to."

"But he didn't?" Susan said.

Mr. Brannon shook his head once, stiffly, as if the movement pained him.

"The letter came back," he said. "Someone had written on it, 'Return to Sender.'"

"But maybe he moved," Susan said. "Maybe he never got your note."

Her mind was spinning. She could track down Edward, and tell him how sorry his father was, and that Mr. Brannon probably didn't have much time left—

Mr. Brannon looked at her with eyes so bleak she instinctively stood up and rushed to his side.

"Just rest," she said. She grabbed the blanket off the foot of the bed and tucked it around him. "We can talk more later."

"He got the letter," Mr. Brannon said, his voice barely a whisper. "On the back of the envelope, he wrote, 'Don't try to contact me again.' I still recognize his handwriting."

# Chapter Twenty-Six

**Newport Cove Listserv Digest**

*Re: Dog Poop

Unbelievable! After a few blissful poop-free weeks, I stepped in it again this morning. Something HAS to be done about this! —Joy Reiserman, Daisy Way

*Re: Dog Poop

Shouldn't this fall under the purview of the Newport Cove Manager? Shannon, I'd like a written plan of action from you soonest. We shouldn't have to scour our surroundings with the vigilance of children conducting an Easter Egg hunt simply to make it to our cars unscathed in the morning. —Bob Welsh, Magnolia Street

*Re: Dog Poop

Thank you for the suggestion, Bob! —Shannon Dockser, Newport Cove Manager

*Re: Dog Poop

Would the trespooper please step forward? —Frank Fitzgibbons, Forsythia Lane

*Re: Remove me from listserv?

There's an unsubscribe link you can click on at the end of the digest, that should solve your problem. —Brandy Zapruder, Blossom Street

• • •

Gigi speared a piece of limp asparagus and wondered how she'd ended up here. She'd been asked to give a speech at an organization composed of chiropractors. Ostensibly, the organization was a charity and held auctions and other fundraisers. But Gigi was quickly suspecting it was actually an excuse for the members to get together and drink too much wine and socialize during a long, drawn-out dinner. Who knew chiropractors were such party animals?

She let the asparagus flop back onto her plate and discreetly checked the program in her lap.

"Forty-five minutes, max," Zach had said when he'd suggested she attend the event. "We'll schedule it so you'll zip in after dinner has started, give your speech, shake hands, and zip right back out."

Cocktail hour had gone on late, though, which meant Gigi had arrived when everyone was on their second martini or glass of wine instead of when the entrées were being served. She'd already been here ninety minutes, and dessert hadn't even made an appearance.

"We just love your husband," the woman to Gigi's right confided.

"Thank you," Gigi said, leaning back. The woman's breath smelled like Chardonnay, and she'd repeated the same exact sentiment twice before.

"He's so cute! Are you sure he's not related to the Kennedy family?" the woman asked. "I mean, that thick head of hair!" She was wearing a low-cut blouse and her boobs appeared in danger of falling out. Was this the kind of woman Joe came into contact with at campaign events? Surely most of them were professionals, but there were always groupies around politicians and athletes. *JohnEdwardsBillClintonAnthonyWeiner*, her mind murmured, before she shushed it.

Gigi laughed as if the woman were completely charming.

"Absolutely sure; it's a common last name," she said. "And we appreciate your support."

"It's too bad Joe couldn't make it tonight," the man on Gigi's other side said. "Not that we don't appreciate you filling in."

Gigi smiled and took a sip of ice water. Zach hadn't mentioned she was a fill-in when he'd suggested Gigi attend the event. But she wasn't surprised; Joe was the star attraction in their marriage.

"More wine?" the waiter asked.

"Ooh, yes!" squealed the woman with Chardonnay breath.

"Excuse me just a minute," Gigi said. She stood up and dropped her napkin on her chair, then left the room. The dinner was being held in the conference room of a hotel, so Gigi bypassed the first bathroom she reached, where she'd be in danger of being cornered by another attendee, and walked down a long hallway until she discovered another restroom.

She went into a stall, closed the lid of the toilet, and sat down with a sigh. After a moment she pulled her cell phone out of her purse with the thought of playing a quick game of Boggle and saw she had a text from Julia.

R U Almost Done?

Gigi typed back: About another hour. What's up? U OK?

Julia's response came a moment later: Guess so.

Gigi frowned and hit the button to call home.

"Hey, sweetie," she said. "What are you doing?"

"Eating pizza," she said. "Melanie ordered it."

"Okay," Gigi said. Something was off in Julia's tone.

"Is Melanie being nice to you?" she asked.

"Uh-huh," she said.

"Can I talk to her a minute?" Gigi asked.

"She isn't here," Julia said.

"What?" Gigi asked. "Where'd she go?"

"I don't know," Julia said.

"Honey, listen, I know she probably told you not to say anything"—threatened was more like it—"but I need to know what happened. Did someone pick her up?"

"Yeah," Julia said. "I think it was that guy. Raven."

*One mystery solved*, Gigi thought. "Okay, can you do me a favor? Go and make sure all the doors are locked."

Gigi listened to the sounds of Julia moving around the house.

"Okay," she said. "They already were."

At least Melanie had taken that precaution. But she shouldn't have left her twelve-year-old sister alone at night without at least telling Gigi. Plus it was a school night, and it was nearly nine o'clock, which wasn't that late in the grand scheme of things, but Melanie had to be up at six. She had a curfew of ten on school nights, but Melanie rarely exercised it. She didn't go out much.

"I'm going to text her and tell her she needs to be home by ten, okay?" Gigi said. "And I should be home around then, too. Just call me if you need anything."

"Okay. Thanks, Mommy," Julia said.

"I love you, sweetie," Gigi said. "Did you do all your homework?"

"Yes, I finished it in study hall today," Julia said. "Oh, and I got an A on my math test."

"That's wonderful," Gigi said.

After she hung up, she quickly typed a text to Melanie: I thought you were going to stay home with Julia tonight. I need you back by 10, sooner if possible.

She sent it, then waited, but there was no response.

*Fuck it*, Gigi thought. Melanie was almost sixteen, and they didn't ask much of her. She rarely did chores around the house and her bedroom was a pit. She shouldn't have snuck out tonight. Maybe the problem was Gigi had been too soft on her.

She dialed Melanie's number and waited through the four rings before it went to voice mail.

"This is Mom," she began unnecessarily. "I need you to call me immediately and let me know where you are and what time you'll be home. I was counting on you to be home with Julia."

She hung up and waited a minute, then called back. This time her call went right to voice mail.

"Dammit!" Gigi said aloud.

She was tempted to walk out of this event—half the people were so sloshed they wouldn't miss her—but her name was on the program and it would look bad for Joe. There was something else bothering Gigi. A few days earlier, she'd gone to light up the bag of weed she kept hidden in the old vanity, and she'd noticed the bag was visible behind the electric toothbrush. Gigi was always careful to keep it hidden, just in case one of the kids or a cleaning person opened the vanity. *Melanie*, Gigi had thought. Maybe her daughter had progressed from cigarettes to pot. But Gigi couldn't be sure, so she'd taken a snapshot of the bag in order to better gauge the contents level. She'd check it when she got home.

She stood up and straightened her skirt, then reapplied lipstick in the mirror before she headed back to her table. She kept her cell phone on vibrate so she'd know the minute a text or call came in.

But all through the next interminable hour, while dessert was served and Gigi was finally introduced and gave her speech and stopped to chat with a half dozen people on the way to the exit, her phone remained still.

By eleven, Gigi was back at home, tucking Julia into bed. Julia would be exhausted tomorrow, but she was too scared to fall asleep when she was the only one in the house.

By eleven thirty, she'd called Melanie five more times and Joe twice.

By midnight, Joe had come home. But Melanie hadn't.

• • •

Jason suspected something. Kellie was certain of it.

First, there was the iPhone incident. And yesterday, he'd

asked about her coworkers: "Anyone you've become friends with?" Jason had been pulling a pair of socks out of a drawer, but he'd paused and turned to look at her.

The phrasing of his question seemed deliberate, as did his sudden scrutiny. "Oh, everyone in the office is great, it's a nice group," Kellie had responded, not untruthfully. But she was aware she'd evaded the specifics of his inquiry.

Perhaps he'd read the same magazine article she had, titled "Is Your Spouse a Cheater?" Apparently if your husband or wife began dressing better and losing weight, you should be worried. And if he or she disappeared at odd hours and became unusually protective of his or her cell phone? Then you were in big trouble.

Kellie had done all of those things. But she'd never even kissed Miller, let alone slept with him. They'd shared one dance, a few outings, and lots of eye contact and conversation.

An emotional affair could be every bit as damaging as a physical one, the article had said. And it was true; she'd fallen into obsessive thoughts about Miller. She drifted off to sleep imagining being in his arms. She dreamed about him while she was caring for the children and cooking dinner and watching television with Jason. She stared into the mirror, wondering what her skin would feel like under his hands. She checked her cell phone constantly to see if he'd texted, feeling an electric jolt when she saw a new message. She'd read about that sensation; apparently it was due to a chemical called dopamine that was released in your brain—that pleasurable, unpredictable rush was the basis of the science casinos employed to keep people pulling the slot machine handles hour after hour.

She was addicted to Miller.

Thoughts of him consumed her, leaving her alternately euphoric and agitated and jittery. She constantly wondered what he was doing, if he was thinking of her, or laughing with his wife. Or making love to his wife. Jealousy would surge within

Kellie, only to be extinguished by a smile from Miller, or a text, which would spin her into a new daydream. She woke up thinking about him, and imagined it was Miller's hands on her instead of Jason's at night. Guilt and desire and confusion battered her like a hurricane.

She had to stop this, she thought as she stepped out of the shower and wrapped herself in a towel. That night at the bar—if Susan hadn't intervened, something might have happened. If she and Miller had found themselves in a dark corner, and he'd leaned down to whisper something in her ear, and she'd turned so that their lips were close together . . . Would one of them have broken that final barrier?

She covered her mouth with her hand to prevent a small, sad noise from escaping. It made her feel physically ill to think about hurting Jason or their kids. She'd made a commitment to Jason when she'd been in high school, and she'd been faithful to it, to *him*, for more than twenty years. She'd worn his letter jacket proudly. They'd gone to the same nearby college, even though Kellie's sister, Irene, had scoffed at her: "Don't you want to date lots of guys?" But Kellie hadn't. Jason was the only man she'd ever wanted. She'd watched friends cry over boys, and chase after them, and break hearts and have theirs broken in return, and all the while she'd felt lucky. Jason adored her. He brought her roses on Valentine's Day and kissed her every single day.

This wasn't his fault. Jason hadn't changed.

She had, though.

She and Miller had fallen into the habit of going to A Piece of Cake every Friday afternoon. They'd share a treat, sip coffee, and talk.

They discussed their kids, and though she never mentioned Jason, Miller had brought up his wife once. "It's nice to be able to talk to you about business," he'd said. "My wife . . . Well, she's more interested in shopping." He'd given a little laugh, and Kellie had smiled, too.

She knew what she'd say to a friend if one had come to her seeking advice on this identical problem: *Can you imagine inviting him over for dinner with your family and watching him talk to your husband?* If the answer was no, there was a problem.

Kellie had a problem. Her relationship with Miller existed in a gossamer bubble. It could never drift into her real life. She couldn't fathom the idea of him watching her wipe down kitchen counters and screech at her kids to stop arguing. She couldn't imagine ever walking into the bathroom and interrupting him on the toilet reading the sports page, like she had with Jason earlier this week.

It was a fantasy, that was all. She had to shake it loose, reclaim her brain.

Had anyone noticed their attraction? She was pretty sure Maria, a senior agent who loved to gossip, suspected something. A couple of weeks back, Kellie had been leaning toward Miller at their table in A Piece of Cake, their eyes locked together, smiling as he told a story about his college fraternity days. A tap on the window had startled her, and Kellie had jerked back. Maria was standing there, inches away. She'd given a little wave, then had continued walking.

Maria's smile had seemed knowing. Or maybe that was just Kellie's guilty conscience.

Today was Friday. When Miller came to her desk and asked, "Ready?" she would shake her head.

"I'm sorry," she'd say. "I'm completely swamped."

She imagined surprise, even hurt, filling his light brown eyes. "Sure," he'd say. "Another time."

But there wouldn't be another time, she told herself as she smoothed lotion over her face and neck. She wouldn't see him outside the office again. She'd keep their interactions warmly professional. She'd treat him the same way she did the matronly receptionist.

Well, maybe that would be unnecessarily abrupt. She didn't

want to be rude to Miller. A gradual withdrawal would prob-ably be the smarter route. Maybe one final treat together, then she could say she was cutting out sugar.

She walked over to her closet and examined her clothes, reaching for her black pantsuit. She felt like she was in mourning.

She looked down at her cell phone, feeling a heaviness in-fuse her body when it showed no new messages. Maybe Miller had come to the same conclusion; maybe he was planning to start withdrawing, too. He could be with his wife right now, curled against her in bed as his warm hand lazily drifted down her thigh—

"Honey?" She jerked her head up at the sound of Jason's voice coming from the kitchen. "Can you send the kids down for breakfast?"

"Yes, yes," she called back.

Kellie went into Noah's room where, predictably, he'd fallen back asleep despite the fact that she'd woken him up before going into the shower. He lay half off the bed, one arm and leg dangling, his head buried under a pillow.

"Time to get up, sweetie," Kellie said. She removed the pil-low and opened the blinds to flood the room with sunlight.

"Mgrf," Noah said.

"Up," Kellie said. "Don't forget to put on clean underwear."

"Ew, do you really have to remind him of that?" Mia asked from the doorway. "Who forgets to put on clean underwear every day?"

"Seven-year-old boys," Kellie said. "Come on."

She made sure Noah was stumbling toward the bathroom before she went downstairs. As she walked into the kitchen, the aroma of fresh coffee and the smell of frying eggs hit her. Jason was standing at the stove, spatula in hand.

"Why aren't you at work yet?" Kellie asked. The hardware store opened at eight a.m., which meant Jason always left at seven thirty, and it was past that time now.

"I told my dad I'd be in a little late today," Jason said. "I wanted to have breakfast with my family."

"Oh," Kellie said. "I mean, that's really nice!"

"Do you have any special plans this weekend?" Jason asked.

"Nope," Kellie said. "Since I don't have any houses at the moment, I won't need to do a showing." A lump formed in her throat at the thought of Miller's absence from her life. Everything would seem so gray and ordinary.

"Good," Jason said as he slid an egg onto a plate and handed it to her.

He'd set the table and fried bacon for Mia. There was a pile of carrot sticks, Noah's preferred entrée, on his plate, along with a piece of toast. Steaming coffee trickled from the machine into the glass carafe.

"Wow," Kellie said, looking at it all. "What got into you?"

"I just want my wife to know how much I appreciate her," Jason said. He caught her eye and smiled.

Yes, she thought as she bowed her head, too ashamed to let her wonderful, loving husband see her face. Jason was definitely suspicious.

# Chapter Twenty-Seven

**Newport Cove Listserv Digest**

\*Ants

I know it won't be springtime for a while yet, but for the past few years we've had an invasion of ants coming through our kitchen window. I squash the little buggers, but they're relentless. Any suggestions on how to prevent this from happening this year? I'd like to be proactive. —Lev Grainger, Crabtree Lane

\*Re: Ants

I use Ant Begone! Exterminators. Give them a call, they'll take care of the problem. —Gloria Wakeman, Blossom Street

\*Re: Ants

I'd be wary of using harsh chemicals, especially in the kitchen. We're becoming a very toxic society. I use nothing but vinegar and hot water to clean my house. A few ants don't bother me. —Tally White, Iris Lane

• • •

Melanie didn't come home until nearly one a.m. Joe was slumped on the couch while Gigi peered out the window yet again and saw headlights finally ease down their street and pause in front of their house.

"It's her!" Gigi cried. "She just got out of a car . . . It looks like Raven's."

"I'm going to ground her for a month," Joe said. "No, two months."

"We shouldn't start by yelling," Gigi said. "Let's ask her what happened. Maybe there's a logical explanation. Maybe they got a flat tire."

"Yes, at the exact moment all cell phones in the universe stopped working," Joe said.

Gigi smiled despite herself. The sweet relief rushing through her, weakening her knees, made her realize just how terrified she'd been that Melanie had run away. The pot in her Ziploc bag looked as if it hadn't been touched, either, which was reassuring. But by the time she heard Melanie's key turn in the lock, her relief was already churning into anger.

The car peeled off, its engine loud in the quiet night, and the front door creaked open.

"Oh," Melanie said when she saw her parents. "Hi."

Tears flooded Gigi's eyes. This was what people meant when they said that having children meant wearing your heart on the outside of your body, where it was most vulnerable. The little baby who'd cuddled at her breast, warm and soft and cooing, had turned into a tall young woman overnight. In a few years, Melanie would be gone. Would she ever have the chance to know her daughter again?

"Where were you?" Gigi shouted. "Do you know how worried we've been?"

She felt, rather than saw, Joe's look: *So much for asking for an explanation first.*

"I'm sorry," Melanie said, which pulled Gigi up short.

"Sit down, Mellie," Joe said. He was the only one who could get away with calling her by her old nickname. Melanie walked over and joined him on the couch. Gigi looked at her carefully. Melanie's eyes weren't red, and she was walking fluidly, which seemed to indicate she was sober.

"I know I should have called," Melanie said. "But I broke up with Raven tonight, and he was really upset. I needed to talk to him for a long time."

Gigi looked at Joe, who was looking back at her, mirroring the surprised expression she knew she was wearing. Melanie had revealed more about her life in the past thirty seconds than she had in the past three months to Gigi.

After a moment, Gigi cleared her throat. One of them had to take the reins here—or take them away from Melanie, who seemed the only one in control of the situation.

"Well," Gigi said. "I guess it's okay."

"Just this once," Joe added quickly. "But next time, you need to answer your phone. Your mother was worried."

"So was your father," Gigi said dryly.

"Yes," Joe said. "I was worried."

"I'm sorry," Melanie said. She looked different tonight. She was in her usual black jeans but she was wearing a red top. The vibrant splash of color made her face look brighter. Her hair looked more styled, too.

Gigi bent down to hug her, discreetly sniffing to see if she could detect the aroma of alcohol or weed. But all she smelled was sweet shampoo. Melanie didn't hug her back, but she didn't pull away, either.

Was her baby finally returning to her after all? All that worrying . . . it could have been for naught. The hope fluttered up through Gigi's chest like a butterfly and lodged in her throat, making it difficult for her to swallow.

"You need to get to bed," Gigi said. "If you want to sleep in tomorrow, I can drive you in after your first class."

"It's okay," Melanie said. "I'll wake up. I don't deserve to sleep in after staying out so late."

Melanie hugged Joe, then left the room as Gigi stared after her.

• • •

## Before Newport Cove

Danny Briggs, the Young Rangers leader, was a widower who had two grown sons. He had a firm handshake. He looked you in the eye when he spoke. He didn't trigger any warning signals in Tessa.

At least not on the first night they met.

Addison had run off to play with the other kids while Tessa sat in one of the metal folding chairs set out around the perimeter of the room. There was a table in the back with bottles of water and juice boxes and cookies. Lots of parents were hanging out, chatting or peering at cell phones—it wasn't worthwhile to drop off the kids, drive home, and come back again when the meeting only lasted an hour.

When all the kids had arrived, Danny gathered everyone into a circle and talked about all the fun things they'd do. There were fourteen boys in the "Ranger Pack" as Danny called it (*Adorable*, Tessa had thought) and they'd go on hikes, earn badges, and even build a derby car to race. There would be a service project—the kids would get to vote on which one—and in the late spring, an overnight camping trip.

"I'm going to need a lot of parent volunteers to help with that one," Danny had said, laughing. "Ever tried to wrangle fourteen boys in the woods while building a fire to cook dinner?"

"Can't we just order in Domino's?" one of the dads had called.

"And Starbucks in the morning?" another had added, and everyone had laughed.

What a wonderful group, Tessa had thought, looking at the bright, eager faces of the little boys. This would be so good for them. They'd get away from Minecraft and Plants vs.

Zombies—Addison would play those games in his sleep if she let him—and spend more time out in the fresh air, all while learning about teamwork.

And it would be good for her, too, she'd thought, settling deeper into her seat and releasing a sigh. Maybe she'd make some new friends among the parents here. And now that the kids were in school, she'd start exercising again. Maybe she'd take a Zumba class; it sounded like fun. Life was easing up, she'd told herself. She was finally catching a break.

She'd gone to shake Danny's hand at the end of the meeting, buoyed by a sense of optimism.

"Thank you for doing this," she'd said.

He'd grinned, his eyes crinkling at the corners. His hands were warm and dry. "My two sons live so far away I barely see them, so it's fun for me, too," he'd replied. "Boys are such a joy to be around."

*What a nice guy*, she'd thought, smiling back at him. "Our kids are lucky to have you."

•  •  •

Susan eased into the big leather chair, slipped on her earphones, and leaned toward the microphone. It was time for her radio show. For the next half hour, she'd take calls from worried sons and desperate daughters. A man would bluster about how irresponsible his mother was being for not creating a living will (he was terrified of losing her, hence the bluster), or a woman would rail about the fact that her siblings weren't stepping up and doing enough for their bedridden mother (she'd be right; Susan would suggest a family meeting with a therapist to determine which tasks the siblings needed to take on or pay to have outsourced).

During the first few weeks of her show, her producer had called in questions from the next room when there were gaps in the airtime. Now, all the lines lit up the moment Susan's voice came over the airwaves.

"Good morning, this is Susan Barrett, here to talk to you about how to best support your aging parents," she said. Her producer, a young woman with colorful tattoos covering both forearms, signaled that the first call had come in. "Diane in Charlotte," the producer said into Susan's earpiece.

"We're going to chat with Diane in Charlotte now. Hello, Diane," Susan said.

"Hi," Diane's voice came over the line. Callers always sounded uncertain during the first few seconds, as if they'd just discovered they'd made a horrible mistake and were on the verge of hanging up.

"I'm glad you called, Diane," Susan said quickly. "Tell us what's on your mind."

"Um . . . okay. I'm worried about my father's driving," Diane said. "He's eighty-eight, and he's never had an accident but I feel like he's just tempting fate now."

"I see," Susan said. "Does he live near you?"

"About twenty minutes away," Diane said. "He and my mother still live in their home, but she has cataracts and doesn't drive anymore. My dad was always a good driver. But I think he needs to stop soon. I'd never forgive myself if he got into an accident. Or what if he hit some kid or something?"

"That is a lot to worry about," Susan said. "Have you talked to your father about it?"

Diane gave a little laugh. "No way. He's a former marine who started his own business while going to night school. He's a very proud man."

"Do you have any siblings?" Susan asked.

"No, it's just me," Diane said. She was almost shouting now. "It's so frustrating! He shouldn't be driving, but I know he's going to make a big deal about it and we're just going to end up in a fight."

Apparently the apple didn't fall far from the tree, Susan thought.

"Here's what you need to do," Susan said. "Starting tomorrow, I don't want you to use your car for an entire week."

"Not use my car?" Diane gasped. "But how will I get to the grocery store? And work? And I have a doctor's appointment next Thursday. And . . . Oh."

"It's hard, isn't it?" Susan said gently. "To imagine losing something that represents so much freedom? And I bet your father has had a lot of losses lately."

"He has," Diane said. She sniffed and her voice lost its angry edge and grew husky. "His best friend passed away last year, and he lost his only brother five years ago."

"No wonder you think he'll resist giving up driving," Susan said.

Diane was quiet for a moment. "Yes," she said. "It isn't just about the driving, is it?"

Susan could see the other lines blinking red and she knew she needed to wrap up.

"It's going to be a tough conversation," Susan said. "But you'll approach it in a loving way, and help your parents figure out alternatives, like taxis. It may be that taking a cab somewhere twice a week will end up costing less than the insurance and upkeep on a car."

"My dad would like that point," Diane said, laughing. "He's a cheapskate. And I visit them every week. We usually just have dinner together at the house. Maybe I can do it twice a week."

"And maybe you'll take them out for lunch at a restaurant instead," Susan said. "And then go run errands with them afterward."

"That sounds good," Diane said. "Thank you."

"My pleasure," Susan said. "And good for you, for being a responsible daughter. Our next caller is Roald from Asheville. Good afternoon, Roald. How can I help you?"

Susan talked to Roald about the handyman he was worried was overcharging his father for unnecessary jobs, then Dottie called in to complain that her mother's new boyfriend wanted to take her to Saint Thomas for Christmas rather than letting her mother cook dinner for the family for the holiday, as had been the tradition for decades (after two minutes on the phone with Dottie, Susan could understand the boyfriend's need for a tropical escape and knew it would be the best thing for Dottie's mom, too). Susan chatted about the difference between revocable and irrevocable trusts with a caller who wanted his parents to set them up for tax benefits, and comforted a bereaved daughter before gently steering her toward a counselor.

With three minutes left to go, Susan accepted her last call from Catherine in Raleigh.

"Hello?" Catherine said. She sounded elderly. "I know this show is more for our children, but sometimes I like to listen to it."

"I'm glad," Susan said. "What is your question today?"

A gentle sigh, then: "I'm ready to give up the family home," Catherine said. "I've lived here for fifty years and it's time to move on."

"I understand," Susan said. "Are you thinking about a retirement community? There are many vibrant ones in your area; I have links on my website."

"I would like that," Catherine said. "The problem is my children, you see. My son comes by to mow the lawn and do yard work, and my daughter hired a cleaning lady to come every two weeks so I don't have to do any heavy housework. She brings by dinner once a week, too."

"Sounds like you raised wonderful children," Susan said. "They must love you very much."

"Yes," Catherine said. "My grandchildren come to visit me often, too. I'm very lucky. Some of my friends don't get to see their families nearly as much. But I'm . . ."

She paused for so long Susan worried they'd been disconnected.

"I'm tired," Catherine said. "I'm ready to leave this old house that I've loved so much. My kids think they know what's best for me. They think I'll be happiest here, with all the memories surrounding me. With my roses blooming in the springtime, and my newspaper delivered to my doorstep every morning. I think they feel proud that they've made it possible. And I'm grateful to them, I really am, but . . ."

"But you're ready to move on," Susan said. "You'd like to try something different."

"Some of these retirement homes have gourmet coffee in the morning," Catherine said eagerly. "Doesn't that sound nice, coffee that someone else makes?"

"It does," Susan said. Sometimes it was the small things that held the greatest allure; she'd love to be brought coffee once in a while instead of having to brew it herself.

"And you don't have to go outside to get the newspaper, and there are swimming pools heated to make old bones comfortable," Catherine said. "And don't laugh at the cliché, but I might even take a knitting class."

"I wouldn't laugh," Susan promised.

"But my kids won't let go," Catherine said. The cadence of her voice slowed, became more somber. "I can't find happiness with them holding on so tightly. They love this house. I think they're planning on inheriting it when I go, and maybe giving it to one of the grandchildren. It's been in our family for so long."

"Catherine, I don't think you need me to tell you what to do," Susan said gently.

Catherine sighed again. "I need to talk to them," she said. "I need to tell them I'm going to sell our family home to use the money to pay for an apartment in a retirement community. It'll break their hearts."

"I wouldn't think of it that way," Susan said. "I think they're just scared of what will happen to them if you move on. They might lose some of their purpose and their identity if they no longer feel they're needed to take care of you. And they'll miss their childhood home, of course. But that doesn't mean it should keep you from living your life. They'll adjust. I promise they will."

"Thank you," Catherine said softly. "I'll do it."

"That wraps up our chat for this morning," Susan said, her tone becoming brisk. "Thank you all for joining us. Please tune in again next week at the same time, same station. I'm Susan Barrett, wishing you a healthy and happy week ahead."

Her producer gave her the thumbs-up as the show's theme music played for a few beats, then Susan removed her headphones and walked out of the studio.

"Good show," one of the sound guys said as she headed to the elevator.

"Thanks," she said. "Sorry—just in a rush. I've got to—"

Thankfully the elevator came before he could get a look at her face, and she escaped into the soundproof chamber before releasing the sob that was building in her throat. She made it to her Mercedes in the employees' lot and turned on the engine, but instead of driving away, she stayed in place, her hands on the wheel, her body beginning to tremble.

How could she counsel other people to let go, to move on with their lives, when it was impossible for her to do the same? She was still frozen in place, her life locked into the moment Randall had left.

*They're just scared of what will happen to them if you move on,* Susan had said. *But that doesn't mean it should keep you from living your life. They'll adjust. I promise they will.*

Sometimes, though, people didn't adjust. She never should have made that promise. She was a fraud.

• • •

Jason looked completely out of place in the doorway to her office. He was wearing a dress shirt, the same blue button-down he'd had for nearly a decade. It strained slightly across his middle.

"Honey?" Kellie had been about to dial a number, but she put down her phone and hurried to his side.

"Surprise!" he said.

"What are you doing here?" Kellie asked, feeling her eyes widen. "I mean, I just— Don't you have to be at work?"

"I took off early," he said.

Jason never took off early on Fridays. Those afternoons, along with Saturday mornings, were the hardware store's busiest time, when all the weekend repair warriors stocked up for projects.

"Wow," Kellie said. "Well, let me show you around! I was actually going to leave in fifteen minutes to get the kids. I'm glad you caught me."

"My mom is getting the kids today," Jason said. "I thought we could go somewhere for happy hour, then get dinner. Just you and me."

"Really?" Kellie looked at Jason carefully. Usually she was the one who cajoled Jason to go out. He was the homebody, she was the social butterfly. "Okay. Sure. That sounds really nice."

Kellie could see the office receptionist watching them, and gossipy Maria peering around from the edge of her computer screen to check out Jason. Jason noticed them, too.

"Don't you want to introduce me?" he asked.

"Sure," Kellie said. She suddenly wondered if Miller was nearby. She hadn't seen him in almost an hour. Maybe he'd left early to show a client some listings in advance of the open houses that were always held on Sundays.

Kellie walked Jason over to the receptionist's desk. "This is Barb, who saves all of our lives by staying on top of everything and keeping this place organized."

"I'm the office mom," Barb said agreeably.

"Barb, my husband, Jason"—Kellie waited while Jason smiled and shook hands—"and Maria, one of our senior agents."

"Nice to meet you," said Maria, who'd progressed from peering around the edges of her computer to getting up and walking over to Kellie's side. The memory of Maria's look when she'd spotted Kellie and Miller in the bakery flashed in Kellie's mind.

"Maria!" Jason said, breaking into a big smile, as he gave a slight emphasis to the second syllable in her name.

Kellie looked at him quickly. "Do you guys know each other?"

"Nope," Maria said.

Kellie frowned. The way Jason had said Maria's name had seemed . . . familiar.

"So, how long have the two of you been married?" Maria was asking.

"Forever," Kellie said lightly.

"Almost seventeen years," Jason said. "We met in high school."

"Aw, high school sweethearts," Maria said. She had the raspy voice of a longtime smoker, which she was, and the ability to instantly carry on a conversation on any topic—a valuable skill in a real estate agent.

"So you were lab partners in biology? Or let me guess—Kellie was the cheerleader and you were the football star, Jason?" Maria continued. "Am I right?"

"That is uncanny," Kellie said, just as Jason began to say, "Well, not exactly the star."

"Oh, Jason, come check out the kitchen," Kellie said. If Jason started talking about his high school football days they might never escape. "Do you want some coffee?"

"No, I'm good," Jason said, but Kellie kept moving, giving him no choice but to follow, cutting short his conversation with Maria. Kellie wanted to get out of the office fast. It felt strange having Jason here. Disorienting, somehow.

She knew she wasn't handling this well. Maria was staring after her, probably puzzled by the abrupt end to the conversation, and Kellie's voice sounded higher and sharper than normal, even to her own ears. She probably seemed nervous. She *was* nervous. Jason had looked at Maria strangely; she hadn't been imagining that. And what about the way Maria had marched over to meet Jason and had immediately started asking about their marriage!

Maria couldn't possibly have looked up Kellie's home number and phoned to warn Jason about Kellie's flirtation with Miller, could she? Was that why Jason had shown up without any warning?

"Sure I can't tempt you with a Keurig Dunkin' Donuts latte?" Kellie offered. "Or a hot chocolate?"

No, she was being ridiculous. It wasn't as if Maria had caught Kellie and Miller going at it in the supply closet. Besides, Maria didn't seem malicious, only nosy.

"Should we head out?" Jason asked.

They'd almost made it to the door when it opened. Jason had to abruptly stop moving to avoid being hit as it swung inward. Kellie knew before he even took a step inside the office that Miller was on the other side.

"Hey, you," he said, breaking into a wide smile when he saw Kellie.

She quickly stepped up next to Jason. "Miller, hi. This is my husband, Jason."

She had to do it like that. She couldn't risk Miller mentioning something about them going to A Piece of Cake.

Jason stuck out his hand and Miller shook it. "Nice to meet you," they said in unison.

"Kellie's mentioned you," Jason said.

*I have?* Kellie thought. But then she remembered the house Miller had sold to Tessa. Kellie had helped him with the listing, so she'd probably dropped Miller's name then. She knew she hadn't brought up Miller in a while, though. Jason's words seemed deliberate. Significant.

Was Jason jealous? She saw Miller through his eyes. Miller was a few inches taller than Jason's five foot ten, and he still had all of his hair. Those sorts of details seemed to matter greatly to men.

"Ducking out early?" Miller was asking.

Kellie smiled, even though her heart was thudding. Why had Jason shown up here? Was he staring at Miller a beat too long? Did he know she'd closed her eyes last night when they'd been in bed and had imagined Miller was the one making love to her? Could she have spoken Miller's name in her sleep?

Kellie could feel her armpits grow damp. Her breath came faster.

"Have fun," Maria called out, waving.

Jason put his hand on the small of her back in what seemed like a possessive gesture, and steered her toward the door. Her husband, the guy who'd always been an open book, was suddenly inscrutable to Kellie.

"Okay, we're off!" Kellie said. "See you."

She walked through the door as Miller held it open, briefly becoming almost sandwiched between the two men, as Jason was so close behind her. She couldn't escape from this place quickly enough.

Kellie exhaled as they turned the corner and reached the elevator. How did women do this? How did they carry on affairs and keep their worlds from colliding? It was too stressful. She needed to end her flirtation with Miller. What she should do was transfer to another branch of the real estate company. There was another office just twenty minutes away, on the other side of town.

But then there would be no sweet texts from Miller telling her he liked her dress. No tingle in her lower belly as she pulled in to the employee parking lot and checked to see if Miller's car was there yet. Her life would deflate back into its old, tired shape.

Maybe she didn't need to transfer, she thought miserably. She just had to tone things down with Miller. If only she knew how.

# Chapter Twenty-Eight

*Before Newport Cove*

THE YOUNG RANGERS GROUP was proceeding exactly as Tessa had hoped. Addison earned badges and learned songs and tried, along with the other boys, to rub together two sticks to start a fire (that was about as successful as Tessa had expected, and after a few minutes Danny had pulled out a Zippo lighter, calling it a "Ranger magic wand"). The kids toasted marshmallows and made s'mores. They argued about what colors to paint their derby car. They laughed a lot.

"He's a saint," one of the other mothers had said to Tessa as she watched Danny give the kids high-fives. "We're thinking about getting him a nice gift card for the holidays. Want to go in on it?"

"I'd love to," Tessa had said. Sometimes Tessa wondered if Harry's being absent from the children's lives during so much of their formative years had created a distance between them. He loved the kids, of course. He just didn't seem terribly interested in them. He'd play with them for a few minutes, then pick up the newspaper or turn on his iPad. He never created forts out of pillows or put shaving cream on Addison's chin and gave him a razor with the blade taken out so that Addison could pretend he was shaving alongside his dad. He didn't do the kind of fun things that sitcom fathers seemed to. Sometimes Tessa would watch Phil on *Modern Family*—clueless, ridiculous Phil—and she'd wished she'd married a guy with a little more Phil in him.

But he'd set up college savings accounts for the kids when they were babies. He'd put up safety gates on the stairs to protect them. He didn't get angry when the kids bounded into the bedroom early in the morning and pulled the covers off him. Maybe he wasn't a great father, but he was a good enough one.

But Danny was present in all the ways Harry wasn't. Danny listened to the kids, and threw back his head and laughed when they said something unintentionally funny. He sat cross-legged on the floor with them. He ate a charred marshmallow at the campfire and made ridiculous faces that practically sent the boys into convulsions.

"Remember, uniforms come in next week," Danny had said at the conclusion of one of the meetings.

"Say thank you to Danny," Tessa had prompted Addison, who'd run over to Danny. Danny had reached down to give Addison a hug. "You're welcome, buddy," he'd said.

Tessa was in a rush to drive home and get the kids bathed and into bed. Harry was out of town again, and it was a school night. They'd be tired in the morning if she didn't hurry.

She, the eternal worrier, still hadn't picked up on a single sign.

# Chapter Twenty-Nine

**Newport Cove Listserv Digest**

*Help Needed for Holiday Decorating Committee!
Please join Newport Cove's Holiday Decorating Committee! We'll be festooning
street lamps with wreaths, wrapping white lights around community bushes,
and planning a very special visit by Santa for all kids (young and merely
young-at-heart). Contact Shannon Dockser, Newport Cove Manager, to sign up.
—Sincerely, Shannon Dockser, Newport Cove Manager

. . .

Kellie started to walk toward the parking lot. "Should we leave
my car here?" she asked. "It seems silly for us to drive two. But
then you'd have to bring me back to work tomorrow . . ."

Jason smiled and put his hands on Kellie's shoulders and
steered her toward the front of the building, in the opposite
direction of the parking lot.

"Jason?" she asked. "What's going on?"

She stopped short when she saw a limousine parked in
front of her office building, a driver wearing a jacket and cap
standing by the open back door of the vehicle.

Kellie blinked a few times, then turned around and stared at her husband.

Jason was smiling. "What are you waiting for?" he asked. "Get in!"

• • •

"Where should we put the cake?" asked Susan, who was wearing bell-bottom jeans and a headband decorated with blue and red peace signs.

Gigi, who was in a sheath dress and white go-go boots, glanced around. "Maybe on that empty table by the bar?" she suggested. "We should probably keep it away from the dance floor."

Jason had booked a private room at the community center for Kellie's surprise fortieth birthday disco party. Right about now, he'd be picking her up at the office. In the back of the limousine he'd rented, he had a bottle of champagne chilling in an ice bucket. After a long, leisurely drive around town and a stop at Kellie's favorite restaurant for hors d'oeuvres, he'd bring her here, where her family and friends were assembling.

Jason had picked up alcohol and sodas and a few appetizer platters and Susan had made the cake—a decadent, fudgy one. Gigi was in charge of the decorations. Tessa had volunteered to bartend, surprisingly. "I used to do it at the charity fund-raiser for my kids' school," Tessa had said. "I can make a mean dirty martini."

The disco strobe light was hung in place, and Gigi was taping up the last streamer. Jason's parents were bringing by the kids for the first half hour of the party, to sing "Happy Birthday" and give their mom a kiss and steal a piece of cake, then the lights would go down and the real party would begin.

Kellie's actual birthday was a month away. But Jason knew she'd become suspicious if he planned a party for the right date.

Easygoing Jason, who was always in the front yard tossing around a football with his son and who'd once shown up at the pool with his toenails painted bright green (his daughter's handiwork), was such a sweet husband, Gigi thought. She wondered if Jason knew about Kellie's flirtation with her work friend, Miller. Maybe that's why he was going all out for the party, to fight for his wife.

Gigi was rooting for him.

Gigi had found an online store that specialized in '70s attire, and she'd bought extra wigs and outfits. After everyone shouted "Surprise!" she'd hustle Kellie into the bathroom and let her pick something fun to wear.

All the elements were in place. Except for the niggling feeling in the pit of Gigi's stomach, a sense that something was amiss.

This morning, Melanie had come downstairs with her hair neatly brushed, wearing jeans and a cream-colored sweater and the brown riding boots that had been buried in the back of her closet.

"You look so nice!" Gigi had blurted before she could stop herself.

But instead of rolling her eyes or rushing back upstairs to change, Melanie had simply mumbled, "Thanks," and reached into the fruit bowl for an apple.

Gigi had been praying for a shift precisely like this in Melanie. Now that it had arrived, though, it felt too dramatic. Too quick.

After she'd eaten half of her apple, Melanie had gotten a mug from a cabinet and filled it with coffee.

"You're drinking coffee?" Gigi had asked. *Way to state the obvious*, she thought. Melanie didn't have to be sarcastic around her; Gigi was well trained enough to do it to herself now.

"Mmm-hmm," Melanie said.

Well, she was almost sixteen. A little coffee wouldn't hurt her, Gigi thought, hiding a smile as Melanie took a sip, wrinkled her nose, and added a huge splash of cream and two heaping spoonfuls of sugar.

"Is Dad around?" Melanie asked.

"No, he and Zach went to some breakfast," Gigi said. "Rotary Club or— No, a seniors group, I think."

"Okay," Melanie said.

"Remember it's Kellie's surprise party tonight," Gigi said.

"Right," Melanie said. "Is Dad going with you?"

*Why are you suddenly so concerned about Dad's schedule?* Gigi wanted to say, but didn't. She knew exactly why.

"Yes," Gigi said. "He might get there a little late, but he's coming." She felt like she was pressing her luck, but she still asked, "So can you stay home with Julia? You know she gets nervous being alone at night."

"Won't Zach be here?" Melanie asked. "Since Dad doesn't have any events?"

"I guess so," Gigi said. "I'm not sure I'd feel comfortable asking him, though . . ."

"It's okay," Melanie said. "I'll do it." Was she smiling? Yes, that was definitely a smile. Melanie had such a beautiful smile. Her front teeth had stuck out when she'd been little, but after two and a half years in braces, they were perfect.

Oh, how she'd missed her daughter's smile.

Now Gigi looked across the room, to where Tessa was stocking the bar. "Half an hour till the birthday girl arrives," Tessa said. "Olives. Where did I put the olives?"

"What can I do?" Gigi asked.

"If you could slice some lemons it would be great," Tessa said. "I'll start on the limes once I find the olives."

"Sure," Gigi said, grabbing a cutting board and a knife. "Is Harry coming tonight?"

"He's in California," Tessa said. "Oh, here they are! Right with the maraschino cherries. Go figure, I was actually organized when I packed this stuff."

The DJ Jason had hired had already arrived and was setting up his equipment. Suddenly "Y.M.C.A." by the Village People blared out of his speakers. Gigi began shaking her hips to the beat.

"This is going to be fun," Tessa said. "I love parties."

"Me, too," Gigi agreed. "And I especially love everything about the seventies."

"Oh! We should come up with specialty drink names in honor of Kellie!" Tessa said. "Like . . . the Kellie Pickler! I can probably make a good green drink with some Midori."

"Great idea," Gigi said. Had Tessa already had a cocktail? Her cheeks were a little flushed and her eyes were bright. Normally Tessa was shy and reserved, but right now she seemed almost giddy.

"The Kelly Ripa?" Tessa was asking. "What should I put in that one? Maybe a gin and tonic with a twist."

"And the Kelly Clarkson," Gigi suggested. "It could have—"

One moment Tessa was reaching for a lime and a knife. The next, the sharp silver blade was cutting through the soft pink flesh on the tip of Tessa's index finger.

"Oh my gosh!" Gigi gasped. "Are you okay? Here." She tore a paper towel off a roll and handed it to Tessa, who was just staring at her finger.

"Tessa? Put pressure on it to stop the bleeding," Gigi said. It must've been a deep cut; blood was running down Tessa's fingers and dripping onto the floor. Gigi hoped she wouldn't need stitches.

"I hate blood," Tessa whispered, staring at the stain on the floor, just before her eyes rolled back in her head and she collapsed.

• • •

Susan had wanted to do something nice for her best friend. So she'd made an enormous batch of chili. She'd threaded strawberries and chunks of pineapple onto skewers, and had made a trio of sweet dips. She'd baked the sheet cake from scratch. She'd stayed up late the previous night cooking, but she hadn't minded losing a little sleep. With Billie Holiday singing in her kitchen, and a glass of red wine by her hand, it had felt cozy. She was showing her love for her friend through food.

She'd made all the food for Randall's fortieth birthday party, too, slow cooking ribs the way he loved them and chopping a dozen cabbages for coleslaw. She'd told him to go out golfing for the day.

"Relax," Susan had instructed, pushing him out the door. In his golf bag she'd put a new putter tied with a big red bow. Randall was a big believer in celebrating birthdays well. For her thirty-fifth, he'd picked her up at work and had whisked her away to the Bahamas for a long weekend. For Cole's fifth birthday, Randall had constructed a tree house for the backyard complete with a zip line and rope ladder before blindfolding their son and leading him outside for the surprise unveiling.

Susan had wanted to make the day special for her husband, to put the kind of thought into it that he devoted to the celebrations he planned for her. But she'd been harried, and had rushed through the cabbage-chopping and rib-basting in between returning work phone calls. Randall's mother and older sister and brother-in-law were coming to the party (his emotionally distant father was claiming he had a cold, which Susan knew would hurt Randall), and Cole was getting over a stomach bug, which had kept him out of school for two crucial days when Susan had counted on doing errands for the party. She'd had to cancel her plan to blow up old photographs of Randall, from babyhood to today, for display. She'd scaled down her menu, swapping store-bought corn bread and appetizers for homemade ones.

But somehow, she'd pulled off the preparations. It was all going to be great. Until it wasn't.

Susan's company was still relatively young. One of her new clients had hired her to do weekly check-ins on his father at a nursing home. His father was showing early signs of dementia, the client had explained in a phone call.

The client—a businessman who seemed eager to convey how important he was—ate lunch all during his phone call with Susan. He lived in Los Angeles. He was "in entertainment," he said. He was a very loud chewer.

"Just pop in and make sure he isn't hitting on the nurses,"

the client had said, chortling. "Last thing I need is a sexual harassment suit."

"Of course," Susan had said, glad he couldn't see her rolling her eyes. "We'll give your father some menu options so we can bring him meals when we visit. Something home-cooked makes a nice break now and then. And we can pick up a Kindle for him as well. The great thing about e-readers is that you can easily enlarge the font size. He can order movies on it, too."

"Sure, sure," the client had said in the slightly delayed, distracted way of a person checking emails. "Put it on the bill."

Susan had planned to visit Mr. Spivey in the nursing home for the initial visit the day before Randall's party. She always did the initial visits. But Cole's stomach bug, the mountain of ribs waiting to be cooked, and the impending visit from the in-laws—it had all conspired to devour Susan's time. Susan only had one assistant back then, a smart, competent woman named Rosa whose kids attended the same school as Cole. So she'd sent Rosa to meet Mr. Spivey instead. Technically she wasn't doing anything wrong, Susan had told herself. She hadn't promised the businessman she'd go to the initial meeting.

The day of the party, just as Susan was about to pull the warm, fragrant chocolate marble cake (Randall's favorite) from the oven, her business phone line and the doorbell had rung simultaneously. At the door were Randall's family members, minus his father. On the phone was the businessman.

"What the hell kind of scam are you running!" he'd shouted.

"I'm sorry, I— What?" Susan had said. She opened the door and gestured for Randall's family to come inside, smiling an apology.

"My father's Rolex is missing," the businessman had said. "Is that your deal? You like to steal from confused old people? Nice racket you've got going, but I will shut you down so fast—"

"Wait!" Susan had cried. She gestured for Randall's family

to make themselves comfortable, then ran upstairs to her bedroom, pulling the door shut behind her.

"Tell me exactly what happened," Susan had said. She'd been breathing hard, aware of the oven buzzer erupting one floor below, reminding her to take the cake out before it burned.

"My father's gold Rolex is missing," the businessman had said. "The woman you sent today took it."

"But you don't have any proof of that!" Susan had protested. "Your father has early-onset dementia . . . he could have put the watch in a drawer or something. I can go tomorrow and look for it. I'm sure there's a logical answer!"

"He told me you sent a Mexican. He doesn't trust Mexicans," the businessman had said, and Susan had drawn in her breath sharply.

"Rosa Gonzales is an American citizen," Susan had said. She began to tremble with anger. "She also happens to be one of the hardest-working people you could ever hope to meet!" Rosa had worked for a monstrous boss—a woman who'd paid her below the minimum wage and demanded that Rosa work twelve-hour days cooking and cleaning and caring for bratty twins—in exchange for a green card. She'd earned her citizenship two years ago. She was one of the finest women Susan knew.

"You've got until the end of today to come up with the watch or I call the cops on you," the businessman had said before slamming down the phone.

The damn watch was in a drawer, or a shoe, or under the bed. Mr. Spivey had left it somewhere. Of course it was in his room!

Susan had raced downstairs, yanked the cake out of the oven, and offered beverages to Randall's family. Then she'd smiled apologetically.

"Can you do me a huge favor?" she'd asked Randall's mother. "Could you frost the cake as soon as it cools? Everything you need is on the counter—see, the frosting's in this bowl, and the spatula is here. I have to run out and do an errand, but I'll be back in plenty of time for the party . . . Cole's upstairs watching TV . . ."

Randall's family had looked bewildered as she'd backed out the door, calling a final apology, and climbed into her car.

Twenty miles. That's how far away the nursing home was located. Susan had driven there in fourteen minutes and was pretty sure she'd be getting a ticket in the mail from a speed camera.

She'd signed in at the front desk, then run down the hallway to his room. "Mr. Spivey?" she'd said as she'd knocked on the door. "I understand you're missing a watch?"

He'd just blinked at her, a confused, sick old man in a T-shirt and faded sweatpants. His eyes had cataracts and he was very thin. Here he lay, abandoned by his family, to spend his final days among strangers. But Susan felt no pity for him, after what he'd said about Rosa.

"Mind if I take a look?" she'd asked, and didn't wait for an answer.

She'd searched through his drawers, sliding her hands in between folded shirts and slacks, squeezing to see if she could feel metal through the fabric. She checked his nightstand drawer, and under his bed. She shook out his shoes. She unrolled his socks and looked inside his medicine cabinet, then stood in the middle of the room, her index finger pressing against her lower lip.

"Let me see your wrists," she'd cried, grabbing them. They were bare.

"It's got to be here somewhere," she'd said. If she found the watch in the next five minutes, she could still make it back to the house before the guests started to arrive.

She searched the laundry hamper and trash can. She asked—ordered, really—Mr. Spivey to stand up and she looked beneath him and shook out the covers in his bed. He watched her, seemingly fascinated.

"You don't like Mexicans, huh? Let's see how you feel about a black woman tearing apart your room," she muttered, too low for him to hear, although she was tempted to raise her voice. She'd be firing him as a client tomorrow, right after she found the watch and photographed it on his wrist and texted the image to his son.

She heard her cell phone erupt with Randall's ringtone. She let it go to voice mail, then texted: Sorry, work emergency but I'm on my way home! See you in a few!

She stopped checking her own watch. She couldn't bear to see how late it was becoming. She was still wearing jeans and a sweatshirt with a streak of icing on it, her hair in a ponytail. She was a mess, but she'd have to walk into the party like this.

She finally found the watch nestled in the soap holder in the shower. He must've taken it off so it wouldn't get wet. She brought it over to Mr. Spivey, intending to shake it in his face. But he'd fallen asleep, his head tilted to one side, his mouth open. Susan had flung it onto his lap, taken the photograph, and run for her car.

She still had time! She could make it before the cutting of the cake. She'd be there for most of the party, she thought as she pulled onto the highway and stepped on the gas.

Then she saw a wall of red brake lights up ahead, as she hit a massive traffic jam.

When she'd finally walked into the party, the cake had been served, and the food was mostly gone.

"I'm so sorry," she'd told Randall. "It was a work emergency . . . and there was traffic . . ."

He'd smiled, and had told her he understood, but his eyes were cold.

Susan realized she'd been standing there in her hippie headband, lost in thought, for too long. Kellie and Jason would walk through the doors soon. She was reaching for a stack of paper plates to set beside her cake when she heard someone yell, "Help!"

Susan turned around, and saw Tessa lying limply in Gigi's arms.

●  ●  ●

"Give her air!" someone shouted as people pressed in around Gigi and Tessa.

"Should we call 911?" someone else wondered.

Tessa's eyelids fluttered a few times, then opened. "Did I faint?" she asked.

"Yes," Gigi said. She eased Tessa to the floor. "Can you sit up by yourself?"

"Give her some water," Susan instructed, and a cold bottle appeared and was thrust into Tessa's uninjured hand.

"I'm so sorry," Tessa said.

"It's okay," Susan said. "I used to faint at the sight of blood, too."

Tessa glanced at her hand, which Gigi was wrapping up in a paper towel that someone had passed to her. "That was really foolish of me," she said. She started to get up, but her legs folded beneath her and Gigi caught her again.

"Give yourself a moment," Gigi said. She put pressure on the wound and sat with Tessa for another moment, then told Tessa to close her eyes.

"I'm going to check the cut," she said. "You may need stitches."

Tessa nodded. She was still pale.

Gigi carefully unwound the bandage. She dabbed water on it, cleaning away some of the blood.

"It actually isn't too bad," she said, wrapping it up again with a fresh paper towel. "The bleeding is slowing down. You may want to get it checked out to see if you need a stitch or two, though."

"Thank you," Tessa said. "I'm sure it's fine, and I don't want to miss the party." She reached for Gigi's steadying arm and slowly stood up. She looked over to see Jenny McMahon kneeling down, cleaning the drops of blood from the floor.

"Are you okay?" Gigi asked. "You're still pretty pale."

Tessa nodded slowly, and kept staring at the blood.

# Chapter Thirty

**Newport Cove Listserv Digest**

*Re: Help Needed for Holiday Decorating Committee!
Wow, a visit by Santa and wreaths. I didn't realize every single resident of Newport Cove celebrated Christmas. —Amy Smith, Magnolia Street

*Re: Help Needed for Holiday Decorating Committee!
Guess we Jews are getting the shaft. Maybe we should form our own holiday
decorating committee? —Deborah Feinstein, Crabtree Lane

*Re: Help Needed for Holiday Decorating Committee!
Um, I hate to break it to you, but FYI there are more religions than simply Chris-
tianity and Judaism. How about a Kwanzaa Decorating Committee? A Ramadan
Decorating Committee? —Lisa Crane, Tulip Way

*Re: Help Needed for Holiday Decorating Committee!
We'll also be decorating Newport Cove with menorahs and symbols of other
religions! All suggestions and decoration donations welcome! —Sincerely,
Shannon Dockser, Newport Cove Manager

• • •

She had to tell Jason. Of course she had to tell Jason.

She watched him sip from a flute of champagne in the back of the limousine, and noticed a stain on the collar of his blue shirt. Her messy, sweet, loving husband.

She thought about him standing next to Miller in the office, the two men assessing each other. She knew she hadn't imagined the hitch in their energy, or the way they'd locked eyes for an extra beat. They seemed like different species. One tall and trim and smooth; the other—her Jason. The man she loved, but had betrayed many times over.

"Cheers," he was saying as he held out his flute. "To my beautiful wife."

She clinked her glass against his and took a sip, but her stomach twisted and she had to force herself to swallow it.

"This is nice," she said. Jason put his hand on her knee and gave it a squeeze. Her throat contracted, and she turned to look out the window so he wouldn't notice the tears flooding her eyes.

She wished she'd never gone back to work. Life had been so simple—dull, yes, but pleasantly so—before she'd met Miller. He'd opened up possibilities she hadn't known existed. The tingle of attraction that now felt as necessary as oxygen.

Jason's hand was still on her knee, steady and strong. She covered it with her own, feeling his warm, thick fingers wind between hers. She was filled with a deep sadness.

*How do I find my way back to my husband again?* she wondered, aching to know if it was possible.

Maybe it started with a confession. If she told Jason about her flirtation, the element of secrecy would be stripped away. He could hold her accountable. He wouldn't want her to continue working in the same office as Miller, and if she was going to save her marriage, she'd have to agree. Jason would force the choice she seemed unable to confront.

Maybe she'd take some time off, and go to couples therapy with Jason. She would make him special dinners and give him back rubs and curl up against him at night. Fake it till you make it, wasn't that the saying?

Jason might look at her differently, though. She would no longer be his golden girl. There might be confusion, or worse, hurt, in his eyes. The next time that blonde came into the hardware store and hung on his arm, he might smile down at the woman and move in closer.

Jason could decide he didn't want her anymore. He could leave.

But she deserved whatever was coming, Kellie thought, remembering the nights she'd imagined Miller while she'd been making love with Jason, the lies she'd told, the way she'd compared the two men and had found Jason wanting. She gulped the rest of her champagne, shuddered, and turned to Jason. He was texting on his cell phone; probably checking in with his mother to see how the kids were doing.

"Honey," she began in a trembling voice. She bit her lower lip hard so the burst of pain would hold back her tears.

Jason looked up quickly. "What is it?" he asked, a look of concern spreading across his face. His kind, dear face.

She'd seen Jason cry a few times before—in joy when their children were born, in sorrow when the black Lab he'd had since the age of twelve had died—but her behavior had never been the source of his tears. He'd planned this beautiful night for them to reconnect as a couple; of course he knew something was wrong. He was fighting for their marriage, and she needed to do the same.

"Kell?" he asked.

She shook her head.

"What is it?" he asked again.

"I'm sorry," she said. "I'm so sorry." She tightened her grip on his hand. "The guy in my office, the one you met today—"

"Miller," Jason interjected. "The tall one."

Kellie nodded. "I didn't sleep with him—" she blurted.

"*What?*" Jason jerked his hand away from hers.

"Oh God, I mean, I didn't— I didn't do *anything* with him," she said. "I didn't even kiss him!"

Jason was looking at her with something akin to horror. "Why are you telling me this?"

Kellie swallowed hard. "I had a crush on him . . . more than a crush. We became friends but then I started to feel something more . . ."

Her voice trailed off.

"You're in love with him?" Jason asked. His brow furrowed. "Is that what you're saying?"

"No!" Kellie cried. "I don't know—I'm just so confused, Jason. Please, don't be mad. I thought you knew . . . the way you looked at him when you came into the office . . ."

"I knew something was up," Jason said. His face looked different now. He was clenching his jaw and his eyes were narrowed. She'd thought he'd be hurt, but he wasn't. He was angry—no, furious—another emotion she'd rarely seen him display.

"All those new clothes you bought," he said. "The way you haven't wanted to be with me . . ."

She'd thought Jason didn't see her anymore, but he did. He'd noticed everything.

"It wasn't you!" she blurted. "It wasn't anything you did . . . I've just been at home for so long, raising the kids. I kind of lost myself. And then when someone looked at me as if I was an attractive woman . . ."

"You're saying I don't look at you that way?" Jason asked, leaning back from her. She should have thought this through; everything she said was making it worse.

"You do, you're wonderful," she said. "It wasn't about us."

He gave a little laugh that sounded more like a bark. "Like hell it wasn't."

"Jason, I'm so sorry," she said. Her heart was pounding so loudly it seemed to be invading her mind, making it impossible to gather her thoughts. Why had she told Jason? "I want to stop it," she finally said. "I don't want to be with Miller."

"You need to tell me exactly what's going on," he said. "You didn't fuck him?"

Kellie winced at the harsh word, but shook her head. "I swear."

He exhaled a measured breath. "Did you ever see him outside the office?" he asked.

She wanted to lie, but she nodded. "We went to scout houses a few times and had coffee sometimes."

His eyes were so hard! They were no longer Jason's eyes; she didn't recognize them.

"Anything else?" he asked. "You better tell me it all now."

She dropped her gaze from his. "Once he came to a bar when I was out with the girls, and we danced, but that was it."

"You brought him out with your friends?" Jason's tone was dangerously calm.

"I'm sorry," she whispered. She started to reach for him, then withdrew her hand. "You knew something was wrong, didn't you? That's why you planned tonight . . . to reconnect. And I want to do the same."

"No," he said. "That isn't why I planned tonight. I didn't ever think you'd ever do something like this. Fall for some jackass in a nice suit."

He wasn't even looking at her now. He was staring out the window, his body rigid.

She'd made an enormous mistake. She should've pulled away from Miller. She was a coward who'd expected her husband to save their marriage when she was the one who should've found the courage to do so.

The limousine pulled to a stop and the driver got out and opened the back door. Kellie thought Jason might ask him to just take them home, to cut the night short, but instead, he got out without looking at her.

"Where are we?" she asked. She looked out the window and saw the community center where Mia had taken dance classes as a young girl and where Gigi taught occasional art classes. "Is something going on here?"

He nodded, and began to walk ahead without waiting for her. "Guess we're both getting surprised tonight," he said over his shoulder.

• • •

Gigi finished setting up the bar, stealing another sidelong glance at Tessa, whose finger was now properly bandaged, thanks to the mini first aid kit Susan kept in the trunk of her car.

*We all have secrets*, Gigi thought. Even Melanie, at the tender age of fifteen, had an internal life that she closely guarded. Julia would probably follow suit. The dozens of women Gigi passed every day—the women peering at the covers of tabloids in the grocery store checkout lane, and waiting in line with a preoccupied gaze at the bank, and putting on lipstick at the red light in the next car over in traffic—were all holders of mysteries.

Susan was affixing a silver banner with the embossed words "Happy Birthday" to a wall with tape, and someone had dimmed the lights. Dozens of guests had arrived by now. John Lennon glasses and short floral dresses and disco shirts abounded.

Gigi felt an arm wrap around her waist as lips touched against the back of her neck.

"Be careful," she said. "My husband's going to be here any minute." She felt the rumble of a chuckle against her back. Before she could twist around to kiss Joe, her cell phone buzzed and she dug in her pocket to pull it out. Jason had promised to send an alert when he and Kellie were en route.

His text read: 10 min.

"They're coming!" Gigi shouted. The lights were dimmed, the music was shut off, and everyone crowded behind the bar to hide.

"Think she'll be surprised?" someone asked.

# Chapter Thirty-One

WHATEVER YOU WERE THE most desperate to escape from always caught up to you, Tessa realized as she crouched behind the bar and stared at her still-throbbing finger. Wasn't that the way it worked in nightmares and horror movies? You turned a corner and ran straight into the killer. You pulled back the shower curtain to see a ghoulish face staring at you. You hid in the basement and heard the stairs creak as someone moved closer, ever closer.

Tessa could feel her past stalking her now, its breath hot on her neck, its jagged fingernails clawing at her.

The police knew. Of course they knew! She and Harry hadn't been very good under questioning. The investigators were circling again. They'd find traces of blood on the kitchen floor. DNA testing could link it to Danny.

The blood. The floor. That night.

The man to Tessa's left jostled her arm and whispered an apology, and someone else began to giggle, but Tessa's mind was drifting across the miles, spinning back in time.

It had started with the uniforms.

"Would you parents mind bringing the boys by my house to pick them up?" Danny had asked at the end of a meeting, smiling his broad smile. "I coach two Young Ranger groups, so there's a lot to hand out . . . shorts and shirts and caps and sashes. Oh, and I have some samples of things like binoculars and water canteens from the group's catalog, in case anyone would like to order those."

So Tessa had brought Addison, her precious son—her baby—to Danny's house, and because she'd gotten a phone call from the pediatrician about Bree's allergies just as she'd pulled into the driveway, she'd sat there and taken the call.

The pediatrician was busy. Tessa had been waiting two days to talk to her. She had to take the call.

She'd looked up at the house, a redbrick Colonial with a basketball hoop in the driveway. Danny's sons must have played; it was probably left over from when they'd lived here. It was sweet that he still kept the hoop up; maybe he encouraged the neighborhood kids to use it, she'd thought.

"Go ahead, I'll be there in a minute," she whispered, and Addison had opened the car door and slid out and gone to knock on Danny's door. When it opened, Tessa had gestured to the phone and made an apologetic face.

Danny had waved and smiled. *No problem*, he'd mouthed.

And then the door had shut, sealing Addison inside. Tessa had expected Addison to grab a uniform and come right back out, but even though the pediatrician had to put her on hold for a minute to take an urgent call, the front door didn't open. Finally, Addison appeared, wearing the uniform, his clothes bunched up under his arm.

"Everything okay?" Tessa had whispered. Addison had given her the thumbs-up.

And Tessa, the woman who could sniff out a threat even when it didn't exist, had turned her focus back to her phone call, completely oblivious to the danger engulfing her son like a dark fog.

· · ·

"I shouldn't have told him," Kellie said.

She was standing in the bathroom, her shoulders still heaving from the last of her sobs. She'd burst into tears when everyone had leaped up and shouted, "Surprise!" and although she'd tried to play off her reaction as tears of joy, Susan and Gigi had instantly known. Girlfriends always knew.

They'd whisked her away, saying they needed to get her into a costume. Kellie wouldn't be missed for a few minutes; Gigi could hear the Bee Gees wailing over the speakers and the sounds of bottles clinking and laughter filling the room.

"You were right," Kellie was saying as she looked up at Susan. She'd told them about her limousine confession, and Jason's reaction. "What you sensed that night, it was real . . . I told Miller we were at the bar because I hoped he'd show up."

Susan's lips tightened slightly, but she only nodded.

"Here," Gigi said, holding out bell-bottoms and a tunic. "Try these on."

Kellie blew her nose into a tissue, but didn't reach for the clothes.

"Come on, honey," Gigi said. "Jason went to all this work planning the party. And your kids are here with your in-laws and parents. You need to get through tonight, then we'll come up with a plan."

Kellie rubbed her index fingers beneath her eyes, removing the specks of mascara she'd loosened by crying. "Okay," she said. She pulled off her dress and slipped into the pants and shirt.

"Let me put some eyeliner and lipstick on you," Gigi said. "Maybe a little powder, too. Then you'll be ready to go back out."

She pulled a smoky black liner from her purse and steadied Kellie's chin in her hand. Kellie's eyes were red and watery.

"Do you have Visine?" Gigi asked.

"I think so," Susan said, opening her purse.

"Is he going to leave me, Gigi?" Kellie asked, then shut her eyes.

Gigi used her pinky to brush away the tear slowly rolling down her friend's left cheek, then she drew on a thick layer of liner, winging it up a bit at the outer edge.

"No," she said.

"How can you be so sure?" Kellie asked.

"Because he loves you," Gigi said as she moved on to the other eyelid. "You hurt him, Kellie, but he'll forgive you."

"I don't deserve him," Kellie said. Gigi had been about to dab on some pink lipstick, but she stilled her hand when she saw Kellie's lips tremble. "I'm not even thinking about Miller right now. I was so sure giving him up would be awful . . . but if I lose Jason, lose our family . . ."

Susan moved in with a filmy scarf and wound it around Kellie's hair, securing it like a headband and smoothing errant blond strands into place. Forgiveness imbued her gentle gesture.

"But I had to tell him," Kellie said. "It would always be between us. I'd always know."

"It was eating away at you," Susan said.

*Yes*, Gigi thought as she powdered Kellie's reddened nose and cheeks, *dangerous secrets are as corrosive as acid.* She thought of Zach's finger slowly stroking the file, like he was petting a cat.

"Ready, Kellie?" she asked.

Kellie nodded.

Susan opened the door to the bathroom, and Kellie stepped out. Gigi could see Jason standing by the bar, chatting with a few guests. He turned to look at Kellie, and in his face Gigi saw intermingled pain and anger and yes, love, too.

*Forgive her*, she thought.

• • •

Kellie was holding it together. She'd danced a few times— once in a loose circle with Jason and her kids, though Jason kept a physical distance between them—and she'd blown out her birthday candles. Susan knew exactly what she was wishing for.

Now the children were gone, the lights were lower, and the dancing was more enthusiastic. Frank Fitzgibbons wore a white silk shirt unbuttoned halfway down his chest, doing a credible imitation of John Travolta's *Saturday Night Fever* routine.

Susan cut him a wide berth and wandered over to the food table, realizing she hadn't eaten yet. She took a little paper bowl and was reaching for the chili spoon when her hand collided with another.

"Sorry," she heard a man say. "You go ahead, I'm just coming back for thirds. That's the best chili I've ever eaten."

She turned and found herself looking up at a tall man she'd never before seen. A very tall man. He had to be six foot three. Oh, Randall would hate that.

No, she told herself. All roads could no longer lead to Randall.

"Thank you," Susan said. "I'm glad you like it."

"You made it?" the man asked. His voice was deep and rich, his nose was wide and strong, and his eyes were deepset. There was a little crescent scar on his chin. She wondered about the story behind it. About the stories that composed him.

No wedding ring, she saw.

He was probably gay. He was handsome and fit and seemingly unattached.

"I did," Susan said.

"I'd love the recipe," he said.

She felt her shoulders slump. Of course he was gay.

"Sure," she said. "You like to cook?"

Was he blushing?

"I'm, ah, trying to learn," he said. "My ex—she was the cook in our relationship."

"Oh," Susan said. She could recite the recipe off the top of her head, then go join her friends on the dance floor. She should probably check on Kellie, and give Jason a hug. And Cole was at home with a new babysitter; she needed to call and check in.

Instead she took a deep breath, then spoke two simple words, words she'd said thousands of times before, that made her feel as shaky as if she were poised at the top of the first big hill on a roller coaster.

"I'm Susan," she said, and reminded herself to smile.

# Chapter Thirty-Two

**Newport Cove Listserv Digest**

*No Parking Signs
It has been brought to the Newport Cove Manager's attention that some residents have been posting large, professional-looking signs reading "No Parking" on trees that line the curbs in front of their homes. A pleasant reminder that the trees are the property of Newport Cove and all signs need to be removed promptly. Thank you! —Sincerely, Shannon Dockser, Newport Cove Manager

• • •

"A few more months until the election," Joe said as they drove home. "Roughly a thousand hands to shake—need more Purell—and forty Rotary Club meetings . . . and church spaghetti suppers . . . and a junior high school Bake-Off to attend."

"Seriously? A school Bake-Off?" Gigi asked.

"Lots of voting parents will be there," Joe said. "Soccer moms. One of my key demographics." He sighed and eased off his shoes and adjusted the passenger's seat, tilting it back

a few more degrees. Gigi had only consumed a single glass
of wine, while Joe had indulged in a couple of vodka Jell-O
shooters, so she was behind the wheel.

"You're tired," Gigi said. "I'm glad we left early."

"Yeah," Joe said. He reached over and slid a hand beneath
her skirt, running it up her thigh, as she turned down their
street. "Not too tired, though."

She smiled. "Think the girls are asleep?"

"They better be, it's almost midnight," Joe said. He yawned.
"Fun party. Kellie seemed really surprised."

"She was," Gigi said. She debated telling Joe more, but decided against it. He had enough on his mind.

Joe withdrew his hand and closed his eyes as she drove
toward home, slowly and steadily, gliding to stops, just as she
had when the girls were babies and she'd put them to sleep
by driving in endless loops at naptime. The circles under Joe's
eyes were darkening; he could use a catnap.

She'd forgotten to call home and check on Melanie and
Julia. She'd meant to do so around ten, to make sure Julia was
in bed. But Kellie had caught her eye just as Gigi had been
reaching for her phone, and gestured toward the bathroom.

"Jason won't talk to me," Kellie had said, her voice quavering.
"Every time I go to stand near him, he moves away. Someone
tried to get a picture of us and he put his arm behind me but
he didn't touch me. What have I done? I've destroyed our life!"

"Just get through the night," Gigi had advised. "Don't drink
anything. Give Jason a little space."

"Okay," Kellie had said, but then she'd begun to cry again,
and by then, Gigi had forgotten all about her phone call.

She turned down their street, smiling as she noticed two
large NO PARKING signs affixed to the trees in front of Mason
Gamerman's house. She coasted into her driveway, tapping the
brakes and killing the engine. Joe was sound asleep now; she
hated to wake him.

She turned off the headlights and stayed in the driveway.

The night was cold, but the car felt stuffy, so she cracked open the door for a little air. She could hear Felix barking.

Gigi frowned. They never let Felix out after ten, by agreement with the neighbors who lived behind them, because his barking had awoken their children once. She glanced at Joe, then slid out of the car and headed for the backyard.

Felix was by the fence, still barking.

"Shh," Gigi commanded, grabbing his collar. He gave one last bark, as if to prove he was in charge, before allowing himself to be led away.

Gigi guided him up the steps to the deck, to the sliding glass doors that led to the living room. Then she stopped.

The living room was illuminated only by the blue light of the television. She could see two figures on the couch. She could only make out the general forms, but one of them looked too big to be Julia, who was small for her age. Melanie and . . . Raven? Maybe they were back together again.

She lifted a hand to shield her eyes; the back porch light was shining into her face, obscuring her vision. The figures on the couch weren't moving, and Melanie and whoever she was with were both upright—thank God—but they were close together. Too close?

Felix gave a loud bark, startling Gigi. She looked down and gave his collar a little tug to shush him, and when she looked back up, Melanie was pulling open the door.

"Mom!" she said. "What are you doing out here?"

"Felix was barking," Gigi said.

Melanie shouldn't have had a guest over without permission, but she wasn't going to lecture her daughter, not now. She'd ask Raven or whoever it was to leave, then she'd talk to Melanie. This time there would be consequences. Maybe she'd lose her computer for a week.

But when Gigi's eyes adjusted to the dim light and the tall form standing up from the couch took shape, she realized it wasn't Raven.

It was Zach.

"Hi, Mrs. Kennedy," he said.

Gigi locked eyes with him. How close had he been sitting to Melanie on the couch? She thought she had an impression of his arm being slung over the back of it, behind Melanie but not touching her. She couldn't be sure, though.

And Zach's clear blue gaze revealed no guilt or fear. He looked . . . bemused.

"It's late," Gigi said, her tone delivering an unmistakable message.

Zach nodded. "I was about to get Felix, sorry about that. Well, now that you're home I'll head to bed."

He exited the room, his hips slim in faded jeans, the definition in his arms showing through his plain black T-shirt. Of course Melanie wouldn't be able to resist his attention.

But why was Zach giving it to her?

Gigi turned to her daughter, wanting to ask a question but not knowing how to phrase it. She and Joe had invited Zach into their home. She couldn't fault Melanie for watching a movie with him.

Melanie yawned and stretched her arms over her head. "I'm tired," she said. She stood up, walked out of the room, and headed upstairs. But not before Gigi saw the smile that had flitted across her daughter's face. A small, involuntary smile. The kind girls gave when they had a secret.

*Take ten deep breaths*, Gigi instructed herself. It was the advice a therapist had once given her, after she'd sought an appointment following the shoplifting arrest.

Ten deep breaths would force your body to calm itself. It would help quash rash impulses, and prevent rage-fueled words from pouring out of your body. Gigi shut her eyes and breathed.

Ten exhalations later, she opened her eyes.

She headed for the front door, to go wake up Joe and let him know that if his slimy, soulless campaign director touched her baby, she'd kill him.

# Chapter Thirty-Three

*Before Newport Cove*

TESSA HAD BEEN EASING a handful of pasta into a pot of boiling water when Addison spoke up. It was a warm, lazy weekend evening, and her body felt loose and relaxed from the first Zumba class she'd taken that afternoon. Pasta, a glass of wine, the kids sleeping through the night—life looked pretty good at the moment.

"I wonder if I'm taller than Jacob," Addison had said.

He'd been sitting at the kitchen table, playing a handheld Nintendo DS game, his thumbs moving quickly.

"I dunno," Tessa had said. Shoot, she'd forgotten to buy lettuce at the store, so they wouldn't have salad. She checked the vegetable bin and decided to cut up carrots and celery instead.

"I'm going to ask Danny," Addison had continued.

"Ask him what?" Tessa had said.

"Whose are longer," Addison had said. "He checked our legs."

"Danny checked your legs?" Tessa had asked. "At Young Rangers?" She didn't recall seeing it, though she could have been chatting with another parent.

"No, at his house," Addison had said. He slid off his stool and wandered toward the living room, still intent on his game. "He said mine felt really strong, so he gave me a special hug."

Tessa had stared after him as he flopped on the couch, then she'd turned down the water on the pasta and followed him.

"Addison?" she'd said. "Can you put that down for a minute?"

"One sec," he'd said.

"What kind of special hug?" Tessa had asked.

"Huh?" Addison had said, his focus on the game.

"Addison, what kind of special hug did Danny give you?"

"An extralong one," Addison had said.

Tessa had frowned. "Why did he check your legs?" she'd asked.

"To see if my uniform fit," Addison had mumbled, his eyes still on the screen.

She'd felt that icy stirring again, the prickling in her chest, just as she had that day with the nanny, and on the afternoon in the park . . .

But she'd been wrong before.

"Addison," she'd said. She'd knelt down in front of him and removed his game, shushing his protests. "You can have this back in a minute. Show me how he did it."

Addison had sighed and stood up from the couch. As Tessa had stared, feeling oddly immobile, Addison had reached down and demonstrated what Danny Briggs had done, tracing a slow line with the palm of his hand along the inseam of his pants, from his ankle up to his groin.

"Can I have my game now?" Addison had asked, dropping back onto the couch.

# Chapter Thirty-Four

KELLIE LAY IN BED, listening to the sounds of Jason brushing his teeth through the partially opened bathroom door. He hadn't spoken to her the whole ride home, not when she'd thanked him for throwing the party, not when she'd whispered, "I'm sorry."

She could hear the water turning on, and Jason gargling, a noise that used to bother her. How many times had she called to him to shut the door—earlier on in the marriage in a joking voice, but lately in one that didn't disguise her irritation? She didn't deserve him.

Maybe she should touch his shoulder when he came to bed, or try to hug him. Gigi had told her to give Jason time, but Kellie worried it would increase the distance between them.

She glanced at the shirt he'd left on the floor. She could still make out the faint stain on the collar. She got out of bed, smoothed it out, and hung it in the closet.

The bathroom door was opening. Kellie's stomach muscles tensed.

Jason wore a T-shirt and athletic shorts, instead of the boxers he usually slept in. His face seemed to have settled into permanent hard lines in the space of the past few hours. He walked over toward her and for one heart-lifting moment, Kellie thought he was reaching for her. But he just grabbed a pillow and left the room, shutting the door behind him. Closing it like a soft slap.

She collapsed onto Jason's side of the bed. It smelled like him. She breathed in deeply and curled up in a ball, knowing she wouldn't sleep tonight. She should be the one to sleep on the couch, but she didn't want to bother Jason by asking him if he wanted to switch. She'd try to talk to him tomorrow. She'd offer to set up counseling, to quit her job. She'd do anything.

She lay there, staring into the darkness, feeling her body ache as if with the flu. When she turned her head a little later, her eyes had adjusted enough to the dark for her to make out the framed wedding photo on Jason's nightstand. In it she was staring at the camera, smiling broadly. Jason was looking at her, not smiling, but with an expression so tender it made fresh tears roll from her aching eyes.

Their wedding day had been so wonderful. It hadn't been fancy; there wasn't enough money for an elaborate reception. But Kellie had worn a poufy white princess gown—if a girl couldn't wear a big dress on her wedding day, when could she?—with flowers woven through her hair. Jason had rented a tux, the only time she'd ever seen him in one. He'd been so young and handsome. He'd started crying when she'd begun to walk down the aisle, and his tears had set off her own. When she'd finally reached him, he'd leaned down to kiss her, and she'd wound her arms around his neck, then they'd both burst into laughter, realizing they were supposed to wait until after the ceremony. The guests had all laughed, too.

They'd danced at the reception, with Kellie waltzing with Jason's father while Jason twirled around her mother, then Kellie was passed around by Jason's groomsmen while he danced with her sister and bridesmaids, but they always found their way back to each other at the end of every song. They'd been so busy with their guests that they'd forgotten to eat dinner, but Jason's mother had brought along a picnic basket and packed up leftovers for them to take to the hotel. They'd gobbled down pasta and salad while sitting cross-legged on the bed, then Jason had moved away the plates and silverware and had pulled Kellie to her feet, for one final, slow dance with no music.

How had she thrown that love away? Kellie rolled over in bed, holding Jason's pillow against her chest, wondering if he was awake one floor below her, too.

As dawn approached, she realized it was the first time in recent memory that she had gone hours without thinking about Miller at all.

• • •

Susan awoke to weak sunlight streaming in through her bedroom window. She knew immediately she'd overslept; usually she arose by seven. But it had been a late night. A strange night. Plus she'd had three cocktails, which her mild headache reminded her was unusual. And Cole was at Randall's, so there wasn't any need to get out of bed.

She never lazed around in the morning, though. Then it would be too easy to think. Better to head directly to the shower, to get on with the day, to start moving and never stop.

She stretched her arms over her head and conjured up an image of Peter from the party. His intent eyes, slightly receding hairline, and lanky frame. Last night had marked the first time since her separation that she'd found a man attractive. And Peter had asked for her phone number, which she'd written down on a little piece of paper from the Moleskine notebook in her purse. "Do you like Mexican food?" he'd asked, and she'd nodded, feeling her mouth dry up as shyness had overtaken her.

She was curious about how Kellie and Jason knew Peter, but she couldn't call and ask. Kellie had far too much to deal with today. Her mind flashed to the memory of Kellie leaving the party, trailing Jason as he marched ahead to the limo.

Susan heard a little whine and looked down to see Sparky's pleading eyes.

"You need to go out," she said. "Sorry, boy."

She got up and slipped on jeans and a long-sleeved cotton shirt, then swallowed an Advil and a long drink of water before brushing her teeth and splashing cold water on her face. She found Sparky's leash and hooked it on, then put on her shoes and coat and headed out the door.

It had been relatively simple to meet guys at age twenty-two, even though she hadn't gone on many dates before marrying Randall, she thought as Sparky sniffed a bush in her front yard. A few movies and dinners, one serious boyfriend during her sophomore and junior years of college, another during the summer after graduation.

Now, though, dating seemed fraught with peril, as treacherous as scaling Everest without supplemental oxygen. Life was so much more complicated! What if Peter hated kids? What if he had a psycho ex? What if she got all dressed up and went out with him, feeling the faint stirrings of hope as she had last night, only to learn that he was actually still married?

It seemed impossible that she'd ever find another man who did the small, sweet things Randall had done for her, like packing snacks for her to bring to work while she was pregnant. He'd filled Ziploc bags with cut-up carrots and pita chips. He'd checked the tires on her car every month to make sure the tread was still safe. He'd fallen asleep with his hand curved around her belly.

How would it feel to roll over in the middle of the night and reach for a warm body, to feel strong arms slide around her again? To watch from the doorway and laugh as someone else danced across the cold winter sidewalk on bare feet to retrieve the newspaper?

For a moment she let herself sink into the fantasy.

But instead of hopeful, it made her feel unsettled. Her life right now, while not joyous, wasn't unhappy. It was . . . under control, not like in those raw, roiling months after Randall had first left, when tears would pour from her eyes in the strangest of places: at the ATM machine, the dog groomer's, the swimming pool between laps.

She'd ensconced her heart in Bubble Wrap, and her grief had slowly ebbed away, like a dropped oar drifting from a rowboat. The ache of losing Randall still consumed her, but most of the time it was a low, steady throb. Only occasionally did it erupt into breath-stealing pain.

She knew how Mr. Brannon felt, sitting in his room at the nursing home, looking at the imprint of his son's hand, forever captured in a block of concrete. Sometimes the future you yearned for was forever lost to you.

But her life was . . . manageable now. In order. If she started to date, everything would change. And her heart, her poor, bruised heart, would be at risk once more.

She felt almost angry at Peter, for asking her out, for awakening long-dormant feelings in her. Yes, she wanted to love and be loved again. But she didn't have time to date. She was a single mom, she ran a business, she had a house to take care of . . . Sparky was looking at her, his head cocked.

"Yeah," she said, kneeling down to scratch his ears. "Excuses, excuses."

Sparky tugged the end of the leash, and she forced herself to take a step, then another. They'd go for a long walk, then she'd eat a light breakfast—scrambled eggs with bell peppers, maybe—then she'd text Randall to see when he'd be bringing Cole home. She had to do laundry, and unload the dishwasher, and maybe she and Cole could have popcorn and movie night . . . Okay, so her life wasn't all that glamorous.

But if Peter or someone like him became part of it . . . Oh, to have Cole on one side of her on the couch, and Peter on the other, while they laughed at a movie together. To feel a big hand wrap around hers, and to sense the warmth of a strong leg as it rested an inch or two away. To climb the stairs with someone at night, knowing that if she awoke at three a.m., she'd see the reassuring outline of another form under the covers next to her.

She shook her head. It was a little soon to be shopping for a wedding dress. She'd have a margarita and some nachos with the guy.

That was, if he even called.

• • •

## Before Newport Cove

Tessa hadn't reacted to Addison's revelation immediately. She'd gone back into the kitchen, pulled the carrots and celery out of the vegetable bin, and had begun to slice them as she re-played her son's words over and over in her mind.

Could there be a simple explanation?

There could, of course. She was just at a loss to come up with one.

The prickly sensation she'd felt all over her skin—the same warning system that had failed her before—hadn't subsided.

She'd reached for a bottle of wine to pour a glass, then pushed it away. She'd tell Harry as soon as he got home. Her logical, left-brain husband would weigh the information and come up with a conclusion.

Addison was safe, and there wasn't a Young Rangers meet-ing for another few days. She'd proceed cautiously this time. After all, this wasn't like making some accusation against a stranger in the park or a nanny she didn't know very well.

This was Danny Briggs, the tireless leader, the man kids and parents alike adored.

The more she thought about it, the more Tessa convinced herself there had to be an innocent explanation.

# Chapter Thirty-Five

SHE WAS AFRAID TO go downstairs. She didn't know what she'd find. Would Jason be at the breakfast table, drinking coffee and reading the sports page? Maybe he'd greet her by saying "Good morning"—although a curt nod seemed more likely—and indicate he was ready to talk.

Maybe he wouldn't be there at all.

Kellie strained to hear the clatter of silverware or the gurgle of the coffeepot, but she couldn't make out a thing.

The kids were still asleep, so she'd better face her husband now. She didn't bother changing out of her nightshirt or checking the mirror. She knew she looked horrible, with her eyes puffy from crying and her face drawn from lack of sleep, but she didn't care. For Miller, she'd always made an effort to look her best. New clothes, makeup freshly applied, hair curled . . . But that was a façade. Jason had seen her with the stomach flu, and with her face covered in a bumpy red rash from an allergic reaction to a skin cream, and even with a perm that had fried her hair and turned it an orangish shade when she was just nineteen. None of it had mattered to him.

Kellie checked the living room first. The blanket Jason had used was at the end of the couch, his pillow resting on top.

The blanket wasn't folded neatly, of course. It was a lumpy bundle, with its ends flopping out. Kellie's eyes pricked with tears at the sight of it.

She went into the kitchen and there he was. But he wasn't reading the sports page; he was just sitting at the table.

"Hi," she said.

He turned to look at her.

"Can I make you some coffee?" she asked.

He shook his head. Was he going to speak to her at all?

She took the chair opposite his. "I am so sorry," she began. "Nothing happened . . . nothing physical at all—"

Jason cut her off: "You said that last night."

"What do you want to know?" Kellie asked. "I'll tell you anything . . . Jason, it was a crush that got out of hand, that was all . . . It was so wrong of me."

His posture was rigid. He was furious, but hurt and scared, too, Kellie realized. If she could just touch him, and hug him, and let him know how terribly sorry she was . . . She stretched out her hand. Jason closed his eyes, then opened them.

"Can I hug you?" Kellie whispered. "Please."

She could see his face soften. He was going to say yes. They were going to be okay. She would hold on tight, and tell him a million times how sorry she was . . .

She was aware of an electronic ping, but it didn't register that it was coming from inside her purse until Jason's head whipped around and he stared at her bag on the counter, just a few feet away from them.

"Sounds like you're getting a text," he said. "Shouldn't you check it?"

"Jason," she said, her voice breaking. "Please . . ."

"No, it could be work," he said. "Could be important. Check it. Here." He stood up and reached for her purse and handed it to her, but he didn't move away. He loomed over her, waiting.

She reached into her bag for her phone, praying it was a client, Susan, anyone . . . but she knew even before she saw the text that it would be Miller.

Up for scouting houses today, beautiful?

She kept her eyes on the screen for too long, because she couldn't bear to look up at Jason.

"Is it from your boyfriend?" he asked.

"It's from Miller," Kellie said, her mouth twisting around the words.

Jason held out his hand and Kellie gave him the phone.

He glanced down at it, then his fist closed around her phone and Kellie thought he might hurl it against the wall. He wanted to; she could tell.

"You should go out with him," he said. "Sounds like fun."

"Jason," Kellie said. "Please . . . I'll text back and ask him to not ever contact me again, if that's what you want."

"If that's what I want?" Jason's laugh was incredulous. "This guy hits on my wife, destroys our family . . . Uh, yeah, Kell, it's probably a good idea to stop dating him, don't you think?"

*Destroys our family?*

Panic swelled within Kellie. Jason couldn't leave her; she didn't know how to live without him!

"How often do you guys text each other?" Jason asked. "Every day? Every night? Good thing you put that passcode on your phone."

His voice was laced with sarcasm. No, worse—contempt.

"Tell me what to do," she begged. "I'll do anything you want."

She stretched out her hand, but he yanked his back, out of her reach.

"You can't give me what I want," he said.

"I know," she said. "You want this never to have happened. I do, too, Jason. I wish I'd never met him. I wish I wasn't so . . . so weak. It was just about me, my ego. I felt like I was getting older, and was just this frumpy mom . . . and I know you never saw me that way, but I felt it . . ."

Jason started to hand her back her phone, but he gave it a

little toss at the last second so she had to catch it. Probably because he didn't want to risk having their fingers touch.

"Tell me what to do," she said again. Her nose was running and she grabbed a napkin from the dispenser on the table and wiped it. "Please let me try to fix this."

When he spoke again, the contempt was gone from his voice, replaced by sadness, which felt so much worse.

"I don't know if you can," he said. He stood up. "I'm going to take a shower."

Then he left the room.

Kellie looked down at her phone, wondering if she should reply and tell Miller there would be no more outings together. She stood up, feeling a weariness that had nothing to do with lack of sleep, and put on the coffee. She had no appetite, but she'd make waffles for the kids and leave an extra one for Jason, just in case. She'd warm the syrup, and make fresh-squeezed juice, if there were enough oranges.

A few minutes later Kellie heard Mia yelling at Noah to get out of her room, and she stopped stirring the waffle batter and hurried upstairs, to smooth over the squabble, to get the kids dressed and downstairs. Jason would see them all in the kitchen, eating breakfast, a chair waiting for him. He'd have to stay.

He couldn't just . . . leave. Could he?

•  •  •

"Mom? Can we go shopping today?"

Gigi was stirring oatmeal at the stove, and her hand actually froze at the words, before she consciously directed it to begin moving in slow circles again.

Melanie wanted to spend the day with her. Shopping. The two of them, together. It was such a normal mother-daughter activity.

She couldn't overreact, Gigi warned herself, aware that she was acting like a girl who'd been asked to the prom by the star football player.

"Sure," she said. "Where do you want to go?"

"Just the mall," Melanie said. "Thanks." She came up behind Gigi and peered in the pot. "Smells good."

"Help yourself," Gigi said. She hid her smile as she moved away from the pot, to gather bowls and spoons. Julia had spent the night at a friend's house, and wasn't due to be picked up until early afternoon, since she and her pal were working on a science project together and had planned to devote the morning to it.

It would be just Gigi and Melanie today, as it had been so many years ago, when the two of them had been inseparable.

• • •

Two hours later, Gigi was on a chair outside a dressing room, checking the messages on her phone. Campaign duties beckoned, but she ignored them. Melanie had disappeared into the room with an armful of clothes. At first Gigi had been hesitant, holding back while Melanie considered various items, not wanting to annoy her daughter and shatter their newfound peace.

But Melanie drew her in: "What do you think about this?" she'd asked, holding up a blouse. So Gigi began to give her opinion: "It's a bit dark for you. Try this green one instead?"

By the time they'd made it through the store, Melanie seemed to have chipped away at the wall she'd erected between her and her mother during the preceding months. They'd even laughed when they spotted a mannequin posed in such a way as to look as if she were spanking the butt of another mannequin.

"Is that intentional?" Gigi had asked.

Melanie had shrugged. "Funny either way," she'd said.

Coffee, Gigi decided as she checked the messages on her phone. She'd suggest the two of them take a little break and get lattes—the decadent kind, with chocolate syrup and sprinkles—before hitting the next store. Maybe they'd get salads for lunch, too.

Julia had texted that she wouldn't be done working until three, so there was plenty of time.

"Mom?" Melanie said. Gigi blinked and looked up. "Oh, honey," she said. Melanie's dark hair was loose and wavy, and the green, peasant-style blouse Gigi had picked out left her smooth shoulders bare and flattered her figure. "I love it," Gigi said. "Let's buy it."

Melanie checked the price tag. "It isn't that much," she said. "Forty dollars. I have some of my birthday money, so—"

"My treat," Gigi interrupted. She'd taken Julia shopping a few weeks earlier but she hadn't bought any clothes for Melanie, save for a few pairs of jeans and some sweatshirts, in more than a year. This wasn't spoiling a daughter; this was a treat for a mother.

Melanie smiled. "Really? Thanks!" She twisted around to check her reflection in the mirror.

"Go try on the other stuff," Gigi said. "Bright colors look great on you."

"Okay," Melanie said, and she disappeared back into the dressing room.

All those hours of worrying, all those fights . . . It was as if time had reversed itself, and she and Melanie were a team again.

Gigi sank lower into the chair and exhaled deeply for what felt like the first time in months. It was incredible, she thought, how everything could change overnight.

• • •

Susan stared at her computer screen, willing the images to disappear.

Facebook stalking wasn't something she was proud of—and she only did it very occasionally these days, at least compared to the immediate aftermath of her separation—but something had compelled her to check Daphne's page just now. Randall didn't have an account, but Daphne regularly filled hers with photos and cheery status updates. Although Susan had deleted Daphne from her friends list long ago, Daphne hadn't implemented privacy settings, so her page was available for anyone to view.

She'd announced her pregnancy here, a week or so after Randall had told Susan about it. She'd posted a photo of her belly— The little one is the size of an orange now!—and had solicited advice on how to get through morning sickness from her friends.

Ginger chews, Susan had thought when she'd read that post. They had been Susan's salvation when she'd been carrying Cole. If Daphne and Randall had never met—if Daphne were carrying the baby of some other man—Susan would have bought a big bag and driven them over. She would've put her hand on Daphne's stomach to feel the baby move, and rubbed her friend's feet, because they had to be getting sore by now.

She missed Daphne almost as much as she hated her.

Today's Facebook status update felt like a slap: I can't believe our wedding is in one month! Dozens of messages of congratulations filled the spaces below her post.

Susan had known it was coming, of course. Randall had kept her up to date, as had Cole. He was to be the best man.

"That's so exciting," Susan had said when Cole had prattled on about the new outfit Randall was buying him, and how he'd get to hold the rings during the ceremony. He knew exactly where to hold them; in the pocket of his shirt. He'd pull them out at the signal from the minister, Cole had told her. He was going to practice a lot. "You must be so proud," Susan had said.

Meryl Streep had nothing on her.

She *was* happy for Cole, though, and the brightness of that emotion sometimes quieted her pain. Or maybe it was what let her power through the pain. If Randall had been marrying someone awful, someone who hated kids—well, that would've been intolerable. Far worse than him falling for Susan's friend. In a way, she was lucky, all things considered.

The wedding was going to be simple, held in Randall and Daphne's backyard. Just a few dozen friends and family. And their puppy, probably. He'd do something adorable like race down the aisle, or bark when Randall and Daphne kissed, and everyone would laugh.

"I know you wouldn't want to come," Randall had said to her in their last phone conversation. "But you're not excluded from anything, I don't want you to ever think that, so . . ."

"Thank you," Susan had managed to say. "I think it's better if I don't, but . . ."

"Okay," Randall had said.

Neither of them had spoken for a moment that felt heavier than the ones before it, then Susan had brought up Cole—the only bit of glue holding them together, but sticky enough to last the length of their lives—and they'd concluded the conversation civilly.

*Progress*, Susan had thought. She could feel herself inching forward at times, before the weight of hurt and regret jerked her back. Maybe a year from now, she'd be able to smile when she saw Randall and Daphne together. Coo over their baby. Drop Cole off and accept Daphne's offer of tea. Well, that might take a little longer . . . but someday. She could almost see it, like the promise of the sun behind a storm cloud.

Or maybe that was just a lie she was telling herself. Maybe a year from now she'd still be alone, and just as sad as she was now.

One more look at the photos, she told herself, scanning through the shots Daphne had uploaded of her engagement ring—a simple amethyst in a beautiful silver setting, so Daphne—and a silhouette of her embracing Randall at sunset.

She closed the lid on her computer, then she went into the kitchen to make a grocery list, to distract her mind with mundane tasks until it grew dark and she could drink a glass or two of wine.

• • •

## Before Newport Cove

On the day that Addison had revealed how Danny had checked his legs, Harry had gotten in from California on a late-afternoon flight. He'd arrived home after the kids had gone to bed.

"How was your day?" Harry had asked, crunching a carrot.

"Strange," Tessa had said.

He'd looked up. Was there a tinge of wariness in his eyes, some hint of reluctance to hear her latest fear? She'd felt herself bristle.

She'd tell it straight out, she'd decided. She'd report the facts and let Harry decide if there was cause for concern; he was much more sensible about such things. Besides, the Young Rangers group was a tremendous positive in Addison's life. She couldn't disrupt that without real proof. A mother's intuition, that tingling along the back of her neck—maybe those signals were reliable for other women, but Tessa knew they were broken in her.

Harry hadn't said much as Tessa had relayed Addison's story, trying to remember their son's precise words, without adding any inflection or significant facial expressions. She'd told him how long Addison had been inside the house, and how he'd come back out wearing his uniform. She'd finished and had looked at him, trying to gauge his reaction. But he'd been impossible to read.

"What do you think?" she'd finally asked.

He'd finished another bite of pasta before answering. Something about that delay—the moment he'd taken to wind up his spaghetti into a neat coil on his fork, the way he'd chewed methodically, the food making a little bulge in the corner of his mouth—had made her want to scream.

"I think kids sometimes confuse details," Harry had finally said.

"Yeah," Tessa had said. "But this wasn't some story about a spaceship or something. It was really specific. Addison showed me how Danny touched him—"

"You already demonstrated," Harry had said, and Tessa had stayed her hand in its gesture along her leg.

"So you think it's nothing?" Tessa had said.

"Probably," Harry had said. "But I'll talk to Addison when he wakes up in the morning."

Tessa had paused. "Okay," she'd said. "I'm going to get ready for bed."

She'd walked out of the room, but she'd stopped just beyond the threshold of the doorway. Had Harry discounted the story because she'd overreacted in the past? Maybe he thought she was exaggerating.

She was the one who'd stayed home with the kids, who'd nursed them through illnesses and night terrors. They'd only ever called out "Mama" in the night; they'd known Harry wouldn't be the one to comfort them. But suddenly Harry was the expert who had to talk to Addison and decide whether their boy was in danger?

The old Tessa, the one who'd untangled complicated taxes and had run half-marathons, came surging back, imbuing a skeleton of steel in the hesitant, confused woman she'd morphed into during the preceding years. She didn't need Harry to lay down the final pronouncement on the welfare of their children. Maybe she hadn't done everything right, maybe she'd erred on the side of being overly cautious, but wasn't that better than the alternative?

The way he'd . . . *dismissed* her and turned back to his newspaper had stung, as if she were just overwrought, someone incapable of reason. He had no right to treat her with so little respect.

She'd glanced back toward the kitchen. Harry would be at the table awhile—he was a slow eater—then he'd watch TV before coming upstairs. It was his routine.

She'd reached for the keys to the minivan that hung on a shelf by the front door, needing to get out.

# Chapter Thirty-Six

• • •

Sunday meant routine and family, dinner at the in-laws'. Kellie
hadn't been sure if Jason would want to go, but he grabbed
the car keys at a little before five and called out, "Ready?"

He didn't meet her eyes, though. It was scary how adept
Jason had become, in such a short amount of time, at avoiding
her. He stared at a spot just beyond her when it was necessary
for him to talk to her, like now. He edged out of rooms when
she entered them, always casually enough that the kids didn't
pick up on anything.

"We're ready," Kellie said, grabbing her purse. Her cell phone was inside it, but she'd turned it off.

She and the kids followed Jason out to the minivan. Kellie felt awkward sliding into the passenger's seat, as she knew he'd rather there be more space between them. The kids filled the short drive with chatter, with Mia talking about the upcoming Taylor Swift concert and Noah launching into a deliberately annoying imitation of her song "I Knew You Were Trouble"—and then they were at Jason's parents'. It was a journey they'd taken hundreds of times before, but never had it felt so precious to Kellie.

Jason's mom and dad had become an extra set of parents to her through the years. Losing Jason would mean losing them, too. She should have thought of all she was risking, and for what? A few moments of feeling young again, of exploring possibilities that had closed off to her long ago. Now it all seemed so . . . cheap. She'd taken a long, hot shower that morning but the sensation of uncleanliness clung to her like a stain.

Jason pulled into his parents' driveway and Kellie got out, opening the sliding door for the kids. They ran ahead, with Jason close behind them. *Don't cry tonight*, Kellie warned herself.

She walked through the front door, straight into the hugs Jason's parents always gave freely, and instantly her resolve crumpled. Her throat constricted, but she managed to blink away her tears.

"So good to see you," Jason's dad said. "Recovered from the party?"

"Just barely," Kellie said, trying for a laugh.

"Oh, I need to check on the roast," Jason's mom said, hurrying toward the kitchen. "Kids? I got you each one of those books with the magic pens, you know the kind with invisible ink . . . Go find them in the living room."

Jason followed his mother to the kitchen. Usually Kellie helped her put together the finishing touches on dinner—or tried to help; Jason's mom rarely let her do more than throw together a salad, saying that Kellie was busy enough and this was her time to relax. She hesitated, wondering what to do, but then Jason came back out with a beer and so Kellie went into the kitchen.

"I hope it's not getting dry," Jason's mother said, opening the oven door and peering in.

"I'm sure it's delicious," Kellie said. She could see freshly washed lettuce in the salad spinner so she pulled it out and began tearing it into shreds.

"Thank you, honey," Jason's mom said. "So tell me all about the party. At least the parts we missed."

"Oh . . . It was wonderful," Kellie said. "The music and decorations, having everyone there . . ."

She knew her tone didn't reflect her words.

"Were you surprised?" her mother-in-law asked. "Jason really wanted you to be."

"I was," Kellie said. "Truly . . . I'm sorry, I'm a little tired today."

Jason's mother pulled the lid off a pot that was warming on the stove, added a pat of butter, and gave the mashed potatoes a quick stir. "Ten more minutes," she said. She moved to the refrigerator—Jason's mother was always moving, always chatting; she reminded Kellie of a bird—and pulled out a bottle of white wine.

She didn't ask before pouring a glass for Kellie, because that was their routine. The moms in the kitchen sharing a glass of wine, the kids playing in the backyard or basement depending on the weather, Jason and his dad by the fire in the wintertime and poking around in the garage workroom during the other seasons.

Kellie hadn't planned on drinking anything tonight, but she took a sip and found the tart, cold wine soothed her raw throat.

"You know, our fiftieth wedding anniversary is coming up in a couple of months," Jason's mother began.

Kellie shook her head. "That's incredible . . . really."

"We've been putting aside a little money," Jason's mother said. "We thought we'd like to take the whole family away somewhere special."

"That's so generous of you," Kellie said. "But we're the ones who should be treating you—"

Jason's mother held up a hand to cut Kellie off, but she was smiling. "Maybe a cruise," she said.

"Sounds wonderful," Kellie said. She wondered if she and Jason would still be together when the date rolled around. Maybe he'd want to go alone with the kids. She turned her head and tossed the salad as tears filled her eyes again.

If anyone saw her cry, there would be concern. Questions. They'd notice Jason wouldn't be comforting her, and conclusions would be drawn. She'd ruin the family dinner, which no one deserved. And her shame would be multiplied if her in-laws deduced what she'd done.

She felt a soft hand on her shoulder and she bowed her head, unable to look at Jason's mother.

"Marriage is hard," she said. "I say we've been married for fifty wonderful years when anyone asks. But really, the answer is we've been married for forty wonderful years, eight so-so years, and two really bad years."

Kellie lifted her head and turned, her surprise at the revelation erasing her tears.

"You've had hard times?" she asked. "You two always seem like . . . such a pair."

"I almost left him once," Jason's mother said, and Kellie nearly dropped the salad tongs. "After we were first married . . . my father was sick, he'd just been diagnosed with cancer, and I had a miscarriage."

"I didn't know," Kellie whispered. "I'm so sorry."

"It seemed like everything was falling apart," she said. "Ralph tried to comfort me, but he didn't really know what it was like. I was mad at him. Mad at the world."

"So what did you do?" Kellie asked.

"I stayed," she said simply. "It was a choice to keep on loving him, to keep on trying. Marriage is like a muscle. You have to work at keeping it strong so it doesn't atrophy."

Kellie nodded and took another sip of wine, wondering how much Jason's mother had seen. Maybe she'd noticed something amiss at Thanksgiving dinner, and had picked up how important the party was to Jason. She had to have noticed the distance between Kellie and her son Friday night. But she didn't understand the reason, or she wouldn't be speaking to Kellie in this soft, gentle voice.

Jason's mom pulled out the roast and set it on the stove. "Do you want to call everyone in for dinner?" she asked. Kellie nodded. She'd see if Jason needed another beer, and she'd cover up his quiet by chatting during dinner. She'd do whatever she could—distribute as many gestures of kindness as possible—to try to soften the terrible thing she'd done to her entire family.

She turned to leave the room, then went back, to give Jason's mother another hug.

"Thank you," she whispered, and was grateful for the soft, motherly arms that gently patted her back.

• • •

"Is Melanie home?"

Gigi whirled around to see Zach standing in the kitchen. It was eerie how he appeared, catlike, without making any noise.

"No," she said. "Why do you ask?"

"I wanted to give you and Joe a heads-up about something," he said.

Gigi nodded. "In there," she said, jerking her head toward the living room. "I'll get Joe."

Melanie had left for school, as had Julia, and Joe was upstairs on his computer, answering emails. If everyone had been around, Gigi would have pulled Zach outside and de-

manded to know what was going on. His last revelation felt
like a power play, and she was determined to keep him from
knocking her off balance again.

She realized her fists were clenched as she went to call Joe.
He came downstairs so rapidly she knew he deduced from her
tone that it was important.

She sat on the couch next to her husband, with Zach across
from them. He had a folder—of course he had a folder! The
sight of it made her pulse quicken. Gigi spoke up immediately,
not wanting Zach to control the tone or pace of this conversation.

"What is it, Zach?" she asked. "I've only got a minute."

"I thought you should see this," he said, handing them the
folder.

Gigi opened it and couldn't refrain from gasping. She'd
been expecting to have another piece of her past revealed. But
Melanie was the target.

Inside was a printout of a conservative web page; Gigi had
seen the site before when its reporter—there only seemed to
be one writing the stories—had published an "exposé" of one
of Joe's campaign contributions, claiming that it came from
terrorists. Of course it had been a lie, but the comments section showed plenty of people believed it.

The headline on this new story read: Family Feud!

Beneath it was a photograph of Joe, Melanie, Gigi, and Julia.
It was from the session they'd held on the front steps, but Gigi
had never seen this picture before. Melanie's face was furious
as she pulled away from the woman who'd tried to cover up
her pimple, and Gigi's mouth was twisting in anger, too. Joe
was staring off into space, as if bored by the scene, while Julia
looked as if she were about to cry.

Beneath the photo was another, of Melanie fleeing. The
angle was particularly unflattering, and Melanie's shirt was
hiked up, revealing the top of her white underpants peeking
up above her black pants and—oh no!—a hint of her butt

crack. Gigi skimmed the story, wincing as she saw the words "hissy fit" and "out-of-control teenager."

"What the hell?" Joe said. "Who took this?"

"Hard to say," Zach said, steepling his fingers. "A neighbor with a grudge, an aide for one of your opponents who knew about the shoot and happened to have a camera ready at the right time . . ."

"The right time?" Joe asked incredulously. "I will sue their asses . . . Get me the number of whoever runs that piece of shit website . . ."

"The right time for them," Zach said quickly. "The wrong time for us, of course."

He gestured to the folder. "There's more."

Joe flipped the page and saw a photograph of Melanie at a park, seated on the grass next to Raven, taking a puff off a joint.

"She's smoking weed?" Joe asked. The venom drained from his voice; he sounded stunned.

Zach cleared his throat. "That night, when we were watching a movie, I talked to Melanie. I figured it might be easier for her to open up to someone closer to her own age, so . . . She's only tried it a few times. She doesn't like it, really. She says it makes her jittery. That's an old photo, she says it happened at the beginning of the school year. And now that she broke up with that guy, I doubt she'll be trying it again soon. He was really into pot."

"You talked to her?" Gigi asked. She was grateful for the information, but she couldn't understand why Zach had taken such an interest in Melanie. And something was off in the timeline he'd presented, but she couldn't quite discern what it was. The photos had come at her like punches and she was still reeling.

"So do we bring it up to her?" Joe asked Gigi. "If it was just a couple of times . . ."

Gigi gazed down at the picture from the family photo shoot again. The date on the top caught her eye. "This was pub-

lished more than a week ago," she said. "When did you find
out about it?"

"Just a little while ago," Zach said. "I think we should
schedule a new shoot and release our own photos to offset
this. Melanie can wear a nice outfit, maybe have her hair done.
This will be forgotten."

"Not to me, it won't," Joe snapped. "I'm serious, Zach. I
want this taken down . . ."

Joe was still talking, but his voice seemed to fade away as
Gigi remembered Melanie on the couch with Zach. That secret
smile curving her lips.

Melanie's interest in new clothes had been too abrupt. She'd
even asked for a makeover at the Lancôme counter, and had
come home with tinted moisturizer, mascara, and lip gloss.
Gigi had seen her that night, experimenting with the mascara
in the bathroom mirror.

Melanie had lingered around the main level of the house
in her new clothes and makeup that night, instead of retreating to her room, until after Joe had come home. She'd even
helped Gigi cook dinner. Gigi had thought it was because Melanie wanted to be with her, but suddenly she realized Melanie
had wanted Zach to see her new look. Her daughter had been
waiting for him. She wanted his approval.

"What did you do to her?" Gigi demanded.

"Pardon?" Zach asked, swiveling to face her. He must've
seen the angry expression on her face, but he was as calm as
ever. This was theater to him, Gigi realized.

"Does Melanie know about this?" She closed the folder and
shook it near his face. "Is this why she wanted to go shopping
right after you watched that movie?"

"Of course not," Zach said. "I wouldn't say a word about it
to her."

"So what *did* you say?" Gigi demanded. Her breaths were
coming hot and fast now, even though her body felt cold. She
turned to Joe. "The night after Kellie's party, remember? The

two of them were on the couch. Melanie asked me to go shopping the next morning."

She looked at Zach. "You're not telling us everything."

Zach hesitated, then shrugged. "Look, I may have mentioned something about how the girl in the movie looked better with makeup, what great style she had," he said. "You have to admit it's embarrassing for Melanie—for any girl—to be singled out like this."

"You had no right—no right! How dare you try to, to . . . groom my daughter!" Gigi exploded.

"You crossed the line, Zach," Joe said. "You told me you just saw this article. But you talked to Melanie last weekend. You should have come to me, not my daughter. About the pot, too."

"She had a crush on you," Gigi said. "Did you know that?"

Zach lifted a shoulder in a half shrug, acknowledging it. "Obviously I'm not interested in *her*, I was just trying to help."

Gigi thought of the weight-loss book under Melanie's bed, the way her daughter had seemed so sad until recently, but had brightened at Thanksgiving dinner under Zach's attention. He'd used that power.

"I'm not comfortable with you being in our house any longer," Gigi told Zach. "You were here to work on Joe's campaign, not to interfere with our family."

"Are you serious?" Zach laughed. He actually laughed. "Because your daughter has a crush on me?"

"Joe?" Gigi turned to her husband.

"Let me think," Joe said. He massaged his forehead with his index finger and thumb.

"You need me," Zach said. "You think this is bad?" He gestured to the folder. "It's going to get worse. They're going to come after you hard. Wait until they have a photo of you smoking pot, Gigi. Can't you see the headline? 'Like mother, like daughter.'"

"That's enough," Joe said. "Look, why don't we all calm down and take a step back . . ."

Gigi was staring at Zach. His eyes were bright and his cheeks were pink. He was exhilarated.

But all he said was, "Okay. I'm sorry again for overstepping. Should we head out now, Joe, and maybe we can all continue this conversation later?"

"Wait," Gigi said. "What did you mean, 'like mother, like daughter'?"

She saw it in Zach's eyes. He knew instantly he'd made a mistake.

"You were in my bedroom," Gigi said. "When?"

Zach shook his head. "I don't know what you're talking about."

Gigi turned to Joe. "The pot I keep upstairs. Someone took some out a while ago."

"It wasn't me," Zach said.

"He must've been alone in the house at some point," Gigi said. "He probably went through everything."

She could see Zach with his iPhone, searching through her drawers, reading the financial information in their filing cabinet, snapping pictures . . . Creating more files, ticking bombs he could store for the future.

She stepped toward Zach, her fingers itching to slap him, wanting to do something—something!—to get his tentacles out of their family. Then she heard Joe's quick, sharp inhalation. She turned and saw her husband's face transform from anger to shock.

In the hallway was Melanie, holding a lunch bag she must've forgotten and come back for. The lunch she'd so carefully prepared that morning, with cut-up carrot and celery sticks and a yogurt. Weight-loss foods.

Gigi leaped up to follow her daughter, but Melanie was running upstairs, and then came the sound of her door slamming. Gigi tore up the stairs behind her, and a moment later, Joe came thundering up, too.

"I want him out of my house," Gigi said. She rubbed her eyes to push away her tears. "Right now!"

"Okay," Joe said. "You're right, he can't stay here any longer." He knocked on the door. "Melanie?"

There wasn't any answer, but Joe cracked open the door anyway. "Honey?"

Melanie had pulled the covers over her head, just as she had when she'd been a little girl. The sight of that lump in the bed broke Gigi's heart.

She didn't look at Joe for guidance or try to think about the next right step. She instinctively ran to her daughter, and wrapped her arms around Melanie.

"I'm sorry," she whispered. "Oh, baby, I'm so sorry."

She could feel Melanie's body shuddering, but Melanie didn't push her away, so Gigi held on tight. She rocked her daughter back and forth, wishing she could absorb her pain.

# Chapter Thirty-Seven

*Before Newport Cove*

IT WAS DARK OUT when Tessa arrived at Danny's house. She pulled into the driveway, behind his Volvo, and killed her car's lights.

She sat there for a moment, deciding how to proceed. She imagined seeing Danny smile as he opened the door. He'd invite her in, and she'd take a seat in the living room. She'd relay what Addison had said, using the same calm tone in which she'd conveyed the story to Harry. "I'm sure it's just a misunderstanding, but could you explain to me why you needed to touch my son's legs?" she'd ask.

Or maybe she wouldn't put forth that question. Maybe she'd just repeat what Addison had said, then study Danny's reaction. His face would reveal something if it hadn't been an innocent act, wouldn't it?

She got out of her car and marched up the front porch steps and knocked on the door. She waited a few moments, then jabbed the bell with her index finger.

The door remained closed. Tessa glanced at the Volvo in the

driveway. The house appeared occupied; light poured forth from nearly every window. She knocked again, harder this time, until her knuckles stung.

Maybe he was in the shower, she thought, feeling deflated. She started to head back to her car, unsure of what else to do. But she paused on the top step of the front porch, looking at the basketball hoop over Danny's garage. He was sure welcoming to kids.

The thing was, she couldn't think of a single thing Danny could say to prove his touch was innocent. Addison could've just tried on the pants and reported if they were too big or too small; that's what he did whenever she took him shopping. And why would Danny use his palm, running it along the inside of Addison's leg? Then there was the special hug. It sounded creepy. She'd gone over and over it in her mind. It wasn't a misunderstanding. There wasn't a reasonable explanation.

She'd been wrong before. But that didn't matter. Right now, every instinct she had was screaming an alarm.

The certainty propelled her to turn around and try the door handle. It twisted easily in her palm. It was still relatively early; maybe Danny only locked up when he went to bed at night. He lived on a quiet, pleasant street. Maybe he thought he had nothing to fear.

She stepped across the threshold, listening intently. She could hear the distant sounds of voices, then a burst of laughter coming from a television on upstairs. She imagined Danny sprawled across his bed, relaxing, perhaps sipping from a bottle of beer.

The television was loud; it must have masked the sound of the doorbell and her knocking. She'd go to the bottom of the stairs and call out to him, she decided as she closed the door. She'd tell Danny to stay the hell away from her son. Then she'd phone the other parents and let them know what had happened. They could question their own children and decide if they wanted to go to the police as a group.

Tessa walked through the hallway, then paused to listen again. The television was still on. She glanced to her right, seeing a dining room with a laptop computer on the gleaming wood table. A stack of newspapers and magazines lay next to it, along with a pile of Young Ranger uniforms and the selection of binoculars and other items that Danny had mentioned. Tessa looked at the stairs to make sure Danny wasn't coming into view, then crept over and leafed through the publications—they were just newspapers and sports magazines—and opened the laptop. It was password protected.

Danny lived alone. Was it suspicious that he wanted to protect the information on his laptop?

She closed the lid, then walked into the galley kitchen. It was clean and uncluttered, with a coffeemaker and a blue bowl containing apples and oranges on the counter. A single coffee mug and china plate rested in the sink.

Tessa took in the electric bill on the counter by the phone, and the calendar on the wall with mostly empty white squares. Then her eyes landed on a door leading to the basement.

She could still hear the television on upstairs, the tinny laugh track filtering through the walls. Noise traveled through the floors of this house; she'd have to be very quiet.

She reached for the knob, but the door was locked. A bolt was fastened high up on the door—above the reach of a child, Tessa noted, wondering if that was significant. She slid it out of the chamber, grateful it eased away with just a small click. Then she opened the door.

She could only see blackness. She waited until her eyes adjusted and she found a light switch, then she shut the door behind her and turned it on. She crept down the stairs, wincing as one near the bottom groaned.

The basement wasn't finished. The floor was cement, and exposed pipes twisted in a labyrinth overhead. She glanced around, taking in a few suitcases, Christmas decorations stored in big plastic bins, and odds and ends of dusty furniture. There was also a workbench in one corner. Tessa moved over to it, noticing the paintbrushes and neatly stacked cans of stain, hammers, and wrenches. There wasn't anything out of the ordinary here.

But the back of her neck was tingling again. This felt different from when she'd seen the nanny with her crying son and had spotted the suspicious-looking man at the playground. This felt like certainty.

She looked around, noticing for the first time two other closed doors leading off the basement.

She tested the first one. It opened into a laundry room. An empty plastic basket sat by the dryer, and a jug of Tide rested atop the washer. Tessa closed the door and walked over to the second one.

The smell of chemicals hit her the moment she cracked open the door. The room was small, maybe ten feet by eight feet, with a large rectangular table in its center. Atop the table were four plastic trays and a pair of tongs. By the far wall was an easel.

A darkroom, Tessa realized. She hadn't been in one in years, not since a photography class she'd taken in high school.

The door was painted black on the inside and a strip of black felt ran around its seam to seal off the light. Even with the door open, though, it was hard for Tessa to see the images on the photographs stacked at the end of the table. She dug into her pocket for her phone and used its screen for extra light. The photographs were all of flowers, she realized as she used her free hand to riffle through them.

Apparently Danny loved roses and azaleas and poppies. He'd zoomed in on their petals, capturing them in glorious detail. She let the last photograph drop onto the table, feeling the sag of disappointment. She'd been so sure . . . but there wasn't any evidence here.

She'd go back upstairs and exit the house and then reopen the front door and call out his name. She'd revert to her original plan.

Tessa straightened up and as she did so, her phone cast a light over the easel in the corner. There were more photographs attached to it with little clips.

She walked over, her heart pounding. She held up her phone as her eyes scanned the rows of a dozen or so photos, then covered her mouth as nausea roiled her stomach. The photographs were of little boys. Even though she'd expected—wanted!—to find something, she wasn't prepared for this.

At least the neat rows of photographs weren't graphic. The boys were all in their underwear. There were some shots that appeared to be taken in the changing room of a swimming pool, judging from the towels and goggles scattered about. And others in a smaller space—a bathroom. Tessa recognized a few faces from Young Rangers: little Sam, who'd broken his arm last year; Max, a cheerful, pint-sized chatterbox; Henry, who had an irrepressible cowlick right in the front of his brown hair . . .

And Addison. He was on the bottom row. In the photograph, he was struggling to get out of his pants, balancing on one leg as he used his hands to wrestle his jeans off his other foot. The Young Rangers uniform was on the floor beside him. His tongue was sticking out of the corner of his mouth, an indicator that he was working hard at something. Addison had the same look when he was doing math problems.

A wave of rage spread through Tessa as she grabbed the photograph of Addison and tore it away. How had Danny done it? Maybe he had a peephole in his bathroom with a camera attached. Her beautiful, perfect son . . . And all of those other innocent children. Danny had preyed on them, earning their trust. She had to get out of here before she vomited, before she grabbed the hammer from the workbench and slammed it against Danny's skull.

Tessa clattered up the stairs, breathing hard, then raced through the front door, leaving it open behind her as she ran outside. She fumbled through her purse until she found her keys and she started her car, revving the engine. She'd drive home to Harry. They'd call the police together. She had the evidence in her hand. Danny would get locked up. She'd call the other parents, she'd call the newspaper, she'd make sure he never, ever . . .

"Wait!"

She glanced in the rearview mirror and saw Danny standing there, a few feet behind her.

He stretched out his arms in an open, welcoming gesture. He was smiling broadly, the same wide grin he'd bestowed upon her when they'd first met. The one that had charmed her, charmed the other parents. Charmed the kids.

"Where are you rushing off to?" he called. Her hand was already on the gear shift; her car was in reverse. But she couldn't move. Danny was blocking her.

So he knew. He'd probably heard her tearing up the basement stairs.

He would cover this up, she realized as rage blurred her vision. He'd get rid of the evidence before she came back. Trash his computer, destroy the photographs, plaster over the bathroom peephole. All she had was one picture of Addison. It wouldn't be enough to send Danny to jail. He'd probably get probation, and then he'd just move away and start preying on other children.

She wondered what else he'd done. She'd read somewhere that child molesters targeted dozens—or was it hundreds?—of victims before they were caught. Had he actually touched Addison or any of the other kids?

All of those thoughts and calculations flitted through her mind at light speed, in less time than it took Tessa to remove her foot from the brake and press hard on the gas.

Her Toyota shot down the driveway in reverse, in a straight, smooth line, barely slowing as it smashed into Danny and he disappeared.

She didn't stop until she reached the street, then she glanced up at the driveway. Danny was lying motionless in the middle of it, his dark clothing blending in with the asphalt.

You could barely even tell he was there. He might as well have been a pile of crumpled rags. She put the car into drive, still holding the photograph of Addison, and stepped on the gas again, more gently this time.

Some time later—ten minutes? An hour?—she became aware that she was in her own driveway, her head collapsed onto the steering wheel, her body ice-cold.

It wasn't until a thought seized her that she was able to muster the strength to lift up her head and stare at the house: *Harry*.

She could see him through the kitchen window, still reading the newspaper. Calm, logical Harry would know exactly what to do. He could fix this.

She exited the car, closing the door carefully behind her, then went inside to tell her husband what had just happened.

# Chapter Thirty-Eight

• • •

"What was it like?" Kellie asked. "I mean, if it's not too painful
to dredge all that up."

She was huddled on Susan's couch, clutching a throw pillow to her middle, ignoring the tea and croissants Susan had
set out on the coffee table.

Susan took a sip of cinnamon tea before answering. "It was
the worst pain I've ever gone through," she said simply.

Kellie nodded. Her face looked drawn, and there were dark
circles under her eyes.

"Imagining the two of them together, not even in bed,

though that was wrenching . . . just laughing, and hugging. Being together," Susan said. "There was something kind of, I don't know, perverse about knowing their joy was the source of my pain."

Kellie inhaled a deep, shuddering breath. "Jason knows I didn't love Miller," she said. "I explained it was a crush that got out of hand . . . but it's still a huge betrayal. I don't even know if it was a true emotional affair, because Miller didn't really know me. He knew the woman who was always dressed up and smiling. It's easy to be that person for a few hours a day. But he didn't understand the messier parts of me, all of the things you can hide when it's not a real relationship."

"Have you talked to Miller lately?" Susan asked.

Kellie shook her head. "I've been calling in sick to work. I don't know if I'm going to tell him I can't talk to him anymore or just . . . disappear."

"How do you feel about that?" Susan asked.

"A week ago it would have been devastating," Kellie said. "Now? It's nothing." She hesitated. "Almost nothing. I miss the feeling I had . . . of someone thinking I was pretty, that I was special. That thrill of the new. But it wasn't about Miller. It was about those sensations."

Susan nodded slowly. It was the difference between a crush and true love. Randall wouldn't—or couldn't—give up Daphne, but Kellie was going to walk away easily.

"Should I quit work?" Kellie asked.

Susan thought about how Jason would feel, knowing Kellie would be near Miller every day at the office. "Yes," she said.

"Yeah," Kellie said. She drew up her knees and rested her chin on them. "I'll call tomorrow. Maybe in a few months I can join another office . . . I don't know."

Susan leaned forward. "Do you really want to know what I think?" she asked.

Kellie cringed. "Of me?" she asked.

Susan reached out and touched Kellie's arm. "No, honey,

that isn't where I was going. I was going to say I think you need to do everything you can to show Jason how much you love him. It's going to take time. But he'll come around."

"I was thinking I'd start cooking him special dinners," Kellie said.

"Little gestures like that are good," Susan said. "And you could arrange a date night once a week. Maybe a getaway down the line."

"I would love that," Kellie said. "I've been remembering all the reasons why I fell in love with Jason. His kindness, his steadiness . . . He hasn't changed. Maybe that was part of it; we've been together forever. And it was just the . . . monotony of being with the same person day in, day out. Talking about who needs to take the kids to soccer practice. Wanting some orange juice and realizing Jason had two glasses and it was all gone. The excitement disappeared."

"So you'll work to get it back," Susan said. "Lingerie. You need to go buy some."

Kellie smiled. "Jason would love that." Her smile dropped away. "Or he would have."

Pain washed over her face and Susan could see her swallow hard. "I know this is hard for Jason, but what I never realized is how hard it would be for me, too. To know how badly I've hurt him."

Susan dropped her eyes to her teacup. She had never before thought of what Randall might be enduring. She'd been too busy imagining his joy.

She'd been so immersed in her own agony she'd never considered the fact that the pain of their divorce might have affected him. Randall was a decent man; a kind man. He'd always carried spiders outside, rather than squashing them. Maybe he'd invited her along on Halloween because he still cared about her feelings, not because he cared what other people thought.

"Do you really think I should buy lingerie, or is it too soon?" Kellie asked.

Susan tucked away her new revelation, to turn over and consider more carefully later, and looked back at her friend.

"Do it. All that effort you put into looking good for Miller, into thinking about him?" Susan said. "Turn it on your husband."

"Yeah," Kellie said. "I'm going to try."

"That's my girl," Susan said. "Try to make this the best thing that ever happened to your marriage, odd as that sounds now. Now eat a croissant or I'll hate you because you're getting too skinny."

She handed one to Kellie, who broke off a corner and nibbled at it.

"So I've got a question for you," Susan said. "I met this guy at your birthday party . . . Peter?"

Kellie furrowed her brow, then her face cleared. "Oh, *Peter*! Yeah, he was one of Jason's fraternity brothers in college. I didn't see him at the party, but Jason must have invited him. I know they've gotten back in touch. Peter moved back to the area a few weeks ago, after his div— Oh my God!"

"Settle down," Susan said, laughing.

"No, but he's a really good guy! Did you talk to him? Of course you did, that's why you're asking."

"We did," Susan confirmed. "He asked for my number, but he hasn't called yet."

"Well, it's been, what, only two days?" Kellie said.

"I know," Susan said.

"I'll give you the scoop," Kellie said. "He has one kid, but a bit older." She furrowed her brow. "Twelve, thirteen, maybe? A daughter. He got married young, that I remember, because Jason and I went to the wedding. His wife was gorgeous but she seemed like a cold fish. That's my completely biased take from talking to her for thirty seconds at her wedding, but if you're not all smiling and happy at your wedding, when would you be? Jason really liked him, but they lost touch for a while even though Peter didn't live that far away. I got the sense his wife was kind of controlling and they just did stuff with her family and friends."

"Are you making that up?" Susan asked, giving Kellie a nudge.

"Nope," Kellie said. "So, will this be your first post-divorce date?"

"If he calls," Susan said.

"When he calls," Kellie amended. "You're the perfect woman. How could he not call you? He's counting the minutes. He read *The Rules* and knows he has to wait a few days or he'll scare you off."

Susan rolled her eyes and handed Kellie the rest of the croissant. "Eat," she ordered. "Then I'm going to take a couple more hours off work so we can go lingerie shopping."

Kellie got in the last word: "Only if it's for both of us."

•   •   •

There was no worse pain than knowing your child was suffering, Gigi thought as she stood outside Melanie's door, listening.

She'd been terrified that Melanie would shut her out again. But after she'd cried, Melanie had fallen asleep, even though it was still morning. When she'd awoken an hour later, Gigi had brought her a tray of chamomile tea and toast.

Joe was staying home today, having canceled his campaign events. Gigi didn't know where Zach had gone. She didn't care, as long as he was out of the house.

"Sweetie?" Gigi asked, tapping on Melanie's partially opened door. Her daughter was still a lump under the covers, but at least this time her head was showing.

"Can I get you anything else?" Gigi asked. Most of the tea was gone, but the toast was untouched.

"No," Melanie said.

Gigi hesitated. Normally she'd give Melanie space, figuring that was what Melanie wanted, but she went against that instinct and sat down on the edge of her daughter's bed. She wished she had a manual for times like these. When Melanie had been young, it was so easy to find solutions. After Melanie broke one of her new crayons at age three, Gigi had used a match to soften the wax and weld it back together. When Melanie had been left out of a birthday party at age ten, Gigi had taken her out for a special dinner and movie.

But how did you guide a troubled, defiant teenager?

Melanie was quiet for a moment, then: "Zach told me he thought I was pretty. He said if I just"—Melanie's voice broke but she continued—"if I just wore some makeup and nicer clothes, I'd be a knockout. So why'd he say 'I wouldn't be interested in *her*' like that?"

Gigi closed her eyes, wanting to absorb her daughter's hurt. "Because he's a horrible person," Gigi said. "I wish I could give you another reason, something to make you feel better, but there's something wrong with Zach."

"Why don't you and Julia ever have to diet?" Melanie asked. "Why am I the only fat one in the family?"

"Sweetie, you're not," Gigi said. "And you are pretty. You're beautiful."

"Don't say on the inside," Melanie said. "No one cares about that."

"Inside and out," Gigi said.

She wondered if she should tell Melanie about her shoplifting arrest. She thought about the weight-loss book under Melanie's bed, and that sad, crumpled lunch bag of carrots and yogurt. Melanie needed to know that everyone struggled; that even her own mother—her aggravating, bossy mother—had stumbled and fallen and gotten back up again. Soon, Gigi decided, but not today.

"Did he ever kiss you, Melanie?" Gigi asked. "Please tell me."

Melanie shook her head. "But he put his arm around me when we watched the movie." She lay back against her pillows and closed her eyes. "Is he still going to live here?" she asked.

"No," Gigi said. "And not just because of what happened to you . . . He made me feel uncomfortable from the start."

"He's a jerk," Melanie said.

"Worse than that," Gigi said.

"Do you know when we went to serve dinner to the homeless on Thanksgiving, he didn't do any work? He was supposed to peel potatoes but I saw him checking his iPhone the whole time," Melanie said.

"I'm not surprised," Gigi said.

Melanie sighed. "Can I have some more tea?" she asked.

Gigi stood up. She wanted to reach out and smooth her daughter's hair, but she decided not to press her luck. Instead she gave Melanie's foot a quick squeeze through the blanket.

"Of course," she said. "I'll be right back."

# Chapter Thirty-Nine

*Before Newport Cove*

DISBELIEF HAD FILLED HARRY'S eyes. He hadn't even realized Tessa had left the house, or that the woman now standing before him was no longer the same person who had cut up
carrots and boiled noodles for his dinner.

"Here," she'd said, handing him the photograph of Addison. She shuddered as she passed it to her husband; the glossy
paper was imbued with evil.

"Where did you get this?" Harry had asked. So she told him
the story again. It had just tumbled out of her, without inflection or emotion, like she was reciting a list of things for him
to pick up at the grocery store. But then her hands started to
shake. They fluttered wildly, like trapped birds that had been
attached to her wrists and were desperate to be freed.

"I'm going to be sick," she'd said. She bent over the trash
can and retched.

Her physical state, more than her words, seemed to convince Harry. He leaped up from his chair and ran outside.

Tessa had followed him as he circled her car, checking the rear bumper. "There isn't even a scratch," he'd said.

So maybe it hadn't happened after all. Had it only been a dream? The car blurred as Tessa's vision swam and she reached out an arm to steady herself against the vehicle. But the photograph! Harry was still holding it. Tessa stared at that rectangle with the jagged edge, wondering if she was losing her mind.

Harry bent down and looked under her Toyota. He pulled out his iPhone and aimed it at a certain spot, apparently using the screen's light for a better look. Just as she had done earlier in Danny's basement. When his face came into view again, something had changed in his eyes.

"What is it?" Tessa had whispered. Was Danny still— *No, no,* her mind recoiled at the thought. Besides, she'd seen him lying in the driveway, motionless.

"I need to think," he'd said. He circled the car, his face intent. Tessa watched him pace, feeling oddly numb, her mind's bandwidth taken up by the work it required to keep track of Harry's movements. Shock. She knew she was in shock.

"Take a shower and seal your clothes into a plastic bag, even the shoes you were wearing," Harry had told her. "I'll be back soon."

"Where are you going?" Tessa had asked, but Harry merely went inside, came back out with his keys, and moved her Toyota into the garage. She was still standing there when Harry pulled out in his Honda, the one they rarely used because the Toyota was roomier.

Harry pulled up alongside her and rolled down the window. "Tessa," he'd said urgently. "The shower, now. Go!"

Tessa had nodded.

"Don't answer the phone. Don't answer the door. Just wait until I get back."

Shower. Plastic bag. Tessa's mind had latched on to those words as if they were life preservers. She'd think only of the tasks ahead, and block everything else out. She turned and walked into the house and headed for the shower as Harry pulled onto the street, heading in the direction of Danny Briggs's house.

# Chapter Forty

**Newport Cove Listserv Digest**

\*Missing Package

A UPS package that was supposed to be delivered to me today is missing from my front porch. I'll be filing a police report, but wanted to let fellow Newport Cove residents know that we may have a thief targeting our community. —Betty West, Crabtree Lane

\*Re: Missing Package

I have your package, Betty! I just got home from work and it was left on my front porch mistakenly. I'll run it right over! —Polly Whelan, Crabtree Lane

\*Re: Missing Package

Another wonderful reminder that we live in one of the twenty safest communities in the country! —Sincerely, Shannon Dockser, Newport Cove Manager

• • •

Kellie pulled the steak out of the refrigerator, where it had been resting in an olive oil, pepper, and Worcestershire sauce marinade, and checked the timer on the stove. Fifteen minutes until the baked potatoes were done; she'd start grilling the steaks now. A big green salad was waiting to be tossed with her homemade Caesar dressing, and for dessert, she'd baked snickerdoodles. She never wanted to eat brownies again.

It was chilly outside, with a drizzling rain, so she pulled on a coat and baseball cap and went to fire up the grill. She could've broiled the steaks, as she usually did during winter months, but Jason preferred them grilled.

As she waited for the meat to cook, she glanced up at the second-story bedroom window. Jason had gone straight into the bedroom after work. She wasn't sure if he was watching television or showering or packing a suitcase, because he'd closed the door behind him. She wondered if he'd thrown away the lunch she'd prepared for him, the one with a thick turkey and cheese sandwich slathered with spicy mustard and a bag of barbeque chips and a Pepsi, which was Jason's favorite guilty pleasure drink.

She'd thought about knocking and telling him what she'd done earlier that day, but in the end, she'd decided to let him be. He'd eventually learn that she'd removed the password from her iPhone, because she planned to leave it on the counter, unguarded, in case he ever wanted to check it.

She'd also called the office to say that she could no longer work there. "Family emergency," she'd said, and had felt guilty when the motherly receptionist had expressed concern. She'd gotten two texts from Miller—the first read Everything okay? and the second, Give a call as soon as you can, worried about you.

She'd texted back, I'm fine. I just need some time to be alone with my family.

He hadn't responded. She'd stared at the screen for a while, then she'd deleted the history of messages between the two of them, the ones she'd read so many times she'd committed them to memory, and she erased Miller's contact information from her phone. She'd felt a tiny pang as the sweet, flirty messages had evaporated—Miller had called her babe in one, in a joking way, but the sexy term of endearment had made her heart flutter—but she reminded herself that she was missing a feeling, not a person.

When the steaks were nearly charred on the outside and pink on the inside, just the way Jason liked them, she went inside and climbed the stairs, knocking on the closed bedroom door.

"Dinner's ready," she said, and held her breath. Jason might not feel like eating with her. If that was the case, she'd keep cooking his favorite dinners, every night, until he was ready.

But he opened the door, still in his work clothes, and came out. His hair was rumpled, sticking up over one ear like Noah's sometimes did when he awoke, and Jason's eyes looked tired. He passed her without a word and headed downstairs while she rounded up the kids.

The children had been a little subdued today, Kellie reflected as they gathered around the table. They must've picked up on the tension in the house. Even Mia's voice was unaccustomedly soft.

She tried to offset any anxiety they might be feeling by chatting normally, asking the kids to tell the best and worst thing that had happened to them that day at school. She'd read about the ritual in a magazine—some celebrity parent claimed it was the way she connected with her kids—and had been meaning to try it.

"Best thing?" Mia asked. "One of the dumb boys tried to kick a football at recess and missed it and fell over on his back."

"Like Charlie Brown," Kellie said.

"Oh, wait, can I change my best thing?" Mia asked.

"No," Noah said, but Mia ignored him: "The best thing is I'm going to be a patrol next year."

Kellie could just imagine Mia striding into a crosswalk, holding up her raised palm, and giving a death-glare to cowed drivers while she shepherded younger kids across the street.

"Congratulations," Kellie said. "You'll do a great job. What about the worst thing?"

Mia shrugged. "We had to do work sheets in math."

*Oh, to be ten again*, Kellie thought.

"My best thing was Dylan dropped an Oreo on the floor at lunch and didn't want it so I ate it," Noah said.

"You're repulsive," Mia told him.

"Mia," Kellie admonished.

"He *is*," Mia said. "He probably got leprosy from it."

Jason was being quiet—too quiet. He was just chewing his food and watching the kids.

"What about you, Mom?" Noah asked. "What was your best and worst?"

"My best?" Kellie cleared her throat. Now was as good a time as any. "My best was telling my job I'm going to stop work so I can just be with my family," she said. Jason was bending over his plate to cut off another piece of meat, but his head rose sharply and he looked at her, his hands still poised above his steak.

"Did you get fired?" Mia wanted to know.

"Nope," Kellie said, shaking her head for extra emphasis. "It was my decision. I'll be here with you guys every night and weekend now. No more going out to show houses. I might go back to work at a different office in a while, I don't know. We'll see."

"Okay," Noah said. "So what was your worst?"

She winced, hoping no one had noticed. The worst was hurting Miller. She imagined how she'd feel if she were on the receiving end of her blunt, unfriendly text. No, the worst was seeing Jason come home and knowing she wouldn't feel his warm arms wrap around her in a hug. He'd hugged her every single day at the end of work, something she'd taken for granted until it was lost to her.

The kids were staring at her. "The worst was stepping in dog poop when I went to take out the trash," Kellie fibbed.

Noah laughed, spitting out water on the table as he did so, which caused Mia to shriek, and Kellie jumped up to get paper towels.

"Dad's turn," Mia said.

"My best and worst?" Jason asked. He'd cleaned his plate, which made Kellie feel a little better.

"The best is being here with you kookaburras," he said, reaching over to ruffle Noah's hair and to wink at Mia.

"Tell the worst!" Mia said.

This wasn't such a good game after all, Kellie realized, as Jason took a sip of water and the smile fell from his face. Kellie reached for more salad that she didn't want, to give herself something to do.

"The worst?" Jason echoed.

Kellie's stomach muscles contracted. She deserved whatever might be coming; she'd absorb whatever angry message he wanted to convey. Jason looked at her for the first time in days and she forced herself to meet his gaze.

"I stepped in the same dog poop as Mom did," Jason said.

The kids erupted into laughter, and Kellie released a small, relieved giggle, too.

"Is it still on your shoe?" Noah wanted to know.

"I dunno, want to sniff it?" Jason cracked, lifting up his foot.

"Eww!" Mia yelled.

"Keep your voice down, honey," Kellie said. She'd never thought she'd be glad to repeat that particular admonishment.

"Who's ready for dessert?" she asked, standing up and clearing the plates from the table, reaching for Jason's first.

"Thank you," he said.

She smiled, knowing her eyes reflected the words back to him.

•  •  •

Susan hadn't planned to visit Mr. Brannon that day. Her Cole-free hours were already filled to bursting with a long list of business calls, a visit to a new client, and a consultation on her website redesign.

But when she checked her calendar, she noticed she hadn't seen him in nearly three weeks. So Susan packed the chicken salad she'd made for her own lunch into Tupperware, added a baguette, some pears, and two bottles of sparkling water, and headed for her car, where she could put on her Bluetooth headset and knock out some of the calls while she drove.

She made good time to Sunrise, but when she pulled into the parking lot, she realized she'd forgotten to let Mr. Brannon know she was coming. But she'd dropped by in the past without warning and he'd always been happy to see her. Mr. Brannon rarely left the nursing home, save for their outings.

She supposed it was part of the natural funneling of the end of a life, his geographical retreat. In his twenties, while serving in the army, Mr. Brannon had fearlessly traversed the world, devouring adventures. Now his journeys were confined to his mind, laced with regret and sadness. She wondered how much time he had left, and whether he was looking forward to that final release, hoping to see his wife again. To seek the forgiveness that had eluded him in this world.

"So I think this will really work," Susan's potential client was saying in her ear. The client, a man who lived in Miami, was concerned about his mother, who had been widowed the previous month. He wanted to hire Susan for what she'd termed "bridge services"—to help support his mom until she learned to do the things she'd relied on her husband for, like fill the car with gas. He also wanted to make sure his mother had an active social network, since she'd been consumed with taking care of her ailing spouse during the preceding year and seemed to have lost her way.

"We'll help her get back on her feet again," Susan promised as she turned off the car. "Maybe find a support group, or if she'd rather, we can look into local book clubs, things like that."

"She loves to read," the client said. Susan could hear the concern in his voice. Cole would grow up to be like this, she thought. He'd be caring and conscientious. That wasn't just a reflection on her, or her parenting. It was also due to Randall.

"Good," Susan said. "Her local library has a fiction group that meets the first Tuesday of every month. We can go with her the first time or two, if she'd be more comfortable. And another one of my clients joined recently; she's a sweetheart and I know she'll take your mother under her wing. In the meantime, I can send you over a contract later today, and once you review it, you can feel free to call me back with any questions."

Susan locked the car as she concluded her call and tucked her cell phone into her purse. It was a cloudless day and although the sun shone weakly in the sky, the promise of spring perfumed the air. Susan was ready for it. This winter had seemed unusually long.

The sliding doors automatically opened as Susan stepped onto the welcome mat, and she entered the reception area, waving a hello to the woman at the front desk.

"Oh, he isn't here," the receptionist called out.

Susan blinked. "I'm sorry?" she said.

"Mr. Brannon," the receptionist said. "That's who you're here to see, isn't it? He left about an hour ago."

"Oh," Susan said, thinking, *He left?* "Do you know where he went?"

"Sorry, I don't," the receptionist said.

Maybe he'd taken a cab to the bank, or the doctor's, Susan thought. "Do you mind if I leave lunch for him in his room?" she asked.

"Go right ahead," the receptionist said.

Susan took the elevator upstairs and was waylaid by Garth. She ended up giving him the half of the lunch Susan had intended for herself in order to escape. She left a note for Mr.

Brannon, telling him she'd be by over the weekend for another visit and to call if he needed anything, then she headed back downstairs.

Maybe he *had* gone to the doctor. Now that she thought about it, she'd noticed a slowing in Mr. Brannon, a kind of winding down, ever since she'd given him the handprint. He'd been as sweet and gentlemanly as ever, but his face had looked drawn—almost collapsed into itself—the last time she'd seen him. She'd thought it was due to the new resurfacing of his old sorrow, but maybe he was physically ill.

Susan exited the building, frowning, thinking that she'd call him tonight to check in. She crossed behind a red Honda that had pulled up to the main doors and headed toward her car. When she reached it, though, something made her glance back. She saw Mr. Brannon get out of the Honda, moving slowly as he struggled to put his weight on his cane and pull himself upright. Susan hesitated, her keys in hand, wondering if she should go help him.

Then the driver's-side door of the Honda opened and a man got out, hurrying around to Mr. Brannon's side. The younger man steadied Mr. Brannon by the elbow and walked him to the front door. The two stood there, talking, then the man reached out a hand. Mr. Brannon took it, and held it for a long moment.

Not quite a hug, but much more than a handshake.

Susan felt the air leave her lungs as she watched.

She'd pictured Edward as a boy who would still fit into that small handprint, but he was a grown man now, of course. He looked so much like his father, with that tall, lanky frame and full head of hair that was beginning to turn silver around the ears.

Edward released his father's hand, then reached over and patted him on the shoulder. Just once, but Susan could feel the warmth of that touch from dozens of yards away.

Edward reentered his car while Mr. Brannon stood by the

entrance of the building, watching his son drive away. Then he looked up and saw Susan and beckoned to her. She hurried to his side.

"Did you see my son?" Mr. Brannon asked. "Edward came here!"

"I saw," Susan said. "He looks just like you. But . . . how?"

"I've been writing to him since you gave me that handprint," Mr. Brannon said. "Every single day . . ."

"He read your letters?" Susan asked.

"No, not at first," Mr. Brannon said. "I knew I didn't deserve his forgiveness, but I wanted to write the words, to say that I was wrong. So very wrong. I wanted to tell Edward I was sorry, that the greatest regret of my life was the way I'd treated him, and that I'd have given anything to change it. Even if he didn't read the letters."

"But he did," Susan said. She blinked back tears. Mr. Brannon's eyes were red, too, but he was smiling.

"Eventually," Mr. Brannon said. "They stopped coming back to me after a couple of weeks. Oh, Miss Susan, I'm so lucky Edward has his mother's heart . . . I told him I'd like to meet his partner sometime. And they have a little girl. They adopted her when she was just a baby."

"You have a granddaughter!" Susan exclaimed.

"She's eleven," Mr. Brannon said. "Her name is Sara. I asked if it would be okay to send her a letter. Edward wasn't sure, but he said maybe, if he read it first."

"I'm so glad," Susan whispered over the lump in her throat.

"To think that after all this time, I could have a family again . . . ," he said. "When you get to the end of your life, you realize the only important thing is love."

Susan took his arm, which felt soft and frail beneath her hand, and gave it a gentle squeeze.

"I think Edward has your heart, too," she said.

• • •

## Before Newport Cove

Once, Tessa had been called for jury duty, and although she'd just spent the day sitting around a waiting room, her juror number too high for her to be called in on a case, it had gotten her wondering: could she vote to impose the death penalty? She hadn't been sure she could be part of a decision to take another person's life, no matter how severe the crime. That reasoned, sensitive woman seemed like a stranger to her now.

Harry had handled everything. He'd touched Danny's body, tried and failed to find a pulse. He'd taken his own outfit along with Tessa's clothing and shoes, even the towel she'd used after showering, to a Dumpster behind a hardware store. He'd created the alibi by changing the clock and waking up Bree. He'd cleaned up the blood he'd tracked into their house on his shoe.

Harry had also found a television show he'd TiVo'd and insisted the two of them watch it together the next morning while the kids were still asleep. "That's what we were doing that night," he'd said. "Stick to the truth when possible. We ate pasta. I did the crossword puzzle. We watched *Game of Thrones*. Remember the plot. But don't give away too many details, act like you're searching your memory for what we did at first. And don't mention Bree waking up. That's our ace in the hole, if we need it."

Tessa had turned her head away from the television, shuddering. Blood had never bothered her before—Bree and Addison had had their share of nosebleeds and scraped knees, and Tessa had briskly dealt with the cleanup—but the gory battle playing out on-screen had made bile rise in her throat.

"But I must have left behind some evidence!" she'd said. "A fingerprint, or some clothing fiber . . ."

Harry had shaken his head. "You've—*we've*—visited the

house before. Remember the barbeque Danny held a few weeks ago for the Young Rangers and their families?"

When Detective Robinson had come by the house—"Just a formality, we're interviewing everyone who knew Danny," she'd said—Tessa's raw nerves had been cocooned by a Xanax. By then, she imagined, Danny's body had been removed from the driveway and autopsied. Maybe the detective already had clues.

"It's horrible," Tessa had said, sitting next to Harry on the couch and clasping her hands together to keep them steady. "Who would want to kill Danny?"

"Did your son ever mention anything about Danny touching him inappropriately?" the detective had asked.

"What? No! Why?" Tessa had asked.

"There were some photographs in the house . . . ," Detective Robinson began.

"Oh, no," Tessa had said. "Addison was never alone with Danny. He just saw him at the meetings."

Her focus was wrong, Tessa had realized. She should've acted more concerned about the photos, less on the details of the uniform transfer.

"Wait, what kind of pictures?" she'd asked quickly.

"I can't give out that information. But we're suggesting all parents have their children talk to a psychologist, even though there's no evidence of any physical contact," Detective Robinson had said.

Tessa had nodded. "Of course, we'll do that." And she would, down the line. But she knew Danny had been alone with Addison just that one time. Addison wasn't at risk.

Next to her on the couch, Harry had fidgeted, his foot tapping out a rat-tat-tat. Tessa had watched as the detective's eyes had tracked to Harry's shoe.

Tessa had leaned forward, gently bumping Harry's leg with her arm, as if it was an accidental touch. "I didn't know much about Danny," she'd said. "Did he have a girlfriend? Or was he in financial trouble?"

The detective had looked at her sharply, her attention drawn away from Harry.

"Why do you ask?" the detective had said.

"Just curious," Tessa had said. "I read a lot of mystery novels . . . Isn't it usually the spouse or romantic interest who does something like this?"

She'd widened her eyes, hoping she looked like a bored suburban housewife, eager for some drama to brighten her day. Harry had saved her when she needed it; now it was her turn to be the steady one, to guide them through the crisis.

A few minutes later, after handing Tessa her card, the detective had left.

"Call me if you think of anything relevant," the detective had said, pausing at the door, holding her black steno notebook. Tessa was desperate to see what she'd written down. "Even a little thing."

"Of course," Tessa had said, willing Harry to say something, to erase the blank expression on his face. But at least empty eyes were less suspicious than guilt-filled ones.

At night, Tessa lay in the darkness, sensing Harry's wakefulness next to her. She couldn't get over how he'd transformed into someone she didn't recognize to protect her. It was a side of her bespectacled, absentminded husband that Tessa had never imagined existed.

But then, she'd also revealed a side of herself she'd never thought possible.

*I murdered a man*, she'd thought.

When Harry began to crumble—when the weight fell off, when his insomnia struck—she moved into the breach, keeping their family going, arranging for the purchase of the house in Newport Cove. Fighting for their survival.

Sometimes, while she was engaged in the most mundane of activities, like plucking an errant gray hair from her head, or washing her hands, the thought would seize her mind, stealing away her breath: *I'm a killer.*

# Chapter Forty-One

"I'M GOING TO DROP out of the race," Joe said, looking at Gigi across the kitchen table.

They'd ordered pizza and had divided the last few inches of a bottle of Pinot Grigio between their glasses. Earlier, the girls had wandered in to eat, with Melanie taking a single slice before retreating to her room. Now the house was quiet. Julia was upstairs on the computer, and Melanie was dozing again. Gigi knew her daughter's exhaustion stemmed from emotional trauma, which could be every bit as draining as a physical one.

"Are you sure?" Gigi asked, even though Joe's pronouncement wasn't entirely unexpected. What did surprise her was the twinge of sadness she felt at his words.

"Politics is filled with people like Zach," Joe said. "And I feel like a used-car salesman when I go door to door to talk to voters . . . I don't get to see you and the kids as much . . . It would be worse if I won and had to be in Washington during the week . . . Should I go on?"

Gigi reached across the table to take his hand. "You've thought about this a lot."

Joe nodded. "I'm so damn tired. How do they do it? They

say Bill Clinton can meet a hundred people and remember all of their names a few hours later. Then he does it again the next night. He feeds off that kind of thing. And for what? Don't tell me it's all about service. It's about ego. Power."

"Will you go back to your old job?" Gigi asked.

"Yeah, for a while," Joe said. "But I'm going to start looking for something different. I'll call a headhunter."

"Okay," Gigi said. But she was thinking about Joe's excitement the night of the primary election, when everyone had gathered to celebrate his victory. The painkillers and champagne had erased her memory of his speech, but someone had filmed it on an iPhone and forwarded it to them. Joe had been invigorated, determined. Passionate.

But then there was the tabloid photograph of Melanie storming away during the family portrait, and Zach and his folders. That was the flip side of politics; someone was always watching, waiting to exploit a perceived weakness.

Gigi turned her head at the sound of footsteps coming down the stairs. She expected to see Julia, but it was Melanie's face that appeared in the kitchen doorway. She looked especially young tonight, with her round cheeks and the big, dark eyes she'd inherited from her father.

"Hey, baby," Joe said. "Want more pizza?"

"I'm okay," Melanie said. She took a glass out of the cabinet and went to the refrigerator to fill it with water from the door dispenser.

"You should tell her," Gigi said to Joe.

"Tell her what?" Melanie asked, turning around.

Joe patted the chair next to him and waited until Melanie sat down. "I'm going to drop out of the race," he said.

Melanie frowned. "You're quitting? Why?"

"A lot of reasons," Joe said.

"Zach is one of them," Gigi said, remembering her vow to be honest with her daughter.

Melanie took a long sip of water. "Oh," she said.

"I figured you guys would be celebrating," Joe said, looking from his daughter to his wife. He winked. "Unless having me around more is a bad thing?"

"No, no," Gigi said. She mustered up a smile. "I totally understand why you need to do this."

Joe nodded and looked at Melanie. "Honey? What are you thinking?"

Melanie shrugged. "I was just telling Mom about when we went to the homeless shelter . . . Remember that little boy?" she said to Joe. "He wanted to live in a house with a backyard so he could have a dog. And when you were talking to him, you told him you wanted to help people like him."

"Yeah," Joe said. He rubbed his eyes, suddenly looking more tired than ever. "Kevin. That was his name."

"He was really sweet," Melanie said.

Gigi looked at her daughter, not following her train of thought. "Do you want to go back to the shelter and see him?" she asked.

"Maybe," Melanie said. "But the thing is, Dad, if you're quitting because of Zach . . . doesn't that mean the bad guys win?"

Joe stared at her. "It isn't . . . That's not the only reason," he said after a moment. "This is different."

"How?" Melanie asked.

Joe opened his mouth, then closed it. "I don't know," he finally said. He gave a little laugh. "Jeez, Melanie, are you saying you want me to keep running?"

She shrugged, a teenager again. "Whatever." She yawned and stood up. "Still tired. I'm going back to bed."

"Good night," Gigi called as Melanie left the room.

She and Joe looked at each other. "Well, shit," Joe said. "She's growing up."

"I guess so," Gigi said, then began to laugh. "You can explain it to her again tomorrow. She'll understand."

"Yeah," Joe said. He drained his wine. "The thing is, that kid . . . Kevin . . ."

How like her husband, to remember the name of the little boy who wouldn't be able to do anything for his campaign, but to recoil at the idea of having to recall the names of a hundred voters.

"Yes?" Gigi prompted.

"I do want to help people like him and his mom," Joe said. He sat up straighter and pushed away his plate. Gigi watched him. He still had dark circles under his eyes, but he seemed more alert than he had a few minutes earlier.

"It would be hard on you, to have to do everything around here during the week . . . but I'd be home every weekend, and there's a long recess in the summer . . ."

"And the bad guys wouldn't win," Gigi said.

She stood up and went over to Joe and sat down in his lap, winding her arms around his neck. Joe would be victorious and go to Washington; suddenly she was certain of it. And it was time for her to find her own passion again, right here in their hometown. Maybe she'd begin volunteering at the homeless shelter regularly. It could be something she'd do together with Melanie and Julia.

"At least not without us putting up a fight," Joe said, and kissed her.

• • •

Kellie was flipping the pages of a book without taking in any of the printed words when Jason walked into their bedroom.

"Hi," she said, feeling shy. They hadn't been alone together since she'd told him about Miller.

"Hi," he said. Another first: he hadn't spoken to her directly for days.

She expected Jason to grab a pillow from the bed or get something out of the bathroom, but instead, he walked over and flopped down beside her, the mattress giving a little bounce under his weight.

"Do you want to talk?" she asked, setting aside her novel.

He flung an arm over his eyes, blocking out the light. "I don't know," he said.

She held her breath, unsure of what to do.

"You swear you didn't sleep with him," Jason said.

"Jason," she said. "Please look at me."

After a moment, he removed his arm so she could see his clear blue eyes.

"I didn't sleep with him," she said. "I never even kissed him." She was so glad it was true.

Jason nodded. "Is he still texting you?"

"No," Kellie said. "I told him I needed to focus on my family." She waited, but Jason didn't respond.

"If you'd like to go to marital counseling, I can find someone," Kellie said. "It might be a good thing for us to do."

Jason exhaled, a long, slow whoosh of breath. But then he averted his eyes so that he was staring at the ceiling instead of her.

Kellie had the sensation that she was feeling her way through darkness, unsure if the ground would disappear beneath her feet. She felt her throat thicken, but she swallowed hard, not wanting to cry. If Jason was coming to a decision, she didn't want it to be based on pity or obligation.

"What I want to do," Jason said, enunciating every word, "is beat the crap out of him." She could hear the anger as well as the pain threading through his voice.

She reached out a hand and put it on his arm. "I'll never see him again," she said. "You're the only man I've ever loved."

Jason remained still for another minute, then he sat up abruptly and reached for her, crushing her against him. She was so startled she didn't immediately react, then she wound her arms around his neck. His mouth found hers and he kissed her, hard and hungrily. The way he hadn't in years.

The five o'clock shadow on his chin rasped against her skin as his hands moved under her T-shirt and yanked down her shorts, and she felt herself responding instantly.

"Hold on," Jason said, pulling back from her. He was breathing hard.

He jumped out of bed and her heart sank. But he only went over to the door to close and lock it. Then he hurried back, into her arms.

# Chapter Forty-Two

IT HAPPENED ON A lazy Sunday morning, while Harry and the kids ate waffles and Tessa sipped coffee and noticed through the window that the birdfeeder she'd hung on the sugar maple tree was nearly empty. By now, their house in Newport Cove had scuff marks on a couple of walls, and the leaves were tumbling off the trees, in need of a good raking. By now, their house in Newport Cove was beginning to feel like home.

Tessa's old friend Cindy was the one who delivered the news. Tessa had always expected a SWAT team to tear down her door, to be led away in handcuffs while tabloid photographers crowded around and stuck cameras in her face and shouted questions. She could see the headline: *Soccer Mom Slays Predator!*

But the end began, simply enough, with a phone call.

"I'll get it," Tessa said.

But Bree leaped out of her seat and reached the phone first. "Oh, hi!" she said. "Yeah, it's okay here . . . My teacher's pretty nice . . . Uh-huh, she's right here."

Bree handed over the receiver and Tessa heard Cindy's voice.

"Did you hear?" Cindy asked, sounding equal parts exhilarated and angry.

Tessa tapped Harry on the shoulder. When he raised his head, she gave him a meaningful look. "Hang on, let me take this outside."

She stepped onto the porch, closing the door behind her. "What is it?"

It had to be about Danny, of course. Cindy wouldn't call her with breaking news about any other subject.

"They've declared Danny's death a cold case," Cindy said. "They don't have any official suspects."

"So they're closing the investigation?" Tessa gasped. "I figured they'd keep it open at least a year."

"For now, I guess," Cindy said. "I mean, they can always reopen these things. At least that's what I've learned from *CSI*."

So in a decade or two, a sharp young detective, or a seasoned veteran, could run his fingers over files, searching for the one labeled "Danny Briggs." He could read notes about the interviews. Perhaps there were details about Harry's jiggling leg, and Tessa's nervousness. Harry had bought new tires for Tessa's car and changed them before disposing of the old ones at a dump. But maybe the tires could be unearthed, the tread matched . . .

For now, though, they were safe. Tessa exhaled deeply for what felt like the first time in months.

She eased out of the conversation, claiming she needed to get back to the children, and hung up the phone. Instead of rushing inside to tell Harry the news, though, she sat down on the steps. It could wait a few more minutes.

She closed her eyes, seeing Danny's splayed hands, his open face, that wide smile . . .

She was still afraid. She didn't want to go to jail.

But when she thought about how it had felt to push down on the gas, to see Danny disappear from her rearview mirror, to feel that *thud* under her vehicle . . .

She'd been waiting for it to come, but she still felt zero guilt. She'd do it again, if she had to, with absolutely no hesitation. Again and again and again.

"Mom?"

Addison was calling, her sweet boy, the one she'd protect at all costs. Just as she would Bree.

"I'm coming, honey," she said, and she stood up, her heartbeat steady, a smile on her face, and went inside, to her family.

# Chapter Forty-Three

• • •

It was a beautiful day for a wedding.

The sun cast a golden light on the trees and blooms that were just beginning to awaken. Why did most brides want June weddings? Susan wondered. Springtime was better; it symbolized a new beginning. An awakening.

The ceremony wouldn't start until three p.m. It was to be a simple backyard affair. Susan got out of her car and walked toward the house, veering right toward the people clustered in the backyard. Two men were setting up tables and chairs, another was busy filling coolers with beer and wine and soda. Her heels sank into the soft earth as she scanned her surroundings.

"Susan?"

She turned around and saw Randall in a crisp white shirt and tan linen shorts, coming toward her. He took another step forward, then hesitated. Behind him she could see Daphne, wearing a cream-colored sundress. She looked very pregnant, and beautiful. And more than a little nervous.

"Hi," Susan said. "I came to give you this."

Randall looked down at the white gift bag in her hand, then back up at her.

"It's just a picture frame," Susan said. A pretty one, though, in sterling silver. "I guess . . . I also wanted to say congratulations in person. To both of you."

Randall moved closer to her, reached out for the bag. But he didn't speak.

Cole was there, sipping a soda he'd taken from an ice chest, looking adorable in his dress shirt and shorts that matched Randall's. She was glad he was watching.

"Thank you," Daphne said. She cleared her throat. "That's . . . really wonderful of you."

"Susan," Randall said again. Just her name, but she could feel the weight of emotion infusing it. Without thinking, she stretched out her arms and he walked into them, giving her a hard, short hug.

"It's a perfect day for a wedding," Susan said after Randall released her. She could see him wipe his eyes, but she pretended not to notice.

"Are you sure you can't stay?" Daphne asked, then looked stricken. "I mean, if you— I didn't . . ."

"It's okay," Susan said. "I need to be somewhere, but maybe we can catch up next time I bring Cole over."

He was still watching her, her little boy. She was so glad. She walked over to her son and cupped his soft cheek in her hand. At times it surprised her to notice how long and thin his limbs were growing, but she'd always be able to glimpse her baby in him.

"My beautiful boy," she said.

"Handsome," Cole corrected.

"My handsome boy," she said. "I'm so proud of you. Do a good job today."

"I will," said Cole, confident as ever. She hadn't harmed him too much. He'd recover from her year of pain. As would she.

"Congratulations," Susan said again as she encompassed them all—Randall and Daphne and Cole—with a smile. "Have a wonderful day!"

*I forgive you*, she thought, and with those words, something loosened in her chest.

She walked away quickly and didn't cry until she was back in her car. But this time, the tears that rolled down her cheeks were gentle, like rain that washes away dust and grime and pollen, leaving shining leaves and clean streets.

Rain was supposed to be lucky on a wedding day, she thought, but who was to say the luck couldn't envelop her, too?

She put the car in gear and began moving ahead as Randall's house—no, Randall and Daphne's house—grew smaller and then disappeared from her rearview mirror.

Her cell phone rang and she looked down at it. Kellie.

"How are you, sweetie?" her friend asked after Susan answered.

"I'm . . . okay," Susan said, and with those words, she realized it was finally true.

"Do you want me to come over?" Kellie asked.

"How about tomorrow night?" Susan suggested. "I'll cook us dinner."

"Perfect," Kellie said. "But let's order in, and I'll bring the wine."

Susan laughed, and it felt good. "Even better," she said.

"Has Peter called yet?" Kellie asked.

"Yesterday," Susan said. "I'm waiting twenty-four hours to call him back, since that's the rule."

"You really need to see someone about your compulsive habit of making things up," Kellie said. "Call me if you change your mind about tonight."

"I will," Susan promised, but she already knew she wanted to be alone. She'd pour herself a glass of good, cold champagne and toast to her own future. There might be more tears, but they would dry soon enough. She'd put on music and begin to plan, to break free from the emotional limbo that had ensnarled her ever since Randall had left.

First, she'd figure out what to do about the house. She didn't want to move, but she would remodel it, erase some of the memories and make room for new ones. She could redo the whole kitchen and add a front porch and bump out the master bedroom, filling a wall with deep, wide windows to let in the light. Why hadn't she redecorated it before? She'd get new bedding, too, and paint the walls a cheery color. Maybe a pale, fresh green. She'd put a swimming pool in the backyard, with a diving board for Cole. It would be long enough to do laps. She'd always loved to swim. And a hot tub! She could invite the girls over for daiquiris and a soak. It would be good to get to know Tessa better. Susan had felt connected to her new neighbor ever since she'd confided in her the night of Joe's primary victory party. She'd reach out to people more, Susan decided, and start throwing dinner parties. It was time to come out of hibernation and start living again.

She'd begin dreaming tonight.

And tomorrow, she'd start anew.

She turned down her cul-de-sac and did a double take when she passed Mason Gamerman's house. He was pounding a stake into the ground, with a FOR SALE BY OWNER sign attached.

Mason was moving?

She gave him a little wave as she passed, knowing he wouldn't return it. She wondered where he was going. She couldn't see him moving into a retirement home, but who knew?

His house would be snapped up quickly. This was a wonderful neighborhood, after all, and even though Mason was a curmudgeon, he owned a nice rambler on a big lot. In a few weeks or months, a moving van would pull up to the curb and couches and beds and bookshelves would be wrestled through the door while a new family—tired and overwhelmed, probably, as well as a little nervous—would settle in.

She couldn't wait to meet them.

• • •

## Newport Cove Listserv

### *Re: Dog Poop

Dear Newport Cove residents, I'm pleased to report that we have obtained video footage from a camera recently placed on a telephone pole that shows the dog poop perpetrator among us is not, in fact, one of our neighborhood's furry friends. It seems a raccoon has been defecating on the lawns of several neighbors, including Ms. Reiserman's. If any residents would like to view the footage first-hand, please notify Shannon Dockser, Newport Cove Manager.

—Signed, Shannon Dockser, Newport Cove Manager

### *Re: Dog Poop

How much money did it cost for us to film a raccoon taking a dump? —Frank Fitzgibbons, Forsythia Lane

### *Re: Dog Poop

It seems a humane trap and relocation of the raccoon would be in the community's best interest. This is probably a job for the Newport Cove manager to investigate. —Tally White, Iris Lane

\*Re: Dog Poop

Thank you for your suggestion, Tally! —Signed, Shannon Dockser, Newport Cove Manager

\*Re: Dog Poop

POOOOOOOOOP! —Reece Harmon, Daisy Way

# Acknowledgments

As always, my deep gratitude to Greer Hendricks—a spectacular editor, and an equally marvelous friend. It has been an honor to work with you on every single book I've had published, Greer, and I look forward to sharing many adventures, and many bottles of wine, with you in the future.

It's a lucky writer who gets to work with two fantastic editors, and I'm so pleased the smart, savvy, and funny Sarah Cantin is taking this novel on the second half of its journey. My literary agent, Victoria Sanders, is also a superstar: protector, director, connector. Marcy Engelman continues to amaze me—and never fails to make me laugh—and she, along with Ariele Fredman, work tirelessly to spread the word about my books.

My heartfelt thanks to Bernadette Baker-Baughman and Chris Kepner at Team VSA, Haley Weaver at Atria, and also to Emily Gambir and Kathy Nolan for supporting my novels with imagination and energy. Lisa Keim is a wonderful foreign rights agent, and I'm so grateful to her for letting my books see a piece of the world. My appreciation, also and always, to film agent Angela Cheng Caplan. And a thanks to Roald and Leslie Keith for helping me secure a quiet place to write.

To the hardworking and creative gang at Atria Books—Judith Curr, Suzanne Donahue, Lisa Sciambra, Chelsea Cohen, Hillary Tisman, Jackie Jou, Yona Deshommes, and Paul Olsewski—I'm incredibly lucky to be on your team.

My thanks to booksellers, book bloggers, and librarians, many of whom have become friends.

A special thanks to Chris Neralcam for the incredible support.

As always, to my family—I love you.

And I'm very grateful to YOU, for reading this novel. Please find me on Facebook and Twitter so we can stay in touch!

# The Perfect Neighbors

## SARAH PEKKANEN

## A Reading Group Guide

### Topics and Questions for Discussion

1. Throughout the novel, Newport Cove's residents hold their status as one of the twenty safest neighborhoods in the United States as a point of pride. Yet each of the four female narrators feels unsafe in some way, due to the secrets she is holding. Do you think people need to feel emotionally safe in order to feel physically safe, and vice versa?

2. In a series of flashbacks, we observe that Tessa "tried to do everything right" after her baby Bree was born, but quickly "felt as if she was failing her daughter" (p. 22). How does her anxiety about the "right" way to be a mother impact her children and/or her marriage? How have you observed this pressure in your own life, or in the lives of your friends

or family? If you have children, how have your beliefs about how to best raise them been affected by the opinions of "experts"?

3. When it comes to her children's safety, Tessa grows to believe she is paranoid or too sensitive, to the point where she becomes wary of raising an alarm when she thinks something is seriously wrong. Do you think it is generally better to be overly suspicious or overly cautious? What are the drawbacks of each, as portrayed in the novel?

4. Kellie initially thinks that because she and Miller have never kissed, she is not cheating on her husband. Is "emotional cheating" *really* cheating? Why or why not? How would you respond if a significant other acted as Kellie did? Have you ever been tempted to slip into emotional infidelity, and if so, how did you deal with the situation?

5. "Facebook stalking wasn't something she was proud of" (p. 280). Was Susan's Facebook stalking relatable or an invasion of privacy? Is Facebook stalking a normal part of having a crush/getting over a breakup, or is it self-destructive?

6. For much of the novel, Susan feels incapable of letting go of the past, at one point despairing that "[s]ometimes, though, people didn't adjust" (p. 233) to an ex moving on. In what ways does Susan's struggle with her divorce mirror the issues her friends are dealing with? What keeps people from moving forward? Looking at these protagonists, where do you see them ultimately exhibiting personal growth?

7. Susan begins dating only after realizing that her son recognizes that she misses his father. To what extent should the desires of someone's children impact their dating choices—and should a parent end a relationship if her children don't like it? Furthermore, do you think falling for someone new is a prerequisite to getting over a past love?

8. What did you initially suspect had happened to Tessa and Harry before they moved to Newport Cove? What did you think of the ultimate revelation, and how did it affect your feelings toward

these characters? Why do you think the author ended that story line the way she did?

9. "She'd been waiting for it to come, but she still felt zero guilt" (p. 332). Reread this scene as a group and discuss your reactions to this line. Do you think you would have felt the same in Tessa's shoes?

10. Besides injecting doses of humor into the narrative, what role does the Newport Cove listserv fill? What sense of the community, or of the individual characters, does it provide? Were there any messages in the listserv digests that echoed larger themes from the novel? Discuss a few of your favorite emails.

## Enhance Your Book Club

1. Look through the listserv digest sections for some of the characters whose voices we get a real sense of, but whose story is not directly addressed, such as Shannon Dockser, Tally White, or Frank Fitzgibbons. Try writing a scene from their perspective, about the goings-on of the neighborhood or what you imagine their lives are like. Share your writing pieces as a group.

2. In *The Perfect Neighbors*, Sarah Pekkanen has crafted a cast of diverse characters, all of whom leap off the page. If the novel became a film, who would you envision in the lead roles?

3. Consider reading one of Sarah Pekkanen's other novels (such as *Things You Won't Say*, *These Girls*, or *The Best of Us*) for your group's next meeting, and compare the major themes of your selection with those in *The Perfect Neighbors*. You can also connect with Sarah Pekkanen on Facebook and Twitter, and learn more about Sarah's books or invite her to Skype your book club by visiting: www.sarahpekkanen.com.